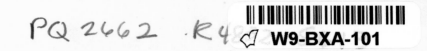

SOFTWAR

SOFTWAR

THIERRY BRETON AND DENIS BENEICH

translated from the French
by Mark Howson

HOLT, RINEHART AND WINSTON ——————— NEW YORK

Published in January 1986 by Holt, Rinehart and Winston,
383 Madison Avenue, New York, New York 10017.
Published simultaneously in Canada by Holt, Rinehart and
Winston of Canada, Limited.
Originally published in France.

Library of Congress Cataloging in Publication Data
Breton, Thierry.
Softwar.
Translation of: Softwar.
I. Beneich, Denis.   II. Title.
PQ2662.R4832S613 1985   843'.914   85-16340
ISBN   0-03-004998-9

First American Edition

Design by Kate Nichols
Printed in the United States of America
10 9 8 7 6 5 4 3 2 1

Grateful acknowledgment is made for permission to reprint
portions of "My November Guest" from *The Poetry of Robert
Frost*, edited by Edward Connery Lathem. Copyright 1934
© 1969 by Holt, Rinehart and Winston. Copyright © 1962
by Robert Frost. Reprinted by permission of Holt, Rinehart
and Winston, Publishers.

ISBN 0-03-004998-9

To the memory of Patrice de Sévin

ACKNOWLEDGMENTS

The researching and writing of *Softwar* was largely a team effort, and we were lucky enough to have a remarkable group of teammates throughout this lengthy undertaking.

First of all, we would like to express our deepest thanks to Patrice de Sévin and Jean-Marie Combes, for advice and assistance above and beyond the call.

Grateful thanks also to the staff of Embassy Computer of New York City and Forma Systemes of Paris and Dakar, for their helpful guidance and oversight, and to everyone in Paris and New York who gave of their precious time in assisting with the revision of the manuscript.

Finally, we would like to thank all those who assisted in the daunting task of assembling the documentary material on which this book was based and who have requested to remain anonymous. Without their generous cooperation, this book would never have seen the light of day.

Paris—New York
May 1984

SOFTWAR

ONE

May 12, 1980   Boston

"C'mon, tag 'im! Get in there! Tag 'im, for crissakes! Use your left!"

Brendan pulled back his head and felt the leather graze his cheek.
He was backed into a corner, and the trainer's voice seemed to be
coming at him through a thick, glowing fog, like the hot breath of a
forge—and it seemed as though every second or so a gloved fist broke
through the fog to find him at the speed of a hot spark flying off the
anvil. Part of him seemed to be watching all this from some distance,
and in spite of the thrill and tension of the contest, he was still able to
observe, to correlate, and to analyze with complete detachment. It
was as if time had split into two parallel streams, and he was horrified
as he saw how slowly his body reacted when he brought up his arm
to block a punch, when he thrust out his fist toward the face of his
invisible adversary, and when he danced back to avoid the counter-
punch.

I'm on a different track, he thought. Back in the world of real time,
where the brain needs several milliseconds to react, he was panting
and ducking and gasping and taking a pretty bad beating, but here he
was only watching.

"C'mon, get *in* there! Start connecting! You hear me? Use your left! Where's your left?"

Brendan shook his head so that droplets of sweat flew off in all directions. *Easy for you to say, my man. I'm still standing up, and that's plenty good enough for me. Okay, now—where's my left?*

Bouncing dutifully to one side, just as he had been taught, Brendan tried to get around his opponent's left; a direct hit to his own right shoulder very quickly put a stop to this maneuver. *I swear I felt something crack. He broke something that time for sure.*

While part of his brain was occupied with this disinterested analysis, he heard a groan escape his lips and felt the ropes cutting into his back. He shot out his right in another attempt to turn his opponent's left flank, and met nothing but empty air.

"Make it count! Put some weight behind it! Get back in there, for God's sake!"

The gloves were almost too heavy to lift now. He tried to bring them up to shield his face, but his opponent got in just ahead of him with a flurry of quick jabs, like the deft strokes of a sculptor or a surgeon, about to make good on the ancient schoolyard threat of rearranging his face. Elbows clamped to his stomach, arms folded tight, head cradled behind his gloves, Brendan fought against panic—another contest he didn't expect he had too much chance of winning. It occurred to him that when the irresistible force that was battering at his gloves finally broke through, the impact on his nose would be no more serious than if, for example, he'd simply taken it up and dropped it from a height of forty or fifty feet.

Okay. Enough for now.

He pivoted to the left, faked to the right, and let go with another left hook. His chin collided with a rapidly moving solid body, something on the order of a meteorite, and his entire body continued to vibrate for several tenths of a second while Brendan felt his remaining strength draining out through the soles of his feet. His legs gently gave way beneath him, and he sank to his knees. The hot fog that encircled him grew thicker, and he switched back to the slow track again . . .

"Out!"

Brendan Barnes, Assistant Professor of Computer Science at the Massachusetts Institute of Technology (with a Ph.D. from the same institution, on top of a B.S. from Princeton), was stretched out on the canvas like a mackerel on a slab. He was visited by one last coherent thought before his mind drifted off into the mist. *Boy, he sure punched my clock back there. How much longer before I'm really dead?* Then a brief inscription in shimmering green letters scrolled through the opaque gray space behind his eyes.

```
10 CLS
20 INPUT. Brendan losing it
30 IF Brendan really dying THEN whole life scrolls before eyes
      ELSE access random memories
40 PRINT
```

"Jesus, Brendan! Let go with your teeth, will you?"

"You hear me, Brendan? Do like the man says."

"Okay, got it."

Someone had plucked out his mouthpiece. He opened his eyes, and his entire field of vision was occupied by two enormous faces. The pleasant-looking one belonged to Tonio, his Puerto Rican sparring partner, grinning with relief as Brendan emerged from the depths; the less pleasant-looking one belonged to Jerry Connolly, his trainer, who was smirking broadly and ironically, as was his invariable custom.

"Whatsamatter, precious? You feel a little shaky all of a sudden?"

Brendan sat up and tried to wipe the sweat off his forehead. They had already taken off his training helmet; he held his hands out to Tonio in a childlike gesture of helplessness, and Tonio started to unlace his gloves. "All right, okay," Brendan muttered to Jerry, "I already know what you're going to say . . ."

"You think I'm not gonna say it anyway? You weren't—"

"—bear-ing *down*, you weren't *con*-centrating," Brendan supplied wearily as Tonio helped him to his feet. Jerry stepped toward him and appeared to be examining him intently from just a few inches away. In Jerry's case, the seamed and battered face of the ex-prizefighter was rendered still more formidable by a piercing, predatory stare and heavy ridges of ancient scar tissue over both eyes, suggesting some prehistoric being of superhuman strength and merely conjectural rationality.

"I got one more thing to say to you, Brendan. You may be a big hit with all the computers over at the college, but around here you're just a lightweight, an amateur lightweight—and maybe you don't have so much of a flair for it, either."

"You're a hard man, Jerry, a hard man." Brendan knew perfectly well that he was not supposed to smile at this point. He had to appear chastened and subdued; it was part of the ritual. Boxing was Jerry's religion, and Brendan was one of his disciples; Brendan would have to provide him with at least a show of contrition before he could be granted absolution. It was true that Jerry Connolly, a former super welterweight champion, had gone into boxing in much the same way that many another kid from Southie of his generation had gone into the priesthood. Brendan had once told him that it was that much easier for Jerry to keep his flock on the straight and narrow, since in his religion an occasion of sin was almost invariably the prelude to a smart rap in the mouth. Jerry had momentarily relaxed his habitual smirk into a grin of pleasure when he heard that one.

"Listen, Brendan," he was saying now, "if I wasn't such a hard guy, then there's no way you'd last even one round in the amateur championships, am I right?"

"And you know I still haven't made up my mind about that. I'm not sure I'll have the time, for one thing . . ."

"You're not gonna start with all that again? Just listen for a second, okay?"

You break the cookie, Brendan said to himself, *you get to have your fortune read.*

"Okay, first of all, I'm not saying you've got no chance. You definitely do—maybe not for the finals, the semifinals even, but at least the quarter-finals, for sure. But you got to concentrate, you got to bear down. I already told you a million times, and now I'm telling you a million and one. Like when you were in the ring just now, what were you thinking about?"

"I was thinking about you, Jerry. You know, somehow I just can't seem to get you out of my mind."

Tonio, who was sliding between the ropes, carrying the gloves and the helmets, sputtered with amusement; Jerry turned around and shot him a venomous look.

"Okay, you wanna be a jerkoff all your life, okay." He turned back to Brendan.

"You were *thinking*, and already that's one thing you were doing wrong. You're in the ring, you've got only one job to do, you got to concentrate all your resources, mental *and* physical."

At this, Tonio assumed an expression of ferocious, punchdrunk imbecility and began throwing wild haymakers at the air with a pair of gloves and a helmet flailing in each hand. Jerry stiffened, looked around furiously—there was nothing worth throwing but a discarded sponge half a dozen yards out of reach—and picked up the thread of his discourse while Tonio continued bobbing, ducking, and dancing his way into the equipment room.

"Okay, second of all, you waited too long to make your move. The footwork was not too bad, and you were taking the punches pretty good. But like the Old Man used to say, Somebody smacks you on your right cheek, you stick out your left cheek. They smack you on your left cheek, you give 'em back your right cheek—and you keep on sticking out cheeks until you get *concentrated* enough to lay 'em out flat on their asses with one good shot. When you're in the ring, same as anywhere else, the whole thing is, you got to know how to take it and you got to know when to stop."

And here endeth the lesson for today, Brendan said, only half ironically, to himself, while outwardly maintaining an expression of grave neutrality.

Brendan lifted his face to receive the scalding torrent from the showerhead, stepped back, and spread his arms wide, palms upward, to enjoy this initial moment of ecstasy. For a long time he let the water stream over his body, burning by turns like fire and ice, as he cheerfully subjected his battered flesh to this final mortification. Jerry had told him that only a maniac who was a danger to himself and others never felt a moment's fear in the ring, but he was still displeased with himself for having let his emotions get the better of him.

He turned off the faucets, groped for the vast terrycloth towel, and began to rub himself dry, vigorously at first, then with a kind of mounting frenzy. He hated himself for having lost control not only of his body but of his thoughts in the ring. He hadn't taken up boxing in order to experience new and uncontrollable emotional states; when he slid between the ropes, he was hoping to leave all that behind him.

"You trying to skin yourself alive, or what?" Jerry shouted as he stepped into the shower room.

"It's good for you!" Brendan replied as he tossed his towel toward the hamper. "You want a lift, or you got your car today?"

"Oh, I got it. I was just gonna ask you the same thing." Jerry concealed his disappointment behind his accustomed crooked smile. He was fond of these little excursions with Brendan; he liked to ask him about his work "over at the college," and even made a praiseworthy effort to retain in long-term memory such arcana as the difference between microprocessors and microcomputers, between binary and octal, between discpacks and diskettes.

"You'll prob'ly be the last to leave," Jerry said. "Click over the little jigger on the door when you do. The night watchman'll be around to lock 'er up pretty soon."

Ten minutes later, Brendan inserted the key in the ignition of his car. No response. He tried again. Still nothing. With an exasperated sigh, he flung open the car door and stepped out on the sidewalk to survey the obscure sidestreet off Dorchester Avenue on which Connolly's Gym was located. The night watchman, an old Italian, extremely hard of hearing, hadn't turned up yet, and when he did, he would be unlikely to provide a solution to the problem. Brendan got back in the car and rummaged in the glove compartment for a flashlight, then walked around in front of the car, opened the hood, peered into the engine compartment, and flicked the switch of the flashlight. Nothing. He had just raised his right hand in an operatic gesture and was about to dash the flashlight to the pavement when he heard a woman's voice coming from directly behind him.

"There's no reason to get so upset. You've got a dead battery, that's all."

Furious, Brendan wheeled around to confront his tormenter. A bright red VW had come to a stop right beside him. The driver had rolled down her window and was regarding him with a disarmingly pleasant smile. It was a pleasant face, as well: very blue eyes—perhaps a little worried looking—a slightly turned-up nose, fluffy auburn hair. The sum of these was sufficiently distracting to make Brendan forget entirely about the delinquent flashlight.

"I realize that. The question is, how did you?"

"I was parked right here about an hour ago, and I noticed you'd left your lights on. Can I give you a lift somewhere?"

Brendan slammed down the hood. "Delighted."

"What happened to you?" she asked when Brendan was perched on the passenger seat beside her. "Somebody beat you up?"

"Yeah, but I really had it coming. I'm taking boxing lessons at Connolly's Gym, and I'm still kind of at that vulnerable stage, I guess."

"Don't you lose a lot of brain cells, getting hit in the head like that?"

"Yeah, but it's amazing how quickly you get used to it."

The young woman laughed. "I'm Sally."

"Brendan. So tell me, Sally, how'd you like to have dinner with me tonight?"

"I see it hasn't slowed you down too much, so far. Think you've got much of a future in the fight game?"

"You're ducking the question, I see. I'm strictly an amateur, so far. Mostly I teach—at MIT."

"A Techie, huh? I bet I know about four hundred people that you know."

"No doubt, but I'd rather go on thinking of you as the attractive stranger that got me off the streets—and that I'm taking to dinner tonight, correct?"

"You did say something about that earlier. But tell me, Brendan, are you also taking the personality course at Connolly's Gym, or do you just naturally come out swinging?"

Brendan assumed his most portentous professorial aspect, folding his arms as if to caress imaginary elbow patches. "The key to a correct analysis of any situation is to decide which of the innumerable processes involved will prove decisive to its outcome. The present moment is especially problematic because it is pregnant with so many contradictory possibilities. You could slam on your brakes, for example, and turn me in to the first cop you meet for attempted mopery or impinging on your personal space. Or we could have a very tedious conversation about whether boxing really does cause irreversible brain damage, or I could retreat into the kind of sulky, brooding silence that our culture prescribes for the macho man with a dead battery and a big, ugly lump on his kisser, who's just been caught by an attractive woman. There are lots of other possibilities, of course, but I suggest we keep two possibly decisive factors in mind: one, now that you've lured me into your car, you're not likely to get rid of me all that easily; and, two, every moment that passes is taking me farther and farther from my original destination. Which brings me back to my original question: What do you think you're in the mood for tonight, poulet Marcel at Another Season or chicken Verdicchio at Felicia's?"

"So we're back to that again, eh?" She slowed down abruptly; they had just passed Mass. General and reached the turnoff for Storrow Drive, with the gilded dome of the Statehouse and the stately homes of Beacon Hill now visible in the distance. "And just what was your original destination, exactly?"

"Oh, you can just drop me right here and I'll get a cab. Thanks. If it hadn't been for your timely intervention, I'd still be wandering around South Boston."

The car had come to a halt, and Brendan started to open the door.

"Listen," Sally said, "I don't want you to get the impression I don't *want* to have dinner with you. It's just that a friend of mine's having a birthday party tonight, very big deal, and it's all the way out on Comm. Ave., and I'm already late."

Brendan was already halfway out the door. "This birthday party of yours isn't at the St. Botolph's, by any chance?"

"Yes!"

"And your friend's name is Elizabeth—"

"Winfield! You know her?"

"She's one of my grad students—one of our many hundreds of mutual friends at MIT, no doubt. Actually, I was supposed to be going tonight, but I wasn't exactly in the mood . . ."

"Is that right?"

Brendan got back in the front seat, slammed the door. "But now I think I might be willing to give it a shot."

May 12, 1980   Vitebsk, Byelorussia

When I got married, I had no idea what that could mean to a woman. No doubt, a woman's perspective automatically makes the appropriate adjustments after she's given up the illusion of personal freedom, stopped dreaming of Prince Charming. I was twenty-eight at the time, and I knew that the little girl in me was gone for good. I could feel myself taking shape, in a sense, becoming more like a woman every day and increasingly aware of the human soul that was living inside my body. But for the longest time I continued to think that there was really something to those fantasy visions of mine. I wanted to hold on to them. I really believed in those phantoms spawned by my imagination, and every night they gently rocked my romantic soul to sleep. "Watch out for the real world," they whispered. "Too many sharp edges and corners, too many dangerous curves." Today I realize that they were deceiving me, that the so-called real world is dangerous only because it is so fragile and insubstantial, as insubstantial as any of them, and because it takes on whatever form one chooses to clothe it in—the same way that we do ourselves.

I suppose that when a woman gets married, she should try to draw up a sort of balance sheet, to draw a bold black line across the horizon to separate the earth from the heavens, the reality from what must always remain a dream. You sort out your emotions, and the ones you won't be needing anymore must be gently put aside. This is what's called putting one's life in order, a process that is supposed to give you a kind of organizational mastery over subsequent events. I doubt that this is really true, but it makes life so much simpler to imagine that it is. Looking back from some years later, I can remember the day on which this line was drawn for me with particular clarity.

Sergei, my new husband, was sitting beside me at a long table in the big banquet hall of the People's Palace. The hall was reserved for

VIP wedding receptions, and the Georgian champagne was flowing like water. Immediately after the ceremony we had rushed upstairs to receive the congratulations of the local party committee, the university, and the organs of state security (my new husband's employers). The first secretary spoke to Sergei for quite a long time, a mark of particular favor that was lost on none of those present—nor were the telegrams from the secretary of the party presidium of our republic and from Colonel Kirshnyev, Sergei's immediate superior. My mother was all the way over at the other end of the buffet when the two telegrams arrived; she managed to intercept them all the same, and shouted out in a voice that resounded across the hall, "Congratulations from Minsk!"

Several of the eminences present may have thought this display of maternal pride a little overplayed, but Sergei merely smiled. The two of them had concluded a nonaggression pact at their first meeting. Everyone has heard the old story from the thirties about the peasant woman who visits her son, a high party functionary of some sort, in his new apartment. "Very nice, my boy," she says, "only pray that the Reds never come back!" My old *matyushka*, on the other hand, was unequivocally delighted by her first sight of Sergei's apartment, and showed appropriate reverence for his collection of records from the West—not so much in appreciation of his musical taste, of course (which is good enough, as it happens), but of his status as one of the *vyezdnye*, who are permitted to visit the West from time to time. Mother listened attentively enough while he outlined the sort of prospects that could open up for a youngish man just starting a career with the apparatus of state security, particularly when he has already had the opportunity to clear up several rather delicate matters to the satisfaction of his superiors, and has been ordered to report directly to Comrade Pavel Pavlovtsev (who reports directly to Comrade Yuri Andropov, the KGB director in Moscow). And Mother annotated Sergei's little speech with nods and smiles and questions whose meaning was unmistakably clear: "Very well, Sergei Denisovich, I have no doubt that a splendid career awaits you in your chosen field, but Yulya knows plenty of other successful young fellows, and you've got ten years on her as it is. At your age, it's high time you started moving up the ladder just a little bit faster than you seem to have been doing so far." Our affair had already been going on for three years; marriage seemed the simplest and most prudent way of ending it.

Sergei had allowed my mother to take charge of the wedding breakfast; a more elaborate formal banquet would be held that evening. She had invited people from Vitebsk for the most part, of course, plus a few of her colleagues from the state farm administration, as well as other rural dignitaries, some old school friends of mine unexpectedly turned out as adults, and a few elderly parties who seemed to be wearing the castoff clothes of sons or daughters much larger than themselves. I smiled as I watched my mother, a sleek little white-haired woman who seemed a bit tired, absently tapping out the rhythm of the inevitable Gypsy orchestra. I suppose she thought that she had seen her duty done and was impatient to get away, to lie down for a while, rub cologne on her temples, chat for a while with her cronies about the splendid marriage her daughter had made, and then get back to her desk as Comrade Director, Office of Heavy Equipment, State Farm "Seventeenth of October."

Sergei laid his hand on top of mine, and I shamelessly allowed my fingers to be possessed by his affable paw. I took note of the coarse blond hair on the backs of his fingers, his blunt manicured nails, his knobby knuckles and fingerjoints. He stroked my hand, lazily and gently, but I could feel so much energy, so much violence, through that simple contact. I didn't love him, and any passion that he might have felt for me was undoubtedly composed of equal parts of ambition and undifferentiated lust. We could both help each other with our careers; Pavel Pavlovtsev was Sergei's marriage portion, Afanasyev was mine. We each had a protector who was a good deal higher up in the hierarchy than our boss's boss; this was an anomalous and unstable situation, since the protégé is invariably drawn up to the level of his protector before very long. That's the way it always works.

That didn't prevent Sergei from continually proclaiming his love for me—doubtless out of simple male pride of ownership—and, of course, my love for him was regarded as a truth so fundamental that it never had to be mentioned. As for myself, I know that love is only a kind of passion that's based on mutual misunderstanding. I've experienced all of its well-known raptures with a man who today, most assuredly, finds it no more difficult to live without me than I do without him.

At the next moment, the violinist leaned over the bride, his instrument emitted a kind of moan, and I felt ashamed, all at once, of the tears at the corners of my eyes, the epigrammatic turn my thoughts were beginning to take, and Sergei's soppy, emotional smile. To be perfectly fair, there was, and is, a certain tenderness between us without which—all of our calculations of self-interest aside—it would not have been possible for us to get married at all. This bond of affection, of emotional complicity between us, came into being on the day that he first made Svetlana laugh, the day she first adopted him as her own. My child, my exquisite little daughter, my reason to live—with your dark eyes on me at this moment, I can't help thinking of your father, and now I think it's time to tell you why.

At first he scarcely noticed me, it seemed. At MIT, I might have had a modest novelty value, for a short time at least, as a participant in the graduate exchange program with the USSR, but essentially I was just another graduate student—not, as you might imagine, a very glamorous stratum of the university community. I shared my dormitory room in Ashdown House, on the MIT campus, with a compatriot, Ludmilla, the daughter of a corresponding member of the Soviet Academy of Sciences. She was endowed with a genuine sense of mission, a subject she would discuss with an earnestness that was truly touching. Sometimes I recognized one of her father's ready-made phrases tumbling heavily from her lips, but, in contrast to the learned academician, Ludmilla spoke her lines with complete conviction, straight from the heart. Inside her little blond head, stale party slogans from the Workers' Motherland seemed to coexist perfectly amicably with the newly minted clichés of the American mass media. Like so many of my countrymen, she was fascinated by American pop culture in all its manifestations.

"He's really a *hunk*," she told me one day, strongly aspirating the *h—khunk*. "He's really got *sex appeal*."

We were sitting on the carpet in our dorm room, with a teapot and glasses between us on the coffee table.

"How do you mean, exactly?"

"I mean that when I *get next to him*, I can feel myself sort of melting inside. Like when he brushes against me in the hall or something, or when he looks right into my eyes . . . Have you noticed the way he looks at you, with those big dark eyes, like a Gypsy?"

"That's quite romantic. Are you sure you don't just mean you're in love with him?" I had been looking forward to a long session of baiting Ludmilla, but this discussion was beginning to make me feel vaguely uneasy.

"Certainly not! It's just that he happens to be very attractive, irresistibly attractive—in a certain way, a physical way. And anyway, if I'm, you know, especially susceptible to his particular kind of attractiveness, maybe it's because he's, like, sort of got his eye on me."

"Possibly." I was in a jealous snit by then, and doubly furious at myself for reacting so idiotically.

"Unquestionably. You know, he asked me to call him Brendan?"

"Must be quite a treat."

"Do you think Americans like to make love in any special way?"

Clearly, Ludmilla's plans for her own squalid seduction should not have upset me as much as they did. As a future Soviet scientist, I should have been pleased, if anything, since if Ludmilla did succeed in getting Professor Barnes where she wanted him, she might very well pick up the odd tidbit of information that the KGB people in our delegation would be grateful for. But obviously all such considerations were very far from my mind. I was entirely eaten up with jealousy—vicious, primal, and malevolent; I was the lusty female hominid, ready to scratch her rival's eyes out to win the favors of the dominant male of the troop—or, in this case, of the MIT Computer Science department. But in spite of the homicidal impulses I was harboring toward Ludmilla at that moment, I think I would rather have died than let her find out what I was really feeling.

"Don't you think you're getting a little bit ahead of the game?" I finally asked.

"Not at all. When we're in the computer center, he doesn't pay any attention to anyone but me. He—he positively showers me with compliments. He told me I had a brilliant mind."

This time it was all I could do not to burst out laughing, and I was suffused with an immediate and total feeling of relief. It had been Ludmilla's father, Academician Mikhail Sevlayin, who had summoned me to his vast and featureless office in the Byelorussian Institute of Computer Science to inform me personally that I had been selected to take part in the exchange program with MIT. At that time I was still quite unaccustomed to the sort of unabashed cynicism to which our leadership sometimes resorts in its less formal moments, and his remarks made a very strong impression on me.

"My daughter is an imbecile," he announced, "but of course she'll be accompanying you to the United States. As you know, ours is a centralized *democracy*, not an intellectual oligarchy—consequently, there's no room for elitism, and we can't allow the specialists to lead us around by the nose. In a delegation of this kind, all points of view must be represented, and a certain proportion of its members must be chosen according to social and political criteria—in addition, of course, to those who are genuinely . . . ah, competent from a scientific standpoint. By the standards of a place like MIT, my daughter is strictly an Epsilon Minus, and I'm counting on you to keep her from making a complete ass of herself. Your professors tell me you have more than enough ability for the two of you. See to it that Ludmilla gets through the year all right, and I can promise you right now that you won't be wasting your time in Vitebsk for very long once you get back. I'm going to have plenty of little tasks for you."

As it happened, I liked Ludmilla, and I was glad to help her out. I hovered over her and forced her to work; I wrote out everything I thought she ought to know on index cards, and made her learn them all by heart so that she wouldn't disgrace herself too badly in front of her professors or the other graduate students. Still, there is quite a difference between not being unmasked as an idiot and overwhelming someone with the naked power of your intellect. None of her professors could possibly have told her that she was "brilliant." She was making it all up, and everything she had said, or implied, about her relationship with Professor Barnes was merely a by-product of her overactive endocrine system. I was surprised—and, once again, very much ashamed of myself—to discover how happy I was to have arrived at this conclusion.

"If he said something like that," I replied after a longish pause, "God knows, he has to be crazy about you."

Ludmilla studied my face carefully. "Are you making fun of me?"

"On the contrary. He's obviously interested in your mind. I'm sure he thinks he's discovered an irrefutable demonstration of the old Cartesian mind-body problem, since in your case your brain and your head are in diametrically opposite locations."

It took a moment or two for this to register, but by then Ludmilla's agreeably freckled face was contorted with fury. "Why are you being such a bitch?" she shouted. "Who the hell do you think you are? You think you're so fucking smart! *You're* the one with the mind-body problem, not Cartesian—"

"*Descartes*—the man's name was René Descartes. He was a Frenchman, for God's sake, not an Armenian . . ." But Ludmilla had already leaped to her feet, crossed the room, and slammed the door. I was left alone.

Then something suddenly occurred to me that produced an unmistakable pang. Of course, what I had just told Ludmilla was perfectly correct. No one could have any conceivable motive for telling her she was brilliant, unless he was making a shameless, all-out effort to lure her into his bed. The pang that had struck me a moment ago had now lodged firmly in my solar plexus.

Ludmilla was swift and terrible in her wrath, but forgiveness came almost as swiftly, and by Thanksgiving the unfortunate incident had long since been forgotten. In the late afternoon of the following day, she burst into our room shrieking, "I don't have anything to wear! I don't have a costume for the ball!" exactly like Cinderella run amuck.

"Nor I," I replied, without looking up from the volume of Lermontov that I was leafing through.

"Then what are you going to do tonight?"

"Write some letters."

"You must be crazy! What about the dance? It's a costume ball, actually—we're all supposed to dress up like the Pilgrims from the *Mayflower*."

"I know, but I don't have anything to wear either, and I haven't had time to make the rounds of the thrift shops—"

"The thrift shops? You really are crazy. You're supposed to try to look beautiful. And remember what the Komsomol secretary told us before we left home: 'Never forget, under any circumstances, that you are representatives of the Soviet Union, but you should also never neglect an opportunity to really get to know the American people.' This seems like the perfect opportunity; I'm sure all the really attractive men are going to be there."

"Such as they are. Does that include Professor Brendan Barnes, by any chance?" I had a little difficulty speaking past the obstruction in my throat.

"Oh, him," Ludmilla replied airily. "That's all over with now. You know, according to what Jenny told me, sooner or later they all go out to their cars in the parking lot and put back the reversible seats as far as they'll go—"

"*Reclining* seats—they're called reclining seats! And you sound like you're all ready to do a little reclining of your own."

"But don't you get the idea? A real American orgy! The fleshpots of the decadent West! I want a taste of what it's really like before I go back to Minsk, and I've wasted quite enough time already!" She rushed over to our communal closet and started rummaging through my clothes.

"What are you up to now?" I asked.

"I'm going through your clothes—I'm sure you've got what they call a basic black in here that would make a fine little Puritan costume, or maybe something just a *little* less old-fashioned would do for Scarlett O'Hara . . ."

"Scarlett O'Hara was two hundred fifty years too late for the *Mayflower*," I muttered with pedantic ill humor. I was a little offended by the way Ludmilla had maligned my wardrobe (even though my mother had picked out most of it). Nevertheless, her enthusiasm for the project was contagious, and when our friend Jenny came by later and assured us that most of the others probably wouldn't bother with costumes, I decided to put off writing my letters until another night.

And, as it turned out, I didn't feel the least bit self-conscious at the dance, nor was there a fleshpot or even a hint of capitalist decadence in evidence. Apart from a handful of frantically dancing Pilgrims, who looked preposterous enough, no one had made much of an effort to dress up. In my great-grandmother's black taffeta, a genuine prerevolutionary relic, I was one of the most elegant women in the room, and if heads turned in my direction, it certainly wasn't because I looked frumpy or outlandish.

The ballroom—one of the undergraduate dining halls, in fact—was immense, with high windows overlooking the concrete-clad banks of the Charles. The entire room sparkled like a Christmas tree; the ceiling was covered with multicolored paper streamers, like a great soft meadow that you'd want to run through in your bare feet. I must have fallen into a sort of reverie, because neither at that moment nor subsequently could I have described the precise sequence of events that led me into the arms of Brendan Barnes. I do remember that in the midst of the joyous cacophony of the dance floor, a curious silence seemed to have enveloped me. I don't remember when we first caught sight of each other; we must have been dancing together at some point, but I have no memory of that either. The one thing I can recall quite clearly is a kind of woodsy, underbrush smell that I became aware of the instant his hand touched the back of my neck to draw my lips toward his.

At this far remove in time, everything I experienced at that moment now seems hopelessly adolescent and self-indulgent, but I'm still very proud, for once in my life at least, to have felt emotions of such extraordinary clarity and purity. I felt certain that we had always loved each other, that we were meant to love each other, and that from now on our lives would flow together as sweetly and fiercely as our lips and our bodies were pressed together. It seemed like a very long time before we broke away from our embrace—when I sneezed. We found ourselves standing on wet grass; a cold mist was rising off the river, loud dance music was still coming from close by. I couldn't see his face too clearly, but I could tell that he was smiling.

"You're going to catch cold," he said softly. "Let's go back in."
But he held me close once more.

"My name is Yulya," I said.

"I know."

"I want to make love with you."

I could feel the muscles in his back stiffen, and he suddenly thrust out his arms, holding me at arm's length, as if to examine me more closely, and looked me squarely in the eyes.

"Let's go in," he said abruptly. He put his arms around my waist and began to steer me back toward the dance. I was watching his face closely, but now his eyes avoided mine.

"Was it wrong, what I said? Did it upset you?"

"No, not really . . . well, actually, yes, I think so. I mean, for one thing, we Irish Catholic boys tend to be a little slow on the uptake, you know, and for another, I've never been seriously involved with one of my students before, and don't you sort of get the idea that this might be pretty serious?"

"Do you think it vulgar of me to want to find out right away?"

We were back inside in a few moments, and I suddenly felt suffocated by the heat and the noise. The harsh lights over the bandstand hurt my eyes, and the gaiety and animation of the dancers seemed to me like a cruel charade—behind each of their smiles I thought I could detect an anxious grimace or a mocking smirk.

"Let's go now," I said.

"In a minute," he replied. "I think we should both try to calm down a little and maybe talk about what's just happened to us, figure out what's going on."

"I don't want to talk, I want to leave right now." There wasn't all that much we had to talk about, in my opinion, and I didn't want to stay there for another second, even with him. I wasn't sure he understood why I was so upset; I barely understood myself. Perhaps he simply thought I was eager to try out the upholstery of his car, as Ludmilla had mentioned earlier; if so, he should have been relieved that I was willing to take the initiative. Instead he merely seemed hesitant, bemused; perhaps he thought we should be permitted to go to bed together only after a lengthy series of talks, as if we were trying to ban cruise missiles rather than falling in love. But then, perhaps he simply hadn't felt the same thing that I did.

Before he could say another word, I turned my back on him and ran out of the building and across the parking lot. There were shadows moving inside many of the cars; I even thought I could make out Ludmilla's face behind the steamy windshield of one of them—if so, she had bagged an attractive BMW. I thought for a moment of pleading with her to come back with me, and then I thought of what her reaction would be if I attempted to deprive her of her first real taste of American decadence, and hurried on.

I was walking down the sidewalk along one of those interminable avenues by the river, where the wind blows straight down from Greenland; I could hear it whistling in my bones. It seemed like I'd been walking for hours, but I think I'd gone only a block or two when I heard a car come to a stop right behind me. I turned around and was blinded by the headlights. Brendan's voice called out to me, "Get in, Yulya. Don't be stupid!"

I did as he said. I was too cold in just my dress to put up much of an argument; I no longer felt betrayed and panicky, merely sulky and out of sorts. He started the car, and we rode along in silence for a minute or two. "I'm sorry," he finally said. "I didn't realize."

"And *I'm* so sorry I had to cut short our most interesting discussion. It's so rare that one finds a professor here who's so willing to *talk* to his students—taking care to avoid encouraging undue familiarity—"

"Okay, I admit I behaved like a total jerk, and I know I deserve a lecture. Which reminds me, did I neglect to compliment you on your incredible command of the language, to say nothing of your unbelievably charming accent? And then there's the fact that you're undoubtedly one of our most brilliant students, in addition to being breathtakingly beautiful—I can see you riding at the head of a troop of cossacks, laying waste the Old World and the New—though I should also mention that for all your charming qualities, you've also got a rotten disposition."

I couldn't help smiling as this tirade finally wound down, followed by several moments of silence. We were on the Southeast Expressway now, speeding past the nocturnal clutter of Boston Harbor. Brendan took the turnoff to Quincy Market, and when we had arrived at an especially nondescript intersection, he began to circle around and around a desolate traffic island. I didn't think to ask him what he was up to.

"Do you really like me?" he asked suddenly.

"Haven't you already guessed that?"

"I mean, do you *really* like me?"

"And haven't you guessed that too?"

"We seem to have reached an impasse," he said, in a voice that was meant to sound offhand and casual. Then he slammed on the brakes; the tires gave out an unearthly squeal. He cut the engine, tilted the seat back as far as it would go, and threw himself on top of me . . . and that was the beginning of the happiest year of my young life.

On the other side of the wall, Sergei is sprawled across our bed, sleeping the sleep of the contented if not the just. As I finish this first installment of my confessions, I want you to know, my only reader, my dear Svetlana with your beautiful Gypsy eyes, that I'm not making any excuses for what I've done. Sergei and I have entered into what, in capitalist terms, might be called a limited partnership— we're responsible only for that fraction of our assets which we've invested in this entity, and we've kept a great deal in reserve. If our bodies can give us pleasure, then there is no need for our dreams to become involved; he has his own secret garden of political intrigue, to say nothing of the periodic delights of a "rest cure" at a Black Sea health resort. I, of course, have my memories.

But you must realize that this tacit understanding which exists between your stepfather and me in no way prevents me from respecting him for what he really is, and by its very terms I am barred from indulging in irrelevant comparisons and from reproaching him for what he is not. I know perfectly well that Sergei belongs to the real world, the world we have to live in, and Brendan belongs only to the world of dreams and regrets. Still—there was so much between us, an absolute trust that came into being almost with the very first moment. It seemed ludicrous then that I had been so jealous of Ludmilla, but less so than it did to him, when I finally confided my suspicions some six months later. The fact that she had played such a crucial role in bringing us together—quite unwittingly, of course—made me feel a special, sisterly tenderness toward her, though I admit I had to make a special effort to sustain this feeling through many sleepless nights of coaching her for our first round of qualifying exams and preparing all of her seminar papers, as well as my own. Ludmilla's outpourings of gratitude made me feel a little ashamed, of course, since I knew perfectly well that it was not simply out of friendship—or because she had become a sort of mascot to our love affair—that I was doing all this for her.

And as it turned out, we both did quite well—remarkably well, under the circumstances—and as soon as we got back home, Academician Sevlayin admitted that we had surpassed his highest expectations. Two days after our first meeting, he called me back to his office to meet Afanasyev, who explained the broad outlines of the plan to computerize all the information systems of the Soviet Union and even suggested what role I might be able to play in all this. Sevlayin, too, had more than lived up to his part of the bargain.

I had never imagined for a moment that I would not be returning home when my year in Cambridge was up. This was something that Brendan had never been able to understand.

"You don't really love me," he would insist.

"Brendan," I replied on one particular occasion, "don't you know that you break my heart every time you say something like that? First of all, I have to think of my mother—she'd lose her job if I didn't go back, and she'd end up sweeping the streets or something. I could never do a thing like that to her."

"We could fix it for her to come over here—"

"You know perfectly well that that's not true. Anyway, even if it wasn't for her, I'd still have to go back. I love my country. I know our system's still far from perfect, but I think that if it's capable of improving, it will be because of people like me. Scientists and engineers are the only ones who stand a chance of overcoming the collective inertia of our leadership; we've discussed this often enough. The computer really will make it possible to do something about waste and profiteering; the rationalization of our economy might very well mean the end of ruling-class privilege and parasitism."

"Possibly, but the odds are certainly against it."

"That's why I feel that it's so important for me to go back. The greater the odds against us, the more I feel like they really need me."

"But not as much as I do."

"Why are you being such a hardhead? You know you can't make me change my mind, but you can still make me feel rotten and guilty if you really want to. We'll find some way of seeing each other again. You don't realize that the very idea of losing you is enough to make it all seem like nonsense, to make me think I'm about to go crazy . . ."

I burst into tears at that point, and Brendan took me in his arms; once more, the incredible magic of our bodies could undo all the complicated spells our minds had woven around us. We made love with a passion that was, as they say, born of despair. Svetlana, by the time you read this, I will probably be quite old, perhaps out of this world altogether, and I'm sure the idea of your old mother indulging in these operatic transports will seem to you quite preposterous, if not actually indecent. But I want you to know that it was as a result of these few minutes of ecstasy at the edge of madness and desolation—or, more specifically, between a political discussion and dinner at a Chinese restaurant—that you were born into this world, my Svetlana, my beautiful little daughter with your big, black Gypsy eyes.

May 12, 1980   Boston

Tonight, the St. Botolph's Club, traditionally the resort of brahmins, literary men, and the more eminent academics from Harvard and MIT, presented an unaccustomed aspect of restrained festivity, like a butler after his second drink. Though the clubroom and the reading room remained undisturbed, the ballroom had opened its doors to nonmembers—for perhaps the dozenth time in living memory—to celebrate the twenty-first birthday of Miss Elizabeth Winfield, daughter of the club treasurer. The portraits of distinguished members of an earlier era turned a serene or dyspeptic gaze on the rented tropical foliage and the painted cast-iron lawn furniture that had been tastefully deployed around the perimeter of the dance floor.

Brendan and Sally danced for a couple of minutes, then talked for a great many more. He discovered that his new acquaintance was the daughter of a physicist, though she herself was interested exclusively in literature. Sally decided she approved of her companion's sharp features and raven-black hair, though she planned to reserve judgment on the purplish, egglike lump on his chin. He was only an inch or two taller than she was, carried himself confidently and even gracefully, and seemed, thus far, to be free of the more obvious personality disorders that were endemic to his profession. He even had a nice ironic gleam in his eye. And, like a typical graduate student in the humanities confronted with a captive scientist, she felt disposed to bait him a little.

"This *debugging* that you do—is that something I'd think was interesting?"

"It *is* interesting, in spite of what you seem to think. What I teach my students to do, essentially, is to eliminate bugs, all the little errors that creep into the coded instructions that make up a computer program. When you consider that a really sophisticated program might require something on the order of a million lines of code . . ."

"And the rest of the world is so perfect that you can't tolerate one little mistake in a million lines of code?"

"Big or little, a programming error—though not in every case, I admit—can have literally disastrous consequences; a bug could conceivably put a company out of business or kill a patient on the operating table, cause a plane crash or a shipwreck. Okay, consider this—a modern supertanker is almost entirely automated. Its course is plotted by an onboard computer, with a little help from a satellite weather relay, radar, and all the rest of that good stuff. Very little human intervention is required to pilot a ship of more than a million tons' displacement."

"But if an oil tanker gets into port a day late, that's not necessarily the end of civilization as we know it, right?"

"Maybe not quite, but bear in mind that the onboard computer on every one of those tankers may be using essentially the same program, and if that program fails, that means that maybe fifty percent of the world's oil supply is going to be treading water until somebody can figure out what's wrong."

Brendan smiled to himself. He had lifted this little speech, almost word for word, from a conversation he had had three days earlier with his distinguished senior colleague, Clive Woodward. His mind suddenly flashed on a shock of ruffled white hair and long, nervous fingers fiddling with the eyepiece of his glasses. Woodward was a South Carolinian—an old-time Charleston type—who looked, dressed, spoke, and even smelled exactly like an Englishman. Trim, tweedy, and unapproachable, he was an almost legendary figure out of the days of Turing and von Neumann. Brendan had found a note in his mailbox requesting him to look in on Woodward at his earliest convenience. This was puzzling; since Brendan had joined the faculty, he had hardly exchanged more than an occasional nod with Woodward. A few minutes later, when Brendan tapped on the door-frame and stepped into Woodward's office, his perplexity was only partially dispelled by the sight of a copy of the current issue of the journal *Computers and Society* on Woodward's desk. The moment Brendan's foot crossed the threshold, Woodward began to speak to what was apparently the matter at hand.

"This article of yours, Mr. Barnes—I must say, from what I hear of you, it seems to be cast very much in your own image. Thoroughly sound, but perhaps just a bit . . . precipitate. Permit me to illustrate . . ." In a crisp, precise voice, which seemed to acquire a thin crust of irony as it went on, Woodward read aloud a passage from Brendan's article in which he had suggested that sophisticated computer technology might be useful as a weapon against Soviet ideological penetration of the West, as a means by which an informationally open democratic society might compensate for its extreme vulnerability with respect to an informationally closed totalitarian society.

"So it seems," said Woodward when he had finished reading, "that you're not simply one of our brighter backroom technical boys, but you've also taken the time to have an idea or two—in fact, to have evolved rather far-reaching views on the political, I might even say the *geostrategic*, implications of what we're up to."

"Does that surprise you?"

24

"Well, I won't say it's unheard of, but it's rare enough. Be that as it may, the real reason I wanted to see you was to ask you if you'd be interested in doing a job that would allow you to start putting some of these advanced ideas of yours into practice—that is, unless you have some objection to being directly under contract to the Defense Department?"

"Well, of course, I'd have to know more about what you have in mind."

"The fact is, I'm speaking on behalf of a number of old gentlemen like myself—most of them not nearly so old as myself, of course—who have come up with some notions remarkably similar to those set forth in your article—clearly a case of 'what oft was said, but ne'er so well expressed'—and we look forward to having you join us in our deliberations. I've been asked to form a working committee with a view to setting up something called DISSA, the Defense Information Systems Security Agency—I didn't pick out the name, you understand—an autonomous body that will be funded primarily by the Pentagon and the National Security Agency. The basic idea's been knocking about the Pentagon since the early seventies, when some of the cleverer generals began to notice that they were paying out more for military software than they'd originally plunked down for the machines themselves."

"Certainly it's not always that obvious to the consumer why the software should end up costing twice as much—or ten times as much—as the hardware," said Brendan.

"Perfectly true, and in this case the greatest single item of expense—half of the total, in fact—could be attributed directly to the language problem." Woodward was referring to the fact that programs are currently written in about fifty different, mutually unintelligible computer languages, so that a programmer who wants to insert a brief routine written in Fortran, for example, into a program written in Cobol generally ends up rewriting one or both of them from scratch.

"When the chorus of Babel became positively deafening," Woodward went on, "the planning and security sections at the Pentagon were obliged to announce an international open competition in order to put together a team of programmers capable of creating a standardized computer language for all military applications. I daresay you've heard a word or two about that." The objectives of this project were to create a language that could be readily transferred from one machine to another, that would maximize the speed and efficiency with which calculations could be performed in real-time application (that is, in situations such as an aerial dogfight or a medical emergency, which require the machine to respond almost instantaneously to a rapid sequence of events in the real world), and that would be designed to make debugging as easy as possible. In 1979, the Defense Department spent more than $500 million on debugging military programs; it was estimated that a comprehensive review of all the programs used by the navy alone would cost $24 *billion*. The winner of the competition was a Frenchman, Jean Ichbicah of Honeywell Bull; the language his team devised was called ADA, after Ada, Countess of Lovelace, mistress of a nineteenth-century logician and usually considered to have been the world's first programmer.

"I know a little bit about ADA," Brendan said. "One of my classmates is working on that one with Ichbicah."

"What I trust he hasn't told you is that ADA has been *officially* operational for at least a week. One of the first tasks entrusted to DISSA will be the thoroughly unenviable one of rewriting most of the programs used by the military. Next, we hope to implement a scheme for what you might call 'preventive debugging'—to rule out bogus alerts and other costly blunders of the sort that you're familiar with—that will systematically be applied to all such programs in the future. The department I've been asked to supervise has been charged with this phase of the operation, as well as with a number of other more general—and, I trust, more interesting—projects that may fall within the ambit of that most interesting passage I quoted to you a few minutes ago."

In spite of all his efforts to the contrary, Brendan was grinning broadly. "'To respond forcefully to Soviet attempts to gain access to high-level technology that it has been the conscious policy of the West to deny them'? I'm quoting from memory, of course."

"Yes, though that's looking a bit far down the road for now. To begin with, the working committee is going to indulge in a little catastrophe planning—studying the effects of various sorts of massive systems failures that were *not* caused by computer mishap, but which very well might have been, such as the New York City blackouts and the far more extensive failure of the French power grid last year. The 'oil crisis' of 1973, as we now know, was inspired by a computer simulation that was run at OPEC headquarters in Vienna."

After he had tried out the French power grid and the OPEC computer simulation on Sally, Brendan realized that, like a supertanker deprived of its satellite guidance system, he was not making very much headway.

"I see I can't possibly convince you of how glamorous and exciting it must be to do what I do"—he gestured with his empty glass—"so what would you say to another drink?"

Sally nodded, and as he got to his feet, he noticed one of the portraits on the wall, half hidden behind a voluptuous philodendron.

"Robert Frost! I had no idea he was a member here!"

"One of the best," Sally said. "You're fond of Robert Frost?"

"The desolate, deserted trees,
    The faded earth, the heavy sky,
  The beauties she so truly sees,
  She thinks I have no eye for these,
    And vexes me for reasons why.

"Not bad, huh? I know that whole poem practically by heart—I learned it to impress a literate friend of mine," said Brendan.

"Very impressive, for a hopelessly right-brained debugging teacher. Sounds like the view from our country house in November, as a matter of fact. It's a cabin, really. Maybe sometime I'll take you there."

"I think I'd like that very much. Listen, since they seem to have closed the bar down hours ago, and I can't just go on sitting here without an unmanly display of emotion—do you think I could possibly have this dance?"

TWO

September 3, 1983   7:30 A.M.
Neuilly-sur-Seine, just outside Paris

Cynthia Thompson always professed to be amazed by the ease with which her husband could awaken out of a sound sleep and plunge right into the deepest thickets of the international press—generically referred to in the Thompson family as "the Hungarian hog reports," since Richard Thompson was the Paris correspondent for a New York–based monthly called *Eurobusiness*. Richard Thompson was also a communications specialist for the CIA, attached to the Paris embassy, and it was this second career that kept him from getting home in time for breakfast on a great many nights. Last night had been one of them.

He got out of bed even before the alarm watch had started to bleat beside his pillow, threw open the curtains, and cast a baleful eye on the gray and watery vista outside the bedroom window; then, still in his pajamas, he padded into the adjoining room and sat down at the desk. The entire house was perfectly quiet; in a way he felt safer here—and not just in the jargon sense of "safe house"—than he did inside the fortress complex of the embassy on the Avenue Gabriel.

He extracted a bulky file folder from a drawer, and glanced at the labels on the dozen or so manila folders inside until he found what he was looking for—a thin sheaf of single-spaced pages of thick bond paper with the legend DEPARTMENT OF DEFENSE—CONFIDENTIAL emblazoned at the head of every page. "Hog reports," he muttered to himself, and began to read:

Working Committee on Information Systems Security
Case Study No. 1—Franco-Soviet Computer Software Sale as a Vector for Projected Aggressive Application
Restricted distribution—6 copies

"France has acquired a solid international reputation as a producer of computer software; our goal should be to do whatever is necessary, and by whatever means necessary, to secure the product loyalty of our current customers in order to avoid being overwhelmed by our American competitors. We should take care to emphasize in all our dealings with our trading partners— with French-speaking countries in particular—that computer software can be a *powerful means of cultural infiltration*. A program effectively contains all the cultural traditions of its country of origin in highly concentrated form. We should emphasize that in this respect we can offer a reasonable alternative to cultural colonization by the United States—a fact that is already clear to the Council of Ministers, which has recently decided to give top priority to the exportation of French computer software in determining future policy on foreign trade."
—Pierre Fromentin, chef du cabinet (undersecretary), Ministry of Research and Industrial Development, in *En-Jeu*, February 1983

Background
In 1975, a Soviet trade delegation offered to purchase the outmoded Univac mainframe on which Air France had developed its famous Alpha 3 program for coordinating passenger information worldwide. The Soviet offer was especially generous in that it would virtually guarantee the replacement costs of the system

at current prices; also, the Soviets were willing to pay in cash, which furnishes another indication of their desperate need to obtain computer equipment, even a relatively low-powered vintage model like the Univac, at almost any price. Air France was Univac's oldest client, and in order to maintain good customer relations, Univac was helpful in walking through the necessary export clearances in Washington. Authorization for the sale was granted at the end of 1975, and the sale occurred shortly thereafter.

Two years later, Anatoly Kasparov, director of Aeroflot, requested a meeting with Maurice Daniel, the Air France executive in charge of data-processing operations. After lengthy preliminary negotiations had been concluded, Kasparov came to the point: Soviet programmers lacked the experience and the technical wherewithal that would enable them to write their own software. It would be a matter of several years before they could expect to have even the most rudimentary program running. The purpose of the meeting was to sound out M. Daniel on the possibility of selling the Alpha 3 reservations program to Aeroflot.

This request was passed on to the directors of Air France; the president of the airline conferred personally with government officials at the highest levels. Permission was granted for the sale. Once again, the Soviets were prepared to pay an exorbitant price in order to acquire this mammoth program, on an unmodified, strictly "as is" basis; Alpha 3 consists of several million lines of programming code, which, even assuming that the capability existed, might have taken ten years for the 152 computer specialists at Aeroflot to replicate successfully.

Since a similar transaction is currently contemplated by the same parties, on a similarly extensive scale, the Working Committee proposes to conduct a detailed study of this earlier transaction and ultimately to report on the feasibility of targeting the product introduced into the Soviet data bank as the subject of an "experimental" Aggressive Application, as that term has previously been defined in . . .

Richard Thompson glanced at his watch. In four or five previous readings, he had already virtually memorized the next few pages, and it was time for a news broadcast that he was particularly eager to hear. Mechanically he flipped through the remainder of the report; his eyes rested for a moment on the list of names at the bottom of the last page:

Distribution:
Two (2) copies to Dr. Clive Woodward, director (designate) of Special Task Force on Counterintelligence Applications, chairman of the Working Committee
One (1) copy each to:
Dr. Arthur McDonald, director (designate) of Research and Development Section
R/Adm. John M. Eckleberry, director (designate) of Operations Section Archives
Richard Thompson, diplomatic liaison, U.S. Embassy Paris
Dr. Brendan Barnes, preparer of the foregoing report

September 3, 1983 8:15 A.M. Paris

When the miniature clock-radio delivered its wake-up call to the tune of "La Cucaracha," Françoise opened her eyes and, contrary to her usual custom, leaped energetically out of bed. She retrieved her crumpled bathrobe from the floor and paused in front of the three-piece mirror to give her slim, brown body its first critical inspection of the day before making her way down the hall to the kitchen alcove. As she plugged in the coffeemaker, the last chorus of "La Cucaracha" finally died away, to be replaced a few moments later by the thundering, overamplified tones of ORTF commentator Ivan Levaï.

"MONSIEUR LE MINISTRE, I'VE ASKED YOU TO JOIN US THIS MORNING SO YOU CAN HAVE THE OPPORTUNITY OF EXPLAINING TO OUR LISTENERS EXACTLY—"

Françoise dashed back into the bedroom, lowered the volume a quarter-turn, and remained crouched expectantly by the radio while Levaï boomed relentlessly on.

"—what this computer deal with the Soviet Union is all about. As you know, a Soviet delegation, headed by Academician Konstantin I. Afanasyev, is expected to arrive in Paris this morning to begin negotiating for the purchase of a bank of high-powered computers from the National Meteorological Center, together with all the computer software that has been designed to go with them. Now, what strikes me first of all is that the machines themselves are Craig 1's—strictly *made in U.S.A.*, in other words—whereas the programs were developed by our own computer experts . . ."

Françoise reached out with one finger and depressed the "record" button on the minicassette recorder that was built into the radio.

". . . So, to help our listeners get a clearer idea of what's really at stake in these negotiations, I'd like to start you out with three questions.

"First, if this deal goes through, we'll be furnishing the Russians with sophisticated computer equipment that may conceivably be of great strategic value. Is this the result of a conscious policy on the part of the government to expedite the flow of high technology in an easterly direction?

"Second, why are we trying to sell them *American* computers? We have a computer industry of our own, right here in France—an industry, I might add, that's just been subsidized by our fellow taxpayers to the tune of two billion francs paid into the sadly depleted coffers of Honeywell Bull. Are we to conclude from this that the French computer industry simply isn't competitive on the world market?

"And my third and final question: Don't we seem to be rather at cross purposes here? By that I mean, on the one hand, we're seriously committed to a policy of discouraging *private* entrepreneurs from selling advanced computer technology to the Eastern bloc, while at the same time the *government* seems to be on the verge of making a no less serious commitment to turn over some of the most powerful computers in the world to the Russians—to help them catch up in the one race, at any rate, that they seem thus far to be losing to the West. Could it be that the presence of several Communists in the government has induced it to adopt this extremely *flexible* approach? And the Americans—how do you suppose they're likely to react to all of this?"

As the insinuations mounted, Françoise slipped back to the kitchen alcove and gulped down a cup of coffee. A dancer's barre was bracketed to the wall between the two high windows in the living room. There was a clean leotard draped over the barre; she shrugged out of her bathrobe and started to put it on. She was just lacing up her ballet shoes when she realized that Levaï's special guest, René Duvallon, Minister of Research and Industrial Development, had begun to speak his piece. Gripping the barre with both hands, she arched her body forward while the point of one toe shot outward and upward in an extraordinary arc and a mocking half-smile appeared on her face.

"Now, my dear Levaï," Duvallon was saying, "I hope you'll agree that there's really no place for red-baiting in a discussion of this kind. Also, we're talking about selling our entire computerized weather-forecasting system—the whole thing, mind you, not just the computers. We're offering the software, the peripherals, everything around and *inside* the computers as well. These machines were made in the United States, but, if I may say so, they've learned to think in French. We mustn't lose sight of the fact that computer software is at least as important as hardware in a case like this, since it's the program that tells the computer exactly what you want it to do.

"The fact is that France is second only to the United States among the world's leading exporters of computer software. If we want to maintain our position in the world market, we'll have to play hard. If we've been dealt a winning hand, then why not play it?"

"You'll forgive me if I keep mentioning it, Monsieur le Ministre," Levaï said, "but we're not just talking about computer *programs* here. No doubt the Russians are going to use our programs to tell them whether or not it's going to snow tomorrow in Minsk or Vladivostok, but how do we know they're not going to use the *computers* for less peaceful purposes?"

"I can answer that quite simply—we're offering to sell the Russians a weather-forecasting program, but we're never going to sell them military software—not today, not ever."

"But you're still not answering my question. What's to prevent them from writing their own military software, and running it on the Craig 1 computer?"

"In theory, nothing, but the real possibility that these programs could be modified, or that military software could be produced from scratch to run on the Craig 1, is not all that great—the Soviets simply don't have the technical capability. Also, experience has taught us that the maximum number of programmers who can work efficiently on a given program is about a hundred and fifty. Once you get past that point, management and communications problems tend to get out of hand, the law of diminishing returns sets in, and overall productivity begins to decrease. The weather-forecasting program we've been talking about consists of some six million lines of programming code; the daily output of the average programmer is about thirty lines of debugged code. That means it would take a team of a hundred and fifty programmers, of roughly similar competence, at least *six years* to come up with an equivalent program. Now if the Russians sat down to do this today, even if they did succeed, it would take them six years, by which time their program would be hopelessly obsolete— to say nothing of the fact that the average useful life of a computer mainframe is only about *five* years. So you can see that, in the circumstances, there's really no way the Russians can catch up to us at that rate, and if they want to buy our computers, they'll have to use our programs as well. The risk that this material could be used for any purpose more sinister than forecasting the weather is virtually nil."

"Unless they get hold of the appropriate software by some other means."

"Perfectly correct, but let me repeat that the computer programs we are talking about this morning are entirely *in*appropriate, indeed completely useless, for any other purpose than forecasting the weather."

"Very good. So much for the software, then. But let's get back to what I believe was my second question, Monsieur le Ministre. Why aren't we trying to sell them French computer *hardware* as well?"

Françoise was sitting under the barre with her legs tucked underneath her, trying to catch her breath. She'd had bad dreams last night—unhappy memories, rather—of the tin-roofed shack near St. Pierre, at the foot of Mount Pelée, that was her childhood home. *Martinique, an earthly paradise . . . if you have someplace else to come home to.* She had dreamt about her father, actually; he would have been proud to see her today, in this expensive apartment, surrounded by all these beautiful things—even though he would have been shocked to the depths of his respectable West Indian soul by some of the prints she had hanging on the walls . . . and by the way she left her clothes lying around, of course. She laughed and got slowly to her feet; the past was pain and helplessness and poverty, and none of those things had any claim on her now.

"Monsieur Levaï," Duvallon was saying now, "the Americans are turning out the most powerful computers in the world. To give your listeners some idea of the orders of magnitude involved—the Soviets' top-of-the-line computer, the Elorg, is rated at 1 MIPS (in other words, it's capable of executing one million instructions per second). Our most powerful computers are rated at 10 MIPS, and a high-powered American machine like the Craig can get up to 50 MIPS. Our strong point is writing programs, so that's the main thing we've got to sell."

René's in pretty good form for this early hour of the morning, Françoise thought to herself. *Lots of techie talk to let everyone know he's done his homework, and he managed to sidestep that business about the two billion francs quite nicely.*

"Let us speak frankly, Monsieur le Ministre. Does the government have some ulterior motive in making this deal with the Russians? And are you sure the Americans are going to give it their blessing? After all, why in the world should they?"

"I really can't speak for the Americans, of course, but what we're hoping to do, quite frankly, is to stabilize the position of our own computer industry, in anticipation of the day—perhaps only three years hence, in 1986—when the Japanese supercomputers are expected to make an appearance on the world market. And in fact, we have *every* reason to believe that the Americans will extend their blessing, as you put it, to this transaction with the Soviet Union. A team of American computer specialists is also arriving in Paris today. They'll be examining the programs we're offering to the Soviets to make absolutely sure that no strategically sensitive material is included."

"And don't you find it somewhat humiliating to have an American inspection team going through your luggage, as it were?"

"As you know, France, along with fourteen other Western nations, is a member of an international organization called Cocom, which is chiefly concerned with preventing high-technology products with potential military applications from falling into the hands of the Eastern bloc. France is a loyal and responsible member of every international organization to which she has pledged her faith, be it Cocom or the European Common Market. Our sovereignty and our dignity as a nation are by no means impaired because we have done our duty by honoring the simple, formal requirements of such an international accord. Furthermore, this is a formality that must be observed, if we intend to continue the fight for new markets overseas, if we intend to take part in one of the first great commercial battles of the Information Age. This is a rendezvous with destiny that France must not, for any reason, fail to keep."

"Monsieur le Ministre, I thank you very much."

Françoise returned to the bedroom to turn off the radio and the recorder, trailing the loose ribbons of her ballet shoes behind her. René had actually done rather well for himself, particularly that last business about the dignity and the destiny of the nation. In reality, this was a touchy question, as Françoise well knew; she had written a memo on the subject, "Enforceability of American Statutes Restricting High-Technology Exports," for the senator for whom she was working as a parliamentary assistant—a position she hoped to be leaving before long. Duvallon had furnished her with a great deal of information, not much of it very soothing to French self-esteem.

To begin with, Cocom—the Coordinating Committee on Multilateral Export Controls, the object of such fervent protestations of loyalty on the part of Duvallon—was a so-called international watchdog agency, most of whose bark and virtually all of whose bite was supplied by the United States. Set up at the time of the Korean War,

Cocom had originally included Japan and all the NATO countries except Iceland. A few more had been picked up since then. In addition, all advanced American computer equipment—such as Duvallon's Craig 1's—was subject to the fairly stringent provisions of a variety of official trade embargoes and export control legislation.

As far as enforcement was concerned, it could work in either of two ways. A French corporation found guilty of bootlegging computer hardware to the Russians could have its assets confiscated in the United States, or its officers or employees could be arrested the moment they set foot on American soil; alternatively, the contracts for all overseas computer sales executed by the Americans could contain a clause binding the purchaser to abide by the terms of the relevant Export Control Acts and whatnot. This meant, in effect, that if the Americans thought you were up to no good, they could declare the purchase null and void and get a judgment against you to that effect in a French court; such a clause was deemed to be enforceable under French law as long as it was "not contrary to French public order." In the bad old days of colonialism—of the British in Egypt, for example, or any of the European powers in Imperial China—this sort of thing was called "extraterritorial jurisdiction," and was not commonly reckoned to have a very salutary effect on the other fellow's dignity or sovereignty as a nation. Françoise wondered what Duvallon would have had to say if Ivan Levaï had asked him, "Is it true, Monsieur le Ministre, that where computers are concerned, the Americans can force French courts to compel French citizens to obey American law?"

Amused by these reflections, Françoise slipped out of her leotard and made her way to the shower. She thought she could hear the phone ringing over the rush of the water, but decided to ignore it. When she came out, it was still ringing.

"Where were you?" Duvallon's voice sounded annoyed. "I let it ring for at least ten minutes."

"Five. I was in the shower. You're not going to start cross-examining me again, are you?"

"Sorry, *chérie*, but I had to talk to you right away. Did you hear it? How did it go?"

"You said 'actually' once or twice too often, but otherwise you were great. I've got the whole thing on tape."

"Seriously? You're not just saying that?"

"Absolutely. You didn't put your foot in it once. You're a natural for radio—you can tell the microphone really loves you."

"Now you're making fun of me. All right, I'll let you go now. I have to drop by the ministry before we go out to greet the Russians at the airport. I'm afraid I can't see you tonight. We're having them all to dinner, ours *and* theirs. I'll call you tomorrow, all right? *I love you.*"

Françoise assured him that the sentiment was mutual, and hung up the phone.

September 3, 1983   11:00 A.M.
In French airspace

Yulya smiled and shook her head; Afanasyev nodded emphatically as the stewardess took his empty plate and replaced it with another piled high with blinis and sour cream, smoked salmon, and a pot of caviar on a bed of crushed ice. Starting about fifteen minutes after their Tu-154 had taken off from Sheremyetevo Airport, the flight crew had been fussing around the first eight rows of seats occupied by the delegation, plying the academicians and the bureaucrats from the Ministry of Foreign Trade with champagne and costly tidbits. In response to Yulya's admonishing glance, Afanasyev spread his hands, palms upward, above his plate.

"I can't seem to stick to a diet when I leave Moscow. They have a special dietetic menu, you know, for the fat boys on the Central Committee, and somehow, when we're all sitting there in our modest refectory on Nikitinov Street, suffused with the spirit of fraternal solidarity and self-sacrifice . . . but look here, there's another half-bottle of champagne, and they haven't switched the real glasses for plastic yet. Join me?"

Yulya held out her glass. "To the success of our glorious mission!"

Side by side, they made a curious pair. Yulya was trim and businesslike in a tailored blue suit and a plain white blouse. Afanasyev was cast in the more traditional image of Soviet officialdom—thick-necked, jowly, and paunchy. Yulya sometimes felt almost queasy in the presence of a man with the ambitions of a Caesar and, within his own scientific and political domain, the arbitrary despotic power of a sultan. Intellectually and ideologically, at least, there was complete sympathy between them.

Thanks in part, as they said in the papers, "to the vigilance of the organs of state security," Soviet science and industry could produce a reasonable facsimile of a jetliner like the Concorde (the Tupolev-51) or a second-generation IBM computer (the ES-1060s that Yulya and her colleagues worked with). Getting the planes off the ground was a relatively simple matter; the shortage of adequately trained personnel and sophisticated software made it quite a bit harder to make good use of the computers. Soviet engineers had turned out extremely complex programs for certain applications to which the state had already devoted a relatively high proportion of its resources—the military and the space program, for instance—but in the realm of communications and database management (particularly critical in view of the highly centralized economic and political structure), the Soviet Union was falling farther behind by the week. Afanasyev and Yulya believed that this deficiency could best be remedied in the obvious way, by importing software from the West. Indeed, as far as their current mission was concerned, the programs that had been written for the Craig 1 were hardly less impressive a prize than the high-powered computer itself.

Afanasyev smiled and set his glass back on the tray. "You know, there's a substantial body of opinion within the French government that we're not entirely to be trusted. For one thing, there was that business about the computer that was supposed to be used for the Olympics and turned up unexpectedly on the premises of the Committee for State Security . . ."

Yulya tilted her head back a few degrees, indicating the KGB official who was seated farther down the aisle. "Our friends are always with us, of course, but somehow I don't think the higher-ups are really all that interested in the Craig 1."

Afanasyev's smile abruptly vanished, then reappeared as he

placed a beefy hand on top of hers on the seat divider. "My darling Yulyochka, doesn't that handsome husband of yours ever tell you anything? Acquiring a new machine that will increase our computational capability by a factor of fifty—to us, that seems like serious business. But to the politicos it's just a tiny chip—if you'll kindly excuse the expression—in the high-stakes game between Andropov's bunch and the other bunch, the wooden-headed old Brezhnevites who are opposed on principle to anything that seems to put more power in the hands of the technocrats."

"It seems to me that, given the state of the economy, the politicos should be glad to let someone else take the blame for a while," Yulya observed.

Afanasyev chuckled. "Very prettily said, and I couldn't agree more. But you know, Yulyochka, that I'm in complete sympathy with the announced objectives of Andropov's bunch—modernization, self-motivation rather than collective responsibility, reduction of waste and good old Slavic inefficiency, an increase in freedom of initiative—but only up to a point, of course. On the other hand, that certainly won't stop me from supporting an entirely different set of principles if the other bunch gets back in. As long as we have history and the laws of historical materialism on our side, what does it matter if the official line takes a momentary turn in the wrong direction?"

Yulya snatched her hand away with a show of mock indignation. "Why, you're just a cynical old careerist, after all!"

"It's merely a case of knowing when to go with the psychological moment, and when to beat a tactical retreat, as you just did when you took your hand away. Listen to me, Yulya," he added, in quite a different tone, "you must never forget that this sort of conversation—speaking from the heart, saying what's on your mind—you mustn't talk like that with anyone but me, you understand? Frankness can be an effective tactic, but only if you know when to use it—such as when you have absolutely no intention of telling the truth."

Yulya screwed up her face. "Another of your idiotic epigrams. In any case, frankness isn't a tactic, it's a quality; there are some people who just naturally tell the truth and there are people who tell lies—just the same as there are good programs and programs that are nothing but garbage."

"A typically petit-bourgeois point of view," Afanasyev replied, as he refilled their glasses.

September 3, 1983   11:30 A.M.
Charles de Gaulle Airport, Roissy

The officer of the Police de l'Air et des Frontières handed back his passport, and Brendan slipped it into an inside pocket. Just then he caught sight of the highly visible figure of Richard Thompson bearing down on him from across the concourse—over six and a half feet tall, with blue eyes and flaming red hair, wire-rimmed glasses and the slightly rumpled trenchcoat without which, as Thompson invariably claimed, "the French always seem to think my press credentials are bogus."

"So," said Thompson with a grin, "the Rat's come out of his hole at last."

"Only I'm not a Rat anymore. It seems I've been kicked upstairs."

They had met for the first time about a year ago, in the cavernous underground structure occupied, in part, by the working group that had been recruited by Clive Woodward and now bore the characteristically grandiose and imprecise designation of Task Force on Counterintelligence Applications. It soon became apparent that the search for an automatic method of debugging programs could have occupied any number of systems programmers for any number of lifetimes, so it was decided instead to concentrate on the more accessible problem of devising a way of deliberately and undetectably *inserting* bugs into a program—presumably someone else's. This, in fact, was what Clive Woodward had really had at the back of his mind when he had first summoned Brendan Barnes to his office at MIT.

So it was that Woodward's section of the newly established Defense Information Systems Security Agency had taken on at least a shadowy existence in a high-security facility in suburban Virginia—not many miles from CIA headquarters at Langley—which housed a number of vaguely similar and equally mysterious "working groups" sponsored by the National Security Agency or the CIA. Brendan Barnes and his colleagues were immediately dubbed "the Rats" by the denizens of the other corners of the futuristic subbasement that had been set aside for their use, perhaps simply because, as veteran programmers, they seemed to take quite naturally to this underground and largely nocturnal existence. The nickname even seemed to have been afforded a kind of quasi-official confirmation, judging from the innumerable white-stenciled inscriptions that read RE-SEARCH AND TECHNICAL SECTION and had subsequently appeared on almost every door and wall, equipment locker and instrument panel in the immediate area.

Richard Thompson had been brought in as soon as a Paris-based operation was envisaged, and since their initial meeting, Brendan had had several opportunities to enlarge on their acquaintance in the course of brief reconnaissance missions to Paris. As a man whose knowledge of the French bureaucratic terrain and the personalities involved would be essential, Thompson would continue to stage-manage the opening phases of the operation.

"Tonight," he told Brendan as soon as the initial pleasantries had been dispensed with, "I'm going to introduce you to someone who knows most of these people very well and should be able to run the whole thing down for you pretty thoroughly."

"Does he know who he's going to be talking to, exactly?"

"It's a *she*—currently working for a French senator, also very tight with Duvallon, apparently, but she's bored with all that and she wants to get into 'international journalism,' God help her. I told her that if she could write up a coherent account of this Russian computer deal, I'd put in a word with the boys at *Eurobusiness*—and that she could do *me* a favor by talking to my friend Dr. Brendan Barnes, who's over here with the Cocom verification team and would really appreciate a confidential deep background on . . . ." He smiled. "Anything you'd like to know?"

"Ideally, of course, I'd like to find out whatever I can about exactly what their political motives are in putting this thing through, and also if they've implemented any special debugging procedures for the weather-forecasting program itself. Finally, I'd like to know what sort of arrangements they've made to maintain the program once the computers have been installed in their new home in Krasnoyarsk. Your friend will probably know more about the political end of things; let's hope the bona fide verification guys can get a line on the rest of it when they actually check out the programs and talk to the technical people at the Meteorological Center."

They fell silent when they reached the crowded bank of elevators that led down to the parking lot. Conversation resumed only after they had climbed into a black Renault—Brendan took the wheel—and turned onto the autoroute in the direction of Paris.

"I've got some bad news for you," Thompson said, "and some bad news. Security's got to be much tighter this trip. That means, first of all, the Concord Lafayette is strictly off limits, and, second, it looks like you'll be bunking in with yours truly, at my little gray home in Neuilly. We've got kind of a low-grade alert on these days; there's been some talk of a new wave of terrorist attacks directed specifically against Americans."

"The Middle East?"

"Always. Also, they tell me there are a few new faces in town, from the Caribbean—sort of the French equivalent of the FALN. Seems they're pretty pissed off about Grenada. However, I want you to understand that the actual *risk* involved is minimal; it's just a form of what we in the business world like to refer to as 'key-man insurance.' Also, we'd feel pretty stupid if you ended up getting wasted by this Club Med Liberation Front or somebody, just when we'd finally gotten your ass out of that damned basement."

September 3, 1983   9:30 P.M.   Paris

Dinner was served in a splendid second-floor room of Duvallon's Paris town house; the tapestries on the walls provided conversational fodder for the first couple of minutes, then Virginie Fromentin, the wife of Duvallon's deputy, asked the Soviet delegate if she preferred to be addressed as Mme. Voron*kov* or Voron*kova*. Yulya replied that the more modern tendency seemed to be to abandon the feminine ending, which, grammatically at least, implied that a wife was her husband's possession.

Duvallon, who regarded this sort of conversation as both frivolous and potentially subversive, hastened to change the subject. "And it does seem that in so many ways East and West are moving closer together every day, toward a single global society, sometimes one of us furnishing the model, sometimes the other."

Afanasyev raised one eyebrow expectantly, as if waiting for Duvallon to start making sense, and Yulya replied, a little sharply, "If you mean that we're still following the Western model as far as data processing is concerned, then I'm afraid I have to disagree. We're not imitating the West—we have our own model information system, just as in the past we have had our own Soviet models of industrialization and the collectivization of agriculture. Admittedly, the Craig 1 will allow us to approach quite a bit closer to that model . . ."

Duvallon had stopped listening. The essential thing was that both of the Soviet delegates had been talking all evening as if the sale were a foregone conclusion. They had spent the late afternoon at the embassy, they must have been in communication with Moscow, and they had obviously gotten the Kremlin's final approval. The rest was just playacting. Then Duvallon realized that, deprived of his conversational stewardship, the others had drifted back to the subject of tapestries.

"I don't know," his wife was saying, "if criticism can ever hope to penetrate to the real, essential meaning of a work of art. In my opinion, a painting or a tapestry simply offers itself up for one's appreciation, like a beautiful woman standing naked before her lover . . ."

There was no immediate reply to this from the rest of the French contingent. Afanasyev was grinning broadly, though perhaps the better to accommodate a heaping spoonful of charlotte aux rougets. Yulya seemed merely preoccupied. Duvallon suddenly remembered that today, September 3, was his thirtieth wedding anniversary. Something had to be done before all hell started to break loose.

"You're definitely in fine form tonight, *ma chère*," he muttered to his wife, then turned to Afanasyev. "I have something to show you that's truly unique, Academician Afanasyev. It's an original photograph of Lenin, taken when he was in exile in Switzerland. My father sometimes used to play chess with him at the Café Voltaire in Zurich . . ."

"Sounds very interesting," said Afanasyev. "I'd like to have a look at it, after dinner."

"Actually," said Duvallon, rising hurriedly to his feet, "why don't I get it right now? It's just in the library, I won't be a moment."

The dining room was separated from the library by a folding door and a short hallway. There was a telephone in the hallway, and Duvallon picked up the receiver and dialed a number as noiselessly as possible. When a woman's voice answered, he cupped one hand around the receiver, pressed the mouthpiece right up to his lips, and spoke in a whisper. "Françoise, *mon amour*, I so much wanted to hear your voice."

"Can't you talk any louder? It's not a very good connection."

"No, I can't. Listen to me, Françoise . . . I miss you very much."

"What's going on? Are you afraid the Russians have got your telephone bugged?"

"Of course not! It's just that I . . . can't exactly afford to be overheard just now. Why else do you think I'd be putting myself through all these contortions?"

"I can't imagine. You do behave rather strangely sometimes, you know."

"But what's really strange is that an old man like me should be carrying on like a lovesick adolescent. How are you right now?"

"I'm fine."

"That's not what I mean. I mean, are you dressed?"

"No, I'm stark naked. I'm in bed with a whole family of Chinese acrobats. Right now I've got three of them in the air and one of them flat on his back."

"Françoise, I'm serious, don't start up with me like that."

"All right. Seriously, René, you know perfectly well that I haven't gone to bed yet, so I'm still dressed."

"But I have to know what you're wearing. It helps me . . . to visualize you the way you are at this moment. It's ridiculous, I know, but indulge me just this once."

"Very well. I'm wearing the red lizard shoes you bought for me, and my white dress from Patou. Are you sure that's all you wanted to talk about? How are you getting on with the Russians?"

"Splendidly. It's in the bag. Apparently Moscow just gave the go-ahead."

"That's wonderful. You must be thrilled."

"Oh, you know, after twenty years in politics, you can't really get too excited over something like this. That little pimp Fromentin, my so-called deputy, he's the one who should really be pleased by all this. Listen, I have to get back to my guests. But I have a favor to ask of you. It's extremely important. I need a cake. There has to be an inscription—"

"What are you talking about? Are you drunk?"

"Certainly not! Listen to me, Françoise. It's our thirtieth wedding anniversary—Gilberte's and mine, that is. I'd forgotten all about the damned thing. I can tell she's likely to make things very awkward for me if I don't make the appropriate gesture. That's why you have to get hold of a baker or a caterer for me, have them send a cake over right away."

"Isn't it a bit late for that sort of thing?"

"Of course not. There should be plenty of places still open, on the Champs-Elysées and in Saint-Germain. Hurry, though. It's essential that we not have another of those dreary episodes this evening. Oh, and you'd better call a florist as well, and have them send up a nice big bouquet—"

"Will there be anything else? A big box of those Cuban cigars you like? Something nice for breakfast, perhaps?"

"Please don't be angry with me, Françoise. You know I wouldn't be calling you like this if the situation wasn't absolutely critical. I'll call you again, just as soon as I get a moment."

"Just don't make it too late, okay?"

Damn, she's really furious, Duvallon thought, as he removed a tiny framed photograph from the wall.

"He says it's in the bag," Françoise informed her two visitors, Richard Thompson and Brendan Barnes. Something in her expression had dissuaded the two of them from so much as cracking a smile during her phone conversation with Duvallon. Perched on the edge of her bleached-oak desk, like a secretary in a film from the 1930s, she crossed her legs as she reached over to hang up the phone, giving Brendan the chance to admire a well-tended stretch of thigh. "I have to make a couple more calls," she went on. "The liquor cabinet's downstairs. Help yourselves. I won't be long."

The entrance hall of Françoise's duplex led directly onto a kind of balcony on the upper level that overlooked the living room with its high windows, which in turn provided a view of the Square des Guillemites in the historic Marais district of Paris, now in the full throes of gentrification after centuries of genteel poverty. Thompson poured them each a drink from a bottle of Scotch, and they sat down at an elegant counter finished with white lacquer streaked with red. Brendan amused himself by watching Françoise's cinnamon-colored calves swinging back and forth behind the rails of the balustrade, to the rhythm of her mounting exasperation. From the torrent of rapid French he could pick out the words *Villa Montmorency, Seizième Arrondissement*, and *immédiatement*.

The three of them had adjourned to Françoise's apartment after a fairly perfunctory dinner in a neighborhood restaurant, since she was reluctant to talk about Duvallon or any of his doings in a public place. Brendan glanced at Thompson, surprised that he could regard his "contact" with such stolid indifference—tempered, perhaps, by a vague contempt for the transparency of her ambitions but apparently without a flicker of appreciation for the beauty of her delicate, almost Oriental features or her slim, sinuous body.

Upstairs, negotiations with the bakery had apparently broken down. Françoise slammed down the receiver and began dialing another number. Brendan shifted around on his stool to look out through the window at the square. It was just a few blocks from here, Thompson had told him, that the killers of the Rue des Rosiers had vanished without a trace, putting an end to one of the most mysterious episodes in the bloody annals of international terrorism. It occurred to him, not for the first time, that he and Thompson were terrorists of a sort; they certainly would be considered so if they were working on their own, or merely on the instructions of a government far less powerful than their own. As it was, their activities were certainly no less furtive and underhanded, and would be considerably more destructive—if successful—and only less bloody by virtue of the fact that very few actual flesh-and-blood humans were likely to be involved.

Françoise slammed down the phone again, and dialed another number. By now she was working on the florists. Richard Thompson emptied his glass and stood up. "I've got to get going. I trust you two will get along all right without me. Try to find out if she does know anything about whatever provisions have been made to maintain the program once the machines have been delivered. It'd be instructive to know what the first-stage reaction is likely to be on the part of the French, once we get going. I'll see you tomorrow morning, then. Harry's Bar, ten A.M."

"I'll be there."

Thompson scuttled up the spiral staircase to the balcony level, pausing briefly by the desk until Françoise—still in the midst of soothing an irate florist she had just awakened out of a sound sleep—acknowledged his departure with a distracted wave of the hand. Brendan poured himself another Scotch and listened as Françoise's voice became progressively more honeyed and enticing, the sums under discussion more and more astronomical. Finally the bargain was struck. Françoise came down the staircase at an unhurried pace, and with what Brendan automatically categorized as a display of unselfconscious slinkiness. "And now, Dr. Brendan Barnes," she said, "I'm at your complete disposal."

As Afanasyev finished off his Bavarian cream with Cointreau, Duvallon involuntarily exchanged glances with Yulya Voronkov. He felt obliged to make some sort of remark; she replied in kind, a social smile on her lips, her eyes as cold as ice. Duvallon felt distinctly ill at ease. He had no difficulty in dealing with someone like Afanasyev—basically a very capable fellow, for all of his rather brutal *muzhik* mannerisms, and really quite predictable, whereas this Mme. Voronkov was another matter.

They drifted into the drawing room for coffee, and when the conversation began to sputter and die, Duvallon cleared his throat in a ceremonious manner and said, "Academician Afanasyev, Madame

Voronkov, if you'd be good enough to step into my office for a moment, along with Monsieur Fromentin . . . I had an opportunity to speak with the Prime Minister a little earlier, and informed him that we seemed to have a firm basis for an accord. Now, I've had a few more thoughts that I'd like to share with you—"

While he was speaking, the butler had come into the salon and murmured a few words to Mme. Duvallon. "Oh, René," she burst out suddenly, "that's really too delightful!"

"What's that, *ma chère?*"

"They've just delivered the cake downstairs."

"Our thirtieth wedding anniversary," Duvallon interposed suavely. "But perhaps, *ma chère*, this is neither the time nor the place—"

"On the contrary!" exclaimed Afanasyev. "No time like the present, after all! And surely the petty concerns of the marketplace should yield to the highest sentiment of which mankind is capable."

"Bring in the cake, please," commanded Gilberte Duvallon, having seized the psychological moment.

"And some champagne as well," echoed her husband, with an air of not entirely graceful capitulation.

A cake decorated with an enormous heart and the inscription *Trente Ans de Bonheur*, "Thirty Years of Happiness," was wheeled in on a cart. While the butler was opening the champagne, Yulya asked, "What sort of a cake is that?"

"It's called a *tourment d'amour*," explained Virginie Fromentin. "Originally from the West Indies, I believe."

"Madame," said Afanasyev, lifting his champagne glass, "permit me to kneel before you and lay at your feet—metaphorically speaking, of course—in honor of this happy occasion, the prize that your husband was hoping to extract from us *in camera* a few moments ago. After tonight, I trust no one will accuse the representatives of the Soviet Union of being addicted to diplomatic secrecy. Monsieur le Ministre, in the name of the Presidium of the Supreme Soviet and the Ministry of Foreign Trade of the USSR, I have the honor to inform you that we have accepted all your terms, and when we meet tomorrow, Madame Voronkov and I will be pleased to sign the draft agreement."

Brendan stumbled over the first step on the stairway; the renovators had lovingly preserved the narrow staircases and aimless corridors of the original eighteenth-century tenement, and Brendan had no clear idea of what floor he was on. Characteristically, the light in the hallway was controlled by a *minuterie*, a time switch that might enable an extremely agile and well-oriented person to make it down to the next landing before the light switched off automatically. Brendan was not so lucky; he had to grope along the wall with both hands to find the switch. When the light came on again, he gave a violent start. A tall, loose-jointed, light-skinned black man dressed in a threadbare mackinaw and with long, snaky dreadlocks hanging down over his forehead was standing on the next step down, glaring at him with manifest hostility.

The two men stared at each other for several seconds without uttering a word. Brendan was reluctant to force his way past, or indeed to turn his back on, the other. Finally the black man lunged past him and up the stairs, took a key from his pocket, and started to unlock the door to Françoise's apartment. Brendan hurried down the stairs, making some effort to keep himself from turning around and looking back.

September 4, 1983   9:45 A.M.   Paris

Brendan emerged from the Opéra métro station and made for the Rue Daunou. This had become a familiar route by now; at this hour, he and Thompson would have the mahogany-paneled elegance of Harry's Bar virtually to themselves.

"Morning, Richard," said Brendan, as he sat down at Thompson's table. "Everything's running right on schedule. Duvallon called her back later on, while I was still there. Afanasyev made a strong verbal commitment last night. Duvallon's convinced the formal signing or closing, or whatever you call it, is going to happen sometime today."

"They can move pretty fast when they want something badly enough. Did Françoise happen to mention one of Duvallon's other distinguished guests—a lady mathematician called Yulya Voronkov?"

"Not by name. She said Duvallon kept teasing her about entertaining *la belle Ninotchka* in his private dining room. I assumed that was meant to be some kind of joke." Brendan searched Thompson's impassive face for a clue to what this was all about. Was Yulya really in Paris? In all the background material he had seen so far, the name of Afanasyev's deputy was given as Y. N. Voronkov. When he knew her, her name was Yulya Nikolaevna Techayev. She could have gotten married, of course; she seemed to have done very well for herself in other respects. At any rate, when he was cleared to join Woodward's working group, he had made no secret of the fact that he had been seriously involved with a Russian graduate student. Certainly he had been over that a hundred times with those characters from the NSA, or whatever they were. There was no way in the world that Thompson didn't know about it too, so why was he playing these ludicrous "we know that you know that we know" games?

"One more thing," Brendan went on, after a long pause. "I ran into a kind of weird-looking character when I left Françoise's apartment—tall, light-skinned West Indian, I guess, with one of those Rastafari hairdos. He didn't seem any too glad to see me, and he had a key to her apartment."

"That would be her brother—one of the ones I was telling you about, in the forefront of the Antillean independence struggle. Thinks he's sort of a combination of Bob Marley and Che Guevara. So far, strictly words rather than deeds, but he could definitely cause problems for us. We may have to prevail upon our friends in the DGST to send him back home to the islands for a while. They can do things like that over here, you know." He chuckled, sketching a giant tabloid headline in the air. "'SEPARATIST SLAYS SIS, CYBERNETICIST, SELF, IN CARIBBEAN CRIME OF PASSION.' No way we could keep something like that out of the papers."

"Am I supposed to laugh when you have one of these psychotic episodes, or just pretend not to notice?"

"Okay, Brendan. That's just my way of letting you know that this guy's not going to be a problem, okay? We go to the French, to the DGST, and start whining about this dangerous subversive who represents a serious threat to the security of our personnel over here, and they'll be only too glad to get rid of him. I can positively assure you that your paths won't cross again, all right? And the main thing is, if this computer deal actually does go through, it'll be time for us to exercise our sacred contractual right of examining the programs and everything before they ship them out, and you'll get to play your big scene."

The waiter appeared at Brendan's elbow, and they remained silent for a minute or two until he had returned with a cup of coffee. Brendan reached into his inside jacket pocket and removed an envelope, which he slid over to Thompson.

"I've written up all the relevant details of my conversation with Françoise. Not much to say on the technical side, but quite exhaustive as far as the political and what you might call the motivational aspects are concerned."

"Could you give me the gist of it right now?"

"The gist of it is that Duvallon's pretty smart, but he's really only interested in this computer deal as a way of getting a little extra leverage at the ballot box and in the Chamber of Deputies. In other words, no immediate plans to do another deal with the Russians in the future. Fromentin and the guys from the other ministries who've been brought in on the negotiations, they all sound like fanatical ideologues—because they're French, primarily—but basically they're just a bunch of marketing specialists and economists who've been called in for a second opinion."

Thompson mulled this over for a moment, then said, rather unenthusiastically, "That's great. I realize it isn't exactly what you signed on for, and I know you must think we're spreading you pretty thin on this one, but I think you better try to maintain contact with Françoise—"

"I have every intention of doing so."

"—and try to keep us reasonably up to date on their reactions to the operation as it develops. Of course, the moment she seems to suspect that something's not quite *comme il faut*, then you definitely shouldn't press your luck. Veer off as quickly and unobtrusively as you can."

"Of course," said Brendan, puzzled by the bizarre personality change that Thompson seemed to have undergone in the last several minutes. This was explained, at least in part, by Thompson's next remark.

"You know," he went on, in something more like his normal voice, "that I'm extremely fond of Sally, don't you?"

"Certainly. I was delighted that you two really seemed to take to each other the first time you met."

"I like her books, too. I think she's a damn fine writer. You know, you should be able to exploit this contact without doing anything that would hurt her in any way."

Brendan found he had to make a special effort to keep his cup from rattling against the saucer. "I hear you, Richard, for Christ's sake. I'm not sure whether you mean it as advice or as a warning, but I'll certainly keep it in mind."

They both fell silent once again, as they considered the magnitude of the task that lay ahead of them.

"You know," said Brendan, "later on, when we talk about how it all seemed like such a good idea at the time, the time we're going to be talking about is now."

"That's exactly right," said Thompson. "And in a couple of days from now, the *softwar* will be well and truly under way."

THREE

The pale, frozen light of a new day filtered in through the half-opened blinds. Yulya, her face still puffy with sleep, slid one foot out from under the covers and began to probe for her slippers under the bed. Outside, the wind off the western steppes was gathering strength for one last assault on the sheer granite towers of the university. The words of a famous old convict song came into her head: "Brothers, it's a long road that takes us to Siberia . . . but if I'd tried to live a different life, I'd be here all the same."

She smiled and nodded her head to the plodding, lugubrious rhythm of the song. At thirty-seven, she had a husband and two fine children, a palatial five-room apartment, a brilliant career—she had just been chosen by the Soviet Academy of Sciences to fill a new appointment as research director at the Institute for Computer Science and Applied Mathematics at Krasnoyarsk—and she no longer had much time to think about the past. *Diagnosis*, she said to herself, *seasonal depression, aggravated by chronic romanticism. Not a very fashionable ailment for someone in my situation.*

Sergei tapped on the doorframe and walked into the bedroom, clad only in his pajama bottoms.

"It's time! Awake already?" he said brightly, as he spotted Yulya's outstretched foot, still groping for the lost slipper. "And how's my lovely wife this lovely morning?" He sat down heavily on the bed and took hold of her ankle, then shook the bedclothes to uncover one leg entirely as he slowly raised her foot to his lips and seemed to be about to nibble her toes.

"I have to get dressed!" She leaped out of bed and ran barefoot into the bathroom; Sergei admired the planes and contours of her retreating figure with a philosophical eye. He was not about to give up as easily as all that.

"Not too cold today," he called out, simply so that she would have to leave the bathroom door open in order to answer him.

Yulya was standing at the sink, squeezing toothpaste onto her toothbrush. "Not *too* cold, perhaps. Don't you have to get dressed today?"

"You going to be looking your best for Afanasyev?"

"Don't say stupid things when you can help it."

"You went to bed with him when you were in Paris together, didn't you?"

There was no reply. Yulya was industriously brushing her teeth.

"I know for a fact that you went to bed with him, and it wasn't just because you'd had too much champagne, either." There was no answer. Sergei leaned forward on one elbow to get a better view of his wife's full breasts and attractively rounded buttocks; she went on brushing her teeth. His hand touched a hollow in the mattress that still retained some of the warmth of her body. He went on, in a harsher, more strident voice now:

"I hope you realize that your appointment at the Institute has to do with a lot more than just your sterling professional qualifications. You're playing Afanasyev's game now, and there are going to be risks involved. He's a technocrat, he wants to run everything with computers—I know all about that—but he and his kind may have been moving just a little bit too fast. Andropov's on their side now, but who knows how long that's going to last? Maybe before long the people that put me in my job are going to get tired of giving away all the power to the people that put you in yours.

"It's funny," he continued more quietly, "but has it ever occurred to you that our so-called marriage is just like Soviet power in micro-cosm—a marriage of convenience between the bureaucrat and the technocrat? And need I add that it's a highly unstable alliance, liable to go sour at any moment? Maybe I only married you because some-body has to keep an eye on you, did you ever think of that?" Sergei regarded himself as the faithful vassal of the old-line Brezhnev faction of the Central Committee (Konstantin Chernenko among them), whom he assumed had been responsible for his recent appointment as political coordinator for all scientific installations in Central Si-beria.

Yulya put down her toothbrush and began to rummage around in the little cupboard that contained her toilet articles. Sergei slammed his fist into his pillow.

"Let's just hope, for your sake, that *our* marriage lasts just a little bit longer than the other one—" Sergei called out to her.

"You'd better hurry up and get dressed. You're going to be late. And didn't anyone ever tell you that you can get into serious trouble by talking like that?"

As another perquisite of rank, Yulya and Sergei had been given an apartment in a modern building adjoining the university complex, only a few hundred meters from the Institute. Even this, in the depths of winter, could be something of a trial; a black Moskvich sedan with a driver was always kept at her disposal, though she al-most invariably preferred to walk. Today the main building of the Institute was festooned with banners proclaiming the indissoluble attachment of its occupants to the Communist Party of the Soviet Union and welcoming the official delegation that was due to arrive shortly to inspect their most recent acquisition.

She nodded to the KGB man stationed by the main entrance; he handed her an identification badge—the color was changed every day—and she walked to the elevators. Her office was on the second floor; right below, past another, more elaborate checkpoint on the first underground level was the computer room. This, with the con-stant soft clicking of the machines and its unmistakably sharp, metal-lic smell, had always reminded her of a vast underground gallery in an anthill (an anthill equipped with fluorescent lighting, to be sure, and in which the walls were all painted white). Here were housed the data banks for the world meteorological project, including, of course, the new Craig 1 computer.

Permission to enter into negotiations with the French had only been granted after Yulya's fourth or fifth memorandum on the subject had penetrated some inner fastness of the Soviet Academy of Sciences. The upshot was that the French were delighted to exchange their old machine and their massive weather-forecasting program for enough cash in hand to make the down payment on a brand-new Craig 2, the *ne plus ultra* in high-powered computer technology. The meteorologists were delighted, at last, to be able to dig out from under the accumulating mountain of data that had to be processed at Krasnoyarsk every day if they expected to come up with truly accurate predictions. Only the hard-line mandarins in Moscow, the boogeymen so frequently invoked by both Sergei and Afanasyev, were not delightd by the purchase of yet another expensive foreign luxury.

She had no sooner sat down at her desk than someone knocked twice on her office door and stepped inside without waiting for a reply. She smiled when she saw her assistant's untidy shock of blond hair in the doorway; for the first time that day, she was glad to see someone.

"Oh, it's you, Kutuzov. Sit yourself down."

He slumped into a chair. Kutuzov was afflicted with a strange nervous tic that made him constantly seem to be winking one eye. This often put him at a disadvantage in the sort of places where he went to get profoundly drunk two or three times a week. At the moment he was winking like a semaphore, generally a signal of distress or despondency. Kutuzov was the one man in the world that Yulya felt she could trust completely.

"That damned new machine of yours has been acting up pretty badly, you know."

"What do you mean? It was working perfectly yesterday. I checked it myself." She looked at him severely. "If this is just some kind of trick to get me to sit around drinking tea with you all morning, I can tell you right now that I'm much too busy for that."

"No, honestly, I swear. It looks like it could very well be serious."

She followed him to the elevator. To get into the computer room itself, they had to pass through a security lock, a device that could only be opened by inserting a magnetized strip and punching out the correct identification number on a keypad. Inside, they were greeted by the subdued rumbling of a powerful ventilation system. The operators were all going about their business with an air of smooth, abstracted competence, as if they expected the delegation from Moscow to turn up at any moment. Yulya and Kutuzov sat down at a terminal, and Kutuzov tapped out a lengthy sequence of passwords and called up the weather-forecasting program.

"The temperature in Moscow at high noon tomorrow, according to the Craig 1." He tapped out another brief command, and a string of meaningless characters instantly appeared on the screen: XC2459///2+=6

Yulya's eyebrows shot upward in astonishment. "That's not possible," she said faintly. "Let me try for a second." She took Kutuzov's place at the keyboard and tapped out the same command, with no more encouraging results. Fighting her mounting panic, she exited and reentered the system, called up the program again, and tapped out a few more characters.

More gibberish appeared on the screen. Yulya looked imploringly at Kutuzov.

"I've tried everything," he said. "I even checked to make sure the mice hadn't been at the cables again."

"When was that?"

"Last night. I didn't want to disturb you. Besides, you know perfectly well how it is when something goes wrong like this—either you can find it perfectly well all by yourself or you can't, even with ten people helping you look."

"Very wise, but not very helpful in the circumstances. The delegation is actually going to be here in a couple of hours. If we can't show them the Craig and put it through its paces for them, we'll really be courting serious disaster."

"Look, the program's failed, it's spitting out garbage at us, and if the problem's with the software itself, there isn't any conceivable way that we could review the entire program in the few hours remaining, still less so if it's the hardware that's acting up. I've given a great deal of thought to this little problem in the last twelve hours or so, and it seems to me that the only thing for it is simply not to let them see the Craig at all."

"And how are we going to manage that?"

"We'll have to hook up one of these terminals to our stalwart Soviet ES 1060, and then simply hope that they don't ask it too many hard questions."

"And if they do?"

"Then I suppose we'll have to give them their money back. Obviously, we'll be running a certain risk, to put it mildly. But ask yourself this, Comrade Director—'Do I have a better idea?'"

Yulya was compelled to admit that she did not. However foolhardy, this did appear to be the only way out for them. "I suppose those damned Frenchmen will have to straighten all this out for us. It's their machine, and it's their damned program, and it's sure to be their fault. But obviously that's not the sort of prognosis that will go down at all well with the doting grandparents from Moscow. Imagine the fuss if they found out that their new high-powered, high-priced American computer was going to require some sort of perpetual invalid care just to get it running at all. When are they coming—the Frenchmen, the maintenance team, I mean? In a week?"

"Eight days. I checked."

"No chance they'll turn up a little ahead of schedule—like within the hour, for example?"

"On the fifteenth, at the earliest. And I don't think it would be wise to try to get them here any earlier—that would just be like broadcasting our troubles to the world."

"Very well, but what if our guests want to take a look at the actual Craig 1 mainframe, not just little numbers dancing on a screen?"

"Then we'll show it to them, of course. How are they going to know we're running the *program* on the 1060? It'll be like a ventriloquist and his dummy. And they won't see the ventriloquist's lips move, since all we'll show them will be the dummy."

"And you actually propose to perpetrate such a hoax on our comrades from the Academy of Sciences and the Ministry of Planning and Development?"

"Pure poetic justice. And in any case, what are they going to do if we get found out? We're already *in* Siberia, don't forget."

"Bold talk, but your eyelid's stopped twitching altogether, and I can tell you're as terrified as I am. However, you've convinced me. Hook up one of the terminals to the 1060. But before you do that, I think you should come up to the canteen with me for a minute and have some tea."

"Do we have time for that?"

"Of course not, but I think we have to talk about this some more, and I don't want to attract attention by fussing around here for too long. It should only take a couple of minutes."

The ground floor of the Institute was largely given over to a formal reception hall and a cafeteria with wide bay windows on two sides, decorated with gigantic photomurals depicting the natural and manmade wonders of Siberia. There was a tea urn—too sleek and chromium-plated to be called a samovar—squatting majestically on a counter by the door. Yulya and Kutuzov filled their glasses, then sat down at a table some distance away.

"I want you to tell me exactly what you think about all this," said Yulya, her eyes fixed on the steam rising from her glass.

"I think, first of all, that the secret of our little deception should probably not be disclosed to anyone else—unless you want your husband's friends from the office turning up at all hours of the night."

"Excellent point," Yulya replied. "And I hope you'll understand what I mean when I tell you that if I have to go through something like this with just one other person—well, in a way I'm glad it's you, that's all."

Kutuzov mussed his fingers through his hair, scraped his chair against the floor, and blinked rapidly. "I understand perfectly. You know, Yulya, that I'd do anything for you—"

Yulya drained her glass before saying, "I know you would, Kutuzov. But that's not really what I got you up here to talk about. The thing is, why won't the program run? The system was working perfectly yesterday. The one very compelling explanation that we've overlooked is deliberate sabotage."

Kutuzov glanced reflexively around them. There was no one else nearby but a couple of technicians who appeared to be deep in a discussion of some new scheme for obtaining black-market stereo components. "That's a word one doesn't actually say out loud, Comrade Director. There we're talking not just about internal exile—to a place far worse than this one—we're talking about nine grams of metal, topically applied, if you know what I mean."

Yulya was amused in spite of herself. "I suppose that 'shoot' and 'bullet' are two more words one doesn't actually say out loud. But answer me this—if it wasn't 'willful destruction of state property' or whatever you want to call it, then why is this happening to us?"

"I must confess I have absolutely no idea. I mean, anyone with access to the machine would automatically be suspect if anything were seriously wrong, and I don't think any of the others could penetrate the security without leaving a few tracks."

"I wasn't thinking along those lines, actually. It seems to me that this must have been engineered by someone on the outside."

"But why would anyone on the outside want to shut us down like that—assuming, purely for the sake of argument, that they could do such a thing? We're not working on anything strategic here. I mean, in certain circumstances it may be militarily useful to have an accurate weather forecast and all, but knocking out this station in peacetime isn't going to deprive us of an *advantage* over anyone else. The data supplied to this station is literally common knowledge, and they're all hooked up to the same network—Washington and Moscow, Paris and Tokyo. Even during the Indo-Pakistani war, the meteorological centers in New Delhi and Karachi kept right on talking to each other all along. Mustn't let the dear old database down, you know. In other words, I just don't see what the point would be."

"And what if it is just the *program* that was tampered with somehow?"

"The only ones with previous access to it were the French. And the consequences for them would be no less disastrous than for us, don't you think? I mean, for things to come unglued at this stage would mean that there'd be a tremendous flap that might scare away all their future customers. No, the only hypothesis that even begins to make sense is that there's a very serious design flaw in the machine."

Yulya did not reply. What Kutuzov was saying made a certain

amount of sense, but there was clearly a great deal more that could be said on the subject, and there was no more time for talk. She glanced at her watch.

"Better go and hook up the 1060 now. We'll talk later. We have exactly an hour and twenty-six minutes until the delegation arrives."

She barely had time to summon her department heads for a final run-through of the day's activities before her desk telephone rang. The delegation from Moscow would be arriving momentarily. In a few minutes, three long Volgas had drawn up in front of the Institute, the limousines' doors were thrown open, and a phalanx of bulky figures in astrakhan coats emerged and started to mount the steps. Afanasyev, walking beside the secretary of the Academy of Sciences, was instantly recognizable, in spite of the sable-trimmed cap he had pulled down over his eyes.

As soon as he caught sight of her standing by the outer doorway, he plunged ahead of his companions, in defiance of protocol, and grasped both of her hands in his.

"How lovely you look, my dear! But much too pale, really. Since you've had a promotion, you shouldn't be working nearly as hard as before, you know."

"I have to talk to you in private," she said softly, trying not to disarrange the welcoming smile on her face. "It's urgent."

"All right, certainly. As soon as we have a few minutes to breathe."

A welcoming committee of Institute staff members and other persons of consequence—including Sergei, tucked away in the back row—was drawn up in ranks in the entrance hall. Yulya and Afanasyev pressed forward to make the necessary introductions. She exchanged a few words with the secretary of the Soviet Academy of Sciences, a waspish old gentleman who congratulated her on having discovered a cure for bureaucratic paralysis. The delegates were relieved of their outer garments, and trooped docilely into the elevators, like schoolchildren visiting a museum.

On the underground level, they were led down long corridors, past glassed-in cubicles where programmers pored over blinking screens and consoles and contrived to look surprised, though certainly not displeased, to be discovered like this in the ordinary, conscientious performance of their duties. When they reached the security lock, Yulya made a rather lengthy speech about the security system, accompanied first by the approving whispers, then by the impatient mutterings of her audience. She realized that she had merely been postponing the moment of truth, or, in this case, of deception; she stepped aside, and one of her deputies began to usher the visitors through the security lock, one by one. Afanasyev caught her eye and stepped back a few paces as well, as if out of deference to the others. When they were out of earshot, she turned to him and whispered, "Disaster. The damned program's blown up."

"What do you mean? What's the trouble?"

"I have no idea. The Craig's been giving us back nothing but gibberish all morning."

"Worse than a disaster, then, for both of us. Is there anything you can do about it?"

"We've got the terminals for the Craig connected to the old 1060, and we've got one of our meteorological programs all ready to run for them. Let's hope it works."

She spoke with the finality of an acrobat who is about to jump from a very high platform into a very small tub of water. If Afanasyev was thinking only of himself at this point, then the most prudent course would be for him to denounce her immediately. He would be compromised, of course; he might be passed over, shunted aside, even demoted for a couple of years. On the other hand, if he chose to say nothing, he was automatically laying himself open to a very plausible accusation of treason and sabotage—and a charge of this kind was not usually required to be very plausible. Yulya watched him surreptitiously for a moment, nodding and smiling to the remaining delegates as they filed past.

He seemed to have shed several layers of his identity in front of her eyes—gone were the affable *bon vivant*, the concerned Soviet scientist, the helpful protector. He certainly did not seem to be remembering that evening while they were leaving Duvallon's in Paris, when, at his insistence, she had given him a few perfunctory caresses, the way one might stroke a very large cat. For the moment, all that remained of Afanasyev was the frightened *apparatchik*, uncertain which way to jump in order to save himself.

The last in line was Sergei. "Aren't you two going in?"

"You go ahead. I just want to have a brief word with Comrade Afanasyev."

The two men shook hands warily, and Sergei disappeared through the security lock. This encounter seemed suddenly to have decided the issue, as far as Afanasyev was concerned.

"Very resourceful, what you've done," Afanasyev told Yulya. "Obviously the correct decision. I'm sure it's going to go off perfectly smoothly, just watch."

The visitors were waiting expectantly in the computer room, and Yulya surprised herself by making a very pretty speech in praise of the Soviet computer industry—in particular of the Soviet research scientists who had so admirably realized the full potential of certain technical innovations that had occurred elsewhere. She let them admire the impressive bulk of some of the recently installed equipment and invited them to gather around one of the terminals, where Kutuzov was about to give a demonstration of the weather-forecasting program.

"This facility," he said, "acts as a clearinghouse for meteorological information from around the world, information sufficiently precise to enable us to prepare an accurate forecast for any locality in the Soviet Union at least seventy-two hours in advance."

"And how long would it take," muttered one of the Ministry of Planning officials, "to switch on the heat in here?"

Seeing that Yulya and Kutuzov were about to embark on a lengthy technical explanation, Afanasyev interposed smoothly, "These machines are all naturalized *Sibiryaki*—true Siberians—and they thrive on the cold. But those of us who may be feeling somewhat depleted by the experience may prefer to start restoring our energies at the excellent buffet that Comrade Voronkov assures me is awaiting us up above."

"Not just yet, if you don't mind," broke in the secretary of the Academy. "I'd still like to see a practical demonstration. Perhaps your machine would oblige us by giving the forecast for Samarkand, for example, in three days' time?"

Kutuzov tapped at the keyboard while a few more of the delegates called out places names, diffidently at first, then with boisterous enthusiasm. "Yalta." "Leningrad." "Let's have some *real* cold—Yakutsk!" "Vladivostok!" When a few more had been mentioned, Kutuzov read off the figures from the screen. "Projected midday temperatures for Samarkand two degrees Celsius, Yalta four degrees, Leningrad minus six degrees, Yakutsk minus twenty-five degrees, Vladivostok minus twelve degrees . . ."

The suspiciously high reading for Vladivostok provoked further muttering, which was stilled when Yulya airily invoked the influence of "warm currents from the Central Pacific." (Fortunately, the only trained meteorologist in the delegation had been bumped in favor of a Party official who had no such embarrassing expertise of any kind.) Afanasyev's repeated suggestion that they adjourn to the buffet was unopposed. As Kutuzov got up and walked away from his terminal with his hands thrust deep in his pockets, Yulya could see them trembling even through the fabric of his white lab coat.

In the reception hall on the ground floor, the murals illustrating the glorious partnership of proletarian science and industry had been further embellished with red streamers, stars, and banners with slogans. A table covered with a superb embroidered cloth was laden with several dozen small bowls of red and black caviar, arranged in the form of a hammer and sickle, as well as glistening slabs of smoked salmon and sturgeon, blinis and bowls of *smetana*, thick sour cream, and a punchbowl filled with frothy *koumiss*, the traditional drink of the steppes, made from fermented mare's milk and popularly thought to ensure longevity. A surprising number of the delegates slighted the vodka and champagne in favor of the koumiss bowl.

There was a lectern draped in red bunting at the other end of the hall; Afanasyev stepped up to the microphone while the others reconnoitered the buffet.

"Comrades! Members of the commission, honored colleagues and fellow workers of the Institute for Computer Science and Applied Mathematics, I address you today not merely in my capacity as director of the All-Union Research Institute for Informational Systems . . ."

Yulya stepped away from the crowd when she saw Sergei approaching.

"What the hell's the matter with you?" he asked in an incongruously soft voice. "What were you playing at with Afanasyev down there? Are you absolutely determined now to make me look ridiculous?"

"Be quiet for a minute, and I'll explain it to you. And I don't have to tell you that you're being ridiculous at this very moment—"

"Vladimir Ilyich once remarked that Communism equals workers' soviets plus electrification. It is thus entirely appropriate that this great industrial city of Krasnoyarsk—site of a six-megawatt hydroelectric facility, the largest in the Soviet Union—should also have been selected as the site of perhaps the most important center for computer research in the entire Soviet Motherland . . ."

"I want you to tell me what's going on right now," Sergei persisted.

"In a minute."

"I want to know right now. Your man Kutuzov looks like he's just come off an eight-day binge. He was shaking like a leaf while he was down there typing on your machine just now."

Yulya stepped back toward the buffet in time to present the secretary of the Academy with a fresh glass of champagne, which he acknowledged with a courtly bow. Sergei was still right on her heels.

As she handed him a cup of koumiss with an ironic flourish, she bent over and whispered in his ear, "The Craig's broken down; we can't get the weather program to run at all. We connected that terminal you all were looking at to the old 1060. The demonstration was a complete fake."

"Are you crazy? There are other people's careers, their lives, at stake here—mine, for one."

Afanasyev had reached his peroration. *"Today we can say, along with Comrade Andropov, to paraphrase our great Vladimir Ilyich, 'Communism equals workers' soviets plus computerization!'"*

Thunderous applause. Yulya had to shout into Sergei's ear to make herself heard. "Don't you love having secrets! I think that's the sort of thing that keeps marriages together, don't you?" She ladled out another cup of koumiss, raised it in a silent toast, and drank it down.

FOUR

The wheels of the taxi threw out a spray of dirty water as the driver pulled up to the curb. Brendan handed him two bills and grasped the handle of his attaché case. *"Merci, monsieur."* The driver grinned and said something about his needing a mask and flippers to get across the street. Brendan replied with the only French phrase he could think of that seemed appropriate to the occasion: *"Bon pour les escargots!"* Nice weather for snails!

At four in the afternoon, the Place de l'Opéra was deserted; the rainstorm that had broken while Brendan was driving in from the airport had become a deluge. The marble bulk of the Opéra, a hundred yards away and almost hidden behind an opaque curtain of rain, seemed to be receding into the distance, like a huge, ungainly galleon going out on the tide. The taxi had left him off just a few paces from a phone booth. He lunged inside, thrust a coin into the slot, and only then did he realize that the receiver had been violently removed, leaving a foot or so of shielded cable dangling uselessly from the box. The rain felt like ice.

Holding his attaché case over his head, Brendan sprinted across the avenue and down the steps of the métro, and finally located a phone in working order.

"Françoise? It's me. I just got in from the airport. I'm in the Place de l'Opéra."

"And you're not going to waste a moment in coming to see your exotic island love, am I right?"

"Got a meeting. I'm already late. See you in an hour and a half at Harry's Bar. How about that?"

"Okay, but not Harry's Bar, all right? There's a nice little bistro on the Boulevard des Capucines; it's called Le Trou dans le Mur, the Hole in the Wall."

"Yeah, I got that. Can't wait. Okay, see you in an hour and a half. *Je t'embrasse.*"

Brendan smiled to himself; an almost childlike feeling of excitement had already erased the cumulative fatigue of the last few days of shuttling between Cambridge, Langley, and Paris. He ran back up the steps of the station and along the Boulevard des Italiens, then ducked into the entrance of an ornate, neoclassical building, where an old-fashioned cage elevator lifted him slowly up to the third floor. He rang the bell beneath a brass plate inscribed COORDINATING COMMITTEE ON MULTILATERAL EXPORT CONTROLS—AMERICAN MISSION. After an interminable pause, while the water ran in rivulets off his raincoat and onto the carpet, the door was opened by a tall man in a blue suit who looked very much, Brendan thought, like a plainclothes marine, if there was such a thing.

"They're expecting you, sir. Looks kind of like you had to walk the whole way back from the States."

"Only the last two blocks, thanks." He was shown into a large, brightly lit conference room where half a dozen men were already seated around a long table. Richard Thompson, apparently acting as chairman, had a pile of newspapers in front of him.

"Take a seat here beside me, Brendan," he called out. "Now I think we're ready to begin. First, we've made a simple comparison of the international weather reports in *Izvestia* with the *International Herald*, both from four days ago. It's been raining here in Paris for a week now. The *Herald* gives the correct temperature—thirty-eight degrees, and, of course, rainy. *Izvestia* has six degrees for Paris—that's about forty-three degrees Fahrenheit—with clear skies. A difference of five degrees. Similar discrepancies can be observed in the case of Bangkok, New Delhi, Milan. There's no doubt that the weather center at Krasnoyarsk had effectively been paralyzed during the previous day, a condition that persisted for a small number of hours; an emergency call went out to the French support team at least a week in advance of their regularly scheduled visit. When they arrived, the Craig was discovered to be in perfect working order. We've sprung the trap and turned them loose again, and they still have absolutely no idea what hit them."

Thompson's announcement of the incorrect temperature reading in *Izvestia* had produced a chorus of subdued applause and various gratified exclamations. Now there was silence until, as if on cue, the man sitting next to Brendan said softly, "That's really incredible!"

"Fortunately," Thompson went on, "it's also true. Everyone at the home office is very pleased about this. Congratulations are in order all around. But of course, this is just the first round—not even that, really, since they haven't started throwing punches yet. The situation seems to justify an attitude of cautious optimism rather than complacency. Let me leave you gentlemen with the reflection that if the other guy's got his head in a potato sack and you're jabbing him with a pointed stick, then when he finally gets the bag off his head and sees you standing there with the stick, he may not be satisfied with just an apology."

The meeting dissolved into a general hubbub of conversation, and Thompson took Brendan aside. "I want a word with you. There's an office next door where we can talk." Catching Brendan's involuntary grimace of impatience, he went on, "I'll only keep you for a moment, Brendan. And if the reason you're in such a hurry is what I think it is, then it's time for us to have a talk."

"What about?"

"About Françoise Vimard. I realize that recently you've been cultivating your relationship with her, chiefly for personal reasons, but this, like the man said in the movie, is business, not personal. Okay?"

"Okay what?"

"We need to know what the French reaction was to what happened at Krasnoyarsk. What do they think actually happened? What do they propose to do about it? Do you think you'll be able to find that out for us?"

"Maybe, but that's not exactly the way I'd planned to spend the evening."

"Brendan, I want you to understand I'm not trying to come on like a hard guy. However, let me just point out that, *one*, this is something we very much have to have; *two*, you've already agreed to serve as the conduit through which this information can reach us; *three*, when you've agreed to do a job and you decide you don't want to do it anymore, then the best thing to do is to resign; and, *four*, as far as your career is concerned, this isn't really the sort of job you can resign from without leaving a few tailfeathers behind. Okay? Over to you."

"I hear you, Richard. If I can find out what you want to know, I'll certainly tell you all about it."

"Tomorrow, at Harry's Bar, ten A.M.?"

"Okay, but mightn't that be a little conspicuous, especially at ten o'clock in the morning?"

"The principle of the purloined letter—hide in plain sight, right? And what better place to hide two gringos in Paris than in Harry's Bar at ten o'clock in the morning. I won't keep you any longer, Brendan. *A bientôt.*"

According to legend, the actual hole in the wall which, only slightly enlarged, became the door of the Café le Trou dans le Mur was originally made by a stray cannonball during the Revolution of 1830. Brendan walked back around the end of the bar and into the back room, where Françoise was waiting for him. He paused for a moment to admire her from the doorway. She was wearing a wasp-waisted, silver-gray outfit with extremely broad shoulders that made her look a little like a pulp science fiction magazine heroine from the thirties, an effect that was somewhat redeemed by the addition of a bright red scarf, in the same hot, sensual shade as her lipstick. Set before her was a drink called a porto flip, something on the order of a brandy

Alexander, that Brendan privately considered to be rather disgusting.

"No matter how well you're dressed," he said with a smile, as he slid into the booth beside her, "you always manage to look great, somehow."

"I won't even ask you what you mean by that."

They embraced for a moment or two, then Brendan drew back to examine her face more carefully. "You seem a little preoccupied today. Is everything all right? Or are we just turning into another old yuppie couple already?"

"I won't ask you what that means, either. It may be because I'm a little tired. *Mon sénateur* is up for reelection, you know, and he's been making my life a living hell. Also, I must confess I've really been putting a lot of effort into this computer article. Your friend Thompson told me that if it turns out all right, he'll say a word to an editor he knows on the international edition of *Newsweek*."

"Quite a step up from *Eurobusiness*, I must say. You should be making a big splash in the world of belles lettres pretty soon."

"Let's hope so." She did not seem entirely delighted by this prospect.

Brendan frowned as he signaled to the waitress and ordered a Pernod. Something was definitely bothering her. When she looked back at him, he could still feel some of that wonderful softness and tenderness that had been revealed to him on that first night, when she had let her white dress slip down over her red lizard shoes. Now she seemed tense and not entirely at ease, which for her was most unusual.

It was certainly unusual for her to sound so dubious and disgruntled about the prospect of career advancement. Thompson's rather crude initial analysis of her character had presented her almost entirely in this light—an intelligent, attractive, and overambitious young woman who was "all the more determined to make it to the top from having started out so close to the bottom." She also had a natural gift for making human contact, for getting through to people, something quite apart from her beauty—or her ambition, for that matter.

Duvallon had made her acquaintance in the corridors of the National Assembly; he had been sufficiently captivated to embark on what was, for him, a monumentally indiscreet adventure. Françoise, presumably, was still enough of the West Indian sharecropper's daughter to be impressed that a man of his power and influence was willing to risk so much for her; she also seemed to relish her role as Duvallon's media consultant and confidential assistant. Still, she had no great interest in being a power behind the throne or *maîtresse en titre* to a powerful man, or even in politics as such. She yearned to achieve some sort of recognition in her own right, hence the projected switchover to "international journalism"—for the sake of which she had already committed a number of substantial indiscretions of her own.

Françoise seemed to have read his thoughts; she suddenly put her head on his shoulder and gently trailed her finger along the line of his jaw, pausing when she came to a slightly discolored swelling.

"What happened here? Did your wife have a jealous rage or something?"

Brendan laughed. "No, nothing as interesting as that. I managed to squeeze in a couple of boxing lessons while I was in Cambridge. Sally's nothing like the way you imagine her, apparently. I mean, we're always happy to see each other, but when we're apart, we have our separate lives to lead. You won't think I'm just trying to change the subject if I ask you about your article? Find out anything good?"

"To tell the truth, I don't feel much like talking about all that right now."

The barmaid arrived with his Pernod; he savored the strong anise aftertaste while he pondered his next move. This was it. Françoise had figured it out, or she'd heard something; maybe she'd found out what her friend Thompson really did for a living. Brendan felt a profound sense of relief. For once, his standing orders from Thompson coincided exactly with his own personal preferences: *When she starts to catch on, veer off.* He hated the idea of trying to manipulate Françoise like this, to milk her for information; from now on, as far as he was concerned, their relationship was entirely personal, not business. She was no longer to be considered a *source*, informed, highly placed, unofficial, unidentified, or of any kind whatsoever.

"Nor do I," he finally replied. "Frankly, I *was* just trying to change the subject. So, what to do? How do you feel about dinner, for example? Or would you rather check in at your place first, for any reason?"

To his astonishment, Françoise merely stared at him for a second, then threw her arms around him and buried her face in the hollow of his right shoulder.

"Oh, Brendan! I'm so ashamed," she said miserably.

"Ashamed? What of?" His hand reached around to stroke her hair.

"I'm ashamed that I allowed myself to become suspicious of you." His hand stopped moving, and she pulled away from this rather cramped embrace so she could explain at greater length. "It was because of some things I heard while I was researching my article. I was talking to someone very high up in the Ariane rocket project. We discussed all the various problems that have threatened to ruin the project at one time or another, some of them quite mysterious in origin."

Brendan tried very hard to look curious and concerned without looking too guilty at the same time.

"Anyway, he told me that most of these mysterious problems had to do with computer failure—an American computer, a Craig, as a matter of fact. The program, part of which had been supplied by NASA, contained a number of errors, and this man I talked to was of the opinion that they were made deliberately."

"What for? What would be the point of that?"

"Isn't it obvious? The Ariane and the American space shuttle are going to be in direct competition as commercial satellite launch vehicles. You can imagine the sort of money that's at stake."

"And you don't think your friend was just looking for someone to blame for the fact that they've had so much trouble getting old Ariane off the ground?"

"But the fact remains that certain representations were made to your government on behalf of our government at the highest diplomatic levels, and since then they've had no trouble in getting old Ariane to *stay* off the ground."

Brendan killed off his drink. "So what are we to conclude from all this?"

"Duvallon told me that the Craig computer we sold to the Russians has also broken down, also under quite mysterious circumstances. A repair crew, support team, whatever you call it, was flown out immediately to the research institute in Siberia, but when they arrived, there was no more problem, everything was going okay now. The director of the institute swore them to absolute secrecy. Duvallon tells me that this whole affair is completely inexplicable; I thought that perhaps some of your countrymen might have sabotaged this Craig as well."

"What for? If we didn't want the Russians to have one, we could have prevented it easily enough."

"Yes, but I don't mean the U.S. government as such. I mean private competitors of the French software industry, let's say, people who'd want everyone to think that French computer programs are no good, or maybe they want the Russian market all to themselves when the export restrictions on microcomputers are relaxed." She smiled. "I know all about this now, you see."

"No doubt, but I still don't see where I come into it."

"Well, you seemed to be so interested in the contract negotiations and everything else, I thought that perhaps you might actually be mixed up in something like that."

Brendan almost laughed aloud with relief. "I assure you I don't own a single share of IBM, nor have I ever set foot in Silicon Valley. To tell you the truth, I think your whole outlook is starting to get corrupted by spending so much time with Duvallon. But you still haven't told me what made you realize all of a sudden that I wasn't one of the diabolical masterminds behind all this."

"I could just tell, a minute ago. You really *didn't* want to talk about it. You were trying to get me to stop asking questions about your wife. I could just tell you were sincere."

"Right. I sincerely don't want to hear another word about either of those two subjects. So how about some dinner?"

"Actually, I think I'd prefer, as you said before, to go and check in at my apartment for any reason."

Kutuzov ran his fingers through his hair, yawned, blinked, and stretched until he felt his joints starting to crack. It seemed that every night when he came home, a wave of fatigue swept over him as soon as he crossed the threshold. He took off his shoes, threw his coat and sweater onto a table, took a small tray out of the sink, gave it a swipe with the edge of his sleeve, and loaded it down with a chunk of black bread, a knife, a jar of pickles, an onion, and a bottle of vodka. He carried the tray into the combination bedroom–living room, set it down on one arm of the chair, and turned on the television. It was too late for the news. On one channel, a group of plump farm girls in costume were singing a shrill folksong of some kind; on the other channel was a quiz show, with a boring-looking couple identifying colored slides of native Siberian birds. Kutuzov decided to watch the boring couple; he ate a little, and took quite a few pulls from the vodka bottle. Soon a pleasant drowsiness crept over him.

An hour later he woke up with a start. He had managed to upset the tray; most of the brine from the pickle jar had already soaked into the threadbare carpet. He eagerly swallowed the few drops remaining in the vodka bottle and trained a quizzical eye on the woman reporter on the television screen, who was chattering on about the "miracle of Minsk." "The population of the capital of the Byelorussian SSR," she explained brightly, "has been increasing at a rate *four times as great* as that of any other Soviet city."

"In fifty years, when the glaciers come back," Kutuzov declaimed at the screen, "we'll all be Eskimos, so what's the use?" He was trying to remember how much money he had to last him the rest of the month. There was probably just enough to allow him to top off the evening at Lyutko's. Visions of the languid "hostesses" at Lyutko's mingled confusingly with the clearer outlines of Soviet girl gymnasts bounding across the television screen. One of them was Dalya Kukaity, seventeen years old, with beautiful long legs, her wrists and ankles as fine as a porcelain doll's. In his present state he did not find it difficult to visualize the slim, naked body beneath her leotard, as he watched it twisting and bending back on itself, launching itself into space like an uncoiled spring, filling the screen with its sensual arabesques.

Then Kutuzov felt suddenly ashamed of himself for desiring this supple young girl; he felt not just like a lecher, but like an adulterer as well. He had been unfaithful. He tilted his head back, closed his eyes, and a single word escaped his lips: "Yulya." He got to his feet abruptly, and walked over and switched off the television. The images on the screen were making him feel a little dizzy. He got down on all fours and began to search for his shoes, calling to them softly, *"Sapagí, sapagí,"* as if they were frightened kittens. They were not immediately to be found, so he stood up again, collected his sweater and coat, and headed out the door.

At the bottom of the staircase, the *dezhurnaya*, the concierge, an old woman wrapped up in a collection of fuzzy scarves and shawls, came bustling out of her little alcove by the outside door.

"Kutuzov, you pig, where do you think you're going? To get disgustingly drunk as usual, I suppose."

"Beg to report, Comrade Snitch-to-the-Militia," replied Kutuzov ceremoniously. "I intend, first off, to get drunk, then to get laid, in rapid sequence. I don't suppose you'd care to join me?"

"Akh, Kutuzov, just be thankful your poor mother isn't here to see you like this! Filthy and foul-mouthed, and going out to catch your death in your stocking feet!"

Kutuzov looked down at his socks, then grinned appealingly at the old woman. "Well, I'll be fucked. Must be drunk already. Have to excuse me while I go back and slip into some shoes. Many thanks, O Cerberus, O ever-vigilant Baba Yaga, Our Lady of the Police Blotter. Your timely intervention might have saved me from a terrible fate . . . might have woken up in the tank, might not have woken up on a slab, whichever the case might have been." He turned and padded up the staircase with surprising agility.

Half an hour later, after a further exchange of civilities with the *dezhurnaya* of his apartment block, Kutuzov, half-sober by now, slid in through the service door of Lyutko's, to be greeted by a chorus of cheers and catcalls from the regulars assembled in the back room. Unlike most of the others present, Kutuzov was careful to ration himself to no more than two or three nights a week of total dissipation. "Kutuzov!" one of them called out to him. "Is it Tuesday again already? I must have dozed off."

Like most Russian taverns and cafés, Lyutko's stayed open until very late; the idea of an official closing time would have been totally repugnant to Siberian folkways, and many of Lyutko's patrons ended up spending the night there, either passed out on one of the tables downstairs or tucked in with one of the hostesses in a cubicle upstairs. Apart from routine checkups by a police doctor, all of Lyutko's hostesses made regular reports to the police, and Lyutko's was also a favorite resort for lesser police and Party officials in their off-duty hours. A couple of them had made pets of some of the regulars in the back room, and enjoyed standing an occasional round and listening to their drunken harangues and mutterings—"like the Caliph of Bagdad," as Kutuzov had once put it, "mingling with his turbulent subjects in the bazaar."

A few moments after Kutuzov had sat down at a little table opposite an unshaven old man in a wrinkled overcoat, a waitress appeared and set down a glass and a bottle at his elbow. "Evening, Professor!" Kutuzov said loudly.

"Ah, good evening, Kutuzov," replied the old man, who seemed to have taken no notice of his rather tumultuous arrival. "You know, with respect to that very interesting discussion we were having the other night, you know I do believe that whenever I spoke of *Protagoras*, I meant to say *Parmenides*, and of course vice versa. But even so, that scarcely detracts from the validity of my basic point . . ."

Three or four hours later, the professor had finally dropped off to sleep, after a vigorous session with the pre-Socratics, and Kutuzov was left alone with his thoughts. By then he had drunk so much that he had finally broken through all the barriers of intoxication and emerged on the other side in a state of complete lucidity.

Something was troubling him—actually two things. Why had the Craig broken down? And, even more of a puzzle, why had it suddenly decided to start up again, entirely of its own accord? For an instant these reflections were replaced by a disturbingly vivid image of the white, muscular thighs of one of Lyutko's hostesses; then this in turn was replaced by that of an attractive woman's face, with high cheekbones, dark hair, and pale blue eyes. The first of these visions he could easily have turned into a reality, just by climbing the stairs to the second floor and walking down a corridor. He stood up quickly, ducked out the back door, and started running, then slowed down to a rapid walk after he had gone a few paces. Still, it should take him only fifteen minutes or so to reach the Institute.

At about the same time, Françoise and Brendan were stretched out happily on a quilt on the floor of her apartment in the Rue des Guillemites. Brendan was staring out the window at the bare branches of a plane tree in the square; he could remember another time when he had felt just this way, with the branch of a tree scratching against the window of his apartment in Cambridge and making a thin, melancholy sound. He turned toward Françoise, who was simply staring out into space with wide-open eyes.

"What are you thinking?" he asked.

"I'm thinking about my brother. You know, after he ran into you on the staircase that time, he decided he didn't like your looks. We had a big discussion about it, and I ended up telling him it was none of his business, really. But what worries me is that I haven't heard a word from him since then. I'm starting to think that something might have happened to him. He knows some pretty funny people and all . . ."

"I wouldn't worry about him too much, if I were you. He looked plenty big enough, and mean enough, to get out of any kind of trouble he might get into."

"Let's hope so, at any rate."

The night security man waved Kutuzov by automatically; he worked past midnight on most nights he couldn't afford to spend at Lyutko's—motivated, some said, by a highly developed Socialist consciousness. The rumored arrival of a "superprogram," surreptitiously acquired from India, was expected to require a great deal of advance preparation. Most people in the Institute simply assumed that Kutuzov had nothing better to do, or that he might even be as crazy as he looked.

The rumor about the superprogram was actually true, at any rate; this was a "routing controller," which would permit the Craig to supervise the activities of the central data-processing facilities of the

Soviet Union and also to link the Soviet computer network with the capacious databases in Western countries. This would clearly be a decisive step in achieving the complete centralization of all Soviet computer systems.

But the reason that Kutuzov had spent the last three nights in the unnatural silence of the machine room was quite different, of course. He was searching for the malign alien intelligence that he now realized was lurking somewhere behind the hundreds of thousands of lines of code in the weather-forecasting program. The first night the program had failed to run, he had begun to believe in the existence of such an entity; after the program had unexpectedly debugged itself, he had become convinced of it. So far, he had not shared any of his suspicions with Yulya; he had somehow not dared to tell her that he had come around to her point of view. The implications were simply too frightening to talk about openly.

The first time, he thought to himself, it was just like flicking the light switch and not having the light come on; for this there could be any number of explanations, most of them merely annoying rather than frightening. But the second time it had been quite different—he had felt a deep, unreasoning panic, as if he had been lying in bed, and the light had suddenly switched on in the next room when no one was supposed to be there. Now he had that same feeling whenever he sat down at his terminal, as if he knew that a burglar or a murderer was stalking him somewhere in the darkness beyond the small pool of light that surrounded him.

Kutuzov had tried to imagine what sort of person it was who had set this trap for him. Undoubtedly it was a systems programmer like himself. He liked to imagine the two of them crawling toward each other on their bellies, holding trench knives between clenched teeth, across a muddy no-man's-land. He found the idea of single combat between them strangely exhilarating. He began to forget his fears; he stroked the smooth metal frame of his terminal. He would fight and defeat him, for Yulya's sake.

Whatever the weapons involved, bare fists or ballistic missiles, a contest of this kind had as much to do with the show of force—with ruses, feints, and stratagems—as with force itself. In this case, it was to be a contest of pure intellectual energy, with just the pressure of a finger on a keyboard and the soft glow of hieroglyphs on a screen. And thus far, the damage done by the enemy had been purely, almost trivially immaterial—he had prevented 300 million people from knowing, for a single day, what the weather was like in London or Nairobi. Now what Kutuzov was looking for was a process, a tactic, the track of an idea. This was what he found truly exciting; the object of the game was not to destroy his opponent but to grasp his internal logic, to wrest his secrets from him, to penetrate the core. As he began to flip through a knee-high stack of printouts, he began to feel the exaltation of the sort of totally rational activity that can tap directly into the instincts and the emotions, like the master of Go who can immediately sense a deadly threat in a shapeless archipelago of black stones on a wooden board.

It was right, Kutuzov felt, that one should have a great deal of respect for one's opponent in a case like this, and he could not help but feel a kind of esthetic thrill in contemplating the ingenuity of the trap his enemy had constructed, that had sprung itself so neatly and then obligingly disappeared when its work was done, like a surgeon's dissolving sutures or a gothic storyteller's melting icicle dagger. Computers were not like that, however. They were not spontaneous; they only did what they were told. It was as if, to switch to another metaphor, the weather program had been moving steadily through a minefield; most of the time it knew how to avoid the mines. But at some point it had been *told* to step on a mine and blow itself up. And if this had actually happened, then this was not just another stupid metaphor; these things must actually exist, as instructions, tucked away somewhere among the coils of the vast leviathan of code that comprised the weather-forecasting program.

He tried very hard to prevent himself from being distracted by his other current obsession, which was Yulya. He had never seen so much trouble reflected in her pale blue eyes. It was obvious that she didn't love that KGB thug of a husband of hers; it was just as obvious that he loved her, judging by the way he followed her around whenever he came to see her at the Institute. When he talked to her, she smiled, but there were no signals passing between them. And of course there was Comrade Afanasyev, as well. He looked at her like a greedy little fat boy looking at a jam jar with a lid screwed on too tight for him to open. But she must have loved someone in her life; there was too much sweetness and tenderness in her, he was convinced of that. He would realize it at once if she fell in love again; he knew all her moods and expressions so well. Perhaps she was waiting for a sign, for a flicker of recognition in someone else's face, someone she still had not met. Kutuzov leaped up out of his chair, almost suffocating with delight. *He had figured it out! He had the solution!*

Yulya was waiting, perhaps, for a sign, for a signal of recognition from someone else. It was just the same with the computer—or with the program, at any rate. There were no traps, there was no minefield. There was only a single self-destructive impulse that had been planted in it at its inception, that would be triggered off by a signal from outside—not so much the look of love, to be sure, but a malign wink or leer that was addressed to it by some external, human intelligence—a being very much like himself, in fact, who had spent long white nights in contriving the seduction of a cold metal machine. But unlike a real, ephemeral human wink, the record of this impulse still existed inside the machine. Now there was no need to run through every line of the program. He would just have to ask the machine to list the number of every line of code that the program generally neglected to read, perhaps that it had read only once. This first filtration process would allow him to eliminate many tens of thousands of lines that he was not interested in; by successive approximations, making the mesh a little finer each time, he should finally be able to find the trap, the detonator, the fatal wink, whatever one chose to call it . . .

Thus Kutuzov descended into the hidden depths of the program, and when finally, just half an hour before the Institute was due to open for the day, he realized exactly how the trap had been sprung, he was so impressed by the elegance and simplicity of it all that he almost burst into tears. He got up from his chair, kneading his fists into the small of his back, both legs full of pins and needles. He dragged himself up to the cafeteria for a glass of tea, where he was discovered a little later by the first of his colleagues to arrive, sitting stiff and haggard, like a troll who had been caught by the sunlight.

FIVE

January 11, 1984   Krasnoyarsk

Sergei Voronkov buckled his belt and bent over to lace up his shoes. Long-nailed fingers began to massage the back of his neck; he gave a violent shudder, turned, and glared at the woman kneeling on the bed behind him. She was an exquisite Tartar with skin like burnished copper, the pride of Lyutko's.

"Get dressed and get out." The Tartar woman made a face at him behind his back, picked up a negligee from one corner of the couch, and flounced out into the hall, neglecting to close the door. Sergei sat down on the edge of the couch and got back to his shoelaces. There was a soft knock on the doorframe, and a figure appeared in the doorway. It was the Professor, Kutuzov's drinking partner of a few hours before. When Sergei turned to him and nodded, he began to speak in the same precise, cultured voice in which he had addressed Kutuzov, minus the geriatric and alcoholic overtones he had affected earlier.

"Kutuzov definitely did say something about a computer program that had been tampered with in some way, Comrade Colonel, but by then he was too far gone for me to make very much out of it. One thing of which he was clearly convinced was that the 'French program' had been sabotaged by an agent of the Western powers. He returned to the Institute early this morning in the hope of finding out how it was done. This makes the fourth consecutive night that he's devoted to this particular problem."

"Thanks very much, Pyotr Samoilovich. You've certainly got the head for it, I must say, and in more ways than one. Why don't you go back down and have an eye-opener, on me?" He waited until the Professor had closed the door behind him, went over to the telephone by the head of the bed, and picked up and then replaced the receiver in its cradle. He sat down on the edge of the bed to think for a moment.

In spite of Yulya's bravura performance, it had been impossible to conceal from the authorities in Moscow that there had been a serious machine failure at the Institute. There had been no explicit confirmation of this, of course, especially since the problem seemed miraculously to have corrected itself and the French support team had been unable to find anything wrong. Afanasyev had been in touch with Sergei personally; the situation, as Sergei had come to understand it, was that the technocrats and other patrons of the Institute had thrown themselves on the mercy of the hard-line opposition and had assured them that nothing of the sort could ever happen again. Nevertheless, the incident would still have to be investigated and the responsible parties subjected to discipline. Yulya was not necessarily going to be blamed for the hoax she had perpetrated on the delegates—unless, of course, it turned out she had something to do with the machine's breaking down as well. The delegation had already turned in a rhapsodically favorable report to the Central Committee, and it was thought that it would be inopportune to retract the report so quickly.

Sergei picked up the phone again and dialed a number. "Voronkov. I can't tell you everything now. This isn't a secure line, to put it mildly. In any case, I recommend against taking any action as yet. If we hang on for a couple of hours, we'll be able to pull him in—the crazy one, I mean—and perhaps a key accomplice as well."

"Very well," said the other. "Not too long, though. I'd like to get to the bottom of this business as quickly as possible, you know. Particularly if it turns out to be an *external* matter. Obviously we can't discuss that at the moment. Call back for confirmation in ten minutes."

Sergei hung up the phone, wandered into the bathroom, and spent the allotted time splashing water in his face and combing his hair. When he called back, the same voice answered immediately.

"I've had a word about all this. It's not as I thought at all. They want him picked up right away; they think he's already found out quite enough as it is. Looks like the accomplice is off the hook, I must say. Call back when you've got him in custody, and why don't you see if you can find someplace that's got a telephone that isn't a whorehouse?"

An hour later, Kutuzov and Yulya were sitting opposite one another in the cafeteria at the Institute; Kutuzov had been successfully revived with massive infusions of tea and breakfast.

"The island of St. Thomas!" he was saying; he made a vague but all-encompassing gesture with both hands, knocking over his glass of tea. Heads turned in their direction.

"My God, can't you pull yourself together?" Yulya whispered fiercely. "Now tell me whatever it is you've been trying to tell me all this time. Try to make some sense if you possibly can."

"The island of St. Thomas, U.S. Virgin Islands. Now listen closely. If a barometric reading of precisely 1029 millibars is reported for the island of St. Thomas, and gets fed into the system, *then* any subsequent instruction that's read by the machine has the effect of turning everything that follows into total garbage. It gets worse and worse as you go along, kind of a ripple effect, like a stone tossed into a pond, very attractive. Then along comes a reading of 1028 millibars for St. Thomas—1028, mind you, not 1029—and everything's suddenly all right again. All the bad things have gone away, like a footprint washed away by the tide, on the beautiful, tropical island of St. Thomas." Kutuzov had started speaking in a dreamy voice and appeared to be in a manic state bordering on religious ecstasy.

"Whoever thought this up," he went on quickly, "is a genius, pure and simple. I'd like to meet him—or her, of course—and shake him by the hand and tell him what a pleasure it's been to be working with him, or against him, for the past four, five days, whatever it's been. I'll tell you frankly, Yulya Nikolaevna, a programmer like that—saboteur, CIA agent, or Martian—a fellow like that is one in a billion . . ."

As always, Yulya could not help smiling at Kutuzov's enthusiasm for his craft. "You're right, of course. That was very cleverly done. But can't you try to calm down for a moment? We shouldn't attract any more attention to ourselves than we've already done. You know, just because you've figured it out doesn't mean it's all over. On the contrary, that actually makes it worse than ever. I'm going to have to give some serious thought to the *political* implications of all this, especially for you and me. I'll have to speak to Afanasyev as well, of course." She pushed back her chair and stood up to leave. Kutuzov had turned deathly pale; for perhaps the first time in several days, he had really paid attention to something that someone else had said to him.

"Wait, not so fast, please. Sit back down for a second. Is it really wise to take any of those people into your confidence? It seems to me that the last time you got away with it, but only barely. You know, at the polytechnic they told us that when we got out and got jobs, we'd be doing work of national importance. If anything, that seems to have been an understatement. I have very well-developed instincts for when something's about to turn to shit. Yulya, I just want to be left alone to do my work and think my little thoughts. I want to live a long, unhealthy, productive life, dedicated to the service of the Soviet Motherland and drinking myself sick at Lyutko's no more than three nights a week."

"What are you trying to say, exactly?"

"That the program seems to be running all right now, and the next time it happens, we'll be able to find the source of the trouble immediately and report it to the proper authorities."

"You must be out of your mind again. That's the worst possible thing we could do. Listen, old friend, I'm sure it's going to work out all right. We haven't done anything wrong, or even anything particularly stupid, so far. Quite the reverse, in fact. You're certain to come out of this with a decoration—Hero of Socialist Labor, maybe a modest salary increase to go with it."

"Yulya, don't forget, the first time the program blew up, we deliberately concealed the evidence of a serious crime. That sounds like an automatic twenty-five years right there . . ."

"Leave all that to me to worry about. You've done your part of the job, now it's up to me to do mine. Go home and get some sleep. I'll keep you informed of any developments."

Yulya walked briskly back to her office, and Kutuzov remained seated at the cafeteria table, paralyzed with wretchedness and fatigue. Yulya had brought him his outdoor coat from his locker upstairs. He got slowly to his feet, shrugged the coat on, and walked out into the lobby. There were two men, strangers in street clothes, waiting for him by the main reception gate.

"Fyodor Ivanovich Kutuzov? State Security. We have a few questions to ask you. I think you already know what it's about. Why don't we stop by your place first, so you can pick up a few things that you might need."

January 20, 1984   Near Langley, Virginia

"As you gentlemen are doubtless already aware," Clive Woodward was saying, "the Defense Information Systems Security Agency, DISSA, now comprises two main branches, the first of which, thanks to the lovely ADA, is chiefly concerned with the standardization of all computer software currently being used by our Armed Forces. The second branch, whose existence has not been made public thus far, is the Special Task Force on Counterintelligence Applications, under my direction. The task entrusted to our group has been that of active preparation for the warfare of the future, a kind of war that will be neither hot nor cold, will not be waged with nuclear weapons, but certainly will be far from conventional—a kind of war that a colleague more imaginative than myself has recently christened 'softwar.'"

Woodward was seated at the dais in a large, paneled briefing room, several floors above the underground catacomb formerly occupied by Brendan Barnes and his fellow Rats. There were two other men sitting beside him; each had been provided with a small microphone. The younger of the two was wearing the uniform of a rear admiral in the U.S. Navy; the other was a civilian, shorter and a great deal plumper than Woodward, and wearing a rather startling yellow tie. The steeply rising tiers of upholstered seats facing them were completely empty except for the first two rows. The gathering might easily have been mistaken for a stockholders' meeting of a very small corporation or a sparsely attended real estate or banking seminar, if it were not for the fact that at least two-thirds of the audience was in uniform. Among the other civilians present were two deputy directors and no fewer than four deputy assistant secretaries; so far Professor Woodward seemed to have seized and held his audience's full attention.

"More specifically, gentlemen," he went on, "our role has been to make *bombs* and equip them with the proper detonators. The sort of bombs I'm speaking of now are at once terribly destructive and perfectly harmless; their targets are not armies, factories, or missile silos, but *information systems*, the sort of complex, *useful* information that nowadays tends to be stored and retrieved by computers. These bombs, I repeat, do not kill or maim; they do not destroy; they are, if once again you will allow me the license of coining a word, 'softbombs.'

"In essence, a softbomb is no more than a few lines of programming code that can be surreptitiously inserted into a standard computer program—with the result that as soon as the bomb is detonated, the flow of information that this piece of software represents will be impeded, diverted, or brought completely to a halt. This is done in such a way that the database to which the program is designed to provide access—the vital information without which modern man finds it difficult to make the most routine decisions—will be rendered inaccessible or even unintelligible to the users of the system. The design and testing of these elegantly simple—and, I might add, remarkably inexpensive—new weapons systems are carried out by our Research and Development Section, directed by Dr. Arthur MacDonald, who is seated here at my right."

Dr. MacDonald, the stout civilian, bobbed his head at Woodward and at the audience. "Fortunately," he said, "the delivery system for these new weapons is provided gratis, thanks to the various non-strategic data-exchange networks that now cover the entire planet—transportation and telecommunications, economic and financial, scientific and meteorological, to mention just a few."

"And," Woodward continued, as MacDonald seemed to be on the point of mentioning several more, "the actual *planting* of the bomb is the responsibility of the Operations Section, directed by Rear Admiral John Eckelberry, this gentleman on my left here, and I'm sure already well known to many of you." At forty-eight, Eckelberry was one of the young lions of the Pentagon, first in his class at Annapolis to achieve his present rank and already being mentioned as a future deputy director, assuming that his intelligence background would disqualify him for the Joint Chiefs. "The first of these new weapons to be tested under field conditions, as it were, was successfully introduced into a complex computer program that is now in use at a major Soviet research facility at Krasnoyarsk in central Siberia; this was done under rather special circumstances, which I'll be discussing in greater detail in a moment. Every phase of this operation has been personally supervised by a member of the Working Committee, Dr. Brendan Barnes. Dr. Barnes is a recent recruit from the world of academe, extremely well qualified to conduct this operation—I might almost say *uniquely* qualified, since at one time he was intimately acquainted with Madame Y. N. Voronkov, the current director of the research institute at Krasnoyarsk that I mentioned a moment ago. In planning a battle that is to be conducted on such a miniature—such an *intimate*—scale, the importance of the psychological dimension, gentlemen, should certainly not be undervalued." A chorus of foot-shuffling and muttering from the audience made it clear that as far as a number of them were concerned, a college professor who was on an intimate footing with a high-ranking Soviet functionary was the last person to whom such a mission should be entrusted.

"Finally, and also a bit on the academic side of things, I should perhaps say a bit more about our Working Committee, which has concerned itself with laying out a long-term plan of campaign, of investigating the role that some of Dr. MacDonald's ingenious notions might possibly play in the economic and electronic warfare of the future.

"To begin with, you might care to consider the numerous sectors of national life that have been routinely victimized by 'computer failure'—I'm referring to the genuine article in this case—and would thus have to qualify as the sort of terrain in which the detonation of a softbomb would not necessarily excite suspicion. Under that heading, for example, we have been studying the recent civil disorders in Tunisia, touched off after an IMF computer here in Washington suggested that the Tunisian government improve its balance-of-payments position by desubsidizing the prices of staple foodstuffs. We have also been watching with some interest the reactions of governmental employees in the Ivory Coast whose salaries are currently three months in arrears, as the result of a computer malfunction in the offices of the Ministry of Finance; clearly, the Ivory Coast's reputation as one of the most sophisticated of Third World countries appears to be well merited.

"On a slightly different front, we have a total shutdown of the Soviet telephone system in November 1982; the culprit was identified in *Pravda* as 'the central telecommunications computer in Moscow.' During the previous year, the Soviet shoemaking industry was also paralyzed for several months due to a serious misallocation of raw materials, traceable in turn to a computer programming error. Finally, we have a computer error whose consequences proved to be far more serious than that. According to information furnished by CIA and Japanese intelligence sources, we now believe the death of two hundred forty passengers aboard Korean Airlines flight 007 can be directly attributed to the Elorg ES-1030 computer at Kamchatka air defense command, which, after deliberating for more than an hour, reported an 'eighty-eight-percent probability that the intruding aircraft was engaged in espionage activities.'"

Woodward paused for a moment, savoring the effect of this last remark, then continued, "These are the sorts of situations that the Working Committee has been looking into for some years now—

their causes, whether machine failure or human error, and their consequences—economic, social, and political—and always in as much detail as circumstances permit. Our current project, Operation Softwar, is derived from a contingency plan prepared as long ago as 1975, when an American-made computer and a substantial package of French software were purchased from Air France by Aeroflot. As soon as it came out that the Russians were dickering for a Craig computer and the associated software developed by the French national weather service, the scenario on which this operation was based was drawn up by Dr. Brendan Barnes. The degree of intervention required of us was minimal; we secured an appointment for Dr. Barnes to the Cocom investigation team that was to inspect the software in Paris, and Dr. Barnes introduced the first operational softbomb into the weather-forecasting program that was sold to the Russians.

"Given the complexity of the program itself, the principle involved is quite pleasingly simple. The 'fuse' that detonated the bomb was a specific piece of information furnished by the U.S. naval weather station on St. Thomas in the U.S. Virgin Islands, which, in the ordinary course of things, supplies the World Meteorological Organization with meteorological data for the island; this data in turn is relayed to all interested parties, including the Russians, of course, in the WMO's global network.

"The bomb was actually detonated in the following manner. The station on St. Thomas has been instructed never to report an atmospheric pressure for the island of 1029 millibars. If this is in fact the correct reading, a pressure of 1030 millibars is to be reported instead. The reason for this is quite important. The Craig computer in Krasnoyarsk has been instructed by Dr. Barnes to malfunction critically—to start spewing out gibberish, in fact—in response to any subsequent instruction, the instant it is informed, via the WMO network, of a barometric reading of exactly 1029 millibars for the island of St. Thomas. Now the softbomb has one very interesting aspect that I have so far neglected to mention—however extensive the havoc it might have wreaked, its effects are completely and instantly reversible. In this case, a later report that the barometric pressure on St. Thomas had dropped to 1028 would be sufficient to undo the effects of the original detonation and restore the normal functioning of the meteorological program. I need hardly mention, of course, that a barometric pressure of 1028 would also never be reported to the WMO in the ordinary course of events—not without, of course, some ulterior purpose of this kind."

One of the deputy directors in the front row flicked up a hand to catch Woodward's attention. "One thing troubles me about this, Professor Woodward—two things, in fact. It appears to me that in order to explode your software bomb and still maintain the secrecy and integrity of the operation, you'll have to pick a time when the actual barometric pressure in the area is pretty close to 1029, just to maintain appearances, or else you'll have to come up with a brand-new triggering mechanism the next time you want to blow up another computer program somewhere else. In other words, as I read it, instead of anticipating the warfare of the future here, it seems more like you've projected us back a couple of centuries into the past, when you had only one shot in your musket and you had to make damned sure you kept your powder dry—only in this case you'd have to worry that you couldn't set off your softbomb, say, in the middle of the hurricane season without attracting some pretty undesirable attention."

There was a slight, sulfurous tang of interservice rivalry in the air. Eckelberry signaled to Professor Woodward that he would like to say a word. "First of all, sir, I think you should bear in mind that the restrictions you're referring to—the role of the naval weather station, the reading of 1029 millibars—were entirely self-imposed. This was basically a test situation, and we were deliberately limiting our choices in order to keep our technical and operational parameters as simple and straightforward as possible. However, the impulse that instructs the program to blow itself up can take virtually any form you choose. For example, in this case we could have instructed the program to blow up when the barometric reading for St. Thomas ended in a figure five, only contained three digits, or whatever you choose. This would have solved the security problem you mentioned, but only at the cost of making an accidental glitch of some kind, even an accidental detonation, a little bit more likely. We decided that the risk that would entail was unacceptable.

"Professor Woodward has already pointed out that any sector of a society can be destabilized, even completely paralyzed—industry and defense, civil and military communications, logistics and transport, public administration, the entire economy—simply by a couple of keystrokes on a computer terminal, anywhere in the world. We do definitely see this as the electronic battleground of the future, and we definitely see ourselves as being in the process of seizing the high ground for ourselves before the other side can get there—"

This time it was the other deputy director who broke in with a fresh objection. "But isn't it true, Admiral, that a better analogy might be that of the proverbial ignorant armies that clash by night, since there can clearly be no question of proper battle management when you have absolutely no control over—and scarcely any knowledge of—local 'battlefield' conditions between the time your bomb is planted and the time it goes off? More specifically, isn't it true that the secrecy and integrity of this operation, as someone said a moment or two ago, were both put seriously at risk by a purely chance event—though this one was a snowstorm over Siberia rather than a hurricane in the Caribbean?"

Eckelberry obviously thought that if the story had to be told, it would be best for him to tell it himself. "Essentially," he began, "the facts are these. A delegation of Communist Party bigwigs from Moscow, including several from the Soviet Academy of Sciences, came to inspect the computer center at Krasnoyarsk on the very day that the detonation code was sent from St. Thomas—on a day, incidentally, on which the barometric pressure was hovering right around 1029 millibars. The visit had originally been scheduled for three days earlier, then, when the airport at Krasnoyarsk was shut down by a snowstorm, was bumped back to the afternoon of the sixth. The Krasnoyarsk computer was caught off guard by that one as well, apparently. In any case, our intelligence had informed us of the *original* date of the visit but not of the cancellation. Admittedly, the situation was pretty ticklish for a while; the machine was virtually useless for public-relations purposes at that point. Fortunately, Madame Voronkov, the director of the Institute, seems to have pulled off some kind of murphy game and convinced them all that everything was working just fine. However, if the failure of the program had been discovered, then there would have been a serious official inquiry—"

The second deputy director's voice had risen half an octave and a couple of decibels when he broke in again. "I'd like to correct any impression anyone might've gotten that this near-catastrophe occurred because of faulty intelligence-gathering. When you were informed of the *scheduled* date of the delegation's visit, you were also advised that this was considered to be dangerously close to the scheduled kickoff date for the operation. This was not, in my opinion, a failure of intelligence, but rather a failure of judgment, compounded, as I see it, by an even more reckless decision to send out the cancellation code from St. Thomas and reactivate the program. As Professor Woodward has quite correctly pointed out, we've all come to regard computer *failure* as a routine hazard of modern life, but I'm sure you'll all agree with me that a computer that inexplicably breaks down and then performs a quick fix on itself like that is bound to attract attention."

"In fact, we had very little choice in the matter," Woodward replied. "Once the alarm was sounded, we could expect the French support team to be arriving momentarily. If they had had a chance to investigate the damage while the system was still down, then it would have been relatively easy to discover that the meteorological program had been tampered with—and by whom. Once the cancellation code had been sent out, the danger of detection was actually decreased significantly—assuming that an investigation of some sort was probably going to be undertaken in either case. To sum up, then, I'm sure you gentlemen will be delighted to hear that we've learned a number of useful lessons from all this, which will enable us to refine our methods considerably in the future. First of all, in choosing our detonation code, we shall have to restrict ourselves to a class of nonstrategic data that is entirely nonfalsifiable—that is, in contrast to the barometric pressure on St. Thomas, if we say it's x, then no one can say, Well, it should be y, or Why *isn't* it y? Also, there must be no secondary effects in the real world, outside the target country of course, that derive from our circulating a false message of some sort—as our detonation and cancellation codes—throughout this global data-exchange network; for example, an attempt to disrupt telecommunications in the Soviet Union might very well set the telephones ringing off their hooks in Saudi Arabia as well. But there is another serious flaw in our present modus operandi that I'm surprised neither of you gentlemen has been able to put his finger on."

Woodward paused significantly. Those members of the audience who did not necessarily regard Woodward and Eckelberry as dangerous rivals, or disdain them as late starters in an already overcrowded field, were clearly enjoying this; the two deputy directors merely glowered. "Very well," Woodward continued, "then I shall have to tell you. It would have been possible for a Russian programmer who was a bit cleverer than the others, perhaps, to figure out precisely what had happened without actually running through every one of the several hundred thousand lines of code in the program. It would have been possible for him to enlist the aid of the machine in sorting out those instructions which had lain dormant within the program and had only once been read by the machine. This, by a sort of logical sifting process, would enable him to have the solution at his fingertips in a finite amount of time, a very few days if not hours.

"Of course, there are a number of possible countermeasures that we could adopt. You're all familiar, for example, with the concept of what are called penetration aids—the drones and decoys and other distracting objects that accompany nuclear missiles to their targets and which, from the enemy's point of view, may or may not be equipped with warheads but which he's obliged to try to intercept in any case, because he can't afford to take that sort of chance. Of course, this makes the task of intercepting the bona fide warheads considerably more difficult. In the same way, a vast number of harmless and inactive lines of code might be scattered throughout a program, which would mimic the actual detonation code—in every way but one—and make it all the more difficult, if not practically impossible—for that Russian programmer to locate and disarm the real bomb in a reasonable amount of time—"

By this time the second deputy director was ready to fire his parting shot. "I suggest to you, sir," he said, "that that's not quite good enough. Even if you could insert fifty thousand lines of inactive code into a program, the Russians could still put five hundred of their people to work on it and crack it wide open in a matter of hours—and they would, too, if they thought they could catch us out at something like this. Gentlemen, you have run a successful operation, but only by taking tremendous risks. You have been extremely lucky thus far, but I submit to you that in a case like this, *any* predictable risk of detection is entirely unacceptable. It seems to me, Professor Woodward, that you've got yourself completely boxed in with this, that in future you'll have to be satisfied with nothing short of a one-hundred-percent chance of success."

"That," Woodward replied, "is precisely what we're going to be counting on, in future."

January 16, 1984   Moscow

The usher who led Yulya through the last several anterooms was a man of gigantic stature, almost seven feet tall. He left her in a handsomely furnished drawing room, though the quality of the furnishings suffered severely by comparison with the treasures of the Kremlin that she had glimpsed earlier on. "Kindly wait here, Comrade Voronkov. The Secretary General should be with you in a moment," the colossus announced, and disappeared through a double door. Yulya stared after him and suddenly felt herself in the grip of a complex and almost paralyzing emotional response, compounded equally of pride, intense curiosity, and terror. The words themselves, *Secretary General*, conjured up memories of songs around the campfire in Komsomol summer camp, and the rather tedious political education courses that she had had to endure all through graduate school: solemn-voiced announcers on television, giant heroic figures painted on the walls of government buildings . . .

The colossus had returned, followed by two others like him, their shoulders touching those of the frail figure advancing between them. Andropov's face was instantly recognizable, of course, though much more fragile-looking than she had expected. The two aides assisted—almost carried—him to an armchair, and he dismissed them with a dry, precise gesture. The movement of his lips in that pale, nerveless face, partially concealed behind outsized glasses, seemed surprising, even a little unsettling, as if a corpse had suddenly begun to speak.

"Please sit down, Madame Voronkova." His voice was cordial enough, but feeble, and Yulya was amused by his old-style habits of speech, calling her "madame" and retaining the feminine particle in "Voronkova."

"Let me begin with two extremely commonplace observations—that Comrade Afanasyev has told me a great deal about you, and that I am delighted to have the opportunity of meeting you in person."

Yulya opened her mouth in the hope that some appropriate formula would emerge, but Andropov did not wait for her reply. "I have also read your recommendations to the Academy of Sciences on artificial-intelligence research, and of course"—his eyes glinted mischievously, perhaps maliciously, behind thick glasses—"I've also had tidings from several academicians, who appear to have been very favorably impressed by their visit to Krasnoyarsk."

For what seemed like a very long time, Yulya waited for him to continue. Did he already know all about it? Afanasyev had assured her that the whole thing was as good as forgotten, and she certainly did not relish the prospect of explaining to Yuri Andropov how a minute fluctuation in barometric pressure on an island in the Caribbean could have caused a sophisticated computer program to blow up in Central Siberia, ten thousand kilometers away. Sergei, for his part, had made quite a point of insisting that she say nothing about it, and in general he had seemed strangely disquieted and depressed by the fact that his wife had been summoned to a private audience with Comrade Andropov in Moscow. As for herself, Yulya was content to float with the current of events, whatever course they might take. At any rate, it seemed unlikely to her that the Secretary General of the Communist Party of the USSR would personally take the trouble to dismiss the director of a provincial research institute—or even to interrogate a suspected saboteur, for that matter.

"You know, Yulya Nikolaevna, that I expect a great deal from you." His voice sounded quite different now, as if it were coming from some distance away. "From you and a great many others like you. You are part of a new generation of specialists that our country has desperate need of—to help usher in a new era in human history, to build a new socialist society in a way that will only be possible if we can master the technical skills over which, for the moment at least, the West continues to exercise a virtual monopoly. But tell me, how are you adjusting to your new life in Siberia? You are not a native, I take it?" His voice had suddenly taken on a livelier, more conversational, and more conventional tone.

"I grew up outside Vitebsk, Comrade Secretary General, and I've spent most of my life there. In Siberia it's a bit different, I suppose . . . but to tell you the truth, I hope you won't think I'm being insincere when I say that I've been so preoccupied with my new assignment that I really haven't noticed it all that much—"

"Quite the contrary. It makes me very glad to hear you say that. It may not altogether surprise you to know that such enthusiasm for the task of building socialism is in extremely short supply at the moment." His voice lowered again; the words came slowly. For a moment it almost seemed that he was about to drop off to sleep; then she was seized with momentary panic at the thought that he might be undergoing some sort of medical crisis right before her eyes.

"And as for myself," he continued, after a protracted silence, "I can scarcely muster the energy to conduct a civil conversation with an attractive young woman. Of course, you know that there are quite a number of people who believe I'm not likely to last very much longer—and in the eyes of many, in fact, that seemed to be my most important qualification for the job . . ."

Once again, Yulya tried to produce the appropriate word of protest, but Andropov waved it away with thin, white fingers. "Perhaps ordinarily I might derive some amusement from the efforts of my former colleagues to replace me in what I must now regard as a not very enviable position. However, unfortunately for us, the situation is not really all that amusing." Her friendship with Afanasyev had taught Yulya to be even more intolerant of official cant and rhetoric than the average politically sophisticated Soviet citizen, but now the fact that Comrade Andropov, chief of state of one of the two most powerful nations on earth, clearly meant to include her in the word *us* went straight to her heart.

"It's entirely possible," he went on, "that for a time at least, the reactionary element—the apostles of absolute immobility—will carry off the top prize. But our people will remain at their posts, for the most part, and I trust that you will remain at yours and continue to work for what you know to be right—modernization, individual responsibility, individual initiative, all three of these goals indissolubly linked together. Computerization should help us to stamp out waste and economic crime, the two great plagues that are devouring our society. It was seventeen years ago that I asked our mutual friend Afanasyev to computerize the archives and administration of State Security. And there, of course, we encountered a good deal of the same sort of blind, senseless opposition. Sometimes it takes a lot of effort to convince such people, you know, that they don't want to be left in the dustbin of history." Though he spoke lightly, Andropov's voice and face had become quite animated again, and for the first time Yulya had the impression of tremendous power confined within a frail cocoon of flesh; this was not an impression that made her feel particularly comfortable.

Once again, Andropov had paused for a long time to catch his breath and to control a slight tremor in his lower jaw. "I have spoken about you," he went on finally, "with my good friend Gorbachev. He's the one to talk to about computers, of course—and in future you should feel free to get in touch with him directly. Perhaps you won't be too surprised when I tell you, Yulya Nikolaevna, that you are young and beautiful, that your personality is both forceful and perfectly charming. We feel that you are extremely well qualified to serve as our standard-bearer in the forthcoming campaign for the modernization of our society. I expect that quite soon you will be reading a lot about yourself in the newspapers, for example.

"I don't mean, however, that we intend to turn you into a sort of propaganda puppet—like an athlete or a cosmonaut, or like Stakhanov of blessed memory—but it is true that public personalities of whom people see a great deal on television and in the press undeniably have a certain impact. Nor am I suggesting, I assure you, that you will be subjected to the same sort of humiliating attentions that public personalities of that kind have to put up with in the West. Far from it, in fact. But our people are also in desperate need of fire and élan and inspiration—dreams of the future. I think you can provide those for them; you will become, in effect, the incarnation of our policy, the living symbol of the future of our country." He paused at the end of this lengthy speech and smiled. "In short, I am asking no more of you than this—your task will be to convince everyone that our policy and the future of our country are one and the same, the one is unthinkable without the other."

Yulya recalled that "Stakhanov of blessed memory" was a famous coal miner of the Stalin years who had cut twenty cubic meters of coal in a single day, or something equally impossible; she would have preferred that Comrade Andropov had set her a task like that instead, one that at least could be performed in comparative privacy. All that she said, however, was, "Naturally, Comrade Secretary General, I will do what I can to prove myself worthy of your trust."

"I hope," he replied, "that you will do what you *must*. I also have another, more serious assignment for you. We have it in mind to appoint an oversight committee of specialists to supervise the systematic upgrading of all data-processing facilities in the Soviet Union. You will be the chairwoman of this committee. Your first objective will be to make certain that new equipment and so forth is being allocated among the various facilities according to central-planning criteria that will be promulgated by the Secretariat. Your second objective will be to review and update the catalogue of priority items—computer software, for the most part—that we hope to obtain clandestinely from the West. In this, you and your colleagues can be assured of the unqualified support of State Security. And, of course, in purchasing stolen goods, one cannot necessarily accept the thief's estimation of their true quality or value. Comrade Gorbachev has likened our present dependence on Western computer programs to the situation that prevailed during the first Five Year Plans, when we were compelled to recruit large numbers of British and American engineers to assist in the industrialization of our country. Naturally, there was always the danger that some of them might have been serving two masters, and the possibility of sabotage, though perhaps more apparent than real, was always there to be reckoned with. Your group will also be responsible for initiating and supervising the development of whatever tests or techniques are necessary to review these programs and give them a clean bill of health, so that the possibility of sabotage—or the presence of what I believe are called 'bugs'—can be positively ruled out . . ."

This last speech had obviously cost Andropov a tremendous effort. Yulya listened dully, convinced—especially after Andropov had mentioned sabotage—that the interview could not possibly be concluded without some discussion of the failure of the weather program. What would she say when the moment came? Tell the truth? Hadn't Afanasyev once said something about frankness only being effective when you had absolutely no intention of telling the truth?

But Andropov had stopped speaking several seconds earlier; his eyes were half-closed now. He remained motionless for a long time, then leaned forward slightly; Yulya realized that his foot must be pressing a button that was hidden beneath the carpet. The two colossi appeared within seconds, helped the Secretary General to his feet, and started to lead him away. Yulya rose to her feet; Andropov and his escort passed quite close to her on their way to the door. "Remember," he said softly, "I'm counting on you, Yulya Nikolaevna." He seemed to be completely exhausted. In a moment, the double doors had closed behind them; the interview was at an end.

February 1, 1984   10:00 A.M.   Paris

Brendan walked the length of the bar and automatically acknowledged the bartender's salutation as he stepped into the back room. As always, Thompson had already staked out a table; there were no other customers, and the waiter brought Brendan a cup of coffee without his having to ask.

"We've just had word," Thompson told him, "that a KGB colonel is coming to town to try to find out what went wrong with the weather program."

"The least they could send, don't you think? And judging by

your expression, I'd say you're making a lot bigger deal of this than they are. What's he going to find out, after all?"

"Not much. But the thing that bothers me is that they're reacting to this so slowly. Don't they even know that they've been *had*?"

Brendan swallowed a mouthful of hot coffee. Thompson, he decided, did not believe in letting sleeping dogs lie. He believed in giving them a wake-up call; he believed in kicking them. Brendan glanced over toward the bar. A tall, light-skinned black man had just come in, his face vaguely familiar; he seemed to be looking around for someone. In the second or so that it took for his eyes to become accustomed to the dim light in Harry's back room, Brendan had recognized him. Françoise's brother, the famous separatist, alleged by Richard Thompson to have been packed off to Martinique by the French political police.

He felt a shock of adrenaline in his chest as their eyes met. The newcomer reached a hand inside his jacket. Brendan tackled Thompson high and pulled him off his chair; they were both on the floor, several feet away, when an unbearably loud detonation, accompanied by an expanding star of flame, burst out from beneath their table. Just before he was struck and stunned by a large fragment of ceiling, Brendan had barely enough time to reflect that the Russians seemed to have a lot faster reaction time than Thompson had given them credit for.

SIX

February 10, 1984   Krasnoyarsk

"In the name of the Central Committee and the Presidium of the Supreme Soviet of the USSR, and following the death of Yuri Vladimirovich Andropov, Secretary General of the Communist Party and Chairman of the Presidium of the USSR, four days of national mourning have been proclaimed, for February 11, 12, 13, 14 . . ."

Yulya and Sergei had long since agreed that Friday evenings were to be devoted exclusively to the children. Unlike other nights, Sergei always waited until they were asleep before he left the house again; husband and wife spent the evening perched at opposite ends of the living room couch, conscientiously enacting their roles of twin household gods, while eight-year-old Alyosha sprawled on the carpet watching television, and eleven-year-old Svetlana sat with furrowed brow and with her back ostentatiously turned to the screen, reading *The Life of Isadora Duncan* or *The Mysterious Island*. Tonight the sound was turned down low, both parents giving the screen an occasional distracted glance while the announcer read and reread the same official communiqué that had been broadcast on the radio all day against a background of somber orchestral music.

"On the day of the funeral service, all primary and secondary schools will be closed . . ."

"Does that mean that my dance class is going to be canceled as well?" asked Svetlana, without taking her eyes from her book.

"Certainly it does," replied Sergei. "That's the way we do things, after all. Comrade Andropov was our country's top leader, and we want to show the whole world how sad we are that he's gone."

"And at the moment that the coffin is interred in Red Square, an artillery salute will be fired in Moscow, in the capitals of each of the Union republics, in the heroic fortress city of Leningrad . . ."

"But I'm not sad, especially, I'm just disappointed my dance class is going to be canceled."

"Well, you realize," Sergei went on, with a sidelong glance at Yulya, "that when important leaders like Yuri Vladimirovich die, even grownups are sometimes disappointed for the same reason you are, because they won't be able to do things they've been counting on."

". . . the heroic fortress city of Brest-Litovsk, as well as Kaliningrad, Smolensk, and Rostov-na-Donu . . ."

"All right, you two," said Yulya abruptly, "time to start getting ready for bed." Svetlana appeared once more to be ferociously absorbed in her reading. "Get along now, Svetlanochka, and take your brother with you." Svetlana released a histrionic sigh, took Alyosha by the hand, and led him off down the hall. "I'll be with you in a minute or two," Yulya called after them, just as the announcer had finished with the lengthy roll of cities that would take part in the synchronized artillery salute. She turned toward Sergei and asked in a quiet voice, "What are *we* not going to be able to do that we've been counting on, for example?"

Sergei did not answer immediately, but kept on squinting at the television screen with spurious concentration. Ever since she had come back from her interview with Andropov, he had seemed a little afraid of her and had virtually refused to say anything without carefully weighing the effect of every syllable in advance.

"All work will cease for five minutes in all designated workplaces, including factories, collective enterprises, and state institutions, on Union territory,

with the exception of factories in which continuous assembly-line production methods are employed . . ."

"You know who's going to replace him," Sergei said eventually. "The only thing *that* one's interested in is keeping the old machine oiled and running—no experiments, no improvements . . ."

". . . factories and locomotives, oceangoing and riverine vessels, will sound their whistles for three minutes . . ."

Yulya got up and switched off the set. "Afanasyev's been named to the funeral committee," she remarked in the same mild voice.

"And Gorbachev's high on the list of pallbearers, I know. But allow me to point out to you, my dear, that your own position is not nearly so secure. That means you should be more circumspect in your dealings with others—stop pestering everyone about your friend Kutuzov, to start with."

Yulya simply stared and said nothing. Sergei briefly savored his moment of triumph—it was not often these days that he could get her to drop her customary pose of total imperturbability—and then continued in a voice ripe with self-satisfaction, "You keep trying to go over my head in the department and to get your fancy friends in the Academy to intercede for you. It's not going to work, and it all gets right back to me, in any case. And, do you know, their only reaction is always, 'Can't you do something about that wife of yours?'"

He paused for a moment. "What I've told you is just good advice, however; the rest is official. Your friend Kutuzov has been detained under Article 245 of the Criminal Code, willful destruction of state property, and Article 57 of the Constitution, which I suggest you read for yourself in its entirety. You should shortly be receiving word from the Office of Personnel Services that he's to be dismissed as a result of that ridiculous charade he put on for the academicians—"

"But you know perfectly well that I was the one—"

"No, I don't. I know nothing of the kind."

They could hear Svetlana calling from the other end of the hall. "Mama, we've got our pajamas on! Aren't you coming?"

"In a minute!" Yulya called back, then said in a lower voice to Sergei, "But why take it out on poor Kutuzov?"

"Because every crime has to have a criminal . . . and because he's become too erratic and unstable to be permitted to have access to state secrets. Yulya, you know that as long as you keep butting your head against this thing, you're going to keep embarrassing yourself—and all of us, really."

"Us?"

"You and me . . . and the children."

Yulya simply stared at him for a moment without saying a word. She allowed Sergei to kiss her on the forehead, and then she walked down the hall to the children's room.

February 10, 1984   Somerset, Massachusetts

Brendan stood the cut log upright on the chopping block, took the ax in his right hand, holding it high up on the shaft, close to the blade, and carefully split the log into four triangular lengths of stovewood. He clicked his tongue contentedly as he split the second piece into two perfectly equal halves and tossed the stove lengths into the wheelbarrow beside him. The woods were still covered with old, wet snow, the wheelbarrow cut a long furrow through the brown grass, and his feet squelched damply as he made his way toward the back porch. The cabin was not far away, low and sprawling and extremely inviting on a cold, sunny morning. As he lifted the cover of the woodbox he felt a sudden sharp twinge in his right wrist, which had absorbed much of the shock of having Thompson and a hundred or so pounds of plaster land on top of him in Harry's Bar. Thompson had not suffered any permanent damage, the bartender had required only a few stitches to undo the ill effects of flying glass, and Jacques Vimard, Françoise's brother, had escaped under his own power. It was actually the table that had absorbed most of the force of the blast, and since there were no fatalities and the names of the principal victims, identified only as "U.S. Embassy employees," were withheld "for routine security reasons," the incident had not gotten much play in the international press; certainly Jacques Vimard had not reappeared to tell his side of the story.

After Brendan had transferred the stovewood from the wheelbarrow to the woodbox on the porch, he trundled the empty barrow back to the shed, hung up the ax by the back door, and went into the kitchen to start breakfast. Soon his mind and hands were occupied with a sequence of familiar tasks as the kitchen filled up with the aroma of hot coffee and frying bacon. Breakfast in bed was a much-cherished ritual whenever they came out to the cabin. Brendan filled the tray to capacity with scrambled eggs and bacon, buttered toast and Highland oat cakes, Crosse and Blackwell preserves, and a number of fussy little Bostonian breakfast things that Sally was partial to. It felt good to be back, to be doing ordinary things again, to watch Sally waking up in the morning—torn, on this particular morning, between a hot breakfast and the last delicious wisps of sleep.

"Beautiful morning," said Brendan. "Also beautiful bacon, beautiful coffee . . ." He set the tray down on the bedside table and walked over to open the curtains. This involved making the sort of lateral sweeping motion that he found particularly painful; he gave a sharp intake of breath and rubbed his wrist ruefully. Sally was watching him with wide-open eyes, and unlike her expression on most mornings, her soft, pleasant face looked very grave.

"Brendan, you know I couldn't sleep last night."

"You didn't seem to be having much trouble about two minutes ago. Ready to sit up and take nourishment?" Sally did so, and Brendan propped both pillows behind her back and began to fiddle with the breakfast tray. "Coffee now? Coffee later? *Jus d'orange?*"

"Brendan, I'm serious about this, I'm afraid. Last night I was lying here thinking about what you'd told me about . . . when you got hurt. Maybe it's true they decided to attack Harry's Bar because it's always full of Americans, just like the PLO or whoever it was that shot up that kosher restaurant in the Marais a couple of years ago. But if that's true, why did they do it at ten o'clock in the morning, when there was nobody there but you and Richard? Maybe it wasn't just meant as a warning or some kind of loony symbolic gesture, maybe it wasn't just *any* two Americans they were after, maybe it was you and Richard, specifically. And after I'd thought about that for a while, I couldn't get back to sleep for a very long time."

Brendan sat down on the edge of the bed and poured himself a glass of orange juice. "You know that whenever you've come right out and asked me about anything, I've always told you the truth, right?"

"And you've also noticed that I almost never have, right?"

"Right. Okay. The answer is yes, that guy had come there to find us, Richard and me, and kill us both."

"Why?"

"Well, it's partly political—*mostly* political if you add it up—and partly psychological; *pathological* might be a better word. The guy with the grenade, his name is Jacques Vimard, and his sister Françoise is someone we know, someone Richard and I both know in Paris . . ." Brendan looked over at Sally. There were tears in the corners of her eyes, but her voice was level and controlled.

"And who's her very best friend," she asked, "you or Richard?"

"Me."

"Are you in love with her? Do you love her more than you supposedly love me?" Sally's voice was ice-cold now. Brendan reached over to touch her cheek.

"Sometimes I think I'm in love with her, but it's not the way I love you. All right, I know what that sounds like, but just let me tell you the whole story, and then you'll know all about it. This Jacques Vimard really is a terrorist, belongs to a couple of different ultraleft splinter groups—*groupuscules* is what the French call them, right? Doesn't like Americans, doesn't like whites, doesn't like *me* very much at all. Anyway, he absolutely forbade his sister to have anything further to do with me. Fair enough. She ignored him. A little later, he was picked up by the French police and deported back to Martinique—that's where they both come from. Okay, the police down there were supposed to be keeping an eye on him, but he managed to smuggle himself back to Paris without too much trouble at all. According to those who know, he must have had some very serious people helping him out with this, not just the sort of whacked-out West Indian radicals he usually pals around with . . ." He stopped to take a bite from the slice of buttered toast that Sally had handed him.

"I think you're telling me quite a bit," she said, "but not the whole story by any means. I mean, we've agreed we both have our own lives to lead and so forth, and I've always known that the life *you* lead is a pretty strange one, on the whole. But I think you're telling me about this girl from Martinique partly because it's true and partly to get me upset and throw me off the track, am I right? I think this really has to do with Richard, and that Cocom job, and your going to Paris to inspect that computer they wanted to sell to the Russians."

"Okay, point taken. Drink your coffee before it gets cold. I'm going to tell you all about it, or as much as I'm allowed to, probably more. They're fairly strict about the details, but I'll try to give you the very broad outlines. I want to be able to put what happened to me and Richard in the proper perspective, so you won't think I'm running around trying to be some sort of two-fisted Indiana Jones–type academic, or start worrying that someone's going to put shellfish toxin in my milkshake, or something—because what happened really was kind of a coincidence in a way. This Jacques Vimard was already on my case, and these very serious people I mentioned earlier must've agreed to put the means at his disposal, as they often do—"

"You mean the *Russians*? The KGB, for example?"

"Well, in a way, it's regarded as kind of a good sign that they did it the old-fashioned way—the say-it-with-high-explosives type of approach—instead of retaliating in kind. I guess by now it's pretty clear this has something to do with computers. Anyway, they've proved themselves incapable of really fighting back on the terrain that we've already staked out."

"You mean you were expecting them to do something *worse* than get some maniac to throw a hand grenade at you at ten o'clock in the morning?"

"Well, I get the sense they're kind of like organized crime in that respect. They do favors for people, and they find people to do favors for them. They're always poking around, looking for loose threads, and sometimes somebody comes away in their hand, like Jacques Vimard. On a larger scale, they spent astronomical sums of money just trying to cozy up to various people, and in a much more effective way than we're usually inclined to think. And on a *still* larger scale, they've convinced most of the world that no matter how rotten they are, basically they're all right—whereas most of the world also believes that it's just the other way around, as far as we're concerned. How much do you hear about Afghanistan compared to what we used to hear about Vietnam? They've convinced a lot of people in

Europe that they're more seriously committed to disarmament than we are; they've convinced a fair number of people in America—"

"But you're too smart for them, so they had to find somebody to blow you up with a hand grenade, right?"

"All right, I'm coming to that. If I'm going to unburden myself of all this top-secret, deep-background philosophy, I should get to tell it my way, okay? And to start with, I merely assert that Western-style democracy, for all its faults, has much more of a potential for realizing the kind of future that I personally want than does Soviet-style Communism, for all its theoretical virtues. Unfortunately, however, a democratic *open* society is at a tremendous disadvantage vis-à-vis a totalitarian *closed* society when it comes to resisting the sort of ideological penetration I've just been talking about—when it comes to making certain choices and to keeping secrets, essentially. I'd like to quote from a highly regarded source:

"'On the international scene today, the nuclear balance of terror appears to overshadow all other policy considerations. Certainly the terror is real enough, but the fact remains that a rough equilibrium appears to exist between the arsenals of the two great nuclear powers. On the other hand, the extreme vulnerability of the United States to the current all-out offensive on the part of the Soviet intelligence-gathering apparatus is potentially no less destabilizing than the nuclear "window of vulnerability." Computer science suggests to us a number of ways, however, in which this imbalance might be redressed.' That's from my article in *Computers and Society*—an article you claim to have read, by the way."

"For short-term recall only, not on file. I understand what you meant a minute ago about 'keeping secrets,' but what about 'making choices'?"

"Well, basically all I meant was that *we* have to make them for *ourselves*, and from my perspective, it seems to be critically important that we make the right ones. Computers can actually teach us an entirely new, nonlinear approach to decision-making—to thinking of any kind, really. For example, when kids learn to work with computers, they just sit down and *learn* it, just like that, often much better than adults do, and of course they never bother to read the documentation. Kids' natural approach to the world—feeling your way, learning by trial and error, stimulus and response—also happens to be the best possible approach to the computer. You say to yourself, What is this thing, anyway? It's just a big box full of data, some of which I want, and you kind of circle around it for a while, trying to find the best way to get inside that box. This teaches the kid a kind of nonlinear reasoning—'circular' reasoning, you could almost call it, but in a good sense—or in other words, a mode of thought that's result-oriented rather than pattern-oriented. A good programmer who sits down in front of a big pile of data like that is not going to ask himself, What's the one great unifying principle that holds all this stuff together? He's going to ask, What do I have to do to get at the particular stuff I want?"

"But doesn't that mean that you're accepting a conceptual model that's imposed on you by the machine—that the computer's teaching you to think in a way that's more convenient for *it*, not for you? I remember your telling me about those Frenchmen who claimed that a computer program represents a kind of bonsai version of an entire culture, but if we allow our culture to be transmitted in that form, the way the computer tells us to, then how do we know that it won't become grotesquely transformed or distorted in some way?"

"Well, really, it's the culture that creates the program, not the other way around. And of course I see what you're driving at—computers winning away the hearts and minds of our children, a conceptual model that's imposed on you by a machine. 'At last, a form of totalitarianism that really works,' and so forth. You can imagine it that way if you like, but you should also bear in mind that computers offer us a way of enlarging the format of the traditional political debate, by turning the binary, true-false type of electoral questions—which are actually not very democratic—into multiple choice, with an unlimited number of choices. The way it works now, the minority that loses the election is always subject to the tyranny of the majority, but, oddly enough, I believe that computers can help restore true classical democracy—as in ancient Athens—on a national, perhaps a global scale."

"Tell us, then, O Socrates, how all this is to come about?"

"All right. If everyone has his or her own computer, all hooked into a national database network, that means you could have a national referendum on *every* political issue of any importance—direct democracy, an electronic Agora. Everyone would have the issues at his fingertips, so there'd be no political flimflam. You wouldn't have to waste the afternoon driving over to the junior high school to vote, and there wouldn't be any problem with counting the ballots. Politics would be a routine part of everyday life—the way it was in ancient Athens, as a matter of fact."

"And you think that's what your friends and associates in Washington are really working toward, to be replaced by a bunch of home computers?"

"I don't think it really matters, because this is just the beginning of the Information Age. As long as we keep our options open, who knows what's going to happen? A vision of society that seems hopelessly . . . well, visionary, utopian, to us today may one day seem perfectly practicable to our kids or our kids' kids, who've grown up with computers. Maybe the kind of society that was dreamed of by the philosophical anarchists—the ones Marx hated so much—is really the way it's going to be, a loose confederation of little communities, autonomous microsocieties, with all the logistical and organizational details worked out by tapping into the national database."

"So, instead of engendering a race of slavish nerds, you think the computer is going to give free rein to individualism in its purest form, all power to the imagination and all that sort of thing?"

"Well, after people get used to really living with computers, I don't think they'll be satisfied with anything less. The lead time between the formulation of a need or a desire and its realization will gradually get smaller and smaller, thanks to the computer, but the regulation of *how* that happens will become a completely individual affair. I mean, there will still probably be laws—millions of 'em, if you want—but these little autarchic communities, microsocieties, will probably just pick the ones they want for their own internal consumption, out of the millions on file. And I suppose for more general purposes there'll be a common code of civilized behavior that transcends these local laws and applies to everyone—perhaps much more so than at present, for example."

"So, then, Socrates, you absolutely reject the notion of the computer as an agent of Pavlovian mind control. It's definitely a Good Thing, a time machine that will take us back to the good old days in the Agora, where you used to hang out with your little buddies—"

"Absolutely. The computer's not just a kind of souped-up calculator, it's also the ultimate ballot box and statute book—a *multiplier* of democracy, in a word."

"And what about those places where they have something different?"

"It seems to me that the spirit of the Information Age is antithetical to the idea of a one-party state—even more than to the idea of a two-party state—or any form of society that tries to wrap up the entire universe in a single, all-enveloping philosophical model. It's true over here, too—that ideologies and absolutist creeds of any kind are losing their hold on people, are losing their collective grip on reality as well, as the processes of cultural fermentation and technological evolution make that reality ever more protean and complex. Remember the kid trying out the computer for the first time; the first step for the operator should be to try out various procedures to see if they really work. That's the great paradox in all of this—that artificial intelligence is going to show us the way back to . . . not exactly a state of nature, but at least to a more natural mode of thinking and behaving. So far, technology has shielded us from a lot of the *good* effects of evolutionary change—spontaneous mutations that result in new and vigorous life forms. In the Information Age, every microsociety will be out there on its own, will have to evolve its own organizational model in accordance with this one fundamental axiom: If it *could* work, try to make it work; if not, try something else . . ."

"I'll tell you what," said Sally. "I'll give up all my rebuttal time if you'll just clarify one little thing for me. I'm not sure I really like this business about the time between *formulating* and *gratifying* a desire getting shorter and shorter . . ." She slipped her hand inside Brendan's shirt and began to stroke his chest. "I mean, is that going to be compulsory, or what?"

Two days later, after passing through four successive checkpoints manned by skeptical-looking MPs, Brendan was ushered into a small conference room. Clive Woodward was already there, deep in conversation with a man whom Brendan recognized as the deputy director of one of the intelligence agencies that had originally sponsored the formation of Woodward's Working Committee. Lately, according to Woodward, they had expressed serious misgivings about the wisdom of going any further with the project. Woodward introduced him to the deputy director and plunged immediately into the matter at hand.

"At our last meeting, sir, you presented us with a challenge—to devise some means of planting and detonating our next software bomb with no predictable risk of detection. I believe we have done just that. But first I'd like to say an introductory word about our 'Indian connection.' Some years ago, the Indians invented zero and the game of chess; today they are among the best programmers in the world. The first Indian programmers were trained by IBM, who also furnished the country with its first computers; some time later, by offering Mrs. Gandhi a number of very helpful hints with respect to her nuclear weapons program, the Soviets managed to obtain a number of interesting trade concessions—henceforth, for example, the Indians agreed to replace their IBM computers with the Soviet Elorg.

"This was more than just an impressive marketing coup, since the Soviets were interested in using India as a kind of staging point for the clandestine flight of Western computer technology. Their ES-1060 computer, for one thing, is capable of emulating the IBM 4341 . . ."

"Excuse me," said the deputy director, "but 'emulating' in what sense?"

"In the sense that an ES-1060 can talk to an IBM as if it were another IBM, can run programs written to run on IBM machines, and so forth. Having encouraged the Indians to take on these Russian computers that are, in effect, IBM-compatible, the Russians then encouraged them to follow up by acquiring American software, which—suitably modified by a group of brilliant Indian programmers—has subsequently found its way into their hands. When they bought a Craig 1 computer from the French and installed it as the centerpiece of their meteorological project at Krasnoyarsk, we suspected, of course, that they had a strong ulterior motive. We now know precisely what it was, in fact; they hope to acquire, in the usual roundabout way, a sophisticated piece of software called a 'routing controller' from the Indians.

"This will enable them, among other things, to orchestrate and monitor the operation of every computer in the Soviet Union and to link them not only to one another but also to the extensive non-strategic databases in Western countries that we spoke of when last we met. The particular routing controller they have it in mind to buy was developed by the Megasoft Corporation of Minneapolis, and is unquestionably the best of its kind in the world. The Indian government will be applying for a special exemption in order to acquire the routing controller; we are urging very strongly that it be granted to them. And in the course of the normal verification procedure—as prescribed by Cocom—we intend to plant a software bomb, one that will be truly undetectable this time, in the routing controller. This is not for the benefit of the Indians themselves, of course, but for the third-party beneficiary of this transaction—the Russian computer research facility at Krasnoyarsk."

Woodward fell silent, and Brendan took up the tale from there. "As you know, sir, we originally envisioned a safeguard system that would involve a large number of inactive lines of code, on the analogy of the MX 'shell game' deployment or the offensive penetration aids that accompany a ballistic missile to its target. This proposal was discarded for the reason that you yourself suggested—the Russians could crack it by brute force, with a kind of programming 'human wave' attack, if they suspected that something was not quite right."

"Quite right," echoed the deputy director. "What we really want from you, to put it baldly, is an absolutely foolproof technique of non-nuclear blackmail. Something that will enable us to put pressure on the Soviets—far more effectively, I trust, than any kind of economic or diplomatic sanctions that we've been able to devise so far— by denying them access to their own database, by paralyzing their entire society. And as far as accuracy goes, you're obviously going to have to turn in a perfect scatter pattern every time—this is one weapons system that's going to be completely worthless if it's not one-hundred-percent effective. I'm sure it's occurred to you gentlemen that we aren't going to be able to present the Russians with an ultimatum of some sort—that we're going to bring them to their knees if they don't pull their troops out of northern Pakistan, or wherever they might have gotten to by then—and end up putting them in a hold that they're going to slip right out of. In the sight of our allies and of the entire world, that would clearly constitute a public-relations disaster of incalculable proportions."

"The solution we finally arrived at," Brendan went on, "should rule out that possibility altogether. The system actually has two separate components—the first is the softbomb itself, the second is another program that might be described as a random switching code, which actually changes the apparent *location* of the bomb within the original program *every time* that program is run. That also means that the switching element is constantly being activated along with the program itself, so it won't be leaving any inactive or infrequently activated lines trailing behind."

"But the bomb itself is going to have to remain inactive," the deputy director broke in, "until such time, at least, as we decide to set it off."

"Yes, but its location within the target program is constantly going to be changed in order to evade detection."

The deputy director considered this for a moment. "I have some trouble visualizing that, but to a layman, at least, it sounds pretty convincing. Certainly I, for one, can find no fault with it."

Woodward smiled contentedly. "Nor can we, sir, I assure you."

"Then the only problem that remains," said the deputy director, "is that of the detonation code . . ."

"We've given some thought to that as well," said Brendan. "This time there are no real-world constraints—no snowstorms or hurricanes—to mess things up for us. This time we're going to be in complete control of everything."

SEVEN

April 12, 1984   Paris

As it was Thursday evening, René Duvallon had told his chauffeur to wait for him some distance away from the entrance to the ministry, in an unmarked blue Citroën CX instead of his official car, a forest-green Renault 30. In spite of such precautions as these, the members of his staff were perfectly well aware that Monsieur le Ministre was off to see his mistress, as always on Thursdays; he seemed keyed up and impatient, especially eager to clear his desk by late afternoon. The day's business had been somewhat more than routine. The Socialist government's latest scheme for "industrial redeployment," Japanese-style, with a heavy emphasis on aerospace, electronics, and high technology, had not gone over well in the Rust Belt of Lorraine and the north; the President's last press conference had only chipped away a little more of his original mandate from the left without winning him any additional support from the right. Duvallon leafed fretfully through a couple of file folders as the Citroën sped past the quais of the Seine along the Avenue de New York before turning off toward Passy.

"To Mademoiselle's," he told the chauffeur, quite unnecessarily.

As the car approached the Rue de Raynouard, where he had rented an apartment exclusively for these occasional trysts with Françoise, Duvallon began to relax, and his face resumed its normal expression—that of a man who was at peace with himself but had long since lost all his illusions (it was also the expression that enabled him to place high up in the standings in the women's magazine polls of "our ten sexiest politicians"). The thinning hair at his temples and his aquiline nose gave him something of the look of a Roman bust; by origin he was a Huguenot from the Cévennes, in the south. On Thursday evenings his face almost regained the firm lines of definition, his skin the glowing tones, that he so conscientiously sought in a health club on Tuesday afternoons—to make it a little easier to face the reporters and their cameras with a smile after the Council of Ministers' meeting that evening. This evening he had even regained the smile. An affair with a beautiful young woman like Françoise— which he made only the most conspicuous efforts to conceal from the curiosity of the press—might even have been filed under the same heading with these other vanities of late middle age. He had once remarked to her, "You know, for a man to have reached my age without acquiring a mistress, that's enough to make him seem like a pretty suspicious character."

The car had pulled up in front of the vaulted entryway to the courtyard of a handsome building. The chauffeur also had been instructed not to get out and open the door, as a final security precaution. *"Bonne soirée, monsieur,"* he said cheerfully instead. Duvallon grunted a reply as he slid off the rear seat with a couple of bulky dossiers under each arm. The apartment was on the top floor, and had a spacious garden terrace from which one could easily make out the soft glow of lights on the Seine. Duvallon lived his public life on the Right Bank, his private life on the Left; it was comforting to have a river between them.

He had first encountered Françoise at a cocktail party, the kind of boring semiofficial function to which he sacrificed so many of his evenings. From the first instant he had seen much more in her than a challenging conquest or an elegant status symbol. Behind the all-absorbing ritual of seduction, he had sensed in her an unusual energy and a streak of cold ambition that seemed ever more remarkable in a woman of her age. It was his deputy, Pierre Fromentin, who had introduced them, and when Duvallon first set eyes on that exquisite face, he felt immediately, violently, and irrationally jealous of Fromentin. Later on, when the latter was comfortably out of the running, Duvallon had occasionally remarked to Françoise, "That asshole Fromentin hasn't any idea how lucky he is." Outside the ministry, Duvallon never referred to his capable chief assistant in any other way, as if "asshole" were an official title, like *chef de cabinet*. He had found him thoroughly unsympathetic from the beginning, when he had been obliged to take him on his staff as a concession to certain dark and implacable forces within his own party.

"And why is he so lucky?" Françoise would ask.

"Because he's known you for so much longer than I have," would be the reply.

It had only been a couple of weeks longer, in fact. Fromentin had not dared to propose himself as a serious competitor, and Duvallon had liberally enlarged on the venomous hatred he felt for Fromentin to include every other man he had ever seen in her company. There had been several of them, since she and René traveled in the same circles and it had taken Françoise some time to yield to what a nineteenth-century novelist would have called his "furious entreaties." He had risked a wildcat strike of the policemen's union, for example, by sending white-gauntleted motorcycle cops streaking across Paris with feverish love notes stuffed into envelopes sealed with the minister's personal seal. His colleague at the Ministry of the Interior took him aside one Tuesday evening and warned him that his conduct was on the verge of becoming notorious.

This in itself was enough to make him feel, like Rimbaud and Gauguin before him, that the air of France had become too thick for him to breathe. He sped immediately from the Elysée Palace to the Rue des Guillemites in order to ask Françoise to leave the country with him immediately, to throw it all over and live the natural life in Martinique. Duvallon could not really recall how close he had actually come to being serious about all this. In any case, the question was academic; they had become lovers that very evening—after

Françoise had extracted a promise from him that he would start to behave more reasonably in future.

Memories of their first night together were stirring pleasantly within him as he stepped out of the elevator on the top floor. Françoise appeared in the doorway wearing some sort of filmy, translucent shift that made him all the more eager to assert his prerogatives as a lover.

"Let go of me, René," she said sharply. "At least let me get the door closed first. And look, you're spilling your papers all over the floor . . ."

René bent down awkwardly to retrieve the folders, fortunately all securely tied with red ribbon. "They could hardly get into a greater state of chaos in any case. What I really need is a drink—lots of whiskey, just a splash of Perrier, please." He dumped the folders on the floor, and went over and slumped on the couch, where he glumly surveyed the Paris skyline and the sparsely furnished living room, his ardor greatly diminished by the thought of the bundle of dossiers and the various crises and catastrophes that they actually contained.

Françoise came over and set a glass in front of him on the coffee table, then sat down beside him. "What's the trouble, then? Are you worried about all those poor steel mills in Lorraine?"

"They tell me to find some way of turning ten thousand steelworkers into ten thousand electronics engineers without actually hiring or firing anyone. They can call it triage if they want, but I call it squaring the circle."

"Why, that's very clever. And anyway, you know perfectly well that that's your job. In France, the left always ends up doing the right's dirty work for it, just to prove to everyone that they're all respectable bourgeois politicians."

"Please, none of your Maoist drivel tonight, my dear. One lunatic extremist in the family is enough, I think."

Françoise's rather superior smile had vanished immediately. "What do you mean? Have you found out something about Jacques after all this time?"

"Nothing directly. Those idiots in the Ministry of the Interior seem to think he's in Libya—based on what evidence, I have no idea.

And in any case, why do you insist on knowing where he is—as long as he's tucked away somewhere where he won't be making any more trouble for both of us?"

"I'd just like to be sure that he's still alive and, wherever he is, that he's not terribly unhappy. You can't imagine how truly adorable he was when he was little."

"You're so right," said Duvallon, after taking a long, comforting swallow from his glass. "And you're wrong if you think I don't worry about him—I'm terrified that he's going to sell his story to the papers somewhere, so he can buy himself a few more hand grenades. 'The terrorist's sister is the minister's mistress'—that sounds almost like poetry, doesn't it? Perhaps we should start drafting my letter of resignation tonight, what do you think? Though, I must say, one thing I don't understand is how he found his way back to Paris so easily—or perhaps I should say it's one thing I'm not sure I *want* to understand."

"You don't have to flex your rhetoric in front of me, you know. Just please tell me, in your own words, precisely what you're talking about."

"These so-called separatist groups he's been involved with have so far proved themselves incapable of robbing a grocery store and making a clean getaway, but look at what they're supposed to have done in this case. Your unfortunate brother evades local surveillance on Martinique, returns to metropolitan France and lives clandestinely for some time, pops up and instantly disappears as soon as the deed is done. What would you need to be able to do that? False papers, an arms cache, safe houses and couriers and that sort of thing, a lot of money—a pretty extensive organization, in short. Make of it whatever else you will, but it does look as if he may have had the resources of a foreign government behind him. And, of course, since his intended victims were Americans, there are many possibilities to choose from. I must tell you in strictest confidence that our best guess seems to be that this business is actually connected in some way with the sabotaging of the weather-forecasting program that was sold to the Soviet Union."

"But that's preposterous! How could Jacques have had anything to do with . . . why would he risk his life for something like that?"

Duvallon finished his drink and set it down on the coffee table. "No particular reason comes to mind, I admit. But what I'm suggesting to you is that the incident he was involved in was intended as *retaliation* for the sabotaging of the computer program. That implies that he was playing for the other side. Of course, this is pure supposition, but consider the old adage, *Cui bono?* Who benefits from the crime? Consider the identity of the two Americans—"

"Don't forget you're no longer talking to one of your well-briefed ministerial colleagues who actually has some access to the *facts* in the case. I'm just another lowly citizen, who only knows what she reads in the captive press, which in this case is precious little. Tell me. I'm curious to know who they turned out to be—Clint Eastwood and Henry Kissinger, I presume."

"My friends at the Ministry of the Interior tell me that the DGST—what you persist in calling our subnormal intelligence service—had persuaded the police to withhold the two men's names from the press, at the request of the American Embassy—a procedure that's often followed in such cases, I believe. One of the victims was a sometime journalist called Richard Thompson, quite a well-known figure in a way—also thought to be a communications expert of some sort for the CIA . . . And where are you going all of a sudden?"

Françoise had gotten up abruptly and walked away. "Can't you see that I'm taking your glass into the kitchen?" There was something very odd about her voice.

"You sound so upset. I thought you wanted me to find out all I could about this business. Please, forgive me. You know I wouldn't upset you for anything in the world." Duvallon got up and followed her into the kitchen, took her in his arms, and began to nuzzle the nape of her neck; she kept her face carefully turned away during this entire maneuver.

"There's no reason to go all to pieces like this," she finally said. "I was upset for a moment, about Jacques, but I'm all right now. Why don't we go back into the other room? And I *want* you to tell me the rest of it, all about it. Who was the other American, for example?"

"That's what I've especially been waiting to tell you, and I'm afraid I am going to have to tell you something rather disagreeable—

though you must remember, of course, that it is still only supposition. Are you prepared for that?"

Françoise, still partially imprisoned in Duvallon's bearlike embrace, merely nodded. She disengaged herself gently, and they walked slowly back into the living room. "We have some reason to think," Duvallon went on, "that your brother may have been in contact with the KGB. I say this for several reasons—first, because we now know for a fact that the weather-forecasting program that was delivered to the Russians *was* deliberately tampered with, very possibly before it left the country, by persons unknown—"

"But surely you can't be accusing my brother of that."

"And second, if you'll just hear me out for a moment, the other American in Harry's Bar that morning was a member of the Cocom inspection team—one of the ones, in fact, who personally examined the weather program before it was turned over to the Russians. A computer scientist named Brendan Barnes, a university professor who also, in our belief, is working very closely with the CIA."

"Don't tell me any more about it now, all right? If Jacques really has been stupid enough to get mixed up with those people, with the CIA and the KGB, then I don't want to have to think about what might have become of him, where he might be by now."

Duvallon put his hands around her waist and drew her toward him; Françoise slipped lightly out of her shift, and Duvallon began tearing frantically at his clothes. A few minutes later, when she judged that the moment was right, she began to groan rhythmically, then emitted a ragged cry of pleasure and was still.

April 12, 1984   Krasnoyarsk

"And this? Tell me, what do you make of this, then?" asked Natalya Georgyevna fiercely, holding up a shapeless mass of green construction paper and turning it around in her hand. "This is the way they spend their time in class!" A bright and baleful light was flashing beneath the somber arches of her brows; her audience was entirely dumbstruck. "At any rate," she went on, "you don't seem to be quite such a talkative bunch as they are." Seeing that the men and women sitting opposite her in the classroom seemed to be suitably chastened for the moment, she began to relent a little.

"Of course, you poor people really don't know all that much about it, I'm afraid. You don't live with them day after day, the way I do; you don't know what they're really capable of. I do, you see; I believe I know them better than most of you do." She added abruptly, in a much louder voice, "It's meant to be an airplane!" She flourished the unlovely object in her left hand and shot out her right index finger in a prosecutorial gesture, pointing it at a tall, startled-looking man who was sitting in the back row. "It belongs to your son," she went on. "He made it. It's by way of being family property, so you'd better come up and get it. And I wouldn't encourage him to take the exam for the Aeronautics Institute just yet." The tall man—a dockworker employed by the river port of Krasnoyarsk—slowly detached himself from the tiny desk at which he was sitting and walked toward the front of the classroom with heavy tread.

Yulya, who found these accommodations no more comfortable than did most of the other parents, waited apprehensively for Natalya Georgyevna to start to discuss the case of Alyosha. For the moment she seemed to be speaking in much more general terms, having embarked on what promised to be a lengthy discourse on "socialist education." Yulya quickly lost the thread of her remarks.

The classroom looked eerily familiar, as such places always did— as if it had been transported all the way from Vitebsk, at unimaginable expense, just to make her feel small and intimidated again. She tried to guess where Alyosha's regular seat would be; she hoped it was not too near the window, since he was a great daydreamer. She could imagine him watching the dust motes in the air as the pale afternoon sun slanted across the room. She could actually see him in his gray school uniform, like a handsome little cadet with his glossy blue-black hair; her "little Pushkin," she called him, though he was much better looking than all the pictures of the real Pushkin . . .

Natalya Georgyevna seemed to be getting down to cases again; the terrible index finger shot out, this time in the direction of the blackboard, where a carefully drawn graph displayed a record of her pupils' average grades over the last trimester, a record of seemingly irreversible scholastic decline. "There you have it in a nutshell!" she almost shrieked. "That's what they've been up to!" She picked up a pile of exercise books and began to hand them out to the appropriate parents, along with a detailed commentary on each one.

Yulya was recalled from her reverie again by the name Alexei Sergeievich Voronkov. She raised her hand, until Natalya Georgyevna finally acknowledged her presence with a chilly smile. "And how, Citizen Voronkov, do you expect me to tolerate this sort of thing?" She produced an especially grubby notebook from the pile; it had quite a few pages torn out, the remainder covered with enormous blots and uncertain lines of script crawling up and down the page like the tracks of a mountain railroad. Yulya bit her lip to keep from smiling; she hoped this made her look suitably contrite. That was just like Pushkin—he had a true romantic's horror of being imprisoned between straight lines.

"However," Natalya Georgyevna went on, "his command of the spoken language is quite a bit more impressive. He talks constantly in class, as a matter of fact. Does he do that at home as well?"

"No more than the normal amount, I suppose."

Natalya Georgyevna suddenly appeared to have softened once again. "Oh, I know what you mean to say, of course. With all your many responsibilities outside the home, it's so difficult to spend as much time with the boy as you'd like to. I quite understand. You know, it's my job, really, to try to take the mother's place, in a way, but obviously he could never look up to me the way he looks up to you . . ."

She could feel the other parents staring at her, and she felt extremely ill at ease. This took her right back to the classrooms of her childhood, and the horrible sticky feeling it gave her when, after tearing some other student's work to pieces in front of the entire class, the teacher turned to her and began to praise her to the skies. This, of course, was just another part of socialist education—positive and negative reinforcement for the paragons and the incorrigibles, respectively—but it was not one of the more pleasant ones for anyone, except perhaps for people like Natalya Georgyevna. She supposed she should be grateful, on the other hand, that the woman had not actually spoken of her "august responsibilities to the Socialist Motherland" or something of the sort.

"He speaks of practically nothing else, you know," she was saying now. "He brought in a newspaper with your photograph in it, and completely disrupted the class by showing it around to all the others. I had to take it away from him, of course. Here it is, in fact. Take a look, then pass it back," she ordered a bemused post-office employee in the first row. When the postman showed signs of lingering over an article on the front page, Natalya Georgyevna merely glared at him until the coughs and titters of the other parents alerted him to the fact that he had made a blunder. Shamefaced, he immediately passed the paper to the woman sitting behind him.

The article in question was on an inside page, under the headline THE ELEVENTH FIVE-YEAR PLAN IN ACTION! A subhead read, "The means of socialist production, a rich and varied cultural life, meeting the informational needs of our people—three sectors of our society, working together to achieve a better new life for all." The first sector was represented by a grainy, old-style Sovfoto cut of uranium miners in the Urals admiring some gleaming new apparatus, the second by a photo of a touring company from the Taganka Theater in Moscow receiving the "tumultuous acclaim" of theatergoers in Krasnoyarsk, the third by a picture of Yulya herself, with a retouched-looking expression of intensity and purposefulness around the eyes and mouth. The caption read, "Y. N. Voronkov, director of the All-Union Office of Information Research, aids in advancing the banner of socialism into the twenty-first century."

"I had to confiscate this as well," Natalya Georgyevna went on, producing a large notebook that she handed directly to Yulya. It was, in fact, a scrapbook half full of newspaper clippings with similar photos and captions: "Yulya Nikolaevna Voronkov, standard-bearer of Soviet womanhood . . ."; "Y. N. Voronkov, director of the All-Union Institute for Computer Research and Applied Mathematics, Krasnoyarsk, RSFSR: 'The fraternal spirit of the Soviet people will provide a decisive advantage in the struggle to surpass the West in information-retrieval technology . . .'"; "Yulya Voronkov, the charm and femininity of Soviet womanhood dedicated to the service of post-industrial development . . ."

She snapped the notebook shut after a moment or two. This aspect of her new appointment was far from agreeable to her, but so far she had submitted without balking too much—except to insist on correcting the grammar in some of her published "interviews." In reality, rather than being a socialist standard-bearer, she was more like a perilously advanced pawn in the game that had recently picked up again between Gorbachev and the "technocrats," as Sergei would have it, and the followers of the old dispensation. However strategic her position, there was little that she herself could do to improve or defend it.

Unlike most of the hand-picked "personalities" touted by the Soviet press, however, Yulya seemed thus far to have achieved some genuine public popularity. As in the case of Gorbachev himself, a measure of personal charm was all the more attractive for its comparative rarity in official Soviet circles, and the more futuristic, science-fiction-like aspects of her profession may have made her public image as a paragon of socialism somewhat more palatable to the average person. (Though Alyosha had no way of knowing it, of course, her name had even cropped up once or twice in the foreign press.)

The parents' meeting broke up after half an hour more. Natalya Georgyevna thanked them all earnestly for "having taken the time to participate in the collective enterprise of properly socializing our children," then turned out the lights of the classroom even before all the parents had left. Yulya's hellish new schedule had made it impossible for her to allow herself the luxury of walking anywhere anymore. The sight of the government car, a long Volga sedan complete with a bored-looking driver slouched behind the wheel in his gabardine coveralls and synthetic-fur cap, made quite an impression on the other parents.

One of the other perks of her new appointment that she was much happier to accept was Irina, a highly competent "mother's helper" who took the children to school in the morning and picked them up afterward, coped with shopping and the apartment, and prepared most of their meals. Tonight, as on most nights, Sergei was not expected to join them for dinner. The atmosphere at the dinner table that night was fairly typical. Alyosha teased his sister elaborately about her dancing class, imitating the soulful sighs and long, fluttering looks into the middle distance that she tended to affect right after she had come back from her class. Yulya was amused by these gestures, the only clues that Svetlana ever deigned to give her family to the way she really felt about her dancing. When questioned directly, she would only say, "Oh, Mother, it was just com*plete*ly exhausting."

She had finally traced a number of these mannerisms to their source when she met Svetlana's dance teacher, a tall, blond young man with very red lips and a fondness for using phrases like "gestural lyricism" and "the poetry of the body." Svetlana's highly successful attempts to reproduce this sort of talk, complete with the original gestures and inflections, was an endless source of hilarity to Alyosha. One of his favorite nicknames for his sister was "Crazy Nijinsky." Svetlana was quite content to go on playing the role of the misunderstood romantic artist, and seemed to find each new evidence of her family's invincible philistinism neither surprising nor even especially displeasing.

When dinner was over, Yulya made herself some tea while Irina cleared the table. This was really her favorite time of day, when she could sit and talk with her children for a while, luxuriating in the feeling that someone else was taking care of the dishes. The tea also helped to keep her awake, so she could get some work done after the children had gone to sleep. Watching Svetlana's serious face with its dark eyes, she began to wonder whether she should ever show her the secret notebook she had filled with her memories of America. When Svetlana was younger, she had asked several times why it was that her eyes were so dark when both her parents' eyes were blue; Yulya had prepared a clever little speech about blond great-grandmothers and Mendelian characteristics, but Svetlana had never asked her about it again. Perhaps she had decided, in keeping with her current views, that it was all a matter of temperament; or, more likely, she was at the age when sensitive young girls discover that they have been stolen away from their real parents, persons of great refinement and distinction, to be raised by hags and peasants. Perhaps this was the time, after all, to tell her that her real father was, if not a handsome prince from across the seas, at least a handsome college professor from America.

"I have a surprise for you," she said at last to Svetlana.

"What about me?" Alyosha broke in.

"Not this time, I'm afraid, Pushkin. You and I," she went on, turning back toward her daughter, "are going on a trip together. And Alyosha will be staying at Grandmother's, in Vitebsk."

Svetlana tossed her head like an unruly pony and scowled. "It's really impossible, I'm afraid, Mama. I do have to keep up with my classes, you know. Maybe next time I'll be able to go to Moscow with you."

"But when did I ever say anything about Moscow? And it's a pity about your classes, because I really thought that you'd jump at the chance to go abroad with me."

"But that's absolutely . . . that should be absolutely fantastic for you," she amended hastily; she was obviously intent on pursuing a staged withdrawal from her original position, not giving in all at once.

"Because that means," Alyosha added eagerly, "that you'll be able to take *me*, instead of the old Lunatic Princess!"

Yulya got up from the table and went over to stroke her daughter's hair. "Are you sure you don't want to go with me, sweetness?"

"I don't know, Mama. I'll have to think about it for a moment. I mean, it would be completely beastly of me to make you go all by yourself . . . or worst of all, with *him*. Very well, yes, I've decided to go with you." She leaped up from her chair, stepped totally out of character, and threw herself into Yulya's arms. "Oh, Mama! I'm so *happy*!"

"But really, it's not fair! What about me?" cried Alyosha. "I don't understand why all three of us can't go."

"I think perhaps you're still a little young to become a rootless cosmopolitan just yet," said Yulya. "And I think I'll only be allowed to take one of you with me. However," she added quickly, seeing that Alyosha was contemplating an outburst of some sort, "there's still plenty of time to make inquiries in the proper quarters, I suppose." Alyosha took this as an unqualified assent; he rushed toward his mother and threw his arms around her waist, so that for a time they were all entwined in a single, complicated embrace.

Svetlana broke away suddenly, struck by a frightful notion. "When are we leaving?"

"Not for a long time, I'm afraid, sweetness. Not till September. Why do you ask?"

"It just occurred to me . . . we're going to be doing *Swan Lake* for our recital this year, in June."

Alyosha, who had attended the previous recital under some duress, said, "Again? You'd better put something different on the posters, or nobody's going to come."

"I just thought that I wouldn't miss the recital for anything in the world. I'd even give up going to Paris!"

"I hope you only mean that as a figure of speech, Svetlanochka. The fact of the matter is that we're not going to Paris, we're going to a conference in Geneva. Whatever made you think it would be Paris?"

"I don't know. I suppose it was just that I really wanted to go there. I wanted to see the Opéra."

"Geneva has an opera as well, though not such a famous one, of course, and a ballet. Perhaps they'll be doing *Swan Lake* when we get there, who knows?"

"But what's the point of going to Geneva, exactly?"

"You know that Geneva is a sort of international meeting place, for summit conferences and so forth; we're going to be going to a conference of computer people from all over the world. I'll take you to the opening session; there'll be lots of very grand people there."

Alyosha had been standing off to one side during this exchange, with a calculating expression on his face. "You know, you're so lucky, Mama, to be able to travel all over the world like that. If I had kids and an important job like yours, I'd always make sure I took them with me, everywhere in the world I went . . . both of them."

Yulya laughed. "Maybe you should try working a little harder in school, if you want to start entertaining such big plans for yourself."

"You're only saying that because you went to parents' night and you've been talking to my teacher. I bet she told you every single thing there is to know about me, except how much she hates me, of course."

"Nonsense, Pushkin. She doesn't in the least, you know. She seemed rather nice, in a way, and I'm sure I agree with her that you'd do quite a lot better in school if you worked a little bit harder and talked a bit less in class."

"Oh, work! Why should kids like me have to work? I'll get plenty of that when I'm old, when I'm old like you."

"But you've only just said that if you had a job like mine, you'd be able to travel all over. And to get a job like mine, as you know perfectly well, you have to work pretty hard in school—or be a whole lot cleverer in the first place than either you or I, I'm afraid."

"Anyway, who says I want a job like yours? I don't! Not in the first place, or the last place!"

So far she had had the impression that Alyosha was merely engaging in argument for its own sweet sake, but this sounded as though he was quite sincere, and quite upset. "There are plenty of other kinds of work to do, of course," she said diplomatically. "But I'm curious to know what's got you so convinced, at this early stage in your career, that you never want to have a job like mine."

Alyosha's face was flushed; he looked at his shoes and said nothing.

"You're so unbelievably stupid!" Svetlana suddenly shouted at him. "You can never shut up until it's absolutely too late!"

"Svetlana, there's no reason to talk to your brother like that," said Yulya, and thought to herself, *At least one of us should be able to get through this conversation without going all to pieces.* "And now, Alyosha, I just want you to tell me why you said what you did. Or, if you like, you can explain to me *why* you don't want to tell me. Either one will do quite well."

The children exchanged complicitous looks, like felons about to be separated for interrogation. Finally Alyosha said, "I don't know . . . They said in school you had all sorts of inspectors and spies working for you, and if you found that anyone wasn't working properly, you'd do like the *zvyenovoi*, the class monitor in school, and report him. And then—I don't know—they said if you *really* had it in for him, you'd send a special report to Moscow and he'd be put into a camp and never be seen or heard from again."

"And who told you all that?"

"Just some kids, kids in my class. Svetlana said it was . . . said it wasn't true. But one of them even said that Fyodor Ivanovich had been sent off to a camp, and it was all because of you." Kutuzov had come for dinner on a great many occasions, and the children had gotten to be quite fond of him. Now she understood why they had scarcely remarked on the fact that a family friend, one they seemed to regard as emotionally almost a contemporary, had simply dropped out of their lives.

"And who told you *that*?" Yulya persisted. "What was his name?"

Alyosha simply looked anguished and stubborn, and fidgeted in his chair.

"I'm afraid you'll just have to sit there until you decide to tell me," said Yulya. Then suddenly she understood; her heart went out to him completely, and she went over to Alyosha, threw her arms around him, and hugged him until he began to struggle in protest. "Oh, Pushkin! Could you ever know how much I love you? But don't expect me to feel this way the next time you disobey me. You didn't want to tell me because you were afraid of what might happen to your friends at school, is that right? My little Pushkin, you really have a heart of gold." She covered his face with kisses, and he started to laugh—relieved, perhaps, that he was not about to be tortured after all. Yulya could not dismiss this incident as easily. Even an eight-year-old could see that there was an official and an unofficial version of the truth. His scrapbook clippings had provided the former; the latter, no doubt, had come from the overheard speculations of parents, a number of whom worked at the Institute, probably not too much embellished in the telling. Alyosha had simply tried to reconcile the two.

"My dear, beloved Pushkin," she said softly, "you must remember that newspapers don't always tell the complete truth, and that people make up stories to explain things they don't understand. It's true that Fyodor Ivanovich is in serious trouble with the authorities, but you must believe that it wasn't because of me or anything I did. I've been looking for him all this time, trying to help him; I'd give anything to have him back here with us again." And I'd *do* anything, she added to herself, except jeopardize the future happiness of my children.

Now it was Françoise, clad only in a splendid robe of gold lamé, who was sitting on the couch, drinking whiskey and looking miserable, while Duvallon sat beside her, one hand stroking her thigh, the other flourishing a whiskey glass, and unburdened himself of his worldly cares in a long, self-pitying monologue. This week, however, it didn't seem to be working; Françoise was distant and distracted, and any further probing on his part would almost certainly result in a quarrel. *I should never have said a word to her about that damned brother of hers*, he thought as he refilled his glass.

"And of course," he went on aloud, "now that we're virtually certain that it was the Americans who tampered with the computer program, we find ourselves, as usual, in a very awkward position indeed. The Communist ministers still haven't got wind of this, but the breeze could shift at any moment, don't you think? At any rate, the Yanks have entirely outdone themselves this time. Why couldn't they have just said a word to us about this first—not asked our permission, heaven forfend, but simply informed us of what their intentions were? They're like that man in the Jules Verne story, with all their wires and gadgets and planes—the Master of the World. But now they've gotten themselves into some very serious difficulties. Are you still listening to me, by any chance?"

"How could I not? And what's going to happen to the Americans now, do you suppose? They seem to have wriggled out of it quite dexterously, in fact."

Duvallon had the clear impression that she was merely feeding him his next cue, so she could be left alone with her thoughts for a minute or two. Nevertheless, he went on, "Suppose the Russians can present firm evidence of sabotage, and make a clear case before what's called the forum of world opinion? Then the shoe would be on the other foot with a vengeance. A propaganda masterstroke, in short.

Just think of it—Uncle Sam's belligerent intentions laid bare for all to see! The workers' Motherland the victim of a perfidious attack! An electronic Pearl Harbor, an act of international banditry! Also, manna from heaven for the pacifists and neutralists—and hardly the proper atmosphere in which to bring up the delicate Pershing missile."

"Then they'll fucking well get what they deserve!" said Françoise savagely, and immediately felt rather sheepish. She realized instantaneously that it was not the Americans she hated so much at this particular moment . . .

"Nevertheless," said Duvallon blandly, "as far as the vital interests of our countrymen are concerned, I think most of them would rather be watching 'Dallas' on Friday nights than televised sessions of the Fifty-fifth Party Congress."

EIGHT

July 5, 1984   Paris

Because of the EEC elections, the French Senate was obliged to remain in session until July 20, so that the venerable Palais du Luxembourg and its honorable inmates were still prepared to welcome several members of the Soviet trade delegation on the fifth. Sunlight glinted impressively on the helmets and metal breastplates of the Gardes Républicains drawn up outside the door. In the back seat of the embassy Citroën CX that was just turning up the Rue de Tournon, Vladimir Zagladyin, deputy chief of the international section of the Soviet Central Committee, was listening distractedly to the tour-guide patter of the embassy's commercial councillor, Konstantin Bakhtov, and wishing that he was not. To his left, Sergei Voronkov was sitting back with his legs crossed, seething with irritation and pretending to be lost in his thoughts.

As the car began to move over the paving stones of the drive that led up to the Palais, Bakhtov suddenly switched his tack and launched into a paean of praise to the trade negotiations that had just been concluded, in the course of which the delegation had persuaded the French government to reverse an earlier decision to limit the export of certain specialized telephone switching equipment to the Soviet Union; they had also struck a very sharp bargain over the sale of electronic control devices destined for the notorious Siberian pipeline.

Zagladyin responded to this fulsome tribute to his skill as a tough negotiator with an undisguised sigh of relief as the Citroën pulled up to a halt beside a number of other cars with diplomatic plates in the courtyard. Bakhtov stepped nimbly out of the car and trotted ahead of the others, as if to salvage the occasion by showing that, for all his faults, he was no stranger to the splendors of the Palais du Luxembourg. As they approached the salon d'honneur, where the reception had already begun, Zagladyin turned to Bakhtov and asked, "One thing you *can* tell me, Konstantin Dmitrich . . . what's that stuff those guardsmen are wearing on their helmets?"

"Ostrich plumes?" Bakhtov suggested cautiously.

"Each of those crests is made from an entire horse's mane," Sergei put in. "First Empire, inspired by the uniforms of Napoleon's cuirassiers. It's all in that sort of guidebook they passed out to us before we left. You can borrow mine if you like," he said to Bakhtov maliciously.

They had entered the salon d'honneur and were instantly absorbed into a dense crowd of diplomats, politicians and their consorts, journalists, waiters, and professional partygoers. The women's jewels and the men's bald heads, orders, and decorations sparkled in the light from four enormous crystal chandeliers. Zagladyin pointed to a distant spot where the crowd was thickest. "Konstantin Dmitrich, why don't you go and get us something to drink?"

Bakhtov plunged obediently into the crowd, elbows thrust outward, as he had learned to do on the métro. As he fought his way toward the bar, he realized unhappily that it would be quite impossible for him to make it back carrying more than two drinks. He approached a barman who was pouring out champagne, and wiggled two fingers in his face. The gesture was misunderstood by the barman as a peace sign, a well-intentioned if belated gesture of reconciliation on the part of another socially retarded Iron Curtain diplomat; he merely responded with a smile. When he finally rejoined Zagladyin and Sergei, he discovered that the French development minister, Duvallon, had joined them as well; a chamberlain was handing around champagne glasses from a tray. Zagladyin had already raised his in a toast.

"Monsieur le Ministre, I've been asked to convey to you the fraternal good wishes of your Soviet opposite number, Comrade Marchuk of the Ministry of Science and Technology. And I'd like to add my own sincere wish that future dealings of this kind between our two nations continue to be 'mutually advantageous.'"

"And may I add to that," said Duvallon, "*my* own sincere wish that they should prove no less so for my country *next* time than they've been for your country this time."

There was general laughter at this. Zagladyin's French was quite good; Sergei and Bakhtov laughed shortly and sharply, out of reflex. Sergei drew Bakhtov aside while the others went chattering on. "Give me one of those glasses, Konstantin Dmitrich, and tell me one more thing. Those fellows over there are Americans, aren't they?"

Bakhtov nodded happily, delighted to have finally found a question he could answer.

"And aren't several of them from the Cocom mission? And isn't there at least one acknowledged CIA official among them?"

"I'm afraid I really couldn't tell you, Comrade Colonel. I look primarily after the economic side of things, and Cocom, as you know, falls within the province of—"

"Permit me to observe, Konstantin Dmitrich, that I very much enjoyed your little talk on the way over here about the buildings and the scenery, but I suggest that in future you devote as much of your attention to present-day political realities as you do to Gothic arches and flying buttresses and all the rest of that nonsense." Bakhtov was no longer listening; he was wondering what it would be like to work for an organization like Cocom, or even the CIA, where a man with a good head for business would not go unappreciated.

In the little group that Sergei had pointed out, there were at least two who fell into the categories mentioned. Brendan Barnes and Richard Thompson were standing by the buffet, exchanging occasional remarks and casting frequent glances at another corner of the hall, where Françoise was working the crowd. She looked serene and supremely confident in an elegant tailored suit of red linen, very flattering to her dark skin tones; she was shaking hands with everyone, calling deputies by their first names, charming journalists by asking after their children by name, senators by asking for the latest gossip from their districts—all the while appearing to be quite charmingly unaware of the splendid impression she was making.

Working for her sleepy old senator, Delépine, and sleeping with Duvallon had brought her, by easy stages, into contact with all of Paris—*le Tout Paris*—or all of *political* Paris, at least. But now it seemed that her life with Duvallon consisted largely of sitting around in a half-furnished apartment, swilling whiskey and flouncing around in foolish, extravagant clothes. In her schoolbooks when she was a little girl, they had always begun the geography lesson by saying that "France was a perfect hexagon"; now it seemed just the same way again, a very small, symmetrical world with rigid borders, and once you had found your way inside, there was no way out again.

"I understand, I sympathize," Thompson was saying, still watching her from across the room. "She's a beauty, all right, but that's *all* she is. Do you follow me?"

"You mean that there are more important things for us to be discussing right now, for example. I agree wholeheartedly. From now on, there's no need for things to be anything but personal with Françoise and me—no further business to transact—so you can take your mind off it entirely. Next case . . ."

"In other words, no, you don't follow me at all. You persist in thinking of yourself as a gentleman volunteer, or thinking that you're on some kind of a damn sabbatical or something. You've still got some work to do for us, and she could easily cause all sorts of problems for you right now. If you'll recall, her brother—"

"I recall all about her brother, for Christ's sake! And you've hardly even met the man. Now tell me what you're *really* worried about."

Thompson made an impatient gesture. "Why do you keep pulling my chain about this? We simply feel that it would be better for you *not* to see her for a while, from an overall security standpoint and from the standpoint of your own personal safety, both of which would appear to be a little problematical at the moment."

"So I have to cable Langley every time I want to go to bed with someone?"

"With *someone*, yes. Now, you know how I hate to be a nag, Brendan, but I think we agreed quite a while ago that there'd come a time when you'd want to radically simplify your personal life over here in order to make it possible for you to honor some of your commitments. And as long as you remain in contact with her, in my opinion, then you're still pretty much hanging right out there on the line, and Jacques Vimard, or an understudy, could come along and take another swipe at you at any moment. And what if I'm not there next time to shield you from the full force of the blast?" Thompson was grinning at him again, but Brendan was no longer amused.

"Aren't the people in the spy books always asking each other, 'What's the point of fighting them, if we're just going to turn around and act like them anyway?'"

"It's not quite as bad as all that, as you well know, and it's only very temporary. After we're over the next one, my friend, you'll have absolutely nothing to lose but your chains. You can submit your resignation at any moment and be discharged, as they say, without a stain on your character."

Out of the corner of one eye, Françoise watched Brendan and Thompson drift away from the buffet table and disappear into the crowd. She tried desperately to think of a plausible pretext for confronting him, then cursed herself because she had let the moment slip away.

"*Eh bien, ma chère*, aren't you thirsty after all?" It was the bespectacled senatorial aide she had been speaking with a few moments before, when she had caught sight of them at the buffet. She had sent him off into the breach at once to get her a glass of champagne, in the hope that something would have occurred to her by the time he got back.

"Right," she replied, refusing to take the glass in his outstretched hand, "but thanks all the same anyway, *mon cher*."

He looked at her curiously, eyes blinking fishlike behind thick glasses. "But what am I going to do with an extra glass of champagne?"

"Sit in it." She flashed a dazzling smile, turned her back on him, caught Duvallon's eye from a dozen yards away, and smiled, but carefully kept her distance.

"Fromentin," Duvallon muttered to his aide, "I'd like you to present my compliments to Mademoiselle Vimard and ask her how old Delépine's getting along these days. I hear that he's taken to his bed, poor fellow."

"*Bien, monsieur*," said Fromentin, and added to himself, *No fear, at least, that he's taken to hers.* Fromentin knew perfectly well that the minister would not have objected in the least if old Delépine had been struck by lightning or devoured by wolves before his eyes.

Brendan and Thompson had forgotten their differences for the moment and wandered through the crowd, using the chatter of a hundred different conversations as a kind of white-noise backdrop to their own. "It all seems to be tracking very nicely so far," Brendan was saying. "The so-called superprogram, the routing controller that's going to let the Russians get all their computers together and talk to each other on one big party line, as it were—it should be just about there by now, in Krasnoyarsk. But of course this is the really sticky phase, the one that's coming up."

"I know that you definitely regard me as one of our leading computer illiterates, but maybe you could explain to me why this one's supposed to work so much better than the last one. I understand there was some objection in the intelligence community to using a detonation code that was subject to unpredictable real-world constraints, like the barometric pressure on St. Thomas."

"The Doubting Thomas Syndrome, as Woodward calls it. This time we're going to try a different tack, a little more complicated but ultimately more reliable, or so they tell me. And it doesn't have all that much to do with computers, you'll be pleased to hear—at least the part that's different doesn't, anyway. The detonation code itself is derived from the quoted price of a share on the New York Stock Exchange."

"Satellite Business Systems."

"Correct. In fact, you probably know more about the financial ins and outs of all this than I do, which is virtually nothing. The point is that the code is going to be a sequence of digits that's guaranteed *never* to appear opposite SBS in the NYSE listings, until the day comes, of course, when we're ready to blow up the balloon."

"But I'm not sure we're exactly in a position to rely on a guarantee like that. And after all, SBS is hardly a dummy corporation. It's a fairly serious business that buys satellite time for computer telecommunications applications and leases it to corporate customers. Also, it's been capitalized, in part, by one of the big insurance companies, a major manufacturer of telecommunications equipment, IBM, no less, and the Defense Department. And high-tech stocks like that are notoriously volatile, so how can your friends be so sure that prices aren't going to go haywire and the button isn't going to get bumped by accident?"

"That fails to take account of the fact that SBS is a joint venture financed, in large part, by the corporate leviathans you just mentioned, as well as the Defense Department. Not too many shares held by widows and orphans that could ever be pried loose by speculators. But the main thing is that Defense maintains a special operations fund, and disbursements from this fund can be used to goose the selling price of the stock back up again anytime it might be about to take a dip down into the red zone. But frankly, I think the real reason that my friends, as you call them, are so intent on doing it this way is that they're secretly convinced that the KGB hasn't figured out how to read the financial pages yet."

"There are a couple of them over there that most definitely have. See those guys in those sort of Slavic-looking suits? That's Zagladyin, the one that's talking, and the one standing next to him is the famous KGB fact-finder you've heard so much about—that's Colonel Voronkov, your ex-girlfriend's current husband."

They had been circulating slowly around the outer edges of the crowd while they talked. Brendan stopped short, and Thompson was obliged to do the same. The babble of conversation behind them, fed on politics and champagne, had reached a kind of chattering, monkeylike crescendo.

"You mean Y. N. Voronkov really *was* Yulya? Are you sure you know what the fuck you're talking about? You know I've found that you're not always totally reliable when it comes to personal matters like this."

"Say what you will, but it's a fact that Yulya Nikolaevna Techayev became Mrs. Y. N. Voronkov in 1975, for the very good reason that she married Sergei Voronkov—the guy who's standing over there sucking up the champagne—then as now of the KGB, and specializing, like yourself, in what you might call the interface between computer science and politics."

"It's nice we have something else in common, anyway. Think I should walk right over and introduce myself? And why wasn't I told about all this earlier, instead of having it spoonfed to me like this, a tidbit at a time?"

"Before you get off on another of your tangents, let's just make sure you understand one thing. Sergei Voronkov—he's the one that's been sent to Paris to find out who's been opening their Christmas presents and breaking them and putting them back in the box. And Sergei Voronkov is definitely the man responsible for security at Krasnoyarsk. So it's probably not such a good idea that you two should meet just yet."

"Isn't that a little bit of a coincidence? That it's him, and that it's me, I mean?"

"From your perspective, it's a complete coincidence. But look at it this way—Woodward was obviously interested in recruiting you in the first place because you had such a brilliant future ahead of you as a debugger, or whatever the hell it's called, and because you'd written those hard-hitting but no less brilliant papers about how we should start whipping it back to the Russians with computer technology. But the fact that you'd also been intimately involved with someone who's now a leading Soviet computer scientist, with a no less brilliant career ahead of her in the Soviet defense-technical establishment—that makes you truly, uniquely qualified for the job. It's a little like—if you'll excuse the comparison—all of *our* Nazi rocket scientists down in Florida in the fifties, who were supposed to second-guess all of *their* Nazi rocket scientists over in Kazakhstan, so we'd always be just one little step ahead of them. Not a very good precedent, I admit, and of course it didn't quite work out the way it was supposed to."

"I can't help getting the feeling that you think I've been programmed—worse than that, *hard-wired*—designed from scratch just to suit Woodward's very peculiar specs. You're not kidding about any of this, by any chance, are you?"

"Not kidding as such, merely speculating. For example, I think Woodward actually wanted you to operate on a kind of preconscious level, almost like a prizefighter, without consciously thinking about it too much. That's why you weren't exactly told outright, at the beginning. He just sort of implanted the suggestion, to get your old intuitive midbrain working on the problem. I think maybe he even imagined that you'd finally be able to anticipate what she'd do next, in response to whatever it was that you'd done to her last. Isn't that what love's all about, after all? And isn't there something you people talk about called a Turing machine—a machine whose primary purpose is to replicate, even to anticipate, the output of another machine? But I suppose I shouldn't be running off about this to you—it might spoil the experiment. And anyway, far be it from me to try to replicate or anticipate the mental processes of someone like Woodward, one of the all-time immortal gods."

"Maybe Woodward's right. Maybe he's got me psyched just right. Maybe I'll be able to look at Colonel Voronkov from across a crowded room, and I'll be able to tell just from looking at him whether he's onto us or not. He'll have *da* or *nyet* written across his forehead, in big, pulsating, liquid-crystal-display red letters."

"I think it's safe to assume that he's onto *something*. I don't think he just came for the drinks. Also, there doesn't seem to be very much doubt that Jacques Vimard and Voronkov—or one of the other colonels—have also reached a very basic understanding. And that brings us back to a point that I believe I tried to raise earlier in the evening . . ."

But that point was already entirely moot, since Françoise herself was bearing down on them at that moment, smiling and looking radiant and a little bit drunk.

"Good evening, gentlemen! Are you having a pleasant time?"

"Mostly," said Brendan. "And yourself?"

"Very pleasant. I find it especially pleasant, exhilarating almost, to watch all these important diplomats and politicians and spies being so pleasant to each other face to face, since of course they're just waiting to spring the trap, or maybe they're just waiting for a chance to lie and cheat and betray . . ."

"Sounds as if our Françoise has had a bad experience this evening," said Thompson, unwisely as it turned out.

"And what makes you think I'm *yours*, Richard? Perhaps I'm one of *theirs*, have you thought of that?" She moved closer to Brendan, a maneuver that enabled her to turn her back on Thompson. "I have to talk to you, privately."

"Go ahead," said Thompson. "Brendan, I'll call you tomorrow. Try to think over what we talked about, okay?" He waved a hand and was gone. It seemed that Thompson had quite a lot to say for himself these days—very free and unguarded with his speculations, equally free with his advice, threats, warnings, and directives. Didn't they talk about a case officer—someone like Thompson, he supposed—"running" an agent, like an experimenter running a rat or a flatworm in a maze? Brendan clenched his fists in a sudden access of rage at Thompson and Woodward and all the rest of them.

"Françoise," he said impulsively, "you know that you can only take it for so long, then you have to start hitting back."

"Perhaps so, but why are you telling me about that now?"

"Sorry. Thinking out loud. Richard's been kind of getting on my nerves, I guess. And the thing is, much worse than that, I'm afraid it looks as if we're not going to be able to see each other for a while. I've run up against kind of a snag in my work—"

"Is that what Richard told you to say? And did you answer him, 'Yes sir, I will, sir, a snag, sir'?"

"What the hell are you talking about? Richard's got nothing to do with it. I'm not a fucking copyboy—or even an international journalist—that he can order me around like that."

"If not, you must be something else. Duvallon's told me all about your work, what sort of work you and Richard do. You mustn't think we're *complete* idiots, you know."

"The thought was never further from my mind. And I suppose

you've come over to tell me that it's all over between us, that you could never love a liar and a deceiver and a stooge of Silicon Valley and Wall Street, is that the idea? And as for me, I've been ordered not to see you anymore, by Thompson, isn't that right? So it works out just fine for both of us, doesn't it?"

"Not really, because, you see, I came over to tell you that I know all about what you're doing, but I still want to see you anyway. I wanted to tell you that I think I'm in love with you."

July 26, 1984   Krasnoyarsk

I'm still searching for a spark of inspiration, the one crucial detail that will allow me to reach out and put my finger on something that I've doubtless been staring at all along. Pushkin has interrupted his precious television viewing for a moment to look up and smile at me. Be with me, Pushkin, in this, my hour of need. I still think about Kutuzov constantly. I am afraid, F. I. Kutuzov, still my only friend in the midst of all this, that I am going to pay homage to your intellectual legacy by marching off resolutely in the opposite direction. Don't feel bad, Fyodor Ivanich, the same thing happened to Marx and Lenin, and if you were still here, I think you would do the same. In short, a different approach is needed. The program that we have acquired from Delhi, through the usual channels, will be vital to the construction of what Afanasyev calls "the informational infrastructure" of our country. I suspect, like our earlier acquisition, that it may also be mined to blow up when the appropriate signal is given.

What is it supposed to do? Since the Craig came to Krasnoyarsk, we have enjoyed the capability—on payment of a fee, of course—to tap into the various databases in the West, those that are classed as "nonstrategic" at least. Perhaps it's not surprising that they've built this great royal road to knowledge, and then decided to put up a tollbooth. This last is not pertinent to my subject, however; I'm going to have to pause to take some of these damned pins out of my hair, or I'll end up with another migraine.

But, to continue with our theme, if the entire Western world makes free with all this information, how can they be sure that when they set their trap they won't be catching some other, innocent creature instead of the dreadful bear? This is only a logical question, and logic is probably not going to be very helpful in this case. I'm afraid I won't have enough time to work out the correct solution, in any case. I'm under a great deal of pressure at the moment, particularly to perform a great many of what I must regard as my less essential duties. This is not a very convenient time for that. Kutuzov used to say that his ambition was to achieve total randomness, so that no one would be surprised anymore by anything that he did. I feel I have come a long way toward achieving it myself, or having it thrust upon me.

July 30: Svetlana and I are perfectly reconciled, I'm glad to say. I've promised her that I'll do everything in my power to ensure that she'll be able to stay on for an extra week. She acted very casual about the prospect of being on her own in a foreign country, but I could tell that she has certain misgivings all the same.

I'm supposed to talk to a certain Chenyshov at the Office of Visas and Registration, to find out if she could possibly spend the extra week in Paris, have someone from the embassy look after her. Perhaps it's just as well that Geneva is not one of the great fleshpots of the West, as my friend Ludmilla used to say. My only worry is that Svetlana will be sure to stumble across the only ballet instructor in Paris more effeminate and objectionable than Shakurov, and fall in love with him on the spot. The child is already showing signs of having inherited her mother's tendencies toward self-destructive romanticism. Perhaps she'll start getting more like her father as time wears on. At the moment, I don't think I could bear it if she got to be much more like herself.

At the Institute, we are luxuriating in all this wonderful data that's coming in from the West, scanning and sifting, filing and compiling, and trying, in a word, to decide how much of it is going to be disseminated throughout the All-Union informational network that is shortly to come into being. The peripheral systems—by which I mean virtually all the other computers across the nation—are all going to be feeding off our own, like a nice fat sow with her piglets. All the programs, all the files, every scrap of information, that we are going to be passing on to them have been examined quite carefully by us here, "pasteurized" as one might say.

Nevertheless, I remain convinced that the system has been sabotaged in some way. This is too much of a golden opportunity, and I suspect that a speck of baser metal has been added here and there. The question is *where*. The answer that suggests itself is *here*, in Krasnoyarsk, but we have still not come across a single line of code that is not precisely what it purports to be—none of those famous inactive subroutines that Kutuzov was so concerned about. The idea that these impurities may have evaded our scrutiny and lodged downstream somewhere, in the peripheral systems, really does not seem very likely. It is still something that will have to be investigated, I'm afraid. This seems like a very daunting project, but perhaps I'm just being like the drunk who drops his watch in the gutter but prefers to look for it under a streetlamp because the light is better there.

July 31: I've given a great deal of thought to the above, since last night. I was too tired to develop it then—as may be only too clear—and a bit anxious as well, though about what I'm really not sure. I'm going to follow one of Kutuzov's excellent precepts by thinking about these things, initially at least, in purely human terms, since, as he was fond of saying, you can always depend on the machine to think just like a machine. This at least, my future reader, should spare you some of the technicalities of what is to follow, though not, I fear, many of the absurdities. But somehow it seems hard to imagine that you will decide to follow me into this thoroughly unrewarding profession.

Suppose, then, that a trapper wants to place a whole string of traps somewhere in a forest. Is he going to put them all in the center of the forest, or in the clearings around the edges? The advantage of putting them in the center is that there are many more animals there, and the paths are more thickly traveled, so that some poor creature is bound to step in each one of them fairly quickly. But after he has tried putting them in the center and has already collected his first string of traps, is it likely that our trapper would decide to conceal his second trapline somewhere else—in the clearings around the edge of the forest this time—or back in the center again? The reasons for selecting the clearings might be, for example, that he is worried that the animals who live at the center of the forest may have already grown too wary, or (since our trapper will definitely not be a Siberian) that he's afraid to penetrate into the heart of the forest for a second time; perhaps he's worried as well that the animals might be eager to have their revenge.

I decided to submit this little fable to Pushkin, our resident specialist on imaginary-animal behavior. I told him all about it just now, when I went in to kiss him good night. He listened with an attitude of respectful attention, thought for several seconds, and said, "In my story, the traps would be around the edges of the forest, but for a different reason. It's not the trapper who puts them there, it's the animals themselves, so that trappers and hunters won't be able to get at them."

This is precisely the sort of logical breakthrough that I've been looking for, but unfortunately it does not seem to suit the facts of the present case as well as it does the fable. For *we*, after all, are the animals; we would have to have sabotaged the system ourselves. Pushkin is a gifted teller of tales, but perhaps he really does lack the proper instincts to be a systems programmer. I should mention in passing that you, Svetlana, my future reader, have started packing for our trip, three months hence, for fear that otherwise you might forget something vital.

August 1 (already): At the Institute, we might just as well be living at the bottom of the ocean—we have lost all sense of time, of the passage of the sun or the seasons, and—another similarity—the pressure has become quite unbearable. In my view, it can actually be dangerous to lose one's sense of cyclical time, to go for days on end without sniffing a fresh breeze or seeing a sunset. It has the same sort of depressing, degenerative effect that the polar night is supposed to have on people, I suppose. The constant clattering of the machines, the snuffling of the ventilation system, do not provide an adequate replacement for real-world environmental phenomena like the sun and the sky. If we ever do regain control of things, I hope to implement a policy of complete decentralization, whose first and only proviso will be that my office, as director, be relocated to the heart of a remote forest, with no telephone lines, and of course surrounded by a minefield.

Back to the realities of underground life for a moment, however. The problem that is driving us all crazy: How could the Americans possibly have sabotaged all the individual computers in the periphery—or was it just the most important ones, or even just one?—without leaving any trace of their activities in the software that's passed through our careful hands at the Institute? The idea that they could have done it is perfectly preposterous, of course, but I believe I owe it to Pushkin—Alyosha, not the poet—and to the glorious memory of F. I. Kutuzov, to investigate it thoroughly all the same.

NINE

"Just explain to me what the point of it all is, please," said Brendan, stroking the soft, cool flesh below Françoise's shoulder blades. Her face was buried in the pillow; instead of answering, she rolled over on her back, pulled the sheet up to her chin, and began staring at the ceiling without saying a word. Brendan got up with a sigh, collected his clothes, and perched on the edge of the bed to put them on. Françoise just watched him, mute and motionless.

"Françoise, it really is kind of stupid for us to go on like this. Don't you think it would be better if we just stopped seeing each other for a while?"

"I love you."

"It wouldn't have to be for a long time. And I swear, when it's over—"

"When? When is it going to be over?"

"I can't name the day right now. Whenever it's all wrapped up, this business I'm working on."

"What business? Have you got someone else who's planning on throwing a bomb at you now?"

"Why bother to ask, if you already know all about it?"

Françoise had moved closer, pulled away the sheet to uncover her breasts, and now she took Brendan's hand and placed it on her belly. He withdrew his hand gently.

"No, Françoise. I'm sorry. It's just not in the cards right now."

"But aren't you tired of having Richard hanging around your neck like that? I know I would be. Wouldn't you like to go back to living your own life, just for a little while?"

"My life is just about the way I want it to be right now."

"So you may think, except it's not yours at all anymore. Your whole life's already been programmed for you, by Richard and by those people in Washington."

A shadow passed over Brendan's face. He had used almost the identical phrase himself, when discussing Thompson's imaginative theories about Woodward and his motives. The idea that his life with Yulya, something that had been too fragile to endure and now seemed completely lost in the past, could have been such an important component of his present existence had seemed completely fanciful at the time. The things that had passed between him and Yulya were not the sort that would ordinarily figure in the calculations of someone like Woodward. The idea that Woodward had been plotting to pit them against each other as adversaries, like a matchmaker making up a fight card, was as distasteful as it was incredible. Finally, other images flashed into his mind: first the mock-heroic image of Woodward as one of Thompson's immortal gods, setting his pet heroes against each other before the walls of Troy; then a sort of animated mathematical image of his entire recent life as a long and tediously predictable expansion series generated by a mad, megalomaniac professor, who was, of course, Woodward.

"Are you listening to me?" Françoise was saying. "Why are you looking like that? Brendan, you mustn't leave me, really. I'm begging you to stay. What is this 'business' of yours that's so important? Does it have to do with sabotaging that mathematical institute at Krasnoyarsk? I know about that, you see, but I thought that was all over with."

Brendan said nothing. He had already said more than enough.

Françoise knew that the softwar was still going on—she knew enough to get her into serious difficulties with all kinds of people: Jacques, Duvallon, Thompson, the DGST, Colonel Voronkov . . .

"You're worried about security," she went on, "that you've talked too much, said something indiscreet? Well, what do you think I've done? I betrayed my country, just to while away the time until I went to bed with you . . . just so I could get my article published in a magazine! You two really make me want to vomit, with your nasty spy games! I would have done better to join up with Jacques and his crazy friends. At least they've got the right idea. I had the right idea myself, that day at Le Trou dans le Mur. Do you remember that, by any chance?"

He remembered it quite well. The name had called up further distasteful speculations, in fact. Looking back on it, he had thought it strange that she had been so insistent that they should never meet again at Harry's Bar. Was it that she objected to the service or the décor, or the clannish Ugly American atmosphere? Or was it that Françoise—a well-known and highly recognizable young woman about town, after all—simply disliked being seen in a place that was so much frequented by Americans? An alternative and more sinister possibility was that she had revealed to her brother, for whatever reason, that Harry's Bar was also a place that was likely to be frequented by Brendan Barnes and Richard Thompson. Had she been afraid that Jacques would find her with them and make an unpleasant public scene? Or was she afraid that Jacques would simply find *him* there, because she knew that Jacques was trying to kill him?

"Why aren't you talking to me?" she asked.

"I don't think we have anything more to say to each other right now. I don't think we really feel as though we can trust each other very much, for the time being—at least I hope it's for the time being." He got up and walked down the hall, up the winding green metal staircase. He turned and looked over the balustrade. Françoise had followed him down the hall and was standing, stark naked, looking out the vast picture window at the first blue light of dawn.

Half an hour later, when the doorbell rang, she was standing in the same spot, though she had thrown a bathrobe over her shoulders in the interim. She gave a start and padded up the spiral staircase to answer the door. It was Duvallon. When she saw the expression on his face, she managed to contain her exasperation, but only barely.

"What are you doing here? I thought the idea was that you were never supposed to come here. What if I suddenly turned up on your doorstep at five-thirty in the morning?"

"Rather exceptional circumstances. Why don't you put some coffee on?"

"Aren't you going to kiss me?" she asked.

"Evidently not."

Françoise ignored him and hurried down to the kitchen to busy herself with coffee and hot water. Duvallon was obviously intent on making some sort of unpleasant scene. She had no idea what he was so upset about, nor did she particularly care at the moment. He sat down, docilely enough, on the couch and waited, without saying a word, for her to bring in the coffee.

"You look like hell," he observed amiably. "Did your boyfriend pay you off last night? Finally outlived your usefulness, is that it?"

"What are you telling me?"

"Brendan Barnes. Computer scientist, professor at MIT, accredited as a representative of Cocom in Paris, attached to the American mission, of course. His name has also been intimately linked with an organization called DISSA, Defense Information Systems Security Agency"—he pronounced the English words carefully and contemptuously—"some sort of highly confidential new intelligence agency of theirs. I have all the details at my fingertips, in fact. And who do you suppose it was who told me so much about the remarkable young man? Can't guess? It was Comrade Voronkov, the Russian gentleman who's coming to Paris to find out why our computer program's gone bad on them all of a sudden. A nice, healthy bit of blackmail there, of course. If we don't lend a hand with his investigations, why, they can start playing the aggrieved consumer and assert the claim, very noisily, that our software was actually responsible for all the difficulties they've been having. How many contracts do you suppose we would lose by that, say within twenty-four hours? And like all sensible blackmailers, they've reserved the option of denouncing us afterwards in any case, after we've done all we can to help them with their investigations. They may decide to start denouncing the Americans as well, of course, and with much better reason. But I'm only telling you this so you'll recognize what your own modest part has been in this affair—assuming, as I do, that you've been furnishing this Brendan Barnes with information."

Françoise merely shrugged her shoulders. "You know that I've never had access to anything that sensitive, except through you, of course. The people I did speak to—I honestly thought one of them, at least, was a journalist. The other was Brendan Barnes, a representative of Cocom—as indeed he is—an international organization in which France, as I understand it, continues to play an active role, in spite of your intrigues with the KGB. Most of what I gave them was merely local gossip, background information on some of our more prominent local politicians, yourself among them."

"Then you don't deny the truth of the accusation?" He seemed genuinely disappointed by this. "You were also very indiscreet in leaving that reception at the Luxembourg with Brendan Barnes. It was Fromentin that spotted you, of course."

"And of course since then you've been having this apartment watched?"

"I regarded it as my duty as a minister of the republic."

"Your duty. Doesn't it leave a nasty taste in your mouth when you talk like that? And aren't you afraid that I'll run right off and tell the Americans about what your friend Voronkov just told you?"

"I'll think they'll find out soon enough, in the usual way. And you're not going to have time to tell them anything, because you're going to have to leave very shortly on a little trip, entirely for your safety."

"Going to ask your comrade to take me back to Siberia with him, is that it?"

"Françoise . . ." he began hoarsely, then reached out to take her hand, an overture from which she recoiled violently.

"A bit late for that sort of foolishness, isn't it? Tell me where you want me to go—or rather, where it is that your duty's going to take me."

"You'll have to go to Martinique for a couple of weeks. I've already fixed it up with Delépine. He understands perfectly. Wait until things have quieted down a bit. I've received informal assurances from the Ministry of the Interior that you shouldn't have any further worries if you simply disappear for a little while . . ." His voice broke off on an expectant rising note.

"Disappear?" she cried, stamping one foot like an angry child. "Where are we now—in Argentina? And what if I don't disappear? What can they possibly do to me if I stay right here? If they find out—officially, not just by you telling them—that I've been talking out of turn to the Americans, then the worst that could happen to me is that I'd lose my job, probably the *best* thing that could happen to me. And of course you'd probably be asked to turn in your precious portfolio—for the good of the nation, don't you think?—but at the moment I couldn't care less about a thing like that."

"At least you should be grateful that you'll never be charged with complicity in your brother's crimes. Now he's gone where they'll never find him—and I'm not talking about Libya this time." He stopped abruptly and made as if to take her hand again, then hastily drew his hand back. "I'm so sorry, Françoise. I hope you'll believe me when I say that I sincerely regret to be the bearer of such bad news. Your brother has been shot, in Marseilles; they think he was about to leave the country."

"Shot! You mean he's dead? Jacques is dead? Tell me what happened, for God's sake!"

"Difficult to say. It happened on the street, at night, no witnesses. He was shot with a .22 long rifle, a weapon favored by amateurs and by professional killers trying to look like amateurs, which sometimes apparently includes representatives of the various intelligence services. In other words, we are no wiser than we were before. His separatist comrades may have decided that he was getting to be too much of a liability; they may have discovered that he had been deviling for the KGB. It may have been that the Russians themselves were responsible, or the Americans . . ."

"Or even the French."

"Don't be idiotic. He had some papers on him—a sort of confession, a highly circumstantial account of the incident in Harry's Bar, which may or may not be authentic, of course. Still, the press is certain to take an interest in this—now that the identity of the assassin, if not those of his prospective victims, has at last been discovered. Your name is certainly going to come up in all this, and if they should happen to find out that you were my mistress as well as Barnes's . . ." Duvallon paused for a painful moment. "You were, weren't you. Brendan Barnes's mistress, I mean?"

Françoise did not answer. She was thinking about home, running through the marketplace as a little girl, playing tag with her younger brother, the sticky-sweet aroma of trampled fruit in the air, and playing hide-and-seek in the canefields after the rain, when the earth began to steam like a red-hot boiler. She thought about her mother, still living on the island, and she looked at Duvallon. "Was I really his mistress? I'm not going to tell you. That will be my parting gift to you," she said with a sultry smile. "I'm going back to Martinique. That'll be one less thing you have to worry about. And now . . . please get out. I want to go back to sleep for a couple of hours before I start to pack."

August 2, 1984   Krasnoyarsk

I have been going quietly mad for quite a while now, and it's surely time for me to pull myself together, stop all this foolishness, and start behaving like a real grown-up scientist. The time has come for more forceful, concrete measures, for grappling with real-world problems—to go down among the computers themselves, in fact. As Kutuzov often said, "They never lie; they're like people who tell the truth all the time, which is what makes them so hard to get along with."

Now that all our tests—Kutuzov's tests, I should say—on the new software for the Craig have come out negative, our vigilant organs of security have finally rallied themselves to take an interest in the problem. They are quite convinced that the Americans have sabotaged the system in some way. This leads me right back to my earlier, most distressing conclusion that the traps have been set all around the edges of the forest. And so, to the periphery I must go.

I've decided, by the way, that it would be wiser for the time being to transfer these frantic reflections of mine from my loyal blue notebook at home to a locked file on a disc here at the Institute. Surely that's the least I can do for security's sake, since anyone clever enough to be able to rummage, electronically, through my files at work must certainly have known about all this from the beginning. Not very much chance there'd be anything *I* could tell *them* at this point (or that I could hope to conceal from them either). In any case, it's a bit more convenient, since the amount of free time I have at home every day can currently be numbered in seconds rather than hours . . .

August 3: I have informed my colleague Nikolai Kruzhkov at Novosibirsk that I am going to be paying him a call—not in person, but over the telephone lines—in my new capacity as inspector general. He didn't believe me for a moment when I told him it was "purely a routine telemaintenance check." He's a bit of a windbag, and very jealous of my august position, of course. He's also part chauvinist swine, part toady—like one of those mythical animals of the Middle Ages. When we spoke this morning, he told me what an honor it would be to be "authenticated by your good self." At least, for his sake, the visit of this thoroughly up-to-date inspector general only involves my sitting down at my terminal and getting our computer to have a lengthy chat with his computer on the telephone—a test of the security cutouts on the lines that connect our two centers, and nothing more. I think the real reason he was acting so terribly slimy was that by the end of our conversation he had convinced himself that Sergei and I had concocted a hellish plot to get him dismissed for some little technical dereliction, and replace him with one of our own. I was shocked to discover that he had not read my own informational offprint on routine telemaintenance procedures. Such are the disappointments of fame.

Same, 11:00 P.M.: I am exhausted. I spent all day putting the machines at Novosibirsk through their paces. All diagnostics negative.

Everything seems to be in perfect working order. Comrade Kruzhkov, your job is perfectly safe. Booting up a new program: nothing to report. Disc backup: likewise. Network configuration file, network protocols, task file, disc storage and files, core memory: all departments running smoothly, and all secure files seem quite impregnable without the proper passwords. Speaking to Comrade Kruzhkov again was something of a trial. His honeyed words—"Delighted to have been able to be of service"—with "dear lady" almost audible in the little puff of breath at the end. But of course what he really wanted to say was, "You see? My yard's just as clean as your yard. Not quite as big, perhaps, but certainly just as clean."

As always, I must be guided by the example of Kutuzov. Never give in to reality. Never even admit that it's there. Reality was never complicated enough to suit him. For example, on that frightful night in January, if he had given in to reality, he would just have assumed that the weather program had failed because of some trifling physical ailment that would have disappeared by morning. It would never have occurred to him to start rummaging through the software instead.

Kutuzov was totally responsive to his intuitions, and so should I be. That means I shouldn't give up the search until I've actually found something. If the system at Novosibirsk all seems to be running smoothly, then there remains the *hardware* to be examined. The word itself suggests something solid, substantial, and conspicuous, like a combine harvester or an open-hearth furnace. I fear that's not quite the case. It's possible that some of the circuitry has been tampered with by the Americans. That, at least, is surely what they would like to do if they could; it probably would be simpler to find out if they've actually done it than to speculate about whether or how they *could* do it. However, that's not the sort of question that can be resolved just by the unaided exercise of pure reason, not by mine at any rate.

I've heard a Taoist teaching story about a disciple who asks his master, as they always seem to do, "Master, what is the Tao?" To which the master simply replies, "Go!" The story does not say, however, if the disciple eventually got as far as Novosibirsk.

August 4: Sunday. I would have stayed at home today, but Pushkin was off on some sort of class excursion and Svetlana has a "full-scale rehearsal." The Institute is running in comfortable slow motion today, and I don't have to worry about the usual interruptions. This first stage of my investigation was purely a journey of the spirit—a task that would be highly suitable, in fact, for an opium eater or a mystical hermit of some sort. Hours of pecking at the keyboard, staring at the screen, watching the little flashing specks resolve into letters and numbers. Thousands of separate memory cells to be examined and interrogated individually. Right now my back is aching furiously, and the UV wavelengths of the console display have etched permanent patterns into my brain. I am deliriously happy. The seventh memory array that I tested happened to exhibit an anomaly. Further investigation revealed that a single one of the tiny memory gates within this array—its full name is 54518, according to the diagram, its address FC 06—seems to have been left permanently open. This memory cell is always being "read," in other words, though by whom, if anyone, and why, I still have no idea. That brings us exactly up to date. The next step is to actually examine the little labyrinth of printed circuitry on a fingernail-sized chip of silicon that is the physical embodiment of this potentially subversive element, FC 06. That is where the Tao is to be sought, in my opinion.

When I was at MIT, they used to talk about "decoys" or "dummy components," nonfunctional kinks and curlicues that formed part of an integrated circuit but served no other function than to make it more difficult to copy illicitly. I hope that this turns out to be something of the same kind; that, at least, would be the only honorable explanation I can think of. I shall have to go to Novosibirsk right away to test this hypothesis. A flying inspection of this kind, of course, is going to reduce Comrade Kruzhkov to a state of helpless panic. Far from being the cause of regret, this may well provide me with the only real pleasure of the journey.

August 5: I thought it only fair, on reflection, to give Kruzhkov a day's warning. I wanted my little fact-finding trip to go off fairly expeditiously, without giving rise to too many stupid rumors. This has proved to be a very good idea. Kutuzov, my old comrade in arms, I remember the morning after that remarkable night, after you had solved the mystery of St. Thomas, how you were practically hovering off the ground in a state of mingled terror and exaltation. Now I believe I know that feeling quite well. I decided, after I had informed Nikolai Kruzhkov of my impending visit in the proper hierarchical way, to perform another simple test. I checked the identical memory on ten different computers from all over the country—Tashkent, Murmansk, Riga, Vladivostok . . . I've forgotten the rest already. The same anomaly appeared to exist in ten out of ten. These units are all being perpetually, as it were, interrogated by persons—or machines—unknown. It was a simple matter to program the Craig to perform the same test and thus considerably enlarge the sphere of my investigations. In a minute or two, it had told me that of 312 different ES-1060s queried, in almost as many different locations, all of them exhibited this same little congenital defect, at FC 06.

As I write this, exaltation has begun to give way to terror. It's all very well to have made such a discovery, but who am I going to tell about it? Kutuzov, at least, had the luxury of being able to come running up to my office in a panic. I'm already there, of course. I've been plowing ahead for the last few days without giving much thought to the consequences of what I've been doing; I've left the plowed lands far behind, to adapt a familiar image, and I'm now quite some distance into the forest, most probably surrounded by wolves.

I hesitate to commit these preposterous suspicions of mine to paper—that the entire "informational infrastructure" of our country has been physically tampered with in some peculiar way. Now that I've found out what they've done, I still have absolutely no notion of *how* they might have done it. An even more horrifying thought, if there could be such a thing, has even occurred to me since. What if it wasn't the Americans? What if it wasn't the hunters at all? What if it was the animals themselves?

TEN

Right by the single passenger-arrivals gate at Novosibirsk airport, a plainclothes policeman lounging in the corridor pursed his lips to whistle at an attractive brunette in a blue tailored suit. His companion, dressed as a baggage handler, caught him in the ribs with an elbow and almost took his breath away.

"Better keep it zipped up this time, all right? That's not a woman, that's a high-ranking official. Didn't you even notice she's got two GBs right behind her?"

"A high-ranking official. With a beautiful ass like that! Who is she?"

"That's what killed Yuri Andropov, if you really want to know."

"Right. I mean, who is she really?"

"Common knowledge. I forgot you're even too dumb to watch television. They say she was practically right there in the room with him when he died . . . may even have speeded it up by a day or two, eh? She's the one that takes care of all the computers. They say Andropov turned over all his secret personal files to her, talking about twenty, thirty years back, so now none of the others can say shit to her. They say she's trying to program her computer so she can figure out how come there's all this profiteering and pilfering going on, so naturally they're all busting their asses to get over on her good side."

"I wouldn't mind getting over on her bad side, even, just for a minute or two."

"Shut up, asshole, she's coming back this way."

In fact, Yulya was stalking rapidly back down the corridor, followed by two panting KGB watchdogs, who had accompanied her on the flight from Krasnoyarsk. She had been disagreeably surprised to find that Kruzhkov was nowhere in evidence. She had scarcely slept for three days, and had finally arrived at that brittle state where the slightest inconvenience was enough to make her seethe with rage. She walked back to the Aeroflot passenger-information booth.

"Could you please page Comrade Kruzhkov of the research institute? He was supposed to meet me here, and I've been waiting for some time."

The woman behind the desk stared for a moment at the watchdogs, then merely nodded and wrote down Kruzhkov's name and particulars with infuriating slowness. "You may wait in there, if you wish," she said to Yulya, tilting her head toward a door labeled OFFICIAL USE ONLY. This opened on a large room full of comfortable plush seats and benches, with a thick carpet as soft as old moss. The VIP departures lounge.

The information clerk appeared in a few moments with a telephone message from Kruzhkov. He was ill and had been unavoidably detained, but would be arriving shortly. Yulya thanked her for her trouble, though not very graciously, and looked around the room. She had actually come to expect that sort of deference from everyone, this sort of special privilege. Like everyone else, she tended to lose sight of the fact that the title that had lifted her out of the middle rank and into the upper levels of the *nomenklatura* was still largely an empty one, and her duties as director of the Office of Information Research were still largely those of a propaganda pinup and a conduit of fatuous slogans, not of her own devising, about "advancing the banner of socialism into the twenty-first century."

It was also true, of course, that she had been actively pursuing the task that Andropov had confided in her, pursuing it past the point of total exhaustion, but so far—apart from imposing herself on the hospitality of the wretched Kruzhkov—she had not dared to make much use of her new authority outside her old principality of Krasnoyarsk. There had been other changes in the landscape after the death of Yuri Andropov. Afanasyev had advanced a little closer to the eighth square, the step that would finally make him a candidate member of the Politburo. There had been a great reshuffling of Party first secretaries and of the upper echelons of the KGB; Sergei was still firmly in place, of course. She had long since stopped wondering whose side he was really on. If asked, he would certainly have replied, "My own."

Kruzhkov, bursting with apologies, was being shown into the departures lounge. "Yulya Nikolaevna! Could you find it in your heart to forgive me for such a disgraceful welcome?"

"Nothing to forgive, dear Nikolai!" she replied in the same chirping tone. "I understand you're not well! You should have sent someone else instead."

"Ah, but Yulya, I can tell from your voice that you're still simply furious at me. I did mention it, of course, but as you know, there's no use in giving instructions if you're not constantly at everyone's elbow to see that they're carried out."

"Still, you must learn to delegate some of your responsibilities, Nikolai. Perhaps you'd manage to stay healthy that way. What seems to be the trouble, may I ask?"

"Medical science confesses itself baffled, as usual."

"Doctors are the last people to ask about that sort of thing. Judging by your color, I'd say it had something to do with an excess of bile."

"A liver problem, do you suppose?"

"Perhaps, but in the old days, of course, they would have said it was caused by an evil humor—an *invidious* excess, in this case. Actually caused by an emotional imbalance—envy, jealousy, that sort of thing."

"Dear Yulya, for a moment you almost had me thinking you were serious! Certainly my admiration for you is boundless, not unmixed with perhaps a dash of envy—but jealousy, never for a single moment in my life!"

Still grinning wolfishly, Kruzhkov showed her to the waiting black Volga limousine. The watchdogs made themselves useful with the luggage; then, with three of their colleagues, piled into a far less prepossessing Zhiguli sedan that was parked nearby.

"Tell me, Kruzhkov," Yulya asked as soon as they were under way, "do you still find your work here as fascinating as you used to?"

"Do you want the answer I'd give to my old friend, or to the director of the All-Union Office of Information Research?"

"The former."

"Yes, I do. I live for nothing but my work."

"I'm the same way myself. Duty and pleasure are indistinguishable to me. But as you know, there are plenty of people out there who are incapable of distinguishing between rendering efficient service to the state and feathering their own disgusting vulture's nests, who work only for the sake of amassing their own little comforts, living entirely at the expense of others. I don't have to tell you, as your old friend, that I despise people like that, and as the director of the Office of Information Research, I'm sure it will come as no surprise to you, Nikolai Alexeich, that I intend to wage a pitiless campaign of extermination against such people until we're well rid of the last of them."

"Quite right!" said Kruzhkov enthusiastically. Yulya found it impossible to make a dent in his tough carapace of amiability, and she was a little ashamed of herself for behaving like a typical bullying *apparatchik* trying to terrorize a subordinate, even if in a good cause. When the car drew up in front of the research institute, she was not entirely surprised to see, draped across the long concrete façade of the building, a banner that read WELCOME COMRADE DIRECTOR Y. N. VORONKOV in enormous, somewhat shakily calligraphed letters.

"There you have it," said Kruzhkov delightedly. "My mystery ailment. I was held up at the last minute, getting things ready."

"Thanks, Nikolai Alexeich, but you know, even though this is an official visit, it's not exactly a state visit, as you all seem to think."

"But everyone will be so disappointed, myself most of all. We've planned a little celebration, of course."

"Very well. I think perhaps I could manage one glass—a toast to your very good health—and then off to work."

"If that's the way it has to be. You actually want to go down to the machine room right away?" Kruzhkov, for the first time, did not seem to fall in with her plans quite so enthusiastically.

Half an hour later, Yulya was face to face with three venerable specimens of the ES-1060. She thought back to the reception in honor of the Craig 1's arrival in Krasnoyarsk; some of the comrades from the various ministries had even seemed pleased that the ES-1060 was such a behemoth, physically so much more imposing than the relatively compact Craig. Yulya smiled, and wished it was really like that.

She was alone in the machine room now; the staff were all upstairs, still celebrating her arrival. She removed the protective panels from the central processing unit of one of the machines to expose the multicolored entrails of the ES-1060—a chaotic jumble of wires and microconnectors, odds and ends of metal and plastic and ceramic, which, taken all together, could be said to constitute a sort of intelligence. In a couple of minutes she had located the silicon chip that harbored the suspect memory cell at FC 06. Then she noticed a tiny wire, as thin, as her mother might have said, "as the hairs on a bullfrog's knees," running across the silicon substrate that supported the memory cell. She took a thread-counter, a small pocket magnifier, and tried to trace the wire to its source. A little further investigation revealed that this particular chip was unique, if not to the whole computer, at least to that particular section of that particular array of memory. Was it possible that the wire represented an afterthought, a design modification of some kind that had been added later by the manufacturer? Highly unlikely, it seemed. The ES-1060 was developed by a state enterprise called Elorg (Elektronicheskaya Organizatsiya); she had served a long, grueling apprenticeship on these machines, and had never come across anything quite like it before. And surely if any special improvements of this kind had been contemplated, she would have been one of the first to hear of it.

She picked up the internal telephone and summoned Kruzhkov

away from his pastries and caviar; she wanted the other two machines shut down so that she could examine them as well. Within the hour she had confirmed that each of the ES-1060s at Novosibirsk had been attacked by this unknown parasitical agent, at whose purpose and origin she could only begin to guess. She deftly removed the alien circuit from the first machine she had examined, replaced the front panels, and informed Kruzhkov that normal operations could resume at his convenience. She was curious to see if this would affect its performance in any observable way. By late afternoon, it did not appear to have done so. She had requisitioned the office of one of Kruzhkov's deputies, just a few paces from the machine room. Kruzhkov had been following her like a spaniel from one room to the next. "Nikolai Alexeich," she said to him as she picked up the telephone, "I'm going to have to impose on your hospitality a little bit longer than I thought."

"Nothing wrong, I trust," he replied heartily.

"Nothing special, really. However, I'd like to see a complete set of your office diaries, plus work logs for all three machines for the last two months, if you wouldn't mind too much."

Several minutes later, after she had called Irina and her new deputy in Krasnoyarsk, a young man named Karimov, she was surprised to see Kruzhkov himself, rather than a burly subordinate, shuffling in with four enormous sheaves of paper, each contained in an outsize ring binder. Yulya laughed out loud at this; she imagined a colossal canvas of the Socialist Realist school, with Kruzhkov as its subject, perhaps entitled something like *We Cheerfully Overfulfill Our Quotas in Order to Advance the Banner of Socialism into the Twenty-First Century.*

"This is a busy place," said Kruzhkov, looking a little bewildered. He set the work logs down reverently on the desk. "Anything else you'd like, dear Yulya?"

"Any leftovers from the festivities upstairs? I haven't really had anything to eat yet today."

"I'll have them send down something perfectly delicious right away."

"Splendid. Thanks. And I'll see you tomorrow, then, Nikolai Alexeich."

"Tomorrow? Right!"

"I mean, I'll probably be spending the night here. If I get tired, I'm sure I'll be able to catch a wink or two in that decadent-looking armchair over there. If this is your assistant's office, Nikolai, I'm really looking forward to seeing yours."

Yulya's parting shot was deflected harmlessly. Kruzhkov merely nodded once or twice, smiled, and stepped backward out of the office like an old-fashioned majordomo. Yulya was left alone.

She opened the drawer of the desk, where she had tucked away the suspect FC 06 for safekeeping. Then she carefully began to pick it apart, to separate it into its various components. It was close work, of course, but not especially taxing if you paid attention to what you were doing. The sort of thing that women are supposed to be especially good at, Yulya thought with some amusement. Most of the components were of Soviet manufacture, a few were American, none of them particularly startling in appearance. To begin with, there was an American Z80 microprocessor, surrounded by the two ROM elements that made up the passive memory of the cell (ROM stood for "read only memory," which meant the information that the elements contained could only be read, not altered or added to in any way). The microprocessor was the real brain of this assemblage, but only insofar as it prompted the memory cell to disgorge its contents at the request of the CPU. The mystery of the tiny red wire was solved quickly enough; it was connected to an adjacent black component about the same size as the Z80, which Yulya recognized as a comparator, whose function would be to make sure that the machine's request for the information, instructions, or whatever it might be that was encoded in the memory cell was expressed in the proper form; this information could only be released, in other words, in response to a particular instruction from the CPU that was also encoded within the comparator itself. The comparator thus acted as both trigger and safety catch, which would allow the memory cell to be fired, but only under the correct set of circumstances.

At once this suggested a great many other questions that all came crowding into her mind at once—most of them, unfortunately, of the familiar, unanswerable kind. One thing that she could do was examine the actual contents of the memory cell for herself, with the help of an ingenious device, also American-made, called an ROM decoder, a little handheld scanner that could convert the digitized information stored in the memory cell to a visual display on its screen. She carried one of these devices, as a sort of badge of office, on the broad leather belt she was wearing. In a few moments she was happily scrolling through a surprisingly lengthy list of instructions that had been encoded in the memory cell. Like an archeologist puzzling over an undeciphered text, she was able to see a general pattern emerging, though most of the specific coded instructions remained incomprehensible. After a few minutes of total bafflement, she decided that, first of all, the memory cell had been programmed to check for a match between incoming impulses from the CPU and a code word that was, presumably, the same one stored in the comparator (and relayed to the cell by way of the microprocessor, and by means of the thin red wire). The code word was in fact an actual word—a Russian word, *venik*—though not a very meaningful one in its present context. And what would the machine suddenly start to do if she sidled up to it—figuratively speaking, of course—like Ali Baba and whispered the password, *venik*? Who had originally implanted this strange speck of alien matter in the heart of the machine, and—perhaps more to the point—would they have any way of knowing that they had been found out? *Venik*, in and of itself, did not seem like a satisfactory answer to any of the questions she had been asking, and many more questions had been raised than she could even begin to answer by herself. At the moment she was not even sure who could. Should she ask the hunter? Or should she ask the bears?

August 7, 1984   Paris

The Soviet Embassy is a squat-looking blockhouse that perversely turns its back on some of the most attractive residential architecture in the city. Thus, instead of admiring the splendid prospect of the Boulevard des Lannes, Sergei Voronkov was impatiently marking time in the ambassador's outer office, trying unsuccessfully, for the fourth time, to invest an oil painting of Lenin addressing the Second Congress of the Socialist Workers Party with an interest that it did not intrinsically possess. The door eventually opened, and the ambassador's secretary appeared to announce that Colonel Voronkov was expected.

Ambassador Arbatov was just hanging up the telephone when Sergei stepped into his office. Arbatov stood up and walked around the massive oak desk, almost the only piece of furniture in the room, to greet him. They shook hands firmly but warily, like prizefighters before a bout. Georgi Arbatov was one of Chernenko's principal vassals; as such, he belonged to a faction that was not all that interested in disputing American supremacy in the realm of high technology. They had insisted, for example, that the retaliatory counterstrike that followed the incident at Krasnoyarsk should be carried out by more conventional means.

"Tell me how the investigation's getting on," said Arbatov cordially.

"So far, I've just been able to confirm what we've really known all along. It was the Americans—the ones with the Cocom mission, to be precise."

"So the fact that our first shot has gone wide of the mark is all the more deeply to be regretted. It seems odd, looking back on it, that this had to become the focus of so much acrimonious discussion at the time. But on the other hand, of course, the gesture was largely symbolic, and I suppose we can console ourselves by saying that the intent, at least, must have been perfectly clear."

Sergei was put in the enjoyable position of apologizing for the failure of an operation that he had strongly opposed from the start. He did so quite graciously. "You're dead right, of course. When it's a question of retaliating in, as you say, a symbolic fashion . . . then the fact that neither of the targets seems to be any the worse for his experience, why, that's entirely beside the point. And incidentally, we have a positive identification on the second American. He's actually thought to be the one who was most directly responsible for the incident. His name is Brendan Barnes, and he is associated with both Cocom and this new defense intelligence agency of theirs, called DISSA. We believe that DISSA may essentially be regarded as the strong right arm of Cocom, at least in matters of this kind."

Arbatov was grinning broadly. "Brendan Barnes. And can't that be essentially regarded as quite a bit of a coincidence?" When Sergei did not respond immediately, Arbatov's smile took on a kind of stretched and patient look, like that of someone growing tired of encouraging a backward child. "I mean, don't you think it's highly coincidental that your own wife was once this man's mistress when she was a student in America? Do you think they're making a special effort to get at you?" He raised an eyebrow as an unmistakable signal that a joke was to follow. "You don't suppose they made a practice of that sort of thing, do you? Perhaps that's the reason they've so persistently refused to ratify the convention on biological warfare?"

Sergei was completely astounded. He still had no very clear idea of what Arbatov was talking about, but a reply was clearly expected. "I've never actually thought of it in quite that light before, Comrade Ambassador. And I had no idea this was a subject of such commanding interest at the moment."

"But, honestly, my *dear* fellow, please forgive me. It was I who had no idea . . . I assumed it was all over *long* before you had arrived on the scene. Perfectly understandable, of course, that a thing like that could happen—she was hardly more than a girl, highly emotional, a bit of a romantic, I expect—and that they could let it happen, her sponsors in the Academy, I mean. Presumably it was all done in the hope that she might pick up some . . . particular pointers that would prove useful later on, might even turn this clever Professor Barnes around for us. Whether that still might be the case one day, I'm sure you know much better than I. But clearly, when it comes to knowing your enemy, after all, she could hardly have . . . don't you agree? And perhaps on the other side they'd been looking on with the same sort of indulgent eye. They kept him on, polished him up, and pushed him up the ladder, with the identical object in mind. At this point it might be difficult to say whether originally it was our idea or theirs—though of course there are so many things in the sciences that seem to fall into that particular category . . ."

Arbatov went on in this fashion, contentedly twisting the knife for quite a long time. Sergei still felt too dumbstruck and humiliated to say a word. Yulya had once made him promise that he would never ask her about Svetlana's father, that he would never make any inquiry of any kind. So far, he had been true to his word. Obviously there were others who had been less discreet. Had they thought so little of him that they had simply never taken the trouble to tell him, or was it that in the past no one had ever had a particularly good *reason* to do so? Whatever it might have been, this information— surely of dubious strategic or security value—had been withheld from him for a very long time, and then had just materialized out of thin air, to be used as a convenient stick to beat him with. As in that preposterous comedy of errors with Jacques Vimard and Brendan Barnes, a first-class tactical blunder had been committed, and— rather more reminiscent of the incident of January 6—an audacious insult had been offered him that would now have to be avenged.

"All the same," Arbatov was saying now, "since the benefits that were expected to accrue from this little experiment may actually never be realized, the Central Committee has been forced to reevaluate our entire position on this matter. It's possible, for example, that, capable as your wife has undoubtedly shown herself to be, she should not be permitted to speak for us at this conference in Geneva. Can you imagine, if the Western gutter press picked up a juicy scrap like that, the business with this Brendan Barnes? And I surely don't have to tell you that the Western press, admittedly of the more respectable sort for the most part, has already taken a considerable interest in your wife's career . . ."

Quite unexpectedly, especially in light of this last remark, Arbatov suddenly produced a bulky portfolio that had been hidden behind his desk thus far; it contained a generous armful of recent Western periodicals, most of which Sergei had seen already. Still, it was impressive to see them spread out all over Arbatov's enormous desk like that, and to consider that the imperious beauty on the cover of *Der Spiegel* or the inside back page of *Paris Match* was a woman he had actually held in his arms, though in recent months not as often as he would have liked. There was a color photograph in *Newsweek* of Yulya wearing a fox-fur hat and a scaled-down feminine version of a KGB leather overcoat; the caption read, "A new generation of Soviet computer scientists—glamorous Yulya comes in from the cold . . ."

Sergei glanced at the two-column article in *Paris Match: "Une ambassadrice de charme pour l'Union soviétique"; Der Spiegel* had run a fairly extensive interview, *"ein exklusives . . . mit der charmanten Botschafterin des 21. Jahrhunderts,"* "ambassadress of the twenty-first century," practically the same idiotic phrase that had appeared ad nauseam in all the Soviet magazines. In the accompanying photo, taken a month or so earlier in Krasnoyarsk, Sergei could easily make out the network of fine wrinkles that had appeared around her eyes since the beginning of the year. Since Kutuzov's disappearance, she had grown hard and bitter, and had come to look upon her husband as not merely an encumbrance or an embarrassment, but as an enemy.

"This is all very well, of course," said Arbatov, "as long as it goes no further than this. We don't want to start reading headlines about 'Yulya's star-crossed romance,' or any of that sort of business."

Sergei was amused in spite of himself. "Frankly, I don't see what harm it would do. It would only prove that we're human, and that we're also liberal-minded enough to entrust an important government post to a woman who's been on intimate terms with a foreigner."

"But I'm not sure the Politburo is especially eager to give a demonstration of its liberal-mindedness at the moment. Your wife's appointment is hardly irrevocable, after all. Certainly no one questions that she's technically competent to speak for us in Geneva, but this is not going to be just another professional conference. Its primary impact will be political, and we must try to be realistic in evaluating what the political repercussions of something like this—the disclosure that our charming ambassadress was once the mistress of a U.S. intelligence agent—could actually be. What we've already gained in propaganda value, we may one day have to pay back ten- or a hundredfold—"

"But in fact, Comrade Ambassador, this is a matter that will certainly be taken up by the Politburo or by the Party Secretariat, assuming that it ever becomes necessary for them to do so. This is not something that *we* are to resolve here and now." Sergei felt that he was finally getting a little of his own back, though he was still very far from feeling at his best.

"Your point seems valid enough," said Arbatov. "Perhaps it

would be better to move on to another topic. That of the late Jacques Vimard, for example. May I take it that this, at least, is not about to erupt into a scandal of major proportions?"

"You may. The other parties involved are no more eager than we are to have their roles in this affair become the subject of extensive commentary in the press. And if I may move on immediately to another topic of far greater importance—the French have also shown themselves to be very susceptible to political pressure with respect to the Geneva conference. The party in power is desperately searching for a 'model' to lead them out of their present economic difficulties. The rank-and-file voter seems perplexed by the spectacle of a socialist government that bows down and prays toward Silicon Valley five times a day. And this new 'politics of austerity' smells far too much like Thatcherism, even Reaganism, to suit the average socialist voter. If these suspicions can be crystallized in the minds of the electorate, then a substantial segment of the government's rank-and-file support could be detached and handed over en masse to the opposition. You may have heard that we're going to introduce a resolution at the conference demanding that all current restrictions of the free exchange of computer technology be lifted immediately. It may not be all that difficult to persuade the French to support our resolution. Next to this, the affair of the unfortunate Vimard begins to seem like a very small black dot on the horizon."

"Let's hope it stays that way. What else have you been up to, Comrade Colonel?"

"Preparing an alternate white-propaganda campaign of a far more specific kind, concerning the French support team's unscheduled flying visit to Krasnoyarsk in January. If the press, either left or right, discovers the *real* reason for this unseemly haste, the Americans may encounter a great deal of difficulty in peddling their computers overseas. They're negotiating with the Chinese at this very moment—having already beaten out the French for the contract. And the Chinese are perfectly well aware that the Americans may not be holding the China card forever; I'm sure they're already scared to death that something like this might happen if they start buying computers from the Americans. I'm going to be speaking to one or two of the technicians who were flown into Krasnoyarsk. I'll have an opportunity to fill them in on some of the pertinent details that have come to light since then, and eventually one of them is sure to tell his story to the press."

"What are you prepared to tell them, exactly?" Arbatov asked.

"That we have discovered the method by which the weather program was sabotaged. The evidence will be there for all to see. It should be easy enough to demonstrate that there were definite irregularities in the barometric reports furnished by the U.S. naval weather station on St. Thomas. However, it may actually be preferable to defer this revelation until the time of the Geneva conference. And in this connection, may I point out that it would be especially advantageous for our chief representative at the conference to be thoroughly conversant with the ins and outs of this entire affair?"

Arbatov smiled thinly at the brazenness of this last remark. Voronkov had recovered his nerve, and his gall, with astonishing swiftness. "I suspect you've already been authorized to do exactly as you see fit, or you wouldn't be telling me about all of this now. If not, I'm sure your proposals will be approved. After all, the bourgeois press, especially here in France, has always been one of our staunchest allies. All the more so in a case like this one, where we can raise the specter of 'American cultural imperialism.'

"It seems to me," Arbatov continued, "that there are too many people at home these days who want to try to beat the Americans on their own ground—electronics, robotics, computers, and all the rest. Certainly the history of our country should have proved to us by now that we always fight best on our own ground—in this case, the battleground of politics and ideology. This business, which you persist in calling 'the incident of January 6,' should also have proved to us that all this advancing resolutely into the twenty-first century only increases our dependence on imported technology—technology that turns out to be no more reliable than our own, if possibly for a different reason. Still, the moral seems clear enough—let science continue to be guided by politics, and not the other way around."

"Certainly it's the duty of each of us," Sergei said blandly, "to wage this struggle as best we can. The idea of Communism itself, as

Lenin said, will always remain our most effective weapon. But remember that Lenin also believed that Communism equals workers' soviets plus electrification. And I'm sure if Lenin were alive today, he'd cheerfully amend that to read, 'plus computerization.'" Afanasyev was a disgusting glutton and a windbag, but always a great source of inspiration when a pompous phrase was required.

"After that, Comrade Colonel, it seems that little remains to be said. I don't want to detain you, and I very much look forward to meeting with you again." Sergei got to his feet; Arbatov walked over with him to the door, then extended a hand. *"Nu, paka do svidanya . . .* that is, I trust our next meeting will be *quite* soon."

"Yet there seems to be some doubt in your mind, Comrade Ambassador."

"We must always be prepared for the worst. Suppose, after all, that your wife is unable to continue at her present post. Then she'll most probably be sent off somewhere else—and she'll undoubtedly need your help in arranging all the little details of her relocation."

August 7, 1984   Novosibirsk

Yulya was thinking not about computers as such, but about linguistics, psychology. The purely intellectual pleasure she derived from solving a complex logical problem now seemed to have acquired an invariable emotional component of uncertainty and terror. She had found the snares at the edge of the forest; she had found the tripwire, the password *venik*, and the Z80 microprocessor that would spring the trap—though she still had no idea what "springing the trap" would involve in electronic terms. Another linguistic puzzle: still assuming that the Americans had planted the chip at FC 06, *venik* was a strange password for them to have chosen.

In ordinary Russian parlance, a *venik* was a little bundle of twigs used as a switch that Russians delighted in beating each other with, across their naked backs and buttocks, in order "to get the circulation"—and sometimes, it seemed, even the respiration—"going again" after a nice long session in the sweatbath, at just about two hundred degrees (and, ideally, just before a nice, invigorating roll in the snow). Code names and passwords of this kind were often supposed to have some sly significance that would not be apparent to the uninitiated. Was it something to do with the word "switch," perhaps? If so, this must have been the result of some CIA man's over-hasty consultation of a Russian-English dictionary. The homely *venik* was not that kind of switch, and had nothing to do with electronics. And it was difficult to see how this ancient folk ritual could have anything at all to do with computers. It was no doubt very clever of the Americans to have thought it up, and it would be even cleverer of her to figure it out, but ultimately not very helpful. There were plenty of other things to think about at the moment.

On the other hand, the notion that she was finally in on the secret, at least partly, was quite a bit more difficult for the unaided human mind to grasp. She now had the power of unleashing whatever genie was bottled up in there, in the bowels of the machine, of every machine all over the vast expanse of the Soviet Union. She thought of Kutuzov again, and she understood as never before what it must have been like for him to have made such a discovery, all on his own like that. She had even found herself getting more and more like him in various little ways—living off sheer nervous energy, for instance. She made a stupendous effort to concentrate once more.

In an hour or so, she had even made some headway in deciphering the rest of the contents of the memory cell. And at the end of another lengthy session with the ROM decoder, she felt a dizzying sense of relief that she had not done what, for a moment or two at least, she had been strongly tempted to do. Now she was certain of what would have happened if she had actually gone in and typed the password *venik* onto the terminal of one of the booby-trapped 1060s in the machine room. The way she had finally figured this out—hunched over a desk with the ROM decoder—had proved to be much more laborious, but far less catastrophic. It had turned out that "springing the trap" would have immediately unleashed a genuine and quite widespread catastrophe, radiating outward from the machine room of the Novosibirsk institute. The Z80 microprocessor on the chip at FC 06 had been instructed, at the command *venik*, not just to give the machine a good, thorough switching, but to beat it sense-less—almost literally to beat its brains out. The real function of the Z80 was to ensure that all the software contained within the machine would be instantaneously erased, obliterated in a sort of a silent, in-visible mushroom cloud that would leave all the hundreds of thou-sands of separate components of the computer totally inactive, and deaf to all future commands (until the machine could be entirely reprogrammed).

This was something she found peculiarly horrifying just to imag-ine, as if she had overheard someone plotting the murder of a child, one of her own children. This was not just sabotage, destruction of state property strategic material; this was the destruction of intelli-gence, the murder of a living brain. If she had been so bold as to feed the password into one of those poor old ES-1060s, for example, the Novosibirsk institute would be paralyzed almost immediately, then waves of devastation would spread, in concentric rings, to encompass all the higher-level activities of the region. Computers were used to monitor production in the larger factories; they were used at various relay points across the electrical grid, at telephone switching stations, at railroad yards and airports. The Soviet press had made much of the American plans to develop the neutron bomb a few years be-fore—a truly diabolical weapon that would kill off all the people in the target area and leave the machinery and buildings intact. This new electronic weapon was like a neutron bomb in reverse—it would leave all the people alive, still fumbling with the switches of their useless, dead machines.

She had a sudden, not very rational urge to pick up the phone, to talk to the children. Perhaps this was perfectly rational after all; there was probably nothing to prevent this electronic holocaust from breaking out at any moment. Then she remembered the time; Irina would be none too pleased to be awakened at this hour, and all calls made on this telephone would doubtless be recorded, to be played back by the resident KGB at their leisure.

Yulya got up from the desk and threw herself into the arms of the decadent-looking chair that she had twitted Kruzhkov about. *Who could have thought of such a thing?* She hated that nameless enemy who had it in his power to unleash a catastrophe at any moment, that, for people like her, would be not much less destructive than a nuclear first strike. Could the country ever recover from such a blow? And perhaps that was just the opening salvo; perhaps a strategic nuclear bombardment would follow while the Soviet Union was still struggling helplessly in the grip of its paralysis . . .

She woke up with a start. She had had a very vivid and disturbing dream. It had started with a twig scraping against a window . . . then men were gathering them into bundles . . . she was helpless, stripped naked, being beaten savagely. That clearly had something to do with *venik*; even her nightmares had been infected by the obsessions that ruled her waking hours. Then she remembered something else. It had not been a birch twig, like a *venik*, but the tip of a little branch of a dogwood tree, scraping against a window. And it wasn't in Russia at all, it was in America. It was scraping against the bedroom window of the apartment on Commonwealth Avenue. *He was one of them now*. Had the idea of *him* gotten hopelessly entangled in her subconscious with the idea of *America*, or had she secretly, unconsciously convinced herself that he was the enemy she hated?

She glanced at the clock. It would already be getting light outside now. When she went back into the machine room, she came across a couple of sleepy-looking operators, who merely nodded and smiled and ignored her. She removed the panels from the CPU, which seemed like much harder work today, then she replaced the chip at FC 06 and returned to the office. She had moved the tray of leftovers that Kruzhkov had sent down over to a countertop to get it out of the way. Its contents, still untasted, looked no more appealing after twelve more hours. She was ravenously hungry, all the same. She consulted the little booklet of internal telephone numbers, punched up the number of the cafeteria, and listened to the phone ring for quite some time. Too early.

There was no point in examining the logs of the machine room; now she knew all about what went on in there. She sighed and decided to start in on Kruzhkov's office diaries instead. These contained a voluminous, detailed account of everything of even the slightest logistical or administrative significance that had taken place at the institute during the period they covered: routine deliveries of cafeteria and office supplies, furniture and equipment, the removal of a subsection of one department to a different floor of the building, or any major events such as the arrival of visitors from other facilities, distinguished or otherwise. Before long her eyelids were burning; picking through the minutiae of Kruzhkov's official life was monotonous enough, but no real substitute for sleep.

She was halfway through the second volume when she began to think that she had found what she was looking for. She was done with the hunters and the bears, at last. Now she knew a great deal more about it. She was investigating a murder, of a sort; critical questions of motive and opportunity still had to be resolved. Thus far she had blithely assumed what the former would have to be, and completely ignored the latter. That approach had turned out to be very helpful, but ultimately misguided. And Pushkin had been right all along.

On June 12, according to Kruzhkov's diary, there had been an unannounced "OIR maintenance inspection visit." OIR, of course, stood for her own Office of Information Research; spot maintenance checks at various facilities had been contemplated for quite some time, but thus far had not actually taken place, at least not at Novosibirsk. That was something of which she could be fairly certain; she had approved the revised inspection schedule only three days earlier. The entire program was shamefully in arrears, but in this case someone seemed to have anticipated even her most optimistic schedule by a month or more.

She was abruptly recalled from these meditations when the office door flew open and a startled male face appeared in the doorway and just as quickly disappeared. Kruzhkov himself turned up not too many minutes later, obviously in response to an appeal from the office's rightful occupant.

"Yulya Nikolaevna! You're an example to us all! At this rate, the twenty-first century should be upon us any day now!"

"Good morning, Nikolai Alexeich. Tell me what you mean by this entry 'OIR maintenance inspection visit' for the twelfth of last month."

Kruzhkov squinted at the typed entry for a moment. "But surely it's just as it says. We'd been expecting one, as I surely don't have to tell you, for some months now, but with all due respect to your good self—"

"Do you remember anything about the men—I assume they were men—who carried out this long-overdue and thus no doubt all the more eagerly anticipated maintenance inspection visit?" She gasped to catch her breath. She was finding Kruzhkov even more of a challenge at this hour of the morning.

"Wait just a moment . . . yes, I recall the entire sequence of events quite clearly now."

"I suppose there's no point in asking whether they had a valid mission order, documents and so forth?"

"Certainly they'd never have been allowed to set one foot among those machines without them! There should be a notation to that effect in the security log for that day—that they each presented the requisite documentation, I mean. Would you care to have a look for yourself?" Yulya nodded briskly, and Kruzhkov picked out a number on the telephone. "Kruzhkov speaking! I'd like all your records pertaining to the OIR maintenance inspection visit that occurred on July 12. You can send them over to Medvedev's office on the lower level, if you'd be so good."

"Very impressive," said Yulya. "Now, perhaps, while we're waiting, you can tell me everything else you can remember about these unannounced visitors of yours—how many there were, and what they looked like, will do very well to start off with."

Kruzhkov looked over at her appealingly, like a puppy who is eager to please but not quite certain what is expected of him. "Ah, there were definitely three of them, I do remember that much. Very thorough, very efficient. In and out in less than an hour. And as to their appearance—well, of course, I only caught a glimpse of them for a moment . . ."

"And you'd never seen them before, nor, I imagine, have you since. And in fact there haven't been any subsequent inspection visits of any kind?"

"Perfectly true, but they did have a valid mission order, you know, and valid identification as representatives of your office. You can be quite sure of that."

The telephone rang, and Kruzhkov bounded over to answer it. "Kruzhkov! . . .Well, look again, damn it! All you people do is sit around all day, fouling the air with your filthy cigarettes . . . I've seen you *all* doing it, don't think I haven't! . . . Then stop sniveling to me about it and go and look some more!" He hung up and turned back toward Yulya. "Security. Though of course I don't have to tell *you* about that. They insist on keeping their records exclusively on grimy little slips of paper, and of course they're constantly being misplaced. I've offered to put it all on a couple of discs for them at least a dozen times. 'But anybody can break into a computer these days, Comrade Director!' It's hopeless, really. Though in fact," he added with an ingratiating smile, "I'm sure they'll come up with exactly what we're looking for, if you'll just be patient a moment longer."

"No time, I'm sorry to say. I really must be off now," said Yulya, snapping the lock on her briefcase. "I'm afraid I'm leaving a terrible mess behind for your man Medvedev. Sorry. Anyway, thanks for your help, Nikolai, and," she added, with a nod in the direction of the armchair, "thanks for the use of your excellent facilities. Do you happen to remember what you've done with my hat and coat?"

"But aren't you going to tell me what this is all about?"

"Very well, since you've asked. Listen to me closely now, Nikolai Alexeich. I'm afraid something very disturbing has come to my attention. A serious breach of security—"

"But I swear to you, we've always observed the correct security procedures, right down to the letter."

"I'm sure you have, Nikolai, and I'm really quite sure that you're not the one to blame for this, nor are any of your subordinates. Ordinarily, I can assure you, a matter of this gravity would almost certainly have to involve the KGB, but until I've formed a clearer picture in my own mind of what's actually happened here, I've decided to take no official action at all. So, for the moment, we'll just keep it strictly between us, in the family."

Kruzhkov had been slowly shrinking back into himself during the beginning of this speech, like a lightly salted snail; by the end, he had brightened up considerably. "Dear Yulya! What does one say? I can't begin to tell you—"

"Best to say nothing. Except, if that grimy little slip of paper you mentioned ever does turn up, I'd like to hear all about it, of course. But I suspect it won't. And remember, one incautious word about this from you, and they'll be positively *swarming* in here, dropping their filthy cigarette ashes all over that lovely low-static carpeting of yours."

The moment Yulya sat back in her seat on the plane, she realized that sleep was still going to be denied her. The two watchdogs, sitting in the seat behind her, had begun a low, growling discussion of the forthcoming soccer playoff match between Spartak and Dynamo, a discussion that flared up into an argument just often enough to keep her from dropping off.

ELEVEN

August 12, 1984   Washington, D.C.

Woodward was rarely willing to be pried out of his suburban lair to make the trip to Washington for any reason. The biweekly conferences at the headquarters of the National Security Agency were all the more to be dreaded. At today's emergency session, the deputy directors of the two sponsoring civilian intelligence agencies, plus a colonel and his aide from Defense Intelligence at the Pentagon, would be in attendance—this, he was convinced, was an ordeal from which he would be lucky to escape with both his sanity and his life.

At the moment, all five of them were sitting in sumptuous leather swivel chairs around a bare white table made of some impregnable white shiny substance; Woodward had equipped himself with an immense black glass ashtray. The colonel and his aide both looked suitably battle-ready and alert. The two deputy directors looked both seriously worried and extremely self-satisfied at the same time; Woodward knew very well why that was.

"Gentlemen," he began, "we are about to become embroiled in a foreign-policy crisis of major proportions. The National Security Council will be meeting in a few days' time to consider what our response will be—and by 'our response' I mean primarily the five of us in this room, because the solution that is ultimately adopted will almost certainly be one of our own devising." He looked around the table; the four others present had clearly decided that since the crisis itself had been entirely of *his* own devising, they had every right to expect the solution to come from the same source.

"I myself," he went on, "am extremely pessimistic about our prospects for the Geneva conference—perhaps almost as pessimistic as one or two of you. The first phase of our experiment, of Operation Softwar, proved on balance to be a success. It showed us that it would unquestionably be possible to wage a form of electronic warfare that would be bloodless, scarcely even destructive, would make virtually no demands on our own resources, and would still conform to the classical definition of warfare as 'the continuation of diplomacy by other means.' This first phase of the operation was still open to criticism as regards what we refer to as the 'muzzle-flash problem'— for technical reasons, the source of the attack could still be identified by an adversary who was sufficiently clever and alert. This was due for the most part to certain heuristic assumptions on our part, per- haps justifiable in experimental terms but inappropriate to real-world test conditions—and also quite easily dispensed with when the time came to design the second phase of the experiment—"

"In other words, Clive," the first deputy director broke in, "when you say 'certain heuristic assumptions,' what you're really saying to us is that you decided it would be okay to stick your neck out a little bit just this once, and now you're trying to figure out how to walk all the way home with your ass in a sling, is that about right?"

"Jesus, Ron," put in the colonel from Defense Intelligence, "let's not start up with any of that just yet. Just let the man say what he has to say, and then we can break for the tag-team matches right after that, okay?"

"I appreciate that, Earl," said Woodward, "but I must admit that Ron has stated the case fairly well. However, the second phase of our experiment has involved us in the design and testing of a much im- proved software weapon—a software MIRV, if you will, with multi- ple warheads that can be independently targeted at any points within the vast Soviet computer grid that have just recently come into being. By means of the international financial data-exchange network—access to a database that is provided gratis, and one to which the Soviets were very eager to subscribe in any case—we now have the capability of disrupting all operations of the central Soviet computer research facility at Krasnoyarsk for an indefinite period, and eventually, perhaps in a year or two, of every single computer throughout this entire network as well.

"For example, suppose that we decide to support an all-out assault on Kabul by the Afghan Mujeddin *without* running the risk that this conflict will escalate into a global conflagration. By taking out the computer banks located at satellite facilities in Tashkent, Samarkand, and Ashkhabad, the normal electronic channels for arranging the reinforcement and resupply of Soviet front-line units will be completely blocked in the three border republics of Kirghizia, Tadzhikistan, and Turkmenistan."

"That's quite a little weapon you've got there, Clive," said the colonel. "I just hope you won't decide to start selling the franchise and put us all out of business."

"For the moment, Earl, there seems to be little danger of that," said Woodward. "Just consider that of 360 generals in the Air Force, only six have any formal training in computer science—and of course, the other 354 have a great deal more lobbying clout in Washington than the steelworkers and the UAW put together. They're not about to let themselves be made redundant overnight. And bear in mind that I've been describing the situation that *may* exist in a year or so; just at present we are only able to affect operations at the central computer facility in Krasnoyarsk; the so-called peripheral systems are still out of reach. We still do not possess that 'MIRV capability' that I spoke of earlier. And this is particularly unfortunate, because at the moment the Soviets are preparing to launch an ideological offensive of unprecedented virulence—"

"The evil empire always strikes back, huh, Clive?" said the first deputy director. "But I think we've pretty much gotten the hang of their major ideological offensives by now, don't you? They certainly haven't been able to stop us from deploying those Pershings in Europe."

"Indeed not, but now the stakes are considerably higher, and the Soviets are playing a much stronger hand. The entire Softwar program—which has finally provided us with a realistic Strategic Defense Initiative, a fully reliable deterrent that does not involve the use of nuclear weapons, and, I might add, will not require an additional thirty-billion-dollar research budget or an armada of giant laser weapons in permanent orbit around the earth—this program is most definitely at risk. This time the danger is that instead of merely provoking massive street demonstrations and inflaming a group of left-wing minority parties against us, with perhaps a cabinet crisis in Holland thrown in for good measure—as was the case with the Pershing missile—the Soviets may be able to drive a very sizable wedge between us and our European allies, perhaps to leave the very fabric of NATO itself in shreds.

"Our initial testing of the software bomb, Mark 1, unfortunately did leave traces that have subsequently been detected by the Russians. They are now convinced that we were responsible for the breakdown of the Craig 1 computer at Krasnoyarsk—"

"But wasn't that the operation," said the first deputy director with leaden irony, "that you were saying was so successful just a minute ago? 'The operation was a great success, but just when they were about to stick in the knife, the patient woke up and punched the doctor's lights out.'"

Woodward glared at his tormentors, and said harshly, "The initial phase of our experiment was planned and carried out in constant close consultation with *both* of your agencies, gentlemen. If you choose to disassociate yourselves entirely from the results, if you have nothing more productive to offer than mere buffoonery, then that makes it all the more regrettable to me that your advice and cooperation were ever sought in the first place." He stopped for a moment to let this sink in, wondering if "mere buffoonery" had been laying it on a little too thick.

"This," he continued finally, "is the situation we currently face. The French are, quite justifiably, furious; they believe they've been stabbed in the back. By using *their* computer software as the delivery system for our software weapon, we may have incidentally put their software industry out of business, at least as a serious competitor on the international market—this is perhaps the greatest single economic setback that a French government has had to face since the grape blight destroyed the vineyards over a hundred years ago.

"There's been talk of the Communist cabinet ministers' resigning en masse. The Communist trade union association is threatening to make even more than the usual fuss, as well. Nothing definite has actually coalesced so far, but there are a great many ominous rumors floating around. It might seem strange that the French technicians who were dispatched to Krasnoyarsk in January seem to have been the original source of these rumors, and yet at the time they were completely unable to recognize the problem for what it was, a clear-cut case of sabotage."

"That would be Colonel Voronkov," offered the second deputy director. "Apparently he's met with several of them, in connection with his current fact-finding mission. But unlike the typical KGB interrogator, he seems to have given much more than he got."

"And if they're also pounding the drums like that," added the first deputy director, "you know they're bound to launch a screaming attack pretty soon. At least with old Andropov, we could almost have sorted this out by now, just sat down and reasoned together, maybe ended up by promising him to scuttle this dirty old Operation Soft-war and never, never do it again—"

"Which would have been a disastrous blunder, in my opinion," Woodward said sharply.

"And that's neither here nor there," the second deputy director put in, "since Good King Andropov's deceased, and now we've got Bad King Chernenko. This is hardly the time to start bargaining away any of our strategic weapons systems, however imperfect they may be, merely judging from the way they've been carrying on about the Olympics! And this time it won't be that they're merely annoyed with us for not putting on enough security to keep the lady shotput-ters from running off to Sunset Strip. This time we've committed a deliberate act of sabotage, possibly to be construed as an act of war, against a top-secret research facility in the heart of the Soviet Motherland."

"An apt comparison," said Woodward. "And I agree that there is a qualitative difference. That's actually why I believe we may be on the verge of something comparable to the Cuban missile crisis. This time we shall have to act with the same boldness and decisiveness as we did then—because this time we may be threatened with the prospect of losing *our* missiles in Europe. European public opinion is certainly going to take a violent swing in the direction of neutralism, and the governments of all our NATO allies—with the possible exception of Turkey—may very well be carried along with the tide."

"To say nothing of the reaction of our own civilian population," said the colonel from the Pentagon. "We've got a President who's convinced them all that God's in his heaven, all's right with the world—there'll be no more Vietnams, no Irans or Afghanistans. Then along comes something like this and suddenly it's 'We're mad as hell, and we're not going to take it!' all over again."

"Excuse me, sir . . . gentlemen," the colonel's aide put in unexpectedly. "Point of information. One thing I just don't see here is how the Russians are going to be able to focus so much public attention on something that, with all respect, ordinarily interests only a tiny fraction of the population. Computer software and so on, I mean. With a thing like the Pershing missile, at least you had an issue where people sincerely thought their *lives* might be at stake."

"The Soviets have been much cleverer about this than usual," said Woodward, with the air of a chess commentator pointing out a move that has been marked with a double exclamation point. "Rather than launching the usual propaganda barrage, simply blaring it out over every available channel, they've decided, as you say, to *focus* public attention, like the blindingly powerful beam of an arc light, on a single individual—Madame Yulya Voronkov, whose name's been mentioned in this room many times before. She's now not only the director of the research facility at Krasnoyarsk, but also of a new kind of government watchdog agency for the Soviet computer industry, called OIR in English, Office of Information Research."

"In Russian IIO. Informaticheskoi Issledovannoi Otdel," the second deputy director noted proudly.

"Correct. And Madame Voronkov appears to be a remarkable person—remarkably personable and photogenic to begin with, especially for a Soviet official. She has the reputation of being a progressive, an extreme liberal by Soviet standards, and she's already made an excellent impression on the European news media. And I'm sure you've all seen her picture in *Newsweek*.

"She's also a protégée of K. I. Afanasyev, their leading computer specialist, though the fact that she has a more sinister *family* connection in Colonel Sergei Voronkov has so far not received much notice in the press. She is almost certain to head their delegation to the forthcoming conference on the International Exchange of Computer Technology. This, of course, will provide her with a bully pulpit from which to denounce us for our transgressions."

"Also," observed the first deputy director, "at the conference they'll be able to make it look like the bad, nasty Americans have been deliberately trying to whip it to her innocent pink ass. There's your sympathy vote, right there."

"Just as you say. And in fact the Soviets are definitely going to introduce a resolution calling for the abolition of all current restrictions on the export of nonmilitary computer technology. A very hasty preliminary study undertaken by our Working Committee has indicated that the French, quite possibly the Japanese, a number of European countries, and the overwhelming majority of the rest will support this resolution.

"And these are only the short-term effects, of course. There is also a possibility that our own computer industry will suffer a significant dropoff in overseas sales—quite naturally, in light of the disclosures to be made by Madame Voronkov, since every Craig, CD, or IBM that's sold overseas will be potentially suspect as a Trojan Horse of U.S. imperialism, or even—and here I use the term in its broadest possible generic sense—a covert operative for the CIA."

"Very amusing," snapped the second deputy director, "but after you brush aside all the verbiage and the stale pedantic wit, I still don't see you coming up with any *solution*."

"I have none to propose at this time. I merely suggested earlier—as a stimulus to discussion—that it was incumbent on us to provide one."

"Not even any bright ideas?" the first deputy director said with a sneer. "Promise first-run cable-TV movies to the Bulgarians if they'll just send someone over to Geneva to pop this Yulya Voronkov?"

"That sounds more like the kind of bright idea that *you* all have gotten to be so famous for," the colonel said scathingly. "The point is to find some way of finessing the Russians so they'll have to keep quiet about this thing at Geneva."

"In fact," said Woodward, "we need to convince them that what happened at Krasnoyarsk must remain a secret that they have no desire to share with the rest of the world, ever. It seems to me that the two people who can best convince them of that are Dr. Brendan Barnes and Madame Yulya Voronkov. We have already recruited the services of one of them; now possibly it is time to go after the other."

August 13, 1984   Krasnoyarsk

"Karimov," said Yulya, "I have an important favor to ask you."

"Anything you like, Comrade Director," replied Karimov, a tall, stooped young man with enormous goggle glasses. He was a formidable debugging specialist, a ferocious Go player; otherwise, though in a much different way from his mentor and predecessor, Kutuzov, he appeared to be dreamily indifferent to the things of this world.

"I have to go to Moscow, maybe for a couple of days," she went on. "They didn't say why—just that I've been 'requested to appear before a commission of inquiry authorized by the Central Committee of the CPSU.' And the thing is, I happen to be right in the middle of something right now . . ."

"So you'd like me—"

"Yes, but don't be too quick to accept. This is something private, you see, something confidential that I've been looking into on my own. Not to be discussed over the telephone—that kind of confidential."

Karimov raised his eyebrows interrogatively and made a quick little gesture with his left thumb. *Na lyeva*—"on the left"—in Soviet parlance meant anything outside the normal channels of socialist legality, something the eavesdroppers in "security" should not be able to play back on their tape recorder.

"That's right. You can always refuse, of course," she said. "And if you accept, that makes you my accomplice, my co-conspirator—for worse *and* for better, I hasten to add. As you know, I've gotten quite used to having a deputy I can rely on completely. And I think that relationship should be one of *mutual* trust. So if there's anything—"

"—I might have heard about how you had poor old Fyodor Ivanovich packed off to camp—or some even say the Serbski hospital, you know, where they put all the really top-class babbling idiots?—and you were about to give me your solemn word that you had absolutely nothing to do with it, and then I was going to say that, of course, I never could believe even for a single instant . . . Is that pretty accurate, do you think?"

It took her a moment or two to recover from this little speech. She had been expecting, with someone like Karimov, that she would have to go through a long ritual of drawing him out and soothing his suspicions before they could communicate with genuine frankness. On the other hand, she had always suspected that Karimov's thought processes were actually two or three times faster than a normal person's. "Well, then I suppose we can go right on from there. This is what I've found out so far. It's beginning to look as though our beloved Kutuzov was taken from us because he had been overzealous in the dispatch of his duties. He accidentally turned over a rock that was not intended to be disturbed for some time yet."

"What kind of rock? And not intended by whom?"

"That I don't know. But there are different *tendencies*, as we say, among the Party leadership . . . It may be that certain of our leaders have recently been trying to extend their authority in a surreptitious, even an adventurist manner . . ."

Karimov smiled, a little uncertainly. "Frankly, none of that political stuff has ever seemed quite real to me."

"Nor me, until very recently. And if you do what I'm about to ask you, I think it will start to seem all too real to you. I want you to get in touch—over the net, of course, not over the phone—with all the other centers, or as many as you possibly can. Ask if they have any record of an unannounced OIR maintenance inspection visit at some time during the last two months."

"But I can tell you that right now. I just drew up the final inspection schedule myself. Surely all my efforts can't have been so quickly forgotten. There've already *been* a few, of course, on a fairly random basis, but we should have records right here of every one of them."

"Nevertheless, if you take the trouble, I think you'll find there's been precisely one at *each* of the centers already, carried out by personnel equipped with valid mission orders, all the right documents."

"But how could that be?"

"It seems that someone out there is so full of advanced socialist consciousness that he's been doing *our* job for us as well as his own. I think Kutuzov was on the verge of discovering his identity, and naturally, being just a modest builder of socialism, he was anxious to avoid the limelight of publicity—"

"But that's incredible—kind of fascinating and horrifying at the same time, if you know what I mean."

"I do indeed. I'm going to call you from Moscow tomorrow evening, early. I'll ask you, of course, how you've been getting along without me. If you say 'Everything's perfect,' that will mean that you've come up empty, nothing to report. 'Everything's in order' will mean that *some* of the other centers have received these unauthorized visits, and 'Everything's under control' will mean that *all* of them have, every one. I don't suppose you'd care to write that down?"

Karimov grinned and pointed to his forehead. "Voice-activated. No problem. Why don't I go down and start right now?"

"So it's all arranged, then?"

"Absolutely. Kutuzov was a good friend, you know, a sort of genius in certain ways. It may sound a little strange to say so, but I really admired him very much."

August 14, 1984   Moscow

The government Chaika pulled up in front of an imposing, almost monolithic building on the outskirts of Luzhniki Park. Yulya snatched up her briefcase and was out the door and about to mount the steps before the driver had even gotten out of the car. As she started up the white marble steps, extremely sharp-edged and vaguely suggestive of ancient temples and human sacrifice, she was slowly replaying in her mind the conversation she had had with Afanasyev the day before.

"'. . . requested to appear before a commission of inquiry authorized by the Central Committee of the CPSU.' You should get the Telex with the official notification any minute now. The hearing's scheduled to begin at eight P.M. I'll be there. There should be plenty of time to talk about it afterwards."

"But can't you tell me what it's about?"

"Tomorrow I will. It's serious, but the best way to prepare yourself is not to worry about it too much."

She found she could repeat the entire conversation word for word. Afanasyev had rarely had so little to say for himself; he had not even asked after the children, which was most unusual. His voice almost had that same brittle, official tone that she had heard in it on that day in January, in the few minutes that it had taken for him to decide that the only course open to him would be to assist her in her deception. She had almost been able to hear the doors slamming shut, the barriers coming down between them; she supposed it would always have to be like that. If they were both running from the wolves, then he would do anything in his power to save them both, but if it seemed as though the wolves would be satisfied with making a meal of just one of them, then he would be sure to be the first one in at the kill. Perhaps it was foolish of her to expect anything more.

She showed her "documents" to a young officer in the entrance hall, who glanced back repeatedly from her face to the photograph in her *propusk*, her internal passport, at least half a dozen times. Don't you recognize me? she felt like asking. I thought you people got to see *all* the foreign magazines! She was met by another earnest-looking young man in civilian clothes, who escorted her wordlessly into the elevator, up to the top floor of the building, then along a series of lengthy corridors that continued the nightmare motif of the marble front steps. The décor was somber—not unattractive, but not terribly friendly, either.

Finally she was shown through a door that looked like all the dozens of others they had passed. There were six massive, late-middle-aged men sitting opposite her at a long mahogany table.

Afanasyev was all the way over on the right; he made a sort of grimace that implied that, had the circumstances been somewhat different, he actually would have smiled. There was an empty chair facing the table, which she took for herself without being asked.

Apart from Afanasyev, there were three others that she recognized on closer inspection. The other two were just the sort of anonymous, putty-faced bureaucrats she had imagined when she had heard the words "official commission of inquiry." One of the others was a computer specialist from the GRU, Military Intelligence, an organization that actually carried out many of the activities popularly attributed to the KGB. Next to him was Chenyshov, from the Office of Visas and Registration, with whom she had conferred about getting permission for Svetlana to stay on for an extra week in Paris; he had seemed harmless enough at the time. Then, over next to Afanasyev, was a KGB colonel—not harmless. A protégé of Chernenko's, he had languished in obscurity under the previous regime, but had recently been reactivated. She knew that he and Sergei cordially despised each other. Even the two putty-faces were beginning to seem familiar, probably from pictures in the magazines, posed stiffly, with half of their faces cropped off, on some official reviewing stand. Here were present, she thought, in dilute homeopathic doses, all the principal "tendencies" within the Central Committee.

"Yulya Nikolaevna Voronkov," one of the unknowns was saying, "this is a formal administrative inquiry into certain charges that have been raised against you. These charges are very serious. In the first place, you are alleged to have concealed information from the duly constituted investigative authorities—vital information that had come to your attention in the course of your official duties."

Yulya suddenly felt very cold and empty, and frightened. On the other hand, all she really had to do was talk to them. "I'll try to answer as best I can," she began. "It would certainly help if these allegations could be made more specific . . . And might I possibly know your name, comrade?" She had heard that in a genuine, intensive interrogation session, the interrogators never revealed their names to the suspect, on principle. But this, she hoped, was a very different situation from that.

And, in fact, the putty-faced spokesman suddenly became almost affable. "My name is Ludkin, secretary of the internal security section of the Central Committee. This is Comrade Antonov, from the Ministry of the Interior. I understand all the others are already known to you. We have been charged with investigating a pattern of irregularities observed in the operations of the institute of which you are currently director, and in connection with other facilities as well. We are primarily interested in your *opinions* on this subject, as a specialist, rather than in any personal avowals of guilt or innocence that you might be prepared to make at this time. Certainly both the considerable services you have already rendered and the critical nature of your present responsibilities will strongly dispose us toward leniency if it appears that a culpable error of any kind has been made. Feel free to speak with total candor, of course."

"I didn't realize I'd made any mistakes so serious they required a special commission of inquiry to investigate them," Yulya replied. "I suppose I've made no fewer than my share, of course, and I'll do whatever I can to correct them as soon as they're pointed out to me."

Antonov, the man from the Ministry of the Interior, picked up a slender file from the table and held it up by one corner. "I remind you that this is not a routine self-criticism session; this is not the Tuesday-night cell meeting at the shoe factory. There is information here from the 'special portfolio.' Do you know what that is, Comrade Voronkov?"

Yulya nodded shortly. Secret resolutions adopted by the Central Committee, the contents of the "special portfolio" were circulated only to those officials most directly concerned with implementing them, then returned and destroyed, with copies retained only by the central archive of the Party. This implied that some of the contents of the folder were also directly concerned with high-level state security matters.

"The weather-forecasting program that we bought from the French," said the GRU official after a moment's pause. "How would you rate its overall performance? Was it totally satisfactory, in your opinion?"

"There were a few disappointments at the beginning. As I'm sure you know, there was an entire twenty-four-hour period when it furnished us with highly inaccurate information. Since then we have had no further complaints."

"And how would you characterize its performance during the much briefer period that your institute was being visited by a delegation from the Soviet Academy of Sciences?" This was from Ludkin.

Yulya looked over at Afanasyev, whose face had remained perfectly expressionless ever since its initial flicker of greeting. "I'm not sure I know what you're referring to."

"The American Craig Computer," said the KGB man, with exaggeratedly precise intonations, "and the French computer program! Were they both running all right?"

She inhaled and decided to take the plunge. "Certainly they were; they were running perfectly. I could easily find you a dozen witnesses to testify to that fact, right here in Moscow. And I believe they've already said as much, in a formal report that was submitted many months ago."

She could see Afanasyev's face relaxing. She suddenly felt that she was on the right track. Kutuzov must have resisted interrogation for a very long time. And after they had finally broken him down, they had still had to reckon with the fact that information obtained in this fashion was often quite worthless (except, of course, for the purpose of securing a confession). They would still need confirmation from some other source. Yulya suddenly realized that this commission had been convened as the result of a political compromise between two factions in the Central Committee, one of which, as typified by the members of the original Academy delegation, had done its best to have the whole affair hushed up while Andropov was alive; the other, in the ascendancy since Chernenko had come to power, had since succeeded in having the investigation reopened. But with the commission split three ways, with two each of hard-liners, technocrats, and nonaligned bureaucrats, they were certain to be deadlocked unless the evidence against her was positively overwhelming.

The fact that, unlike Kutuzov, she had not been arrested and summarily tried for some vague but sufficiently serious offense, like "misappropriation of state property" or whatever it was, only furnished additional proof that the Chernenko people were still not totally in control and that things were not necessarily going to be done the old-fashioned way. That was all to the good, of course, but it was difficult to feel a great sense of solidarity with "progressives" like Afanasyev, who stood to gain a great deal of ground if she was cleared of all these charges, but was apparently willing to watch her being carted off to Lubyanka, if necessary, rather than disturb the balance of power any further if things already looked as if they were about to tip the other way.

"If the American computer, the Craig, and the program had not been 'running all right,' it would have been my duty to submit a report to the Ministry of Foreign Trade and the Office of Science and Technology of the Central Committee," she went on, a bit pugnaciously.

"But you didn't, and that's the substance of the second charge against you," said the KGB man.

"I deny that such a charge has any substance to it at all, and I'd like very much to know if any of these allegations have even a scrap of evidence to support them."

The colonel clenched both of his fists on the table, as if to signal that he had finally reached the end of his patience. "I'll have to ask you not to take that truculent tone with the commission, Yulya Nikolaevna! And also to remind you, once again, that we've asked you here not to teach us *our* jobs, but to explain to us exactly how you've been doing yours."

"But don't I have the right to be confronted with the evidence against me?"

"This is not a trial. This is an administrative proceeding."

"If I'm to be condemned out of hand, without any evidence against me, then what's the point of even having a trial? *Or* an administrative proceeding?"

During this exchange, she had not had much leisure in which to study the faces of the other members of the commission, but it was clear, at least, that they did not wholly approve of their colleague's methods. "We have chosen to begin this investigation," Ludkin said mildly, "by taking testimony from you. Surely you cannot possibly object to that. Now tell us, please, how it's possible that the computer and the program could have been working in such perfect harmony and still conspired to produce such wildly inaccurate results, at least during that period under discussion."

"Even the French technicians, in consultation with the specialists who had designed that particular program, were unable to answer that question."

"But isn't that odd," pursued the KGB man, "that the computer, or the program, seems to have inexplicably diagnosed and healed *itself* within a mere twenty-four hours?"

"Very odd, yes. However, the software—the internal instructions that keep the computer running—is extremely complicated, containing tens of thousands of lines of programming code, with millions of possible connections among these various instructions. Computer programs are also notoriously subject to what the Americans call 'finger problems,' trivial programming errors, often extremely difficult to detect, no matter how ruinous the consequences might be. If I had insisted on having a precise diagnosis of the problems that initially plagued the Craig computer, I would have had to assign an entire team of programmers to the job, which would also have meant, quite simply, that a great deal less of the other work of the Institute would have gotten done during that same period. On the other hand, there was no way of telling whether this problem, even if we ignored it completely, was ever going to occur again. In retrospect, I still feel that I must stand by my original decision." There was a brief silence, during which Afanasyev permitted himself a glimmer of a smile.

"Let us suppose," Ludkin said ponderously, "that your account of this incident is perfectly accurate. You believed yourself to be confronted with a mysterious but transitory malfunction of some small part of the computer, rather than a general breakdown of the system, and for that reason you neglected to notify the competent authorities. However, this does not explain the bizarre misconduct of your deputy, Fyodor Ivanovich Kutuzov." This was totally unexpected. She had assumed, illogically, that because their entire case was founded on a confession that had been wrung from Kutuzov under torture, then for some reason his name would never be mentioned during the course of the proceedings. She had borne a terrible burden of guilt, as well, ever since Sergei had succeeded in convincing her that she would only be endangering the safety of her family by making any further attempt to recall her friend from the frightful limbo to which he had been consigned.

At this point, Afanasyev evidently realized that she was not at all prepared to cope with the questions that would undoubtedly follow. In fact, she was on the verge of tears. "But Kutuzov," said Afanasyev, "was notoriously unstable. He had already attracted the attention of State Security as an antisocial element. Didn't you notice anything abnormal about his behavior during the delegation's visit?"

Yulya merely shook her head, and then burst out with the question that had been burning on her lips for so long. "But where *is* he? What's become of him?"

Antonov, from the Ministry of the Interior, leaned forward to speak to her, elbows outthrust on the table. "You have repeatedly assailed the Party Secretariat, the Academy of Sciences, my own department, and the organs of State Security with petitions for his release, demands that you be informed of his whereabouts. Not only is this clearly prejudicial to good Party discipline, it also seems to me to suggest that you have something of a bad conscience as far as this Kutuzov is concerned."

"Of course. He was my closest associate, my friend, the most brilliant programmer I've ever known. And you're quite right. I do have a bad conscience—just as if I'd known that he was going to take his own life and I'd done nothing about it. I blame myself for not having tried to help him."

"And what do you mean by that, precisely?"

"I mean he was clearly having . . . emotional problems. His mental state seemed so *precarious* at times . . ."

Antonov chuckled unpleasantly. "Your diagnosis has subsequently been confirmed by expert psychiatric opinion. He has, in fact, been diagnosed as an incurable schizophrenic, and accordingly has been committed to a psychiatric hospital for an indefinite period of confinement."

Yulya passed a trembling hand over her face and murmured, "I didn't mean he was actually *insane*—"

"That's of little importance," Ludkin said complacently. "Leave psychiatry to the psychiatrists and computers to the, ah, computer programmers—under the leadership and guidance of the Party, of course," he added hastily, as if shocked by this inadvertent heresy. "However, let us get down to cases." With some ceremony, he opened the cover of the folder on the table in front of him. "On being questioned by State Security, F. I. Kutuzov has stated that evidence of certain anomalies in the operation of the Craig 1 computer were deliberately concealed by him—"

Yulya's heart sank. Instead of talking about the computer "breaking down" and all sorts of imprecise, ignorant nonsense of that kind, they were suddenly speaking of *anomalies*, as if they really knew what it was all about. They had finally dropped the old accusation that she had concealed the "breakdown" from the Academy delegation; now they were onto something different. What had already occurred had just been a rehearsal. This was the real thing.

"—and that these anomalies were the result of an act of sabotage carried out by an agent of the Western bloc. Do you claim to be unaware of this fact as well?"

"I couldn't call it a *fact*, exactly. It is one possible explanation, one originally proposed by Kutuzov, which was closely considered on its merits and subsequently rejected immediately after the incident occurred. If I believed the incident itself to have been too trivial to report to the 'competent authorities,' there certainly would not have been very much point in my leveling accusations of sabotage against a foreign power. Certainly it's difficult to see what would be gained by it—by the NATO powers' preventing us from putting out an accurate weather forecast, I mean, for a period of just over twenty-four hours. The French, on the other hand, as developers of the program, stood to lose a great deal if such a charge was ever made public. I myself finally came to the conclusion that if there *had* been an act of sabotage—'vandalism' might be the better term—it must have been carried out by a single individual, motivated perhaps by anti-Soviet or merely sociopathic tendencies. Computer folklore is full of stories about disgruntled programmers who instruct their machines to erase all their data files, for example, the moment their names are deleted from the payroll records—"

"And how many of these anti-Soviet, or merely antisocial, or mentally unbalanced employees do you suppose you're still harboring at that institute of yours?" asked the KGB man.

"The witness need not trouble to answer the question," said Ludkin. "What you've already told us makes it clear that you're quite incapable of distinguishing between a reliable and an unreliable employee, or between a 'trivial incident' and a matter of enormous gravity. But you admit, at any rate, that from a technical standpoint, the possibility of sabotage could not be ruled out?"

"Of course. One of the primary tasks of the Office of Information Research is to prevent just such a thing from occurring in the future."

"In that case," the GRU official said darkly, "you have been guilty of gross dereliction of duty. Apart from Kutuzov's testimony, we have also established beyond a doubt that this weather program of yours had been tampered with by a member of the American Cocom mission while it was ostensibly being 'inspected' on the premises of the French national weather service. A clear-cut act of sabotage, nothing less."

"Precisely," said Ludkin. "An act of naked aggression, in fact. It's just as if they'd sent in a team of saboteurs against one of our most vital research facilities."

"If what you say is true, then I admit that my original analysis of the situation was sadly in error. I've been guilty, even as you say, of gross, inexcusable negligence, and I'm now prepared to submit to the proper punishment." Even if this was not a Tuesday-night cell meeting in the shoe factory, the dénouement was still going to be the same. It would end with her admitting her fault and embracing the rod of chastisement, then lying back and taking her punishment like a loyal Party member.

"For the moment, however," Afanasyev put in, "no *permanent* harm appears to have been done."

"No *serious* harm," Ludkin chimed in immediately. Yulya suddenly felt like jumping up and throwing her arms around his neck, felt like smothering him with kisses. That meant that the bureaucrats Ludkin and Chenyshov, and the technocrats Afanasyev and the GRU computer man, had decided, through some secret process of extrasensory consultation, to block together on this vote; there would be no "exemplary punishment" for her this time. The GRU official gave her a broad, almost salacious smile, as if to assure her that there had been nothing personal in the accusations of gross incompetence and subornation of treason that he had been flinging at her a few moments earlier. The KGB colonel scraped his chair against the parquet and tried to look bored and uninterested.

"There is, of course," said Ludkin, "one way by which all record of this fault might be *erased*—even as you were performing a service of inestimable value to your country. Quite simply, it all depends on what kind of a job you do at this conference in Geneva."

Chenyshov, the man from the VIRO office, spoke up for the first time. "We will not be able to provide temporary exit visas for both your children. You'll have to be content with taking just one of them." *Pushkin, forgive me*, she immediately thought to herself.

"Now that our business here is concluded," Ludkin said blandly, as if they had all just been discussing whether or not the license on her television set should be renewed, "I'm afraid you'll have to be racing off to another appointment. Comrade Gorbachev is eager to have a word with you about this conference."

This was an even bigger surprise. At fifty-three, Mikhail Gorbachev was the youngest full member of the Politburo. Paradoxically, though he was a man who had risen to the top during the Brezhnev era, and had first distinguished himself in the rigidly conservative agricultural sector, Gorbachev was now being proclaimed as the technocrats' great hope for the future. He was politically a centrist, but had shown himself to be increasingly attentive to the demands put forward by the Andropovite reformers and modernizers (very roughly, the Soviet equivalent of the "Atari Democrats" in the United States). The main thing was that Chernenko was known to be seriously ill, and Gorbachev's chances for the succession were said to be very good.

Several months before the death of Yuri Andropov, Gorbachev

had moved up to one of the topmost pinnacles of the Soviet bureau-
cracy, the directorship of the General Office of the Central Committee, a sort of central personnel department that was responsible for
the advancement and replacement of key officials throughout the Soviet Union. This was seen by interested observers as a kind of bureaucratic fortress in which Gorbachev could afford to relax and await
developments, and from which Chernenko's besieging forces had so
far been unsuccessful in dislodging him. The fact that Yulya was
being sent off to an audience with Gorbachev, rather than with just
an official of the Office of Science and Technology, meant that her
forthcoming trip to Geneva was being taken very seriously indeed.

The welcome she received in Gorbachev's office was certainly far
more cordial than the commissioners' had been. The office itself, on a
lower floor, was immense and sparsely furnished, something like a
Western business executive's, she supposed—a type that Gorbachev
superficially somewhat resembled, with the high color in his cheeks
and slightly puffy features, the receding hairline and smiling, sensual
lips of a high-living Eurobusinessman. Certainly he offered a remarkable contrast to Chairman Chernenko, who had the heavy, brooding
features of a Siberian peasant patriarch.

"And what a pleasure, after all this time, finally to meet the famous Yulya Voronkov," said Gorbachev, taking her hand and holding it for perhaps a millisecond longer than was strictly necessary.
"My wife and I have seen you so often on television, of course, that I
almost feel I know you quite well already. And let me say at the
outset that the television cameras do not begin to do you justice. I'm
sure it must feel a bit strange to be the only one of us who's ever
likely to be mistaken for a film actress or a circus trapeze artist."

"I assure you, Comrade Gorbachev, that it's not that particular
aspect of my work that I find the most enjoyable."

"Nevertheless, the foreign press has fallen in love with you,
Yulya Nikolaevna, and I'm afraid we're going to have to make sure
that the love affair, though not necessarily requited on your side, will
have many opportunities to burgeon and flourish during your forthcoming stay in Geneva."

"But I thought I was to be cast more in the heavy character role—

as the public prosecutor, perhaps," said Yulya, trying hard to keep up with this elaborate, mildly flirtatious banter, "rather than as the romantic lead."

"Nothing nearly as dull as that, I trust. In fact, we intend for you to be no less than the field commander of our vanguard forces in Geneva. Far from being merely a forum for our propaganda or what I believe is called 'photo opportunity,' this conference may well turn out to be the first truly decisive battle in this campaign we've been waging to wrest exclusive control of the technology of the future from the hands of the NATO bloc and the Japanese."

"But all false modesty aside, I'm still not sure that's a job I'm particularly well qualified to fill."

"All you will have to do is tell the truth about what's been happening . . . about what excellent use the Americans have been making of the monopoly they enjoy over this advanced computer technology, which they are so anxious to withhold from us in the socialist world. Of course, you realize this makes terribly good sense from their point of view. The societal infrastructure of the West has been steadily eroding since the end of the war. They are desperate to find some way to reverse this steady process of decay. They long to return to the good old days of the Pax Americana, when it was all their empire, when they had the atom bomb all to themselves. But the fabric of our own society is strong enough that we can eventually shake off this terrible malaise of apathy and disaffection with which the capitalist countries have contaminated the entire developed world. This means that we alone can make truly productive use of this new technology. The task to which Yuri Vladimirovich has summoned us is nothing less than this—to make a serious, all-out effort to wrest this prize from the deathgrip of a moribund Western society that is eaten up with all the diseases of multinational capitalism."

Though she had been expecting that Gorbachev would probably treat her to an exhortation of basically this kind—it was one of Afanasyev's favorite themes as well—she had never heard a high-ranking official, least of all Afanasyev, speak like this, in private, with such apparent conviction. She was entirely at a loss for something to offer in reply. "I'm deeply honored," she said, not very originally, "that I'm to be permitted to continue to devote myself to the task for which Comrade Andropov chose me."

Gorbachev gave her a long, searching look and smiled. "One hears all sorts of remarkable tales in a place like this, you know— even some that happen to involve yourself and Yuri Vladimirovich, for example. The sort of thing that you or I or any other sensible person would be inclined to dismiss out of hand as . . . a medical impossibility, as one might say. I'm very glad to have met you, Yulya Nikolaevna, and to have had this opportunity to confirm for myself that Yuri Vladimirovich's trust and confidence have not been misplaced."

Ordinarily, any sort of allusion to the rumor—a very widespread and persistent one, she suspected—that she had become Andropov's mistress during the last weeks of his life was enough to make her livid with rage. The idea was hardly very flattering to her self-esteem. Physically, Andropov had reminded her of nothing more than a frost-killed spider still sitting in the midst of its frozen web. Gorbachev must have realized that any reference to such things—even if phrased entirely in the negative—would almost certainly be very distasteful to her; it seemed like a very strange way of paying her a compliment. Perhaps that was what people meant when they spoke of Mikhail Gorbachev's "candid and disarming manner."

"And I hope," he was saying now, "that this will be the first of many meetings, now that we've made each other's acquaintance after all this time. We've arranged a very full schedule for you tomorrow— you'll be conferring with representatives of all interested state departments, most notably the Department of External Propaganda, of course, and you'll have a chance to work out all the details with them. And if any problems should arise, feel free to come back and take them up with me personally. I know we've kept you quite a long time this evening, but before you rush off again, I hope you'll be able to answer a number of questions I've come up with about your office, what sort of success you've been having . . ."

As the car sped past Luzhniki Park and down the deserted boulevard, Yulya sank back wearily against the soft upholstery, feeling completely drained. The combined experience of the commission of inquiry and Mikhail Gorbachev had been physically, mentally, and emotionally overwhelming. At least she had acquitted herself well enough at the hearing to have been spared a special session with Afanasyev as well, which might have pushed her over the edge completely. She thought of Kutuzov, lying on dirty sheets somewhere, drugged and helpless in a locked hospital ward. *My poor, dear friend,* she thought to herself, *you've finally gotten yourself locked up in the madhouse, the genuine Seventh Circle, and you probably can't even remember what it was all about anymore. And here am I, on the other hand, riding along in the cushy back seat of a government car; I remember perfectly well what it's all about, and there's absolutely nothing I can do to help you. Certainly nothing that I said today could have done much good. They've torn you away from your beloved machines, from your monumental, antisocial debauches at Lyutko's. You, my poor, crazy, drunken Kutuzov, were too much of a threat for them to bear, these men of such tremendous power that the very thought of them made you tremble like a leaf in the wind.*

It was after 4:00 A.M. in Krasnoyarsk by the time she got back to her hotel room. Karimov answered on the second ring. "I've been waiting for your call," he said brightly. "I'm probably going to be here for a few hours more. I still have a little work to do, while you're back there living it up in Moscow, I suppose. Nothing to worry about here, of course. I've got everything under control." Like an actor with just one line to deliver, Karimov had obviously decided to make the most of it. His meaning was nonetheless clear, for all the embellishments. "Everything's under control" meant that the entire network was affected; every one of those machines had been enlisted into the service of the unknown enemy.

TWELVE

September 3, 1984   Geneva

Until she and Svetlana stepped onto the stage of a large meeting hall in the Palais des Congrès, flanked by a couple of sturdy-looking young men from the embassy, the idea of "the Western press" had only been an abstraction. Yulya was hardly prepared for the sight that greeted her eyes. A howling, disorderly mob of reporters, soundmen, and cameramen, bristling with flash attachments and microphones, were surging down the aisles of the hall, shoving and jostling, some of them even leaping straight over the seats like T-shirted, carefully barbered mountain goats. Yulya, in a spectacular red dress designed by Vyacheslav Zaitsev, the leading Moscow couturier, was appalled; Svetlana, wearing the more conventional red and white ensemble of the Soviet Young Pioneers, faced them down with all the aplomb of a seasoned performer.

She and her mother took their places behind the battery of microphones on the stage; the French and English interpreters, in their glassed-in booth at the back of the hall, signaled their readiness to begin. With their quarry in sight, the photographers responded with a blinding communal flash explosion. The special correspondent of the *Nouvel Observateur* nudged his colleague from the *Daily Express* and pointed at the stage. *"Super! Le look!"*

"Something for everybody!" the Englishman shouted back. "Sex appeal for the gentlemen, haute couture for the ladies, mother love for old Mum and Dad at home . . . not to mention an overall air of crisp technical competence for the gentlemen of the press."

Yulya tapped one of the microphones experimentally, and the mob immediately fell silent. "Ladies and gentlemen, kindly allow me to welcome you all in my native tongue," she said in Russian, then switched immediately to English. "But in the interests of efficiency and better international understanding, I think it might be preferable if I spoke with you today in English." She beckoned to the Russian-English interpreter in the booth. "Take off your headphones, comrade! Why not take off the rest of the day, as well?" The interpreter rose gallantly to his feet and made a deep bow. Yulya waited a moment for the general hilarity to subside, then plunged ahead. "Before I start taking your questions, I have a couple of things I'd like to say. First, I think it's clear that no honest observer can dispute that my country has shown itself to be sincerely willing to work for peace—that the Soviet people are willing, and shall always continue to be willing, in the words of our late, deeply regretted leader, Yuri Vladimirovich Andropov, to 'consider even the most audacious proposal in order to push back the nuclear darkness.'" At the mention of Andropov's name, the professional Kremlin-watchers in the audience all nodded to themselves and scribbled happily in their notebooks.

"And, second, I'd like to make a special personal appeal to all of you—and I certainly hope you won't regard this as a criticism, but just as a simple, personal request—that maybe you could concentrate less on some of the more, shall we say, *superficial* aspects of our visit to Geneva. And of course it would be equally wonderful if maybe some of you could concentrate more on the very serious errand that has brought us all here—and, really, on what I'm here to talk to you all about today—my country's very genuine aspirations toward increasing our current store of scientific knowledge, our sincere desire to achieve equal access to some of the material and intellectual benefits of the great informational revolution that is going on in the world today, and also to assist in sharing those benefits among *all* the nations of the world, and of the Third World in particular . . ."

"Bad move," Clive Woodward was saying. "The press doesn't like to be lectured to like that, doesn't like to be told how to do its job by some little KGB snip."

"She got off to a flying start, though," observed Kenneth Clowder, the chief of the U.S. delegation to the conference. "And that little bit of business with the interpreter? Good enough for Gerry Ferraro!"

These two men, along with Brendan Barnes of DISSA and Howard Jackson of the CIA, comprised the nucleus of the crisis-management team that had been dispatched to Geneva to help counteract what one of the embassy press officers had referred to as "a massive Soviet ideological outreach attempt." At the moment they were sitting in the communications room of the U.S. embassy, watching a simulcast of Yulya's press conference (with the original English audio available through a special feed, rather than the French interpreter's voice-over that was being heard on local TV) on a giant monitor screen. To Brendan, this entire scene, with its grotesque overtones of NASA Mission Control and the Pentagon Situation Room, was totally preposterous. He listened impatiently as Woodward and the others pecked away at Yulya's larger-than-life image, unfolding a tedious nonstop commentary on her every word and gesture. They had it all wrong, of course. Still, after a while he began to consider the possibility that *he* was the one who had gotten it wrong. It was hard to imagine that the proud, fiercely intelligent woman he had known in Cambridge could have been transformed into this lacquered mannequin, this glib Soviet bureaucrat posing as an American talk-show hostess, that he was watching on the screen.

". . . and so that no one will be able to accuse me of trying to dictate your articles to you, I'd be glad to answer any questions that you might have. I promise to be perfectly candid about the purpose of my mission, though there is one important item on our agenda that I'm

afraid I can't discuss at this time. I'll be sure to let you know if anyone happens to mention it. Now—questions, please?"

A German reporter in the front row was lucky enough to find
himself standing right next to the long boom microphone that one of
the young men in Yulya's escort was holding over the edge of the
stage. "In connection with the request you've just made to us a moment ago . . . don't you agree that Madame Yulya Voronkov has been
deliberately promoted by your government as a public relations
phenomenon, and that your government seems to have gone over
wholeheartedly to the side of Hollywood and Madison Avenue in
launching this new propaganda campaign against the West?" This
prompted a vast murmur of approval from the crowd.

"Thank you, sir," said Yulya, "for at least crediting me with sufficient intelligence and integrity to be able to answer your question."
Laughter. "I'm not really in the best position to tell you if there is a
Yulya Voronkov 'phenomenon.' I'm simply trying to do my job as I
see it, and I'm sure that if any of the particulars of my age or sex or
appearance had been any different, I'd still be doing that job in more
or less the same way."

The German had tenaciously retained the microphone for a
follow-up question. "But don't you admit that the Soviet government
is making very good use of these particulars you mentioned in order
to prosecute its latest propaganda campaign against the West?"

"We have a saying about that, with which I'm sure you're all
familiar: 'From each according to his abilities.' The Soviet government naturally attempts to make the best use of the particular qualifications of its employees, as does every other government in the
world."

The special correspondent from *Corriere della Sera* had seized the
microphone. "You know you've been called 'the Scarlet Empress'?
How do you react to that?"

"Just put yourself in my place. How would you react? And isn't
there anyone here today who wants to talk about this conference?
About computers?"

"One more question on the personal side," offered a trim young
woman from *People* magazine. "A lot of people here in the West have

been wondering why you've brought your little daughter along with you to Geneva. In fact, a lot of us are wondering why you brought her here today. Couldn't that be considered as kind of an obvious propaganda ploy?"

"Perhaps you'd like to take that one, Svetlana . . ." Loud laughter. "Why don't you tell everyone why you decided to come to Geneva with me?" Svetlana leaned up close to the microphone. "I'm eleven years old now, so I'm old enough to go with my mother wherever she goes." Appreciative mutterings from the press. Svetlana's English was very good, with just a slightly perceptible accent.

"And now," Yulya went on, "why don't you explain why you decided to come here with me today?"

"Because my mother's promised to take me to the opera tonight, and I'm not going to let her out of my sight until she's kept her promise." Loud laughter and thunderous applause.

"A masterly performance," said Woodward. "Full marks for crowd control."

"Better check on that little broad from *People*, see if she's been taking black money," said Jackson, in a voice that made Brendan wonder if he might possibly be serious. "Seems like they couldn't have set it up any better. And the kid speaks better English than anyone—except you, of course, Clive."

"Probably goes to one of their special schools for 'gifted' children—in reality, exclusive prep schools for the sons and daughters of the Soviet elite. And where are you off to all of a sudden, Brendan? I think it's essential that we get your reaction to the entire press conference."

Brendan sat back down again with a groan.

It was the correspondent from Agence France-Presse who finally asked the question. "For the past several weeks we've been hearing rumors that a French computer program that was sold to the Soviet Union has been sabotaged by the American CIA. Is it your impression that these rumors have any truth to them?"

"That, unfortunately, is the one question that I won't be able to answer today. I invite you all to the opening session of the conference, tomorrow. I invite you to listen very carefully to the address I'm going to deliver then. After all, if I told you what it was all about now, I'm sure very few of you would bother to turn up."

The *Washington Post* correspondent caught the eye of the young man holding the microphone. "Madame Voronkov, your country has been buying computer software from the West for many years now. Would you say that the Soviet Union has finally become self-sufficient in this respect, or are you likely to remain dependent on the West for some time to come?"

"I think that in reality we have both become dependent on each other, to a large extent. This may shock you, but the manufacturers of the products we buy from the West are actually turning a profit on these transactions. We're very good customers; we represent an enormous and largely untapped market, and we generally offer very favorable terms. Why not continue to build on this mutually profitable relationship, then? Of course, the problem is that this relationship is complicated by various political restrictions that have been imposed on the export of computer technology to the socialist world. But that's a subject I'd prefer to develop at greater length, in my speech tomorrow."

A Swiss journalist raised his hand. "Could you tell us something more about the specific objectives of the conference itself? Though of course we're delighted to have you all here, I'm afraid that's a point that a lot of us in Geneva are still fairly vague about."

"We feel that the primary object of this conference *should* be three-fold: to guarantee the free exchange of information all over this entire planet, to recognize that exchange as an absolute precondition to sustained friendly relations among all the world's peoples in the future, and finally to fight for the repeal of those discriminatory restrictions of which I was just speaking a moment ago—most notably the surveillance over world commerce in high-technology products that is exercised by organizations such as Cocom."

The editor-in-chief of *Etudes soviétiques* was recognized instantly by the young man with the microphone. "Welcome, Madame Voronkov! Wouldn't you agree that your country's desire to do away with all these embargoes and discriminatory restraints on the free exchange of information and technology is only one *part* of that greater struggle in the cause of world peace that the Soviet Union has continued to wage on *every* possible front?"

"Precisely. And I'm happy to find that there is at least one representative of the Western press here today on whom our message doesn't seem to have been completely lost."

"That," said Woodward, "was strictly for internal consumption. When the text of this press conference appears in *Pravda* tomorrow, of course there'll be no mention that the friendly Western journalist in question is also a distinguished member of the French Communist Party."

Jackson turned toward Brendan. "It's the Kim Il Sung technique. Take out a couple of full-page paid political ads in the *Times*, then you build a big enough backlog of 'spontaneous tributes from the Western press' to last you a couple of years back home."

Brendan had nothing to contribute to this discussion. He was still trying, unsuccessfully so far, to reconcile his own memories of Yulya with the strange talking image he was watching on the television screen. She had been a patriotic Soviet citizen, to be sure, proud of her language and culture, proud of her country's scientific achievements, sentimental about its music and folklore, even its landscapes. Still, as far as the official political line was concerned, she had always seemed to preserve a healthy skepticism, and he could remember several occasions on which she had subjected sentiments of very much the same kind that he had just been hearing—usually voiced by her friend Ludmilla—to merciless ridicule. She had been far too intelligent to be taken in by that sort of Party doubletalk; she had far too much intellectual honesty to indulge in it herself.

A few days earlier he had had a very strange conversation with Sally on that very subject. "You can't deny," she had said to him, "that you've always made her out to be some kind of angel in human form." They were stretched out on an old sheepskin in front of the fireplace, in the cabin in Somerset. They had just finished making love a few minutes before, but it had not been as pleasurable for either of them as it might have been; the reasons for this were only just beginning to become clear.

"Oh, yeah? I thought angels were *always* in human form. And anyway, how come you happen to be thinking about that just now?" He was stroking her bare shoulder, with his eyes closed, dreamily trying to find a favorite beauty spot.

"Well, just think about the kind of things those people have to do to get up to the top of the heap—considerably worse than here, as I've been given to understand . . ."

"She's bound to be more on the technical side of things. I mean, I don't think she can actually see the Gulags out her office window or anything. She really is a brilliant scientist, by the way."

"I should have known you'd stick up for her, you dog."

He pushed himself up on his elbows, looming over her and staring down into her eyes. "You're jealous, aren't you? About something that happened when you were hardly more than a child."

"So were you. So are you still. And such a romantic affair! Remember *Romanoff and Juliet*, with Peter Ustinov? It's your story exactly, except I'm not sure where Peter Ustinov fits in. Anyway, compared to something like that, *our* story's just a tiny bit prosaic, don't you think? I mean, you seem to positively thrive on being on a different continent from me!"

"You have one sure advantage over her, which is, as you know, that's she's just a memory, a phantom, whereas you're right here, in the flesh—"

"Back off, buster, I'm not in the mood right now. I want to talk about this some more, okay?"

"About Yulya? How come?"

"Haven't you seen this week's *Time* magazine?"

"Well, I meant to check it out at the barbershop in town, but I kinda got to talkin' to some of the boys over to the feed store . . ."

"Fine. Stay right there. I've got something to show you."

"Okay, but I warn you, I've pretty much seen it all by now . . ."

Sally ignored him and switched on a table lamp a few feet away; she quickly located the copy of *Time* she had set aside for him. He looked at the picture she showed him.

"It's just an image on glossy paper. It does absolutely nothing for me."

"But you wouldn't mind seeing her again?"

"Well, I wouldn't *mind*, of course . . ."

"You're still in love with her, right?"

"Well, you know, I think that if you've preserved a beautiful memory of someone in your heart, then far better *not* to seek them out and see what they've become . . . the same reason I've always avoided my Princeton class reunions . . ."

"Brendan, I think I'm just beginning to realize I'm serious about this. I'm also just beginning to realize you really *are* still in love with her, and there's no way you can avoid seeing her at this conference. So what's going to happen then? It just makes the way I feel about your working for those people about ten times worse, is all. Do you understand what I'm getting at here, by any chance?"

"I understand," said Brendan, "I really do," and took her in his arms again. This time, though nothing had really been resolved— least of all in his own mind—the tension was gone between them, and there was no holding back.

"Brendan, are you aware that the press conference has just ended?" It was Woodward who had broken in on his thoughts. "What were you thinking about just now, with such ferocious concentration?"

"I was just wondering what the hell I'm sitting here for . . . that kind of thing." Yulya's face had vanished from the huge dull-silver screen. The others were already on their feet.

"We have a meeting with the U.S. trade representative in twenty minutes," said Woodward, "and I'd like to take a moment to discuss what we've just seen, among ourselves. Please follow me, gentlemen . . . Brendan?" Brendan got wearily to his feet. He thought of another, even stranger conversation he had had some time earlier, with Richard Thompson on the night of the reception at the Palais du Luxembourg. Certainly the idea, advanced by Thompson in its most elaborate form, that he had become what was sometimes called "the plaything of vast, impersonal forces beyond his control" was another one of those ideas that it would be difficult for him to refute just now.

At this point, it was even impossible for him to tell exactly when it was that he had lost control of his life. That same night had been almost the last time he had seen Françoise, the last time but once.

That morning, after he had left her apartment, he had immediately made a reservation on the first flight he could get back to New York. It was time, he decided, to recover a little of his perspective—as much as he could manage in a couple of days, at least. He had come so close to falling in love with her that it was impossible for him to feel entirely blameless about walking out on her like that. The reason he had done it, for one thing, almost had more to do with Thompson—certainly an unlikely figure to crop up in the midst of a blighted love affair—than with Françoise herself. There had always been bad faith between them, and from the beginning they had been so intent on manipulating each other that they had not even noticed that they were both being manipulated by Thompson, and much more skillfully and unobtrusively. He had called Thompson first thing that morning to tell him he was taking a couple of days' R-and-R; all that Thompson had said in return was "Good career move." Apparently, when he had left the reception at the Luxembourg with Françoise, this had been classed by the people who kept track of these things as some sort of disciplinary infraction.

He was at the baggage counter, just getting involved in a dispute with a listless Air France clerk about the status of his overnight bag, when he felt a hand on his shoulder. He spun around; it was Françoise, in the same white dress she had been wearing on the night they met.

"Brendan, I'm so glad! I wanted to see you again so much." She had a heavy suitcase with her, strapped into one of those little wheeled racks that stewardesses always carried around with them. Brendan took it from her, and they rolled cozily over to a little indoor café on the departures level. "I see you're off somewhere as well," he said to her as they sat down.

"I'm going back to Martinique for a while . . ." She turned to face him, her face distorted with pain and grief. "Oh, Brendan, a terrible thing's happened! Jacques is dead! He's been killed."

"What happened, for God's sake? And how did you find out?"

"Duvallon came to see me, just after you left. He told me Jacques was shot. Duvallon said it might have been the Americans who did it, the CIA."

"I'm pretty sure that wasn't the way it happened, Françoise."

"That's what Duvallon said when I suggested it might have been the French who had my brother killed. Only he came right out and told me not to be so stupid. He lacks your gift for diplomacy."

"I'm sorry, really. I mean, I'm sorry for you—it's a little difficult for me to feel sorry for him. At least I'm not exactly pleased about it—the way he undoubtedly would have been if it had been me."

Françoise shrugged noncommittally, then simply repeated what Duvallon had told her about Jacques.

"Thompson was suggesting to me last night," said Brendan, when she had finished her story, "that I'd completely relinquished control over my life, a couple of years ago at least. I guess that's what happened to Jacques. Sounds like it might have started to happen to you now, too."

"At least at some point you must have made a decision of some sort. I assume you volunteered to do what you're doing now."

"It seemed like a good idea at the time, you mean? It still does, pretty much. I just have these ideas that things should turn out a certain way—and I think that *they're* a lot less likely to deliver on them than we are, okay? You can think of it as a simple calculation of probability, if the idea of patriotism seems like hopeless bourgeois sentimentality to you, as it undoubtedly does."

"I'm sure the Russians are equally sentimental, and equally bourgeois if it comes to that. I'm sure they also share your concerns about the future. It's not the people who think differently from oneself that one has to watch out for, or so I've been told. And talking of that, I suppose they'll be sending you to this thing in Geneva. You'd better be especially careful there. I understand the famous Yulya Voronkov is going to lead the charge at the head of her cossacks."

Brendan gave an involuntary start. He remembered that he had used exactly the same phrase, in his very first conversation with Yulya. Had Françoise learned to read his mind now as well, along with Woodward and Thompson? "She's making quite a name for herself these days," he said finally. "She works for K. I. Afanasyev, their big computer man."

"It may be the other way around by now. She seems a formidable figure in her own right. Her no less formidable KGB husband was at the Luxembourg last night, as I'm sure you know. He, at least, seems to conform more closely to type. Duvallon, for one, is terrified of him."

Brendan was eager to divert the conversation into safer channels. "Was it just a happy coincidence, then, our running into each other like this?"

"I called Thompson, of course. He told me where you were off to, the gate number and so forth. And of course, I had to use torture to get it out of him. I told him if I didn't get a chance to say good-bye to you, I'd start taking my story around to all the left-wing papers, just in time for the evening edition." Brendan had been momentarily toying with the notion that Thompson had some kind of rudimentary moral sense, and was trying to make amends in a very small way. The moment had passed quickly enough.

He reached over to take her hand. To his surprise, she pulled back immediately and rose to her feet, almost knocking over her chair. She stared down at him with a masklike, wooden face, as if she had suddenly decided that she hated him after all. "I'm still not sure I should even be talking to you. And I'm sure you still have no idea where you're actually going! Isn't that what gets people into such terrible trouble?"

"You're so right. That's what I'm going back home to think about for a little while. That's what I was trying to say a minute ago, before you insisted on dragging in all this high-level foreign-policy stuff."

"So now you're finally getting around to your great existential crisis! I had mine when I was fifteen, you know—and that was in a very culturally backward area."

"I think it's probably just a mild case of burnout. Existentially, I should be as right as rain in a week or so."

"What we call a *crise des nerfs*? You *better* get over it. Those nerves of yours are going to have to stand you in very good stead when you get to Geneva, you know. What if Colonel Sergei Voronkov finds out you've been dozing at the switch—is that the expression?"

"You're very well briefed today, Françoise. I'd have thought Duvallon would have cut you off the distribution list after all that's happened. Or isn't that all from him?"

"The part about Geneva is actually public knowledge, if you even know what that is. A Tass news dispatch. And let me say at once that I heard it over the radio this morning, since you seem to be implying I have some sort of direct line to Moscow!"

Brendan was suddenly on his feet as well. They could think of nothing better to do than stand and glare at each other for a moment, their faces a few inches apart. Then they both burst out laughing simultaneously.

"Isn't it wonderful," said Françoise when she had finally regained control of her voice, "that we've had a chance to share these last few tender moments together?"

"But I hope we'll see each other again, Françoise. I *know* we will."

"I hope we will too. But you still have some important business affairs to wind up, wasn't that it? Listen, I think they're calling my flight. I have to go. Write to me at the old address, Rue des Guillemites. They'll send it on to me."

"Au revoir, ma belle!"

"Good-bye, my brave little soldier! Take care of yourself, all right?" They embraced quickly, and then Françoise sped off down the concourse with her suitcase. He watched until he could see her, or rather the small white rectangle of her dress, disappearing around a corner at the end of a long corridor.

For the duration of his stay in Switzerland, Woodward had requisitioned a large, luxurious office from some vacationing diplomat. "Take a chair," he instructed Brendan. "You seem a little off-color today. Feeling all right?"

"I'm fine, thanks. But about this press conference. What are these 'reactions' of mine that you're so eager to discuss? I thought it had great production values, but basically lacked authenticity . . . and I hope you didn't get me over here just to watch TV programs, or talk about Yulya Voronkov, or try to turn me into some kind of freaking Manchurian Candidate or something."

"I'm not sure I catch the reference. And if you don't feel like talking about Yulya Voronkov at the moment, then I most certainly do. She's the key to this whole situation, and I'm sure you can't claim to be unaware that it was your personal history with her that made you such an excellent candidate—Manchurian or otherwise—for the position you now hold."

"I thought I was being called in as a consultant on some kind of new intelligence program, not 'I Was a Nerd for the CIA'! What do you want me to do, ask her out for drinks and then try to sweet-talk her into defecting, or just set her up for a hit, or whatever the fuck you guys call it? Or just a simple case of entrapment, perhaps? 'Nerd Snares Scarlet Empress in Swiss Love Nest!' Is that the basic *idea*, at least?"

Woodward was grinning broadly. "Brendan, I had no idea you had such a flair! And since you've asked, any of the various scenarios you've just outlined would be entirely acceptable, except that one contingency, which you just referred to a moment ago as a 'hit,' has been definitely ruled out. I think that otherwise the choice should ultimately be yours, however, don't you agree?"

"I'm sorry I got out of line on that one, chief," said Brendan, with what he hoped was transparent irony. "Just a little jet-lagged out, I guess. Or maybe it's that I forget sometimes that everyone else in the world is crazy except me."

"Yulya Voronkov," Woodward went on imperturbably, "according to our most recent profile analysis, is currently in a very vulnerable position. She owes her entire career to this so-called modernist tendency within the Soviet administration. Now, of course, the old guard has come back into power with the accession of Mr. Chernenko. Gorbachev, of course, is comfortably ensconced in the wings, but he's not strictly a modernist, except perhaps for public-relations purposes in the West, though he is admittedly far less of a dinosaur than either Chernenko or Brezhnev. At any rate, it seems like a safe bet that the trajectory of Madame Voronkov's recent meteoric rise has begun to flatten out in the last few weeks—I'm speaking of genuine power and influence, of course, not propaganda glitter. We know that she was summoned to Moscow to give evidence before a tribunal of the Central Committee that has been investigating the program failure at Krasnoyarsk.

"Obviously, considering all the work they've put into the construction of her public image, the fact that she hasn't simply disappeared from sight doesn't necessarily mean she's *not* still in disgrace, to some extent at least, because of what happened at Krasnoyarsk. She may simply have been released on probation, and primarily for the purpose of accomplishing this one final mission. Then, quite possibly, she'll be recalled to Moscow, and that will be the end of her as a public figure, or even a figure of any kind, I expect. I've been rereading the transcripts of your NSA security clearance interviews, especially those passages relating to Yulya Techayev, as she was then called. One moment, in fact."

He picked up a typed page from a folder on the desk and began to read. "'She believed that ideological differences among nations would eventually become less pronounced. She believed that the computerization of her own country would help to abolish waste and what they refer to as "economic crimes and parasitism"—embezzling and stealing, I suppose. She also felt that the "rationalization" of their economy, as the Europeans call it, would ultimately bring about the abolition of special privileges for the ruling elite, at least for the most part—kind of a Cultural Revolution kind of idea, I guess. She believed that it was far from certain that all these changes would necessarily come about, and she felt it was kind of her duty to go back there and try to make sure that they did. She wanted to go home and fight the good fight is about what it boils down to.'"

"All right," said Brendan. "I think I've finally got the idea now. You want me to help you take her out because she betrayed the ideals we all had during the sixties, right? I'm surprised you didn't read the part about how she thought that Soviet dissidents were 'objective traitors' to their country because they ended up helping the West. I remember that part quite distinctly. She also recognized that her country had a hell of a long way to go before it could claim to be truly socialist, let alone democratic. The woman I knew was your basic fiery young Slavic type, full of romantic ideals—and I can make absolutely no connection between her and that scarlet Barbara Walters that I saw on TV just now."

"I might add," said Woodward, "that she's also the mother of a very charming young girl—and a little boy, as well, who was obliged to remain at home. That means, as I'm sure you know, that the Central Committee is definitely hedging its bets."

Brendan looked at Woodward curiously, trying for a moment to imagine him as a little boy, in Charleston or wherever it was. The experiment was not a success.

Woodward went on, "I know you think that what I've told you is just another of my long-winded, obsessive disquisitions on Soviet policy. In fact, what I've just told you is merely a précis—stripped of its preposterous Freudian jargon—of a report prepared by a panel of psychologists working for the CIA."

"They should be working *on* the CIA, by all accounts. And what role do they see me, the old college sweetheart—the regressive male degradation symbol, or whatever it is—finally playing in all this?"

"You know as well as I do that the subjective element plays a very large part in the formulation of programs, as well as in the detection of bugs, or in their deliberate implantation, I might add. The Soviets have already framed their indictment. They are getting ready to put us on trial at this conference, and as always, they like to know how a trial's going to turn out in advance. They have programmed these events to turn out in a certain way, in other words. You, Dr. Brendan Barnes, are going to be the bug in this particular program. We are going to put you in contact with Yulya Voronkov, and you are going to convince her that it will be entirely in her own interest *not* to carry out her instructions in this matter."

"I tried something like that about twelve years ago, if you don't mind my getting personal all of a sudden, and it didn't work. Not at all."

Woodward smiled. "That was because you didn't know the right things to say. You might begin, for example, by asking her to 'give us a break,' as you might conceivably put it, or to mitigate the force of her accusations against us. She will say that that's quite impossible, because her superiors would never forgive her for a second dereliction of duty while she was still supposed to be doing penance for the first. She'll remind you that the future happiness of her children is at stake and that that imposes a serious constraint on her own freedom of action. You'll ask her just to give you something, some little scrap of information that will do something to counterbalance the disastrous effect that her address is sure to have on our political position at this conference. For example, we have reason to believe the Soviet Union has been unable to resist the temptation to try to turn one or two of the Communist ministers on the French cabinet. In a more general way, it would be very helpful to have some specific information that would enable us to frame our own indictment of the various clandestine channels through which high-technology contraband has still been able to reach the Soviet Union, in spite of all the efforts of your erstwhile colleagues from Cocom."

"And why should she give me anything like that? For auld lang syne, my dear, and nothing more? Is that what all this bullshit 'profile analysis' adds up to? 'Subject will undoubtedly be influenced by the fact that her old boyfriend's turned into such a sorry mess, that he's sunk so low he's become a stooge for the CIA'?"

"A more compelling reason might be found—namely, the threat of a Third World War."

"So you think that Chernenko, this diehard antitechnologist, is really ready to go to war with us over this one? We simply refuse to rescind any of our export controls—whether this damned resolution is adopted by the conference or not. And immediately Silicon Valley is a smoking ember, and Russian tanks are rumbling down Route 128. Is that the way you really see it happening, Clive?"

"I don't think, for all your talk about 'resisting Soviet ideological penetration,' that you fully understand what's at stake here. Consider what Mr. Chernenko would stand to gain by detaching the other technology-exporting countries from their allegiance to Cocom. The removal of these political restraints would result in a significant and virtually instantaneous upgrading of Soviet defense capabilities—at present, for example, the circuitry in the guidance system of the SS-20 is little more than spit and tinsel. The confidence of our

NATO allies has already been profoundly shaken; this might convince them that they'd be better off trying to strike some sort of separate bargain with the Russians. It's easy enough to see how the effects of this are going to be profoundly destabilizing—and a Soviet liberal might very well be alarmed by the prospect of what the government hard-liners and the Soviet defense establishment might be tempted to do in a case like that."

"Still won't wash, Clive. I don't think I can talk her into betraying her country just to save us from taking a beating."

"Very well. Consider this. We are currently in the midst of a presidential election campaign. Jimmy Carter was brought down because he failed to display the proper firmness during a similar test of our national resolve—the Iranian hostage crisis. We are supposed to be in the midst of a great revival of old-fashioned patriotic and nationalistic sentiment—as, I might add, are the Russians. The present administration is likely to have these factors uppermost in its mind in considering its reaction to this Soviet ideological offensive. That reaction is likely to be intemperate; this time, like the Ayatollah on an earlier occasion, they will feel perfectly confident that even the most aggressive measures will receive the full support of an aroused and militant population. Thus, the possibility of a total embargo on *all* commerce of any kind with the Eastern bloc is not necessarily to be ruled out, and the Soviet leaders, in turn, would be under very great pressure to respond with equally vigorous countermeasures to avoid serious economic dislocations within their own society.

"To you, this may seem wildly exaggerated, even preposterous, but I think that, as you say, your basic Soviet liberal idealist might find this particular scenario quite convincing. At any rate, the current administration is determined to resist any further Soviet encroachments on what it has come to regard as its traditional sphere of influence; with the hard-liners in power in both Washington and Moscow, we may rest assured that the next serious world crisis that comes along could quickly develop into an all-out battle of the titans . . ."

"You keep implying that this is some sort of smartass disinformation act that you've cooked up—in consultation with your panel of leading psychiatrists, of course. I'm not sure she's going to go for any of it. You don't even believe very much of this yourself, do you?"

"Indeed I do," Woodward replied. "Some of the things I've told you might have been exaggerated a bit for what might be called promotional purposes, but essentially, yes, I do believe that this thing could very easily push us to within a few millimeters of the brink. I don't mean to imply that you should restrict yourself to these purely political appeals when you make your approach to Madame Voronkov. Anything personal that you can think of . . . I was about to say that no considerations of delicacy should hold you back, but in this case it scarcely seems necessary . . ." Brendan was pleased that Woodward had been unable to resist the temptation to get in a jab of his own.

"Finally," Woodward went on, after letting his last words hang in the air for a suitably long time, "one personal question that I *can* advise you on. She knows perfectly well that the ax is quite likely to fall within days or weeks of her return from this conference. You may offer her every assurance that if she cooperates with us on this, we'll have quite a bit of political leverage to exercise on the Soviets. And in that case, we should have no difficulty in getting both of her children out of the Soviet Union, if she wishes to remain with us . . . for a bit longer than originally planned."

"Okay, I think you're starting to make a little more sense. Just tell me one thing, Clive. Why is it that in all the time we've been working on this thing together, you never even mentioned her name to me before today?"

"I might almost ask you the same question, Brendan. It would have been very easy for you to verify that this Y. N. Voronkov, this new guiding star of the Soviet computerization program, was the same person as Yulya Techayev, who had returned to the Soviet Union over ten years earlier with precisely that idea in mind. Thompson tells me that he himself provided you with an excellent opportunity to do so, many months ago. And I must say, at the risk of provoking further displays of outraged innocence on your part, that this all matches up quite well with your own psychological profile."

"Go ahead. Tell me all about it, and I promise you won't hear a squawk out of me."

"The gist of it seems to be that you have become so deeply attached to an idealized psychic image of 'your Yulya' that you are extremely reluctant to risk destroying or degrading this ideal image by confronting it with the reality of 'their Yulya' and all that she may have become in the interim."

"Okay. So what was in it for you, then? I mean, apart from the purely intellectual satisfaction of nosing around in another person's private life and cynically manipulating his emotions to further your own peculiar designs? If that's not too personal a question, I mean."

"Rather than think of it in those terms, why not think of yourself as having been the beneficiary of a kind of affirmative-action program? There were a number of candidates for the post, all more or less equally qualified, and you happened to have been the only one among them who had ever had a love affair with a woman who was almost certain to become a leading light of the Soviet computerization program. In selecting a candidate for a post of this kind, where the nontechnical qualifications are impossible to define except in a very sketchy, *subjective* way, all sorts of factors have to be taken into account. That was one of them. It was not necessarily the decisive one, except in retrospect, perhaps. It might just as easily have come to nothing. Yulya Voronkov might have taken up a harmless academic post, been denounced by a colleague as 'socially unreliable,' and been shunted off onto a different track at any point during her career. However, as you know, that was not the way it happened.

"There's one other thing I'd like to say to you, Brendan. And while you don't seem to be in a terribly receptive frame of mind at the moment, I would like to point out that *if* you had come to me at any time and said, 'This Y. N. Voronkov? Is she the one? And what the hell do you think you're doing?' then I would have told you exactly what I'm telling you now. It was not my Machiavellian disdain for the dignity of the human spirit that restrained me from letting you in on the secret; it was your own apparently deep-seated reluctance to face the truth that prevented you from coming to me. This was entirely your affair—your own personal business, I mean—and if you were concerned that you were being manipulated in some way that you disapproved of, then it was your responsibility to take that up with me."

Brendan felt more as if he had been argued into a corner than genuinely convinced of the truth of what Woodward was saying. Still, it was true that for a long time he had resisted the idea that Y. N. Voronkov was Yulya; when the evidence became overwhelming, he had still refused to come to terms with it and had preferred to distract himself with complicated conspiracy theories—none of them without some basis in fact, of course—involving Thompson and Woodward and the rest of them. He did think those idiot psychologists had slipped up when they claimed that he had preserved an "idealized image" of Yulya in his mind; at the moment it seemed like a very real one, the exact, living image of a face he had first encountered in the midst of a crowded, cacophonous university dining hall, then blinking in the glare of his headlights on a windy night down by the river, in November of 1972.

"Brendan," Woodward was saying, "you know that it's more in my nature to amplify than to summarize, but I think I can reduce it all to one basic point. The details of your mental and emotional life are really no concern of mine, *except* insofar as they might affect your efficiency, for good or ill, first as a consultant on the Softwar program, and now as an essential actor in a little drama of a very different kind. Certainly I've never made it a practice, as you seem to think, to interfere in anyone's personal life, least of all for the sheer pleasure of it. But I see how you might feel that you've been victimized, and if you still feel that any undue liberties have been taken, then I apologize sincerely. I can only say in my defense, once again, that if you'd come to me earlier, I think you could have spared yourself a great deal of unnecessary anguish."

Brendan simply stared back at him. It was interesting that Woodward's most compelling argument was also unverifiable. It was equally possible that if he *had* talked to him about this at some time in the past, then Woodward would simply have told him whatever best suited his purposes at the time. It did seem as though they were going to be sending out the wrong person to talk to Yulya. If there was anyone who could convince her that everything she knew to be true was false, and vice versa . . . He looked over at the nattily dressed old professor on the other side of the wide, shiny desk—bright, glittering eyes, sharp, patrician features, the shock of pure white hair.

Perhaps he would have to suspend judgment on it altogether—on the questions of whether Woodward was a brilliant scientist with a remarkable intuition into the human soul, or a fascist megalomaniac who had deliberately stripped himself of all human emotions for the sake of operational efficiency. Perhaps this was just another of those mysteries that the human mind was not meant to penetrate. He felt much the same way he always did after he and Sally had had one of their "discussions"; nothing had really been resolved, but somehow the basic tensions and instability of the relationship had been appeased until another time. Perhaps his involvement in this project of Woodward's was not so very different from his relationship with Sally: he could easily and happily imagine it being otherwise in many secondary respects, but he could not imagine the alternative of simply walking away from it.

"Mama, look at that!" cried Svetlana. She was pointing excitedly at an exquisite candy cuckoo clock reposing on the counter, under glass. A waitress in a black skirt and white apron, heavily laden with pastries and carrying a spade-shaped cake knife at the ready, obliged with a lengthy list of ingredients, in French: marzipan, chocolate, chantilly, praline filling . . .

"What's she saying, Mama? What is it?" Svetlana shouted, with a febrile consumerist glint in her eye. Yulya put her arms around her neck and held her for a moment, laughing, before providing a translation.

"And are we going to get that one, too?"

"No, Svetlanochka. We want them to have something to sell to the other customers after we've gone. You know that dancers can't really keep stuffing themselves with chocolate marzipan for very long before it starts to show. Purity of line, isn't that right?"

"Quite right," said Svetlana, fingering her Young Pioneer kerchief and assuming an expression of socialist self-sacrifice.

The two silent young men from the embassy were waiting for them on the sidewalk; passersby would occasionally permit themselves a sly sidelong glance at Yulya or Svetlana. By Genevan standards, the press conference had clearly been an enormous sensation. As soon as they had gotten back to the embassy, Svetlana had started in about *shopping* until Yulya began to regret that she had ever taught her a word in English. They had set out on a slow and methodical sweep of the principal shopping streets; there was something in every store window that caught Svetlana's eye, and Yulya had already dispensed a great many grave warnings about the folly of not deferring at least some of one's hard-currency purchases until one's first day in Paris. It had been a pleasant afternoon; for a couple of hours, at least, she had almost stopped worrying about Alyosha and her opening address to the conference, two subjects that had divided her attention almost equally until then. It was always rather pleasant to be in a Western city, especially so when you were seeing it all for the first time through the eyes of a child. Less pleasant was the fact that the eyes of this particular child seemed unable to overlook anything that was both highly portable and expensive.

"Look, Mama! Is that what they call video games?" Svetlana had plunged ahead for a couple of yards and stopped in front of a window filled with gaudy East Asian electronics. Yulya glanced idly at the display, then at her reflection in the window, and patted a vagrant strand of hair into place. She realized there was someone standing directly behind her. She turned around. It was Brendan.

He looked a little thinner, not too much older, his face perhaps just a little sadder, his eyes and hair as black as ever. He was just standing and smiling at her, just as if it were the most natural thing in the world for them to be running into each other in front of a toy store in Geneva, as if they'd simply arranged to meet there after two or three days apart.

"Brendan!"

"I had a bet with someone that you'd be even more beautiful than the way I remember you. And you are."

"*Mama, kto eta?*" Svetlana asked fearfully as Brendan smiled down at her with a strange, dreamy look in his eyes. Yulya put up a hand sharply as a signal to the two embassy watchdogs that they were not to interfere. "It's a ghost," she told Svetlana, in English. "A very nice ghost . . . a professor I used to know in America."

"*Razvye on Amerikanets, Mama?*" cried Svetlana, staring back at him in disbelief.

"I happen to know that you speak English, and very well, too," he said to her. "I saw you both on television. Here, I have something for you. Welcome to Geneva." He held out a pastry box tied up with red string. Svetlana's eyes opened wide when she recognized the name of the bakery. After he had seen them come out, it had taken him a few minutes to catch up to them after he had gone in and made his inquiries, and then waited while the counterwoman carefully wrapped up the marzipan cuckoo clock.

Svetlana still drew back uncertainly, and Yulya finally took the package from Brendan's outstretched hand. Until that moment they had refused to allow their eyes to meet. Yulya quickly looked down at the pavement. Brendan cleared his throat nervously.

"Yulya, I have to talk to you—I really do. It's pretty serious."

"I'm afraid that's impossible. I really can't."

"I swear, it's important . . ." Brendan glanced back over his shoulder and saw that one of the security men was drawing closer, though still very slowly and tentatively. "I'm afraid I have to insist. It's really more important than anything, for both of us, for all of us." He had removed a little oblong of plastic that looked something like a credit card from his pocket and slid it between two fingers of Yulya's right hand as she grasped the parcel. "The mag card for my room at the Hilton. Come directly there, if there's no other way. If I'm out, ask at the desk; they'll know where to find me."

The trench-coated bulk of the security man had suddenly interposed itself between them. He held up an arm as if to push Brendan away, but Brendan was already walking briskly down the street. "I can't!" Yulya was calling after him. "I really can't!"

He had been back in his room for over an hour when the telephone rang. "Jesus," he said aloud. "Woodward!" But the hotel operator informed him that the call was from the Soviet embassy.

"Changed my mind. If you're free tonight, want to get together for dinner? Just the two of us?"

THIRTEEN

"Don't lean over too far, dear. You don't want to fall down and hurt yourself on one of those lovely tiaras." Absolutely no response. Svetlana was craning her neck out over the rail of the embassy box at the Grand Théâtre; the décor was similar enough to a Russian opera house that she was interested exclusively in the remarkable appearance of the bejeweled ladies and the gentlemen in evening dress in the orchestra below. The great velvet curtain gave a premonitory groan before it began to part, and the house lights went down. At once, Svetlana was settled back in her seat expectantly, and her mother leaned over and murmured in her ear, "I have to go now, pet. Manya's going to take you back to the embassy, so try not to get on her nerves too much. And don't eat too much ice cream during the intermission, all right? I'll try very hard to get back before you're asleep, but whether I am or not, I want you to start getting ready for bed just as soon as you get back, all right?" Svetlana nodded hypnotically, without taking her eyes off the stage. The orchestra launched into the opening measures of *Swan Lake*.

Just as Yulya was reaching for the handle, the door of the box flew open of its own accord. Sergei was standing there in a blaze of light from the corridor.

"Aha, so it's you," said Yulya.

"Is that all the welcome I get? I flew all the way down from Paris just to have a little talk with you."

As soon as she heard her father's voice, Svetlana leaped up from her seat and ran over to him; he bent down so she could kiss him on both cheeks. "Papa! Have you come to watch *Swan Lake* with me?"

"Not exactly, little one. I've got something important to discuss with your mother first."

"Is everything all right? We don't have to go back, do we?"

"No, nothing like that. Aren't you missing your ballet?" Svetlana looked at him anxiously for a moment, then returned to her seat, leaned all the way forward until her chin touched the rail, and was immediately enthralled. Yulya and Sergei remained standing at the rear of the box.

"What's going on?" she whispered. "You look as if you're about ready to strangle someone, for one thing."

"Guess who."

"Wonderful!" She picked up her purse, which she had slung over the back of one of the seats. "I hate to disappoint you, but I'm afraid I have another engagement."

"I know all about it. You're going to visit your American boyfriend in his hotel room, aren't you? He had the nerve to make an open assignation with you in the public street."

"Why don't you shout a little louder?"

"I'll shout as loud as I damn well please!"

There was a chorus of hisses and angry mutterings from the adjoining boxes. Svetlana drew back into her seat, arms clutched around her chest, deeply mortified.

"Don't you think it's a little late for you, of *all* people, to start making jealous scenes?"

"You're perfectly prepared to break up your family so you can go back to him. You're getting ready to defect, isn't that right?"

"If you insist on being loud, at least try not to be stupid. I'm going to have dinner with Brendan Barnes. That's all. The ambassador, for one, thinks it's a splendid idea, and I'm sure your people know all about it too. So why don't you sit down and watch the ballet, before you make a complete ass of yourself?"

"The ambassador doesn't know you as well as I do. He thinks you'd never run off and abandon your own daughter. I know better than that."

"You really disgust me, Sergei! And you're drunk besides. Why don't you go crawl under a bridge somewhere and sleep it off? Don't say anything else you're going to regret. You'll be feeling bad enough tomorrow as it is, by the look of you." Yulya made for the door again, but Sergei caught hold of her shoulder. She struggled to free herself from his grasp; the strap of her purse suddenly gave way, spilling most of the purse's contents onto the thick carpet. She bent down to retrieve them and handed the mirror and compact, the tissues, scraps of paper, and cosmetics all over to Manya, with a pleading look. She was relieved to see that Svetlana was still completely engrossed in the ballet. She got up again, to find Sergei still blocking her path.

"I know that you were lovers when you were in America."

"I thought you'd found out a long time ago. You've always been so good at finding things out."

"And you're always so calm and serene and sure of yourself! I know you despise me! You think that you've gotten where *you* are because you're so damned smart, but I've only been able to get where *I* am because I'm ready to get down in the dirt and I don't care who my friends are, and because I married you. That's what you think, isn't it? You think that fat pig Afanasyev is after you for your brains, don't you? And poor old Andropov, and that slimy pimp Gorbachev? I'll tell you what they're after, if you like—"

Yulya shot him a minatory look that kept him from finishing the sentence. "Do you get some kind of perverted thrill out of talking like that in front of your own child? Is it because that's one of the few disgusting things you can't do down at Lyutko's?"

"She's not paying the least bit of attention . . . and she's not my child!" he added triumphantly, though still not daring to raise his voice very loud. "She's his, his child! You two can march yourselves over to the American embassy right now, for all I care! I don't give a shit about either of you! But Alyosha's mine! My son! And I'm going to keep him!"

"Sergei, my bodyguard's standing out in the corridor, and if you don't leave me alone within one second, he's going to be kicking you right down those four flights of stairs out there, and I'm going to be on the phone to the embassy, telling them you turned up drunk in a public place, raving incoherently about the American embassy and defecting to the West! That's one second you have."

Sergei pressed the palms of his hands together, as if he were trying to obliterate some small, invisible object. He stood glowering at her for a moment, then opened the door and disappeared. Yulya glanced over at Svetlana, still completely immersed in the spectacle on stage. She came up behind her and stroked her hair. No reaction. She was watching the pas de deux between the heroine, Odette, and Rothbart, the evil wizard.

"Ah, Madame will have the frogs' legs . . . *gratin de cuisses de grenouilles*, and I'll have the *cassolette de queues d'écrevisses*."

"The crayfish, monsieur?" said the waiter. "Very good."

"He just wanted to humiliate me by making me try to speak French," said Brendan. "There's a great restaurant in the Parc des Eaux Vives. I wanted to take you there, but this place sounded like it would be a little more private."

"I don't even know where we are, you know."

"Right off the Place de la Taconerie."

Yulya smiled. "No, I mean *when* we are, I suppose. What year it is. It seems just like we've slipped out of time for a moment. It's so strange . . ."

"Maybe it's just all this local color," said Brendan, tapping the tablecloth with his fist. They were alone in the tiny back room of the restaurant; the checkered tablecloth and most of the furnishings were indeed covered with alternating squares of red and beige, the heraldic colors of Geneva, the walls with old-fashioned steel engravings of Jean Jacques Rousseau botanizing in alpine meadows. Brendan had examined these minutely while waiting for Yulya to turn up. "The quintessence," he added, "of the 'pretty nice but a little out-of-the-way restaurant.' And seriously, I do know what you mean. It's like we're castaways on a desert island—an island where they're just about to serve dinner, as luck would have it."

"Is that why there are so many frogs and crayfish about? That reminds me, is that Lotus place still good, out by Fresh Pond, the one we used to go to?"

Brendan laughed. "Jesus, I don't know. I haven't been there in years! I'm glad you haven't lost your taste—"

"Taste for what?"

"You know. Ta-chien chicken, life, and all of life's little pleasures. Three things you were very big on at one time, as I recall . . ."

Yulya wished there were something she could do to prevent the blood from rushing to color her cheeks like that. She hated that tingly, schoolgirl feeling, though the memories that had flooded into her mind were of a slightly later vintage. She felt vastly relieved when the maître d' arrived with the bottle of Chablis that they had ordered. Brendan obligingly submitted to the ritual of sniffing the cork and swishing wine around in his cheeks before the maître d' could fill their glasses.

"No offense," said Brendan, "but did you have to get permission to have dinner with me tonight?"

"Not really. I simply informed the embassy people of my plans for the evening, and there was no objection."

"I must confess that surprises me a little."

"What would be the point of anyone's making a fuss? We're allowed to talk to people occasionally, you know—and if frogs' legs are also involved, then so much the better."

"As long as we agree only to discuss the distant past, is that right?"

"Hmph. I like that word 'only.' Also 'distant.' Not very tactful when you're talking to your old lover, after all. And anyway, I know you're going to want to range free over all of space and time, past, present, and future, so go right ahead. It's possible that we still might have a few things to talk about after all. Even if perhaps I'm not in a position to range quite so freely as you are."

"Why not?"

"Well, you know, the people I work for aren't very tolerant of indiscretion. Though I suppose that might be true of the people you work for, too. Are you even allowed to admit it? That you work for people, I mean?"

"They'd blow me away in a minute if they knew I'd even told you this much. And once again, at the risk of being offensive, has that got anything to do with why you haven't brought your little boy with you? Alexei, right?"

"He's still too young for 'Alexei.' We call him Alyosha. What else do you know about me?"

"Your husband, Sergei, is a colonel in the KGB. He's the 'political coordinator for scientific research in Central Siberia'—sounds like a bullshit job to me, I must admit. Svetlana, of course. Incredibly cute, but still a little on the shy side." He stopped for a moment and watched Yulya fidgeting with the stem of her wineglass. "It's empty. The wine comes out the top, you know, not the bottom. Why don't you let me fill your glass again?" He did so.

"Sorry," she said, "for embarrassing you in front of all these people. It's just that I thought you had something very important to discuss. 'Important for all of us,' is what you said. I left Svetlana at the ballet, with her father, so I could come here and talk to you. If it was just to chat, then I don't know why you went through that incredible charade of slipping me your room key and everything, in front of those two men from the embassy."

Brendan looked at her for a moment in silence, then grinned wickedly at her. "Why do you think I slipped you my room key? I mean, *dinner* was entirely your idea . . ."

The waiter arrived with the appetizers, and for a moment they simply watched the steam rising from the serving dishes and looked at each other inquiringly.

"Why didn't you answer any of my letters?" he asked finally.

"Why do you think? Because I never got them."

"Go ahead, eat. You know, I even went to a conference in Leningrad, in 1976. I asked after you. Somebody thought you were working in Kiev or someplace."

"No, I was still at the same place. First Vitebsk, then Minsk, actually. I believe you about the letters, but you know, if you really had come to see me, the answer still would have been the same."

"I know. I just felt like hearing it again, was all."

"Were you already working for the CIA back then? I know it's not called that, exactly. It's DISSA, isn't it?—and of course Cocom, the people that destroyed my program in Krasnoyarsk. You heard about that, I expect?"

"Okay. The time has come, the Walrus said. I told you I had something very serious to talk to you about. Here it is. I know the way you feel about what happened to your program and all, but I don't think it necessarily means we should all step outside for a nuclear showdown. I mean, the fact that we both got away with it in 1962 means that this time we may not be so lucky. All right, I've just about got it memorized, what I wanted to say to you. So just listen for moment, okay?"

Yulya listened silently and impassively as Brendan began to speak his piece. He had spent most of the afternoon closeted with Woodward's briefing team, trying to refine their lunatic escalation scenarios and conflict-resolution studies into a single, compelling chain of reasoning—something that might possibly convince her that neither of their two governments could be relied on to deal with this crisis in a wholly rational manner.

"There you have it," he finally said. "That's the final position. Not *my* position, necessarily, but *our* position, okay? It's just exactly the same as one of my favorite sayings: 'You got to know how to take it, and you got to know when to stop.' And the point of all this is, this job I have has put me in contact with some very crazy people, and I'm not sure they can be trusted to keep on taking it for very much longer. And I'm sure you could say the same."

"Can I take it you're still interested in boxing?" was the only response to Brendan's carefully prepared twenty-minute oration.

"Yeah, a little, when I have the time. I see that I've just ruined a lovely dinner by running on about this boring political stuff when we could have been talking about boxing and our different hobbies and everything. Sorry. I see that you're just another grimy little foot soldier like me, and unlike me, you've got your little boy at home to worry about . . ."

"You know that what your crazy friends did to that program—that cost me the best friend I have in this world! The only one clever enough, unfortunately, to figure out all that stupid business about St. Thomas and 1028 millibars. I really can't believe it's you that's been doing this, Brendan. That was my worst nightmare, literally, that you'd turned into one of those people. Perhaps one evening you should go to a ballet instead of boxing—*The Sorcerer's Apprentice*, where a foolish young man starts playing tricks he doesn't understand, and gets swept away in the deluge he creates because he's never learned the magic words to make it stop. Only this time you expect *me* to come up with those magic words, don't you? It's as if one of your precious boxers were backed into a corner by his opponent, and he said to him, 'Better leave off hitting me and hand over those boxing gloves, or I might get very angry!' What's the thing we used to say? No more Mister Nice Guy, is that it?"

"That's about right. And in the scenario that I'm dealing with, they've both got machine guns stashed back in their lockers, and if they're still pissed off when they leave the ring . . ." He realized, with a sudden, pleasurable shock, that now at least she was engaging him in an argument, rather than merely laughing in his face.

"You want me to 'give you something' to help soften the blow—is that right?—of what I'm going to talk about tomorrow? Don't you mean I should just sit back and allow you to keep on doing what you've been doing all this time?"

"Yulya, your country's been infiltrating our computer network for years, as you well know. Also, you have all this data of ours, quite literally, at your fingertips—to say nothing of all the 'sensitive' information that you get just by reading our books and magazines, or by watching TV, for Christ's sake. And we don't exactly enjoy reciprocal privileges in that department, do we? In other words, your government continues to use our basic freedoms against us—to subvert our system, presumably, in order to replace it with another system in which these basic freedoms of press and of information will no longer exist. All I'm asking is for a little something to help redress the balance."

"Redress the balance! You mean you want it all put back the way it was, with us down on our knees and you holding the gun to our heads. And I know this is going to sound to you like typical Red propaganda bragging, but I can assure you that our leaders have already done the job that you've been trying to do, and much more thoroughly than you could ever hope to! But I must give you some credit, you've certainly learned to *talk* like them, the way our leaders do—out of both sides of your mouth, is that it? Or as we say, with a wooden tongue. I must say, you seem to have mastered both of those difficult skills extremely well."

"What do you mean, they've actually done the job that we've been trying to do? You've figured out some way of getting into *our* computers?"

Yulya tilted her wineglass from side to side, watching the patterns of the droplets on the inside of the glass. She smiled mockingly at him. "As you know perfectly well, there is no centralized 'computer network' in the United States, since you're so frightfully *de*centralized and, as you're constantly reminding us, you have so many different brand names to choose from. The kind of sabotage that you got away with at Krasnoyarsk would never work for a moment if we tried it on you."

Unexpectedly, she put down the wineglass, seized Brendan's hand in hers, and stared straight into his eyes. "Brendan, I'm afraid you still don't understand. Maybe it's just that craziness for a Russian and an American are two completely different things. You're talking about loss of perspective—'failure to relate to objective reality,' as they used to say in Cambridge, I recall. But you can't imagine what these people I'm talking about are capable of! They're not just unstable or disoriented, they're criminally insane! Like Stalin, only much more powerful than Stalin!" Yulya was practically shouting now, and the maître d' suddenly poked his head around the corner with a mixed expression on his face of curiosity and alarm.

"It's okay, Yulya. Calm down a little. Just talk to me. Tell me what's going on."

"Very well. You know that since the last time I saw you, I've been inducted into a very exclusive fraternity, what's commonly called the Soviet elite, the *nomenklatura*—the people who not only run the Soviet Union, but actually *own* it as well. You remember, I thought because people talked about things like 'the rationalization of the economy' and the modernization of this and that, that I should give them my support. So I did, and they made me part of their club." She had snatched her hand away from Brendan's without warning, knocking over her wineglass. For a moment they simply watched the spreading stain on the checkered tablecloth and said nothing.

"I'm sure you've heard all about this sort of thing," she went on at last, "but you really don't know what it's like. To look at them, I mean, they might even seem the same as your crazy people—because they all have servants and limousines, and all sorts of delectable Western luxuries strewn all over their houses. Most of them are sick old men, of course; some can scarcely walk, or have anything more to do with women or drinking or any of the rest of it. The one single appetite they continue to retain is the appetite for power, and in some particularly horrible way they seem to have rolled up all their other frustrated human desires into this one great pathological obsession. But they're not merely obsessives, they're addicts—and if their precious little hoard is endangered, they're prepared to do anything to hang on to it. And if that includes cutting off the electricity for railroads and hospitals, exposing millions of their subjects to famine and darkness and panic, then so be it!" Her voice broke on a shrill, harsh note, and Brendan refilled her wineglass so she could take a drink.

"I'm afraid I still don't quite understand what this is leading up to," he said, after she had remained silent for a few moments.

She smiled. "I'm sorry. I shouldn't get so emotional, as you say, about a boring thing like politics. I've been under a bit of a strain, you know. And seeing you again, that was as sure to knock me off my feet as if I'd been *drinking* Chablis all night, instead of spilling it." Brendan fought hard to dispel a grotesque, hallucinatory image of Woodward smirking at her and saying, Don't worry, my dear. That sort of behavior fits in perfectly with our psychoprofile analysis.

Yulya was looking at him curiously. "I have a question for *you* now," she said softly. "Are there still dogwood trees on Comm. Avenue?"

"Comm. *Ave.*, remember? There are still a couple, I guess. I haven't been back to check on the particular ones you're thinking of, not for a while at least."

Yulya seemed suddenly to have stopped listening. When she

began speaking again, it was with almost the same annoyingly reasonable and precise intonations she had used during her press conference. "Very well, Brendan. I can't say that your debut as a CIA disinformation agent really deserves to have such a brilliant success, and I know you'll insist on taking all the credit, in any case. However, I've decided to do what you've asked me to do. Not really because of anything you've said tonight—I want you to be very clear on that. But you did at least . . . implant the suggestion that there could be some way out of this. Now listen closely.

"I'm going to go back to my people at the embassy and tell them this: that you threatened me tonight with the prospect of an ideological *counteroffensive*, the one truly effective propaganda riposte to everything I was planning to say in my address tomorrow—and when I tell them what it is, they're going to want to get in touch with Moscow immediately. Moscow is going to tell *me* to tear up my original address and replace it with an extremely boring speech about exploring every avenue in the pursuit of a true understanding among nations and the free exchange of information. It won't get even a paragraph in any of the papers."

"Wonderful. Whenever you feel like telling me about it . . ."

"The entire central computer network—and I assure you that in our country there *is* such a thing—has been infiltrated, sabotaged in fact. But not by Cocom or the CIA. By the KGB and the GRU. Of course, it wasn't at all difficult for *them*, since they had a terrific logistical advantage. All they had to do was send out the usual maintenance crew, in the usual grubby coveralls, all equipped with the proper documents, to pay a visit to each of our computer installations."

"And so? What's the payoff?"

Yulya explained to him how she had discovered the piratical computer chip at FC 06, and what the result would be if its instructions were ever carried out. "And almost at that exact moment," she went on, "I was summoned to Moscow for, among other things, a private interview with Mikhail Gorbachev himself. He paid me a few nice compliments, asked me a few questions about my work, and then told me some things that truly chilled my blood. The basic idea was that all this 'security' has been installed as a massive concession to the old guard, the Stalinist types. It was all quite incredible, I can assure you."

"You're telling me that the Soviet Central Committee has built this incredible Rube Goldberg contraption that, at a given signal, is going to start sawing off the branch they're all sitting on? What's the point?"

It was then that the maître d', having reached the end of his patience with them, returned with the menus for the main course. He did not brighten up appreciably when he saw the wine spot on the tablecloth or the congealed, half-eaten appetizers on both of their plates. Yulya and Brendan put down their menus immediately. She took up her story again as soon as he was out of earshot.

"The point is that the Red Army has its own, entirely separate communications network, including its own computers, of course. It's like a whole separate country *inside* our country. Now do you see the point? If there's some sort of serious trouble—nationalists in the Ukraine or the Baltic, Muslims in Central Asia, or any kind of popular uprising or civil disorder—then the whole affected region can simply be shut down until the army's had time to move in and restore order. It's a little like turning out all the lights as soon as a fight breaks out in a café, I suppose. In short, our leaders have discovered how to use my machines the way the tsars used their battalions of cossacks."

"And if all the machines have been boobytrapped like that, then the effect would be practically instantaneous. As soon as one gets it, they all get it."

"Precisely. And more than anything, more even than the destruction of Cocom and all its works, I want this evil 'contraption,' as you call it, to be dismantled, done away with. I told you I'd lost my best friend because of what you did to the weather program. That's not strictly true. What happened was that the designers of the system were concerned that he might stumble into one of their little traps while he was looking for further traces of *your* handiwork. He was detained by the KGB—for quite a long time, I think. Now he's been locked away in the chronic ward of a mental hospital.

"Naturally, quite apart from avenging my friend, I'm also very much interested in protecting our people from the folly of their leaders. And, of course, a blackmail demand of this magnitude will sound much more impressive coming from you than from me; they know that you've already succeeded in penetrating our computer network, so something like this—something that would make it truly worthwhile for you to penetrate even further—could not be permitted to remain in existence once it had given up its secret."

"But the real secret is the password itself. And if we don't actually know what it is, then are we *really* going to be able to put a big enough scare into old Afanasyev—or whoever the hell it was that thought up this crazy business—to convince him that he's got to run right upstairs and start flushing all those little chips right away?"

"That won't be necessary. The system as it stands is in perfect equilibrium. We each get what we want out of this, and there's certainly no point in being greedy. You'll just have to accept my assurance of that, along with everything else I've already given you, of course."

"But if you give me the password as well—"

"You talk about giving one side a destabilizing advantage! I hate to think what the White House would do if they thought they could get away with something like this! And if things were really permitted to reach that stage, I think everything that I've been working to achieve for the past ten years could almost literally be destroyed overnight. The leadership was suspicious enough of my machines when they merely thought of them as something new and unproven; what happens when they discover they are actually unreliable—the worst of all Soviet sins—and quite likely to be dangerous! Remember what you said about both our governments being too crazy to settle this conflict rationally? I can't believe that your leaders, at any rate, could have suddenly come to their reason within the last hour or so. And as for ours . . ."

"But how are they going to *know* it's not a bluff?"

"I assure you, they'll be so terrified that the password will fall into the hands of some crazed dissident, or someone like Lech Walesa, that they won't be willing to risk it for a moment."

"I just can't believe it's all going to work out so perfectly. I think we need some insurance, and I don't see us getting another chance to call another time-out like this real soon. I still think we have to have that password."

"I was just starting to think you might be human again, and you immediately spoil it by behaving like Agent Barnes of the CIA. Don't you see that you're ruining everything by talking like that? You should be down on your knees, murmuring tearful words of gratitude for what I've given you already, not tugging at my sleeve and asking for more." She looked away for a moment, and then she looked ruefully down at the table. "I think," she said in a very different voice, "we're going to be thrown out of here if we don't order something pretty soon. I think if you could just get me some tea and toast, then we could go on sitting here and talking about nothing for a while, the way we used to do in the far-off days of our youth."

"We're not all that old!"

"True. I'm thirty-seven. You must be forty by now. But even so, if I were still a reckless, romantic young girl, I think I'd fall in love with you all over again. And now it's your turn to tell me something about your life. I don't even know whether you're married or not!"

"I am. To a really extraordinary woman."

"Then you're already luckier than most—" She suddenly seemed to be staring up a fixed point directly over his head. He turned and saw the same Russian security man who had chased him away that afternoon, standing in the little entry hall that led into the main dining room.

"It's my driver," she said. "I'd better go see what he wants." There was a brief colloquy between them. He heard Yulya give a little cry or a sharp exclamation of some kind. He got up and started toward her, but she was already on her way back toward the table, her face deathly white.

"Brendan! This is too much of a coincidence! It looks as though your employers didn't quite trust you to strike a respectable bargain without applying some additional leverage of their own." She quickly retrieved her jacket and purse from the chair where she had left them. He reached out a hand to touch her arm, but she shook it off angrily.

"What the hell's going on? Why aren't you talking to me?"

"I see now that you were merely recruited to play the role of decoy. They didn't even bother to fill you in on the rest of the conspiracy."

"What are you talking about, for Christ's sake?"

"Svetlana is missing. They think she may have been kidnapped. I trust you'll be able to explain to your 'people' that they've ruined everything with their own criminal stupidity. And of course I don't have to tell you that *our* little arrangement will of course remain in abeyance until I've got her back again, safe and sound. And then we'll have to see."

It was only with some difficulty that he could penetrate as far as the outer door of Woodward's office at the embassy. This was eventually opened by an agent, the one he thought of as the "plainclothes marine," who customarily served as Thompson's doorkeeper at the Cocom mission in Paris.

"I have to see Woodward. It's important!"

"Barnes, right? I'll see if the mahster is in." He returned a moment later. "Come aboard," he said dolefully.

Woodward was sitting behind his desk, just as Brendan had left him a number of hours ago. "What's going on, Woodward? Have you got her?"

"Little Svetlana Voronkov, do you mean?"

"You know I do. Her mother's already convinced this is some kind of harebrained scheme of yours—not yours personally, my 'employers.'"

"She's free to believe whatever she likes, of course, and I'm sure the press has already reached that conclusion quite independently."

"And is it true?"

"I think even our own vigilant organs of state security, as represented by Thompson and our friend Ed out there, would have to draw the line at something like that."

"Right. Let me put it another way, then. Do you have any idea what happened?"

"The little girl had been left at the ballet, in the custody of an employee of the Soviet embassy. This young woman stepped away from her post for a moment on some personal errand, and when she returned, the girl was gone. That, at any rate, is what she told the Swiss federal police a short time later. I don't suppose it's occurred to you that the Russians themselves may be behind this—as a means of obtaining even stronger guarantees of good behavior from your friend."

Brendan looked dubious. "To coin a phrase, Clive—they may be that crazy, but they ain't that stupid."

"Perhaps they merely don't show the same solicitude we do for the emotional well-being of their employees. I think something like that would only serve to heighten the dramatic effect when she denounces us from the podium tomorrow."

"I suppose there's no chance the kid just got lost in the theater somewhere?"

"You forget that we are in Switzerland, Brendan. The opera house was virtually disassembled, brick by brick, by the police earlier this evening."

"And they're all out looking for her now?"

"That's right. Of course, she may simply have wandered off by herself for some reason. Children are often quite resourceful in that respect. But that's not really my area of expertise, or yours, for that matter. Perhaps it would make more sense for you to be giving me some account of your meeting with Madame Voronkov?"

"'My Dinner with Yulya'? Of course. But bear in mind that everything I'm about to give you is totally out the window unless she gets the kid back. Then, she says, 'We'll have to see.'" He went on to give a fairly detailed account of their meeting, glossing briefly over the more personal passages at the beginning and the end. Woodward seemed to be quite fascinated by his description of how the Soviet security services had sabotaged their own computers. He had been looking a little worn-down when Brendan first stepped into his office. This news seemed to have had a powerful restorative effect.

"The real question," said Woodward, when Brendan had told his tale, "is why they didn't think of it sooner. Perhaps it was largely a matter of hammering out the boilerplate on the various political compromises that had to be worked out before the system could be set in place. You've done very well with this, Brendan. Surprisingly well. And I'm sure I can count on you to take that in the proper spirit."

"Oh, definitely. And I just hope you appreciate that she just went ahead and *told* me about it—because, for the moment at least, our 'objective political interests' happen to coincide. None of that Cuban Missile Crisis nostalgia stuff of yours seems to have made any impression at all. Nor, in all fairness, did any of *my* stuff about widespread, dangerous craziness in high places—naming no names, of course, Clive. And as to whether any of your CIA psychobabble reports really panned out this time, I guess it's just too early to tell, isn't it? I guess both of us were aware of a certain disparity between what might have been and what we've both become—like, for example, I don't think those hysterical Chicken Little scenarios I was handing out really did a lot for her subconscious image of me as her ideal dream lover.

"But I will admit, Clive," he went on, after a moment's pause, "that I couldn't help getting the feeling we were having our own private little disarmament conference or something . . . like we were definitely in *control* of the situation and even starting to sort it out a little bit. I kind of tended to forget, as I'm sure you would have made sure to remind me, that I was really there only for purposes of damage control, right? I mean, to make sure that if the KGB finally does have to call off this big scam they've been working on all their computers, that isn't necessarily going to queer the pitch for Operation Softwar as well."

"As usual, Brendan," said Woodward, "your instincts are fairly sound, but you still seem to be confused about a number of basic points. True, you are in Geneva, that much I'll grant you, but not for the purpose of strategic-weapons reduction by any means. Operation Softwar naturally *will* continue, in whatever form future circumstances might dictate; I don't think there was ever any doubt about that. The fact that Madame Voronkov refused to give up the password, largely for reasons that you yourself seem to have planted in her mind initially, does not seem terribly surprising; she may prove susceptible to further, more persuasive approaches in the future, though certainly not, of course, to be undertaken by you. And finally, you are quite wrong in supposing that I do *not* believe that our current predicament truly qualifies as a genuine world crisis—and certainly in so describing it to you, it was never my intention either to exaggerate or to deceive . . ."

Even Woodward was finally winding down, however. He glanced at the clock on the desk. "My Lord. Two-oh-three A.M.! Brendan, I think you had better go back to the Hilton and try to get some sleep. You know, as my dear grandfather used to say, 'When you have a problem, and there's no longer any way you can act on it, then it's best to sleep on it instead.'" Brendan could even imagine Woodward's grandfather, back in Charleston in 1861, saying exactly that, perhaps while trying to forestall further useless speculation on the part of his hotheaded Charleston cronies about the possibly destabilizing effects, perhaps, of Abraham Lincoln's election, or the Defcom readiness status of the garrison at Fort Sumter.

He did not feel like taking Woodward's advice, however, and when he left the embassy he decided to leave his car parked where it was and to walk around for a while. He realized, of course, that what he was really hoping would happen was that he would run into Svetlana, scuttling around the next corner in that strange-looking Soviet sailor suit she had been wearing that afternoon.

He ended up walking the streets of Geneva all night, from the Pleinpalais down to the railroad station, from the Place Cornavin to the Rond-Point des Philosophes—yet another local memento, he supposed, of the late J. J. Rousseau. It was there, in fact, that a police patrol car pulled up next to him and insisted on running an identity check, which they conducted with a thoroughness of which even Woodward would have had to approve. He saw several other little bands of Swiss policemen, not all of them in uniform, walking through the parks or down by the quais along the Rhône. There was an unmarked radio car with two detectives sitting in it, parked by the trolley stop for Annemasse; the occupant of the passenger seat looked him slowly up and down, then muttered something into his little microphone. It was nice, thought Brendan, to be able to feel so safe in the midst of an urban jungle like Geneva.

The sun had already been up for some time when he flopped,

exhausted, onto a chair outside a café on the Place du Mollard. He was starting to feel that he had walked off most of the burden of irrational guilt he had acquired during the last two minutes or so of his conversation with Yulya. He ordered a café renversé, a cappuccino served in a glass, and picked up a copy of the *Tribune de Genève* from a passing vendor. The headline left little doubt about how the matter still stood:

DISAPPEARANCE OF SOVIET DELEGATE'S DAUGHTER
PROVOKES WIDESPREAD RUMORS OF CIA INVOLVEMENT

FOURTEEN

September 14, 1984   Geneva

With all the routine opening formulas safely out of the way, the press was deeply disappointed when, at 11:00 A.M. precisely, the scheduled time for Yulya's address, an unfamiliar male figure in horn-rimmed glasses ascended the podium and read a brief statement informing the delegates that "Director Y. N. Voronkov deeply regrets that for personal reasons with which you are all undoubtedly familiar, she will be unable to address you today on behalf of the people of the Soviet Union." Instead, the Soviet delegate went on to explain, and if circumstances permitted, she would return to deliver her address in exactly twenty-four hours' time. During the storm of applause that followed, the senior delegate from India walked briskly up to the podium to propose the resolution that "Madame Voronkov be assured of the profoundest sympathies of this assembly in view of the tragic circumstances which have prevented her from attending this morning's session." After this was adopted by immediate acclamation, he went on to propose a further resolution: that "the strictest possible sanctions" would automatically go into effect in case "it ever becomes the sense of this assembly that the disappearance of

Miss Svetlana Voronkov is in any way proven to have been an act of despicable political blackmail carried out by the agents of an unfriendly government." It was only with some difficulty that the organizers of the conference had prevented some of the more volatile Third World delegates from proposing that the United States delegation should be immediately—and physically—stripped of their credentials and expelled from the hall.

In one of the numerous lounges and waiting rooms that surrounded the conference hall, the chief of the French delegation, René Duvallon, was holding forth to his Italian colleague, well within earshot of a half-dozen journalists. His own government, he was in the midst of explaining, had already started to explore the possibility of withdrawing from Cocom altogether. "What's it going to be next—call in a nuclear first strike on anyone who dares to utter a word of criticism? That seems, after all, to be the logical outcome of all this!"

A small group of delegates and journalists were gathered around a nearby television set, watching a news broadcast, most of which was devoted to the "kidnapping crisis." There had been a brief segment showing a pink-cheeked Soviet news announcer reading a statement issued by Mikhail Gorbachev, in his capacity as chairman of the Commission on Foreign Affairs of the Supreme Soviet, and proclaiming his government's refusal "to allow itself to be intimidated by this shocking act of international banditry." In West Germany, an informal and extremely raucous group of Green Party deputies had stormed the speaker's platform in the Bundestag in order to read out a much longer statement calling on the government "to immediately adopt a more independent stance on this vital question of abolishing all current political restrictions on the free flow of technology and information all over the globe."

The political office of the French Communist Party had called on "all true lovers of democracy" to continue to agitate for a thorough official investigation of "l'affaire de Krasnoyarsk," which, they added, they fully expected to be forthcoming, "given the present government's previous expressions of solidarity with fraternal socialist states." *The Washington Post*, better informed than many of its competitors, had run an editorial instructing the U.S. Congress to conduct a no less thorough investigation of "certain top-secret intelligence-gathering agencies *other* than the CIA." CIA director McFarlane, however, had completely spoiled the effect of this and instantly succeeded in shifting the blame back to himself by issuing a strongly worded denunciation of "these obscene allegations that this agency or any other agency of the United States government could have been implicated in such a contemptible criminal act."

Kenneth Clowder turned around and grinned at Brendan when this was read over Swiss TV. "Well, it was pretty smart of him just to come right out and confess like that, wasn't it?"

"Very shrewd," said Brendan. "Have you noticed that we've practically got this whole set to ourselves, and there are about three hundred people watching the one in the other lounge?"

"Well, boy, as my dear old father back in East Texas used to say"—his voice became low and twangy—"'Son, yuh got yuhself intuh some hip-deep shit this time, Ah guarantee yuh . . .'" Brendan had not been able to resist sharing his speculations about Woodward's secessionist grandfather in Charleston while they were sitting through the opening speeches.

He was trying to think of some reply to this when he suddenly felt a strong hand gripping his right bicep. It was Woodward's doorman at the embassy, the gloomy-faced ex-marine whose name, he suddenly remembered, was Ed.

"Woodward's got us looking all over town for you. Better give him a call right away—you can use one of those public phones right over there if you want—just to let him know you're okay." He looked at Brendan with some interest. He had not taken the time to go back to the Hilton to get cleaned up and was still far from looking his best. "You found an after-hours joint in Geneva and didn't even tell your old buddy?"

"Not exactly. I'll be along in a couple of minutes, I promise. Okay?"

"Okay, fine." He tilted his chin toward the TV screen. "You know, they got 'Dynasty' and 'Falcon Crest' over here in German, French, *and* Italian. Now that's what I call a full-service town." He grinned significantly at Brendan. "Just making conversation . . . since we seem to be standing here and all." He had still not removed his hand from Brendan's upper arm. He only did so when Brendan spun around without a word and headed off toward the lobby.

All of the telephones had been preempted by a jabbering crowd of journalists, but after a few minutes' wait he was put through to Woodward's office at the embassy.

"Office of the trade representative."

"Hello, Clive. It's me. Checking in as requested."

"Where the devil were you this morning? Don't even bother to answer . . . I have only one thing to say to you at the moment. The Wimex has just switched over to full alert."

"This isn't what you'd call a secure line, Clive. There's a guy in a turban standing about two feet away from me who can hear every word you say."

"So much the better! Perhaps the sooner the entire *world* finds out about this, the better!"

"Is that what we call a deliberate leak, Clive?"

"No time for that now. I want you in my office as soon as possible."

After a brief, silent ride with Agent Ed, Brendan found himself sitting in front of Woodward's desk again. The clock said 2:19, a little more than twelve hours after Woodward had sent him off to bed the night before.

"Last night, Brendan, you were scoffing at my 'Chicken Little scenarios' of world crisis. Now perhaps you'll be inclined to listen a little more attentively. Those people in Washington have finally dug in their heels about this. They're not about to lose all of Europe without firing a shot—and whether or not that is destined to remain a figure of speech, I'm sure I can't tell you at the moment. I already *have* told you, most indiscreetly as you pointed out, that the Wimex has gone over to full alert. Surely that must mean something to you."

"Yes, it does. It means somebody's taking this pretty hard. Also being incredibly stupid and reckless, in my opinion."

Wimex—or, more strictly, WWMCCS, Worldwide Military Command and Control System—was a satellite-linked, computerized communications system intended to provide the principal military command posts in the continental United States with current and reliable information concerning the deployment and combat-readiness of all U.S. forces everywhere. This involved 158 separate computer systems located at eighty-one stations around the globe, as well as the full panoply of the U.S. early-warning network of satellites, radar installations, and other, more recently developed primary-alert facilities. The activation of this formidable data-retrieval system clearly meant that, even for Woodward, the Softwar had now become a secondary concern.

"All right," said Brendan, after Woodward had merely stared back at him in silence for several seconds. "I think we're in complete accord as far as this Wimex business is concerned. Now, Clive, what exactly do you propose to do about it?"

"Last night I spoke of making a second approach to Yulya Voronkov. Now the time has come, a little bit earlier than planned, for us to do so—and, also contrary to what I might have said earlier this morning, it is you, Brendan, who are going to be making that approach. The situation is not just critical, but desperate, as I feel sure you are finally beginning to understand. Your opening gambit has been accepted, and with a great deal more enthusiasm, I might add, than I ever dared hope to expect. She is, as you would presumably put it, already into us for quite a bit, from the standpoint of her own personal security with respect to her current employers. Now it is time—if you'll pardon me for referring to your charming friend in such a fashion—for you to go back and pick up the package."

Brendan was surprised to discover that Woodward could be even more obscure than usual when he resorted to simple colloquial English. After a moment's reflection, however, he felt sure that he had fully understood what was now being asked of him.

Ambassador Yevtushenko was panting sharply when he finally reached the suite of rooms in the embassy compound that had been assigned to the Voronkovs for the duration of their stay. The escalator had broken down again; he had had to walk up three flights. It was not in accordance with policy to allow local artisans—even world-renowned Swiss craftsmen—to carry out major repairs of this kind.

It was Yulya who answered his knock. "Any news?" she asked immediately.

"None, I'm afraid." He cast a cold eye at Sergei. "I'm also afraid, Colonel Voronkov, that this is a highly confidential matter I've come to discuss."

"But he's the girl's father, after all," said Yulya, not without some irony. "He surely has the right to that information."

"I'm afraid the Swiss police have exhausted . . . that is, they've begun to search the river."

Yulya sat down heavily in a chair. Tears were already running down her cheeks. "That's too horrible . . . I can't even think about things like that right now . . ."

"There is no need for you to think of such things, dear Yulya Nikolaevna. I myself remain firmly convinced that the Americans are responsible. That is as good a guarantee of her safety as you could wish to have . . . though only for the moment, I'm afraid."

"Do you have any proof of what you're saying?"

"Nothing direct, of course. Merely certain indications that we have received through different channels . . . intelligence channels." Sergei correctly took this as a signal that he was intended to leave the room. He did so.

"Please continue, Comrade Ambassador."

"As I said, I have nothing to tell you that concerns your daughter *directly*. Our KGB station chief has simply reached that conclusion. Though of course it's possible that a rival intelligence service may have been involved."

"Our own, for example."

The ambassador darted his eyes around the room, as if to make sure that Sergei had not concealed himself behind an armchair as part of some elaborate test of his loyalty. "With all due deference, Yulya Nikolaevna, I should point out that though it is permissible to lodge such uninformed accusations at the door of *another* intelligence service, it is hardly advisable to do so in the case of our own—unless, of course, you can furnish convincing proof."

"No, of course not. My accusations are, as you say, totally uninformed. However, you will admit that my daughter's disappearance has generated a great deal of advance publicity, highly favorable I think, for the performance I'm expected to give tomorrow."

"Naturally you're upset—"

"Isn't that one of the first things you have to consider when a crime has been committed—who stands to benefit the most? You needn't try to make me shut up, however. I'm fully prepared to do so, until tomorrow at least. And right now I think I should go over to the Palais to see what they've been up to without me."

"But the press, the photographers! Why subject yourself to such an ordeal when you're already—"

"In a highly nervous state? Scarcely rational? I'm afraid it can't be helped, Comrade Ambassador. I also think that the time has come to renew our contacts with Professor Brendan Barnes."

"To what purpose, may I ask? Allow me to remind you, your first encounter did not turn out very well."

"No need to remind me. Nevertheless, I have only the highest hopes for the second. I admit, of course, that my reasons for wanting to go ahead with this are largely personal. *If* the Americans really have taken my child, and *if* he knows anything about it at all, there's no way in the world he'll be able to conceal the truth from me."

The ambassador gave her a thin smile. "You have some private means of persuasion at your disposal? Or of coercion?"

"I intend to use nothing but sweet reason—reason and logic. I've come up with some fairly convincing arguments since last night."

"But it's entirely possible for the Americans to have abducted your child, and yet for him to know nothing about it. This is not the sort of task that's likely to be entrusted to a computer specialist, after all."

"He's very well informed, as a rule. He's a protégé of Clive Woodward, who might accurately be described as the gray eminence—even the K. I. Afanasyev—of their delegation."

"And even if he does tell you something you want to know, what happens then?"

"If you'll permit me to wax slightly melodramatic for a moment, and somewhat in advance of my scheduled artistic debut—how little you know, Comrade Ambassador, of the secrets of a mother's heart. Just put yourself in my place for a moment. If it were your child, for example—"

Yevtushenko produced a handkerchief from his pocket and began to mop his forehead. "I'm reluctant to authorize such a step without prior consultation with Moscow. I'm responsible for your security as long as you're here in Geneva, and if you could just put yourself in my place for a moment, dear Yulya Nikolaevna—"

"Speaking for myself, I feel perfectly safe, as long as I'm here in Geneva. After what's happened, I think it would be extremely foolish for the Americans, or even that rival intelligence service you spoke of, to seek to apply any further pressure on me of this kind. And if, Comrade Ambassador, by some unhappy chance I should happen to perish as a martyr to the deathless cause of socialism, then I can still console myself with the reflection that the sparks from my funeral pyre might even touch off a much more extensive conflagration that none of the rest of you is likely to survive for long."

"Yulya Nikolaevna, it distresses me deeply to hear you indulging in wild, feverish talk of that kind."

"No, I assure you I have it all on very good authority. A highly placed official source . . ."

Yevtushenko merely nodded, then frowned in a puzzled way. "That's as it may be, of course. And now I think I should go and have a talk with Moscow."

When a small cortège of limousines with hammer-and-sickle pennants flying from their front fenders appeared in the Avenue de la Paix, obviously headed for the Palais des Congrès, the corps of press photographers and cameramen who had been stationed all along this route instantly abandoned their posts and started to jog alongside, like infantrymen accompanying an armored column into battle. The crowd of reporters and the TV crews around the Palais itself was so densely packed by now that the three limousines were forced to slow to a crawl. The Swiss policemen and Soviet security men on the scene had a moment of collective panic when it began to look as if they would not be able to get through at all. After a narrow avenue had finally been opened up in front of them, a rear window of the second limousine rolled down and was instantly surrounded by a bristling phalanx of microphones.

"I have every confidence that the Swiss authorities are going to restore my child to me before too much more time has passed. I know that everything humanly possible has been done. I simply hope that I will have her with me again very soon. And I would like to make a very urgent request to all of you at this time—that the Swiss authorities should be permitted to continue their investigations without any further interference from the press. And as for my own personal feelings in the midst of all this, I think, at the very least, that all the women of the world will surely understand what they must be."

The black Lexan window slid back into place, and the limousines rolled on for a few more yards in order to discharge their passengers behind a solid cordon of police.

After his brief audience with Woodward, Brendan could think of nothing better to do than return to the Palais and try to catch up with the proceedings of the conference. When he arrived, a Japanese delegate was delivering an impassioned antiprotectionist oration. Yulya Voronkov, he soon learned, had not yet emerged from the seclusion of the Soviet embassy compound. The conference hall itself was very impressive, like the ultimate Art Deco movie palace, with its immense bronze doors, faded allegorical frescoes, and two benevolent winged figures hovering high above the speaker's platform at the edge of the proscenium. The panels and furnishings were of dark walnut, striking a slightly more somber note, and, all things considered, this elaborate physical setting—a great, useless artistic legacy of the extinct League of Nations and the War to End War—did not seem very auspicious for this particular conference.

He had been sitting in the great hall for about half an hour when Kenneth Clowder tapped him on the shoulder and motioned for him to follow him out into the lobby. "Yulya Voronkov just drove up out front! She headed straight up to the delegation office. Don't think she'll be seeing any visitors for a while." He gave Brendan an accurate paraphrase of her statement to the press, followed by commentary. "Very nice and dignified. She's much too high-tone to start slinging accusations. And she handled the 'mother' angle very well too, of course. Ever see that one? *The Mother?* Russian silent film, by Pudovkin. Early method-acting technique, a classic. Your friend was right up there with the best of them—real Moscow Art Theater quality."

"So you agree with Woodward that this is all just a hoax, a publicity stunt?"

"Not necessarily. I'm just, you know, a cinema buff. I tend to assume that everybody's playing for the cameras until proven otherwise. And this time"—his voice took on the heavy Germanic intonations of Fritz Lang or Erich von Stroheim—"Vot a shkript! Early Hitchcock vit just a liddle *touch* of Costa-Gavras!"

Clowder had suddenly stopped in mid-harangue. A heavily built man with a worried look on his face was standing at Brendan's elbow. It took Brendan a moment to recognize him as Yulya's chauffeur-bodyguard of the day before. The worried look was apparently caused by the fact that he was about to say something in English. "Please. Director Voronkov asks to see you immediately, in the office."

"Director! Aha, what did I tell you! *That* was the early Hitchcock," said Clowder delightedly. "The scene with the speech and the limos and all? *This* is the Costa-Gavras, coming up!"

Brendan fell into step with the Russian, ignoring the curious stares of the journalists and delegates in the lobby and the corridors. When Brendan finally arrived outside the office that had been provided for the use of the Soviet delegation, he suddenly recalled that he was still wearing the same clothes she had seen him in the night before. An attempt to shave with a borrowed razor in one of the luxurious restrooms of the Palais had left an angry slash across his cheek, perhaps reminiscent of the dueling scars on Clowder's old-time film directors.

Yulya looked a little tired and worn, but certainly no less attractive. She was wearing a light blue suit—which Clowder had earlier described, not unappreciatively, as "the perfect outfit for the Bolshevik working mother." Her manner was markedly formal and distant;

she invited him to take a chair, but did not get up or offer him her hand.

"I'm really sorry . . . still," was all he could think of to open the conversation. "I hope you realize by now that my 'employers' didn't have a thing to do with this."

"Not necessarily. That's still the pet theory with *my* employers, as I'm sure I don't have to tell you. And it wouldn't be the first time that your intelligence services have gotten involved in some sort of grotesque criminal extravagance that ended up completely backfiring against them. They seem to imagine we'll all think it *couldn't* have been the CIA, because everyone knows that only the CIA is capable of such things, and therefore they wouldn't have dared to do it!"

"You'd like my boss, Clive Woodward. He says things like that all the time; only he believes them, of course."

"And you're implying that I don't? That I'm just trying to bait you, to get some kind of reaction out of you? Is that the way you think I spend my time when something like this has happened?"

"This man Woodward I was telling you about? One thing he'd never do, unlike yourself, is to draw some kind of zany conclusion just because it happens to fit in with his personal prejudices, without having examined all the other hypotheses that might just fit the same original set of facts. For example, you might have explored the possibility that your *own* world-famous intelligence service—you know, those kind of *wide*-looking guys that drop by the house on your husband's bowling night—?"

"Stop it! Stop being so stupid! Don't you think I've already thought of that? Don't you know I've been thinking about that all day?" Her voice had become very high-pitched and brittle. Brendan felt immediately like going over to her to take her hand, or still better, running over to her and taking her in his arms. For the moment he thought it would be more prudent just to grip the arms of his chair a little harder and mutter an apology.

"You're right, of course. Very stupid. Totally stupid. I think that was just my tactless and unbelievably callous way of trying to make you realize that I really had nothing to do with it, and don't know anything about it."

"They haven't been able to tell me anything, you know. Every lead the police have investigated has turned out to be the work of some Swiss busybody or some sort of crazy person. They've combed the entire region, and now they're dragging the river!" She turned her face away from him. "I don't feel much like talking about that part of it, to tell you the truth."

"I do. I was down by the quais last night. There's a great big parapet that runs all along the bank—even higher off the ground than she is, I'd say. Svetlana's not really what you'd call the lunatic daredevil type, exactly."

"Hardly."

"So I don't think you have too much to worry about—her going over the high side, I mean."

"She could easily have managed it if she wanted to badly enough, don't you think? Last night, before I went to meet you, I was with her at the ballet, as I told you. Sergei turned up, quite unexpectedly of course, and made a disgusting scene. He said all sorts of perfectly horrible things. I was sure she hadn't heard a word of it, the orchestra was so loud and she was so completely engrossed in the ballet. But what if she *did* hear something? What if she heard every word of it?"

"Well, pardon me for putting it like this, but if every kid who ever overheard her parents yelling at each other went straight out and threw herself in the drink, I don't think the human race would have made it even this far, do you?"

"You don't understand. You weren't there. It wasn't his tone of voice that I'm talking about, it was the things he said." She paused for a moment and looked straight at Brendan. "Sergei was drunk, in a jealous rage. He was jealous of *you*, in fact." Brendan was about to respond with a short, snorting laugh of disbelief, but he was lucky enough to contain it. "He was jealous of you because he'd just found out somehow that you were Svetlana's father."

It felt just like a nice, well-aimed shot to the solar plexus, one with lots of heart behind it. He could almost hear the air rushing out of his lungs. He just had to hold on for a second, without thinking about it. Without thinking about anything. It was also a little like falling off a cliff, then finding out there's another cliff at the bottom.

This was Woodward's famous "psychological block" again, with a vengeance. He had had access to all the relevant data, but he had not been able to bring himself, somehow, to carry out the necessary computations. He knew perfectly well that Svetlana was eleven years old—as did the entire civilized world by now. In the old days, as he remembered quite clearly, Yulya had always shown the cynical Soviet consumer's disdain for any form of artificial contraception—"because those things don't work anyway," she had said. A more recent and considerably more poignant memory came to him; just yesterday he had been standing on a sidewalk in Geneva, looking down into his daughter's dark eyes.

Yulya looked over at him and smiled softly, just as if she had been following his thoughts. "We were children then, don't forget." The smile turned to a grin. "*I* was a child; you, I suppose, were already an adolescent. We behaved very foolishly, in any case. And this is the result. A love affair between two people like us could only have led to catastrophe of one kind or another."

"It isn't our fault that the rest of the world's so screwed up."

"Of course it is. At the moment I can hardly think of two people who deserve any more of the blame than we do. And why do you suppose 'fate' has brought us together again like this? It's obvious that our respective employers have been trying to think of some way to capitalize on this from the beginning. Your Mr. Woodward and all the rest."

"Capitalizers to a man. And your Mr. Afanasyev, wasn't that the guy? And wasn't there something you used to say about paranoia being called 'the Russian disease'? And isn't this getting us a little off the point? The point being, why didn't you ever tell me about Svetlana?"

"For the same reason I didn't tell anyone else. Because it made things so much simpler for everybody. Sergei was really a very good father to her—until the last couple of years, at least. I even wrote out a sort of confession that I was going to let her read some day."

"I swear, if there was anything I could do . . . I don't know where she is, and I'm just about positive none of the rest of them know, either." He folded his arms and leaned back in his chair, and locked his gaze into hers for what seemed like many minutes. Finally it was she who lowered her eyes.

"I believe you," she said. "I believe that you're sincere, but as one of my colleagues once remarked to me, sincerity can be a very dangerous weapon, unless you have no intention of actually telling the truth. In this case, I believe it is your Mr. Woodward and the rest who have no intention of *letting* you tell the truth."

"I don't quite see where this is getting us. I guess you really asked me to come up here so you could tell me about Svetlana, right? Well, Jesus, I'm glad you did, but—"

"But I want you to help get her back for me. I want you to go to Mr. Woodward and tell him that I'll do anything he likes, if I can just have my daughter back with me again. That's all I'm asking for now, you understand. I've put off delivering my address for one day, but it has to be decided by tomorrow—what sort of revisions I might care to make in preparing my final text . . ."

"What did the folks back home say about that? About your postponing your address, I mean?"

"Gorbachev thought it was a fine idea. He thinks that the more tension is allowed to mount, the greater the impact will be when I finally deliver my address."

"I agree that tension can be a very fine thing, but only in moderation. Don't you think maybe you've built up about enough by now?"

"Most assuredly. And this is what I'd like to propose. If I have Svetlana back with me by tomorrow, then I'll speak to Gorbachev again. I'll tell him that the Megasoft routing controller that we acquired through the Indians has *also* been modified by your agency—in such a way that it permits you to monitor all the essential activities of our computer research center at Krasnoyarsk. I won't even ask you to tell me whether that's true or not; the next part isn't. I also intend to tell him that your infiltration of the institute at Krasnoyarsk was what enabled you to discover all the little traps set by the KGB throughout our central computer network.

"I will *also* tell him that, of course, their purpose was immediately apparent. The secret is out, in other words. In return, I'm sure he'll instruct me to deliver an address so full of 'goodwill for all mankind' that not a single one of those reporters will still be awake by the time I've finished. On the other hand, of course, if Svetlana is still not back with me by then, I'll get to read the speech I've already written. Less work for me. The first way, we can all be blackmailing each other, you see. As I think I pointed out last night, the system is in perfect equilibrium."

"Not quite. Because we can't possibly deliver on our part of the bargain. We haven't got the kid. We don't know where she is. That puts us right back where we were when we started, 'in hip-deep shit,' as a colleague of mine recently expressed it. The people in Washington simply aren't going to accept a crushing diplomatic defeat like this; they aren't going to let you break the blockade on high-technology exports. Don't you think if I really did know where your daughter was, I'd be falling down kissing the hem of your garment right about now, instead of giving you a big argument about it?"

"*My* daughter? She's your daughter too, Brendan. Or doesn't that part count?"

"Our daughter, okay. But we still haven't got a deal here until you start facing facts. One will do, to start with. We haven't got the kid. Far be it from me to criticize your methods, such as pegging the outcome of this whole enormous fucking crisis to the fate of one small child, even if she does happen to be y— our own . . ."

"So it's Agent Barnes of the CIA, back with us again. Is that what you think, that I should be more concerned about my computers and 'long-term political objectives' than about our child?"

"Not necessarily. But I think you should be able to step back and look at this rationally for just one second, and then maybe you'd realize that you can't make me tell you something I don't know just by sweetening the kitty."

"What?"

"Sorry. Just by increasing the terms of the ransom, is what I mean. Even if you promised to hand over the damn password and everything—the exact point where our negotiations bogged down yesterday, as you'll recall—" Brendan realized instantly that he had committed a grave tactical blunder.

"So that's the idea? That's what you've been waiting for all along?

And now, I suppose, Agent Barnes, if I do give you the password, you'll just *happen* to remember that you did just *happen* to see a little girl locked up in a broom closet in the American embassy. You know that you must never lose sight of the fact that lying can be a very effective tactic, but only if you remember not to spoil it all by starting to tell the truth." Yulya put her chin in her hands and stared at him in silence for a moment. "You know," she went on, in a soft voice that made Brendan wish even more fervently that none of this was happening, "I've never forgotten what we meant to each other, you and I. I love both of my children equally, I suppose. But I must admit that I love Svetlana in a *special* way that has something to do with a dream, or just the memory of a dream, that had you right there at the center of it. But you're quite right, of course, Agent Barnes. There's no place in our solemn deliberations for any of that soft, emotional, *womanish* sort of thinking, is there? Go back to Mr. Woodward and give him the terms of our bargain. I get Svetlana, he gets the password. All right?"

Before Brendan had time to reply, the telephone on the desk rang. Yulya picked it up. *"Da, gavarit Voronkov. Shto? Kagda sluchilos? . . . Uvidesh' shto skora budyet garazda huzhe! . . . Tak tochna, mozhet byt' cheres tritsat' minutov."* She hung up the phone and began to speak, without turning back in his direction. "Ambassador Dobrynin has just been recalled from Washington 'for consultation.' Gorbachev wants to speak to me. I have to get back to the embassy." They both got to their feet immediately. "If only I was sure I could trust you, Brendan."

On his way back to the embassy, Brendan had learned from the French-language station on his car radio that Gorbachev, speaking as chairman of the Commission on Foreign Affairs, had just issued a strong statement criticizing the U.S. government for "its unconscionable interference" with the scheduled activities of the conference; the Soviet delegation was said to be already on the verge of walking out of the conference, but only after they had unburdened themselves of certain "truly horrifying disclosures" not described in any greater detail. The news commentator on the radio seemed particularly impressed by this "as evidence of the recent ascendency of Gorbachev" in the high councils of the Soviet government. Worse awaited him, of course, in Woodward's office.

He had given Woodward a carefully expurgated account of their discussion (leaving out all mention of Svetlana's true paternity). "Ah, well, then," said Woodward, when he had finished. "The news isn't entirely discouraging, at least?"

"What have I missed?"

"Quite simply the fact that Yulya Voronkov is so clearly disposed to strike a bargain with us. Pity we haven't abstracted the child after all."

"To use as a bargaining chip? To get her to read the Mister Nice Guy speech?"

"I trust you'd strike a harder bargain than that! The password, of course. That's what we're really after in all this. The only guarantee of their continued good behavior that we could accept."

"Fair enough, Clive. Maybe it's time for me to start checking the broom closets after all."

When he left Woodward's office, he was feeling even dizzier and more disoriented than usual. He had not had any sleep for thirty-six hours, he suddenly realized, and decided to head back to the Hilton.

How do you say "daddy" in Russian? was the first of many thoughts that came crowding into his mind during the brief car ride to the Hilton. This was far too much to take in all at once. He decided to adopt Woodward's method of picking away at random until he found a loose thread. And the loose thread, of course, was Svetlana. In return for a brief précis of his most recent negotiations with Yulya, Woodward had offered him a few small crumbs of information, all from the very spartan table of the Swiss federal police, it seemed. The only item of any great human interest was only of incidental value in terms of the overall crisis; it turned out that Svetlana had been able to slip away from the embassy box at the opera without being observed because Manya, the embassy employee who had been deputized to look after her, had been having what Woodward called "a highly personal encounter" with the security man on duty in an adjacent and otherwise empty box. Brendan felt strangely comforted by the news that there was at least one other person in the world with whom Yulya was as furious as she was with him.

He began to think about something else. Why was it, for example, that he and Sally had never had any children? The official explanation, as formulated by Sally, of course, was that "I could never have a child by a man who's probably going to hop right on a plane and then turn up with a panda bear when the kid's sixteen years old." Her frequent references to "living out of three different suitcases" (in Cambridge, Washington, and Paris) and "the lure of the next flight out"—even her occasional references to herself as "Sally Barnes, Standby Wife"—had made it fairly clear what she thought the basic problem was. Perhaps she had realized as well, as she had hinted the last time they were together, that the one person with whom he had been willing to share *that* much of his life had been someone else. It had been Yulya.

He had gotten as far as the lobby of the Hilton when he remembered that he no longer had his magnetic room key. He had left it with her. He would have to speak to someone at the desk, perhaps even engage in tedious negotiations. Anything that stood between him and sleep at that point seemed like an intolerable imposition.

He was also none too pleased to come across Agent Ed reading the *International Herald* in the lobby—even though, in Geneva, this seemed like the logical place to find him. Perhaps Thompson himself would not be far behind. The two men nodded warily to each other as Brendan passed by.

He was pleased to discover another old acquaintance, Jean the night concierge, a fellow boxing enthusiast, on duty at the reception desk.

"*Bonjour, Jean!*"

"*Ah, bonjour, Monsieur Barnes!* And how is your little girl today?"

FIFTEEN

"*My* little girl?" he asked idiotically, though this was not nearly as bad as any of the other replies that had come to mind, including, How the hell did *you* find out so fast, buddy?

Jean was clearly used to excitable foreigners; like all good Swiss hoteliers, and like the trained staff members in expensive Swiss sanitariums, he was able to take a guest's—or a patient's—most irrational and preposterous inquiries entirely at face value. "Of course, monsieur. Your little daughter. I had the pleasure of making her acquaintance last night. She was unfamiliar with the *clé magnétique*. I had to show her how to open the room door." Then, seeing that Brendan seemed to be appalled by his failure to execute the proper security precautions, he added soothingly, "She's very shy, of course. But when she told me that you were her father, why, I could see it right away—your eyes, your nose . . ." He had happened to glance at the unhealed razor cut on Brendan's right cheek and hastily completed his inventory.

"Is she still up there?" Once again Brendan had a very strong sense that he was not asking the right questions.

"That I can't say, monsieur. I've only just come on duty." He finally allowed himself to acknowledge the look of shock and wild surmise on Brendan's face. "I hope this isn't a question of some sort of girlish . . . escapade, monsieur. If I have created a problem of any kind—"

"*Absolutely* no problem," he replied firmly. "It's just that I gave my key to my little girl, and I—" He could think of no possible explanation of his twenty-four-hour absence from the Hilton that was adequately plausible, succinct, and not thoroughly discreditable to his character. What kind of a degenerate would leave his eleven-year-old daughter all alone in a hotel room, all night and practically all day, and what was there to do in Geneva that would make such a course of action necessary or desirable?

"No need to say more, monsieur." He produced a ring with a set of little plastic mag cards, selected one, and handed it to Brendan. "This is a little irregular, of course, monsieur, but I'm sure it will be all right if you'll return it to me when you come down again." He handed over the little card with a flourish. "From one admirer of the great Jersey Joe Walcott to another!"

"Thanks, Jean. You're a great man." He looked at him closely. "May I ask you one more question?"

"Of course, monsieur." Jean had reverted to his original morning-rounds-in-the-asylum voice.

"Don't you ever read the papers? Watch TV? Anything like that?"

"Only what they call the sporting press, monsieur. *Le Monde du Box* and so on. And as for the *télé*, I'm afraid it gives me a headache. Except, of course, I understand that in America they have professional wrestling. Must be quite wonderful—"

Brendan gave him an emphatic nod, to assure him that was indeed the case, and a wave, and ran off at full speed toward the elevator.

He found Svetlana curled up in a kind of little laundry cupboard in the bathroom; she had originally crawled in to escape detection by the chambermaid. The latch had clicked shut, and there was no way to unfasten it from the inside. He scooped her up and carried her into the other room and set her down on the bed. Her eyes were open but seemed to be—a term he associated primarily with TV doctor shows—"fixed and dilated." Her breathing was very shallow, and her pulse seemed remarkably slow and weak. He picked up the phone and dialed the switchboard; they gave him the names and numbers of three different hospitals, one of which—"*la clinique pédiatrique*" in fact—was quite nearby. He hung up, and wondered if he could possibly make contact with her, make her realize she was safe now.

"Svetlana, can you hear me? It's me, Brendan . . ." He could not quite bring himself to say "your father" or, least of all, "papa."

There was no response. He soaked a handkerchief in cold water, wrung it out, and feeling very shy and awkward about the whole thing, tried to cool off her damp forehead. She began to speak a little, brokenly and almost inaudibly, in a mixture of English and Russian.

"*Ya proshu, pust' mama ob etam nikagda nichyevo nye uznayet* . . . please, don't tell Mama, please . . ." and a great deal more that was too faint to be deciphered.

Then she gave a sort of moan and seemed to lapse back into the state of open-eyed unconsciousness in which he had found her. He picked up the phone immediately and dialed the pediatric clinic. The highly competent young woman at the other end of the line took down all the relevant details and assured him that an ambulance would be there in a matter of minutes.

Svetlana seemed to be more or less conscious now, but still disoriented, watching him fearfully with wide-open, staring eyes. He reached down and took her hand and smiled. He was trying desperately to recall some of the stray Russian phrases he had picked up from her mother, but the only ones that came to him were either too humdrum or, as Woodward might have put it, too highly personal to be of much use.

There was a knock on the door, and Brendan felt vastly relieved. The paramedics. His primary-care routines were all just about exhausted by now. But when he opened the door, it was not to admit a paramedical team with a stretcher. It was one of his fellow guests at the Hilton, Agent Ed.

"You got the kid!"

"Sorry?"

Ed ignored this pathetic attempt at subterfuge. He was in a highly exalted state. "Woodward's gonna shit when he sees this—if that's something he ever does, which I personally doubt very much. I saw you were having this big discussion with the guy down at the desk. So I pursued my own discreet follow-up inquiries. Monsieur Barnes and his cute little daught-air, right? How'd you pull it off, prof? Reese's Pieces? Angel dust? You really got the touch, old buddy. I bet you could have a whole *string* of cute little daughters working out for you down on Collins Avenue in Miami, if you really put your mind to it, am I right? Okay, here's the detail. Woodward, needless to say, wants us to sit tight on this till he gets here—which should be about any old second now . . ." While delivering this speech, Ed had managed to insinuate himself all the way into the room and was staring down at Svetlana with an almost greedy expression on his face.

"She got herself locked into the bathroom closet by mistake," said Brendan. "I think she's still in shock. I called an ambulance."

Ed's face froze, all of his hyped-up amiability suddenly gone. "Well, shit, man. Call 'em up and tell 'em the eminent Geneva specialist, Dr. Woodward, is taking charge of this case, and they can just park it right back in the garage."

"For Christ's sake, Ed. She's just a little kid, okay? She's in shock, hardly even has a pulse—who knows, maybe hypothermia, anoxia, apnea, from being in that closet for twenty-four hours. She also barely speaks English. So what's the risk? They can admit her to the clinic as Miss Cecilia Woodward or something, if that's what you're worried about."

"Bull*shit*, she hardly speaks English! Little Miss Cecilia Woodward, right? Fuck, no. When *big* Cecilia Woodward gets here, he's going to want to have your ass on a stick for even *suggesting* a fucking lamebrained scheme like that." He held out both hands, in a gesture of sympathetic but abject impotence. "Sorry, man, but that's the way it's got to be. No discrimination on account of age or sex or place of national origin. She gets treated like any other big-time Soviet defector, from here on in. Woodward, I'm sure, could run the whole procedure down for you in only about two hours or so, so be sure to make a mental note to ask him about it when he gets in."

Brendan was no longer listening. He was thinking about another aged mentor of his, Jerry Connolly—who was also fond of quoting a beloved parent—what was it about—"knowing how to take it and knowing when to stop"? The extent to which he had been taking it so far was staggering just to think about. Thompson had effectively stage-managed his relationship with Françoise from the beginning; Woodward, as it turned out, had been hovering over his relationship with Yulya, if not quite from the beginning, at least during its more recent stages. Even his relationship with his lawful wife, Sally, had been at least a trifle *stunted*, if not exactly blighted, by his involvement with Operation Softwar. And now it was Svetlana, his own daughter. He decided, after all this time, that it was time to give in completely to one of those wild-card "subjective factors" that Woodward was always on about.

He looked over at Agent Ed, who was smiling back at him in a benign but thuggish sort of way. He remembered another piece of advice that Jerry Connolly had given him, on many different occasions. *Tag 'im one, Brendan! Use your left, for chrissakes!* He wound one up a little and launched a solid, technically flawless sucker punch, aimed exactly at the spot where he judged that Ed's liver ought to be. Ed crumpled up and went straight to the bottom.

Five minutes later, Brendan was standing on the curb outside the Hilton, watching the ambulance drive off, escorted by two Swiss federal police cars. From the other direction, a slightly battered Buick with consular plates pulled up beside him; from it emerged Woodward and Clowder, backed up by two well-groomed young men from the embassy. "Great God, man! What have you done with her?" cried Woodward.

Brendan merely pointed toward the ambulance as it disappeared around a corner. He felt obliged, as usual, to give Woodward a brief circumstantial account of the events of the last hour or so. Woodward seemed merely bemused at first. "She ran away, the little girl ran away. A Defcom 2 alert, a major foreign-policy crisis, Dobrynin recalled to Moscow . . . and all because an eleven-year-old child got herself locked up in a laundry cupboard." In a moment, though, he was entirely himself again. "I must say, Brendan, you seem as usual to have followed the dictates of your heart rather than your head, and I'm sure you'll agree—now that the warm, humanitarian glow of the moment has begun to fade—that this single heedless act of yours may have done incalculable harm."

"That's entirely up to you, Clive. I'm sure that you and Ken and these other gentlemen are resourceful enough to deal with this little contretemps. I suggest you head right back to the embassy and put on your breechclouts and warpaint. I'm sure you can convince the press that the little girl was abducted by a Comanche raiding party that was merely trying to forestall the possibility of global thermonuclear conflict . . ."

Woodward naturally ignored this and turned toward Clowder. "Get this to the press at once, Ken. At least some of the more preposterous charges that have been made in this case may finally have to be withdrawn." Then he turned back to face Brendan once again. "I'm afraid this will probably mean the end of your association with us, Brendan. I'm sure you can imagine how our two *parent* bodies— especially those blood-drenched villains of yours at CIA—are going to react to a thing like this. It would only have required another five minutes to arrange proper medical treatment for the little girl *plus* a simple one-for-one exchange with Madame Voronkov—the little girl in return for the password."

"It would never have worked, Clive. We've both been running a scam on those computers of theirs, all right? They blow the whistle on us, we blow the whistle on them. We both take a huge propaganda beating, but who gets hurt the most in terms of what's happening at this conference? All we can realistically threaten them with is something like 'inflaming Soviet public opinion' against the KGB and those bad old men in the Kremlin. The whole rest of the world will be shrieking for *our* blood, but we'll have 'Soviet public opinion' on our side at last. I guess that means Chernenko's really going to be tasting it at the polls in November, right?" Brendan secretly did not find this argument too convincing, but it seemed like a handy stick to beat Woodward with. Woodward, of course, was fully prepared to duck.

"Yulya Voronkov would have agreed to meet our demands *without* bringing her superiors into it in any way. She was perfectly prepared to act on her own initiative. Brendan, I do hope you realize that you've deprived us all of the human intelligence triumph of a lifetime?"

"Humint. That's where it's all happening, right, Clive? I think I'm just about ready to start getting back to good old *artificial* intelligence, myself."

When Brendan called the Soviet embassy, he had some difficulty at first with the switchboard, then was handed over to an affable third secretary, who offered to put him through immediately, "on Madame Voronkov's private line." From the slurpy way in which the secretary had pronounced the word *private*, Brendan had surmised that it would be prudent not to take this too literally.

Her voice at the other end of the line sounded faint and distant, as if she were already back in Siberia. "Brendan! Do you have anything to tell me?"

She had still not been notified by the clinic. He was the first to bring the news. He told her the whole story, in considerably more detail than he had gone into with Woodward. "I think she must have snitched the mag card I gave you out of your purse. She saw me handing it off to you in front of the toy store, I guess. Who knows why she decided to pick on me, though? What do you think, little mother?" This was purely for the benefit of the third secretary, or whoever else happened to be listening in.

"She must have heard me talking about you at the ballet last night. She seemed very intrigued by you, I think. And you know you made a tremendous hit with the marzipan cuckoo clock!"

"Listen . . . it doesn't look like we'll get a chance to see each other again right away. Of course, I said the same thing last night, and I turned out to be totally wrong about that—"

"Everything I said to you last night is going to turn out to be totally *right*! Do you understand what I'm saying?" There was a pause, and when she began to speak again, her voice was barely audible. "Brendan, you know I've never stopped loving you. I've never really loved *anyone* but you."

He decided to do what he could to mitigate the enormity of this indiscretion in the eyes of the KGB, then instantly regretted it. "Say again? I can't hear you! I love you too . . . are you still there?" The line had gone dead, though whether it was Yulya or the KGB who had cut him off, he could not be sure.

Woodward was awaiting him in the hotel bar, drinking Guinness, probably warm. Brendan ordered a Pernod. It had begun to seem to him that every real-time episode of his life was now divided into two different segments, roughly equal in duration—first the actual experience, then telling Woodward all about it. "She said everything she told me last night was going to happen, was going to turn out right. I believe it. I've finally done something to *prove* to her that I can still be trusted. You remember what she told me about her friend, the programmer who ended up in the loony bin because he'd started to figure out what was suddenly going wrong with the barometer on St. Thomas? I think that was what did it for her. She doesn't feel that she can cooperate, that she can be a part of all that anymore."

"From your mouth to God's ear," said Woodward unexpectedly. Perhaps, thought Brendan, it was just the Guinness talking. "But I continue to believe," Woodward went on, "that things would have worked out quite a bit better if you hadn't allowed that password to slip through your fingers like that." Brendan ordered another Pernod while Woodward went on austerely nursing his stout. "And what about poor Ed, by the way? You're quite sure you haven't dealt him a mortal blow?"

"Quite sure. But I locked him in the bathroom. Isn't that something from Shakespeare? 'I'll lug the guts into the neighbor room'? I'm sure the chambermaid will let him out eventually, if he's still not quite up to putting his head through the door."

"Brendan, I'm going to have to have a word about all this with McFarlane at CIA, among others. It's not a conversation I'm exactly looking forward to."

"Clive, you know, you're sort of starting to get on my wick again. Isn't that something they say back home in Charleston?"

"Are you threatening to make some sort of drunken exhibition of yourself? That's your second Pernod, if you'll forgive my pointing it out to you, in about as many minutes."

"I drink to forget, Clive. So I make it only my first. Why don't you check back with me in, say, about *twenty* minutes?"

Yulya Voronkov's opening address to the conference was a terrible disappointment both to the press and to most of her fellow delegates. Much as she had done at her press conference two days earlier, she spoke very briefly and only in the most general terms of "intolerable restrictions" on high-technology exports, and made vague if ominous references to the activities of "the U.S. defense-technological sector," but none of the truly shocking disclosures that had been promised by Gorbachev were forthcoming. Indeed, the whole tone of her remarks seemed to imply that all of these problems could eventually be sorted out by means of good-faith negotiations and a candid exchange of views among the interested parties.

Two main theories were already in circulation within seconds after she had stepped down from the podium: the first was that the bland and even conciliatory tone of her remarks was merely the final installment on the kidnappers' ransom payoff, and the second was that everything that had been happening at the conference thus far was no more than a vast propaganda hoax staged by the KGB. The fact that an American delegate had been instrumental in restoring the child to her mother was more readily explained by proponents of the first theory; Brendan Barnes was thus merely the quasi-respectable go-between who had transmitted the kidnappers' ransom demands to the child's mother. He was alternatively described in the international press as "a onetime academic associate and longtime personal friend of the child's mother" and "a notorious American agent with links to Cocom and other top-secret appendages of the U.S. defense-technological establishment."

The fact that an impeccably neutral Swiss pediatrics clinic had also played a role in the final act of the drama was something that received a great deal of attention from proponents of theory number two. The child had gotten lost, then she had been found. Everything else was KGB disinformation. Others contented themselves with remarking on the apparent ease with which even the most highly respectable of institutions could have been infiltrated by an aggressive foreign intelligence service. Jean the night concierge and the dispatcher at the clinic were predictably closemouthed about the whole affair. Later that afternoon, it was also announced from Moscow that the Soviet ambassador would be returning to Washington immediately after "certain matters of urgent personal importance" had been attended to.

"They were afraid of raising the stakes!" said Woodward triumphantly. "The 'ideological offensive' has been canceled—because the political climate was simply no longer favorable, and no doubt at the personal insistence of Mr. Gorbachev himself. Imagine what we could have accomplished if you'd only got hold of that password! We could have brought them to their knees."

"Face it, Clive, we could have *buried* them—but only about up to their ankles. I just don't think it could have been as easy as all that."

Woodward brushed this aside with an airy gesture. "No point in dwelling on the past, in any case. And I have some rather good news to convey to you—rather better than you deserve, I expect. I have been in communication with Washington, and elsewhere in that general area. As to the disciplinary sanctions that I alluded to yesterday, it has not been thought necessary to put them into effect. You'll be remaining with us as a much-valued member of our little working committee. From this moment, you may consider the entire matter closed."

Easy for you to say, Clive, Brendan thought to himself.

He spoke to Sally on the phone later that night. "You could at least go out and say good-bye to her at the airport, you cad! Think you might ever be getting back this way at all? The leaves are starting to look pretty good back here—you don't get quite as much of that in the Alps, as I recall."

"Nope. In fact, I'm thinking of taking a little personal time, maybe a couple of weeks, maybe more. Think you could stand to have me kicking around the house for that long?"

"At the moment I can't think of a better place for you. This time, try to get back just a little bit *before* you have to take off the next time, okay?"

Early the next afternoon, Brendan found himself stationed outside departures gate 5 at Geneva-Cointrin Airport. Passengers were preparing to embark for the Aeroflot direct flight to Moscow-Sheremyetevo. He was holding an enormous bouquet of flowers and feeling very foolish. The first wave of departing Soviet conference delegates had just pulled up outside the terminal, in the same three black limousines with little hammer-and-sickle pennants on the fenders. The delegates swept on toward the departures area in a tight formation.

Brendan saw her immediately, though her face was almost hidden beneath a shaggy lynx-fur cap. She had seen him as well; she merely shook her head quickly and almost imperceptibly from side to side. This time he was convinced that it was she who was to be made to regret any impetuous "subjective" demonstrations on his part.

He stood aside and watched the Russians begin to file slowly through the security gate. Yulya and Svetlana stepped through almost simultaneously and started off down the companionway. Brendan started looking around for a trash receptacle large enough to accommodate his bouquet. Then he heard a sharp, quick rattle of footsteps behind him. It was Svetlana, running toward him at a gallop. Yulya was calling out to her, sharply, in Russian. He caught her up in his arms and held her out in front of him so he could look directly into her face for a moment before setting her down again.

"Mama told me you saved my life, Brendan. Do you know why I came to find you like that?"

"Sure do."

"I'm going to write to you, you know. That's an absolute promise. And Mama told me a secret she wants me to tell you. But first *you* have to promise not to tell anyone else about it, okay?"

"I swear."

He leaned down and wrapped her in an enormous bear hug for a moment. Then he caught sight of a man in an astrakhan cap and an elegant leather overcoat who was walking briskly toward them. *"Svetlana! Pridi syuda totchas-zhe! Shto delyaesh'?"* He had no difficulty at all in recognizing the famous Colonel Sergei Voronkov.

Svetlana pulled away from his embrace, then kissed him quickly and wetly on each cheek. "Good-bye, Brendan. *Do svidanya.* I almost forgot about the secret. Still want to hear it? It's *venik.*"